The Day and The Hour

by Presley Acuna

Percussion Publishing LLC

New York, NY

To Believers and Non-Believers alike

CONTENTS

"But of that day and hour no one knows, not even the angels of heaven, nor the Son, but the Father alone."
Matthew 24:36

Chapter One: The Numbers Game

New York City, December 31st, 2019

The congregation extended out in all directions; each face basked in a wash of neon, every breath a vapor in the cold, December night.

It was noisy. A dissonance of sirens, music, corks, fireworks and breaking glass, woven through the jangle of the shouting, laughing crowd.

It was New Year's Eve, Times Square, New York City. The Babel metropolis of brick, concrete, metal, glass, neon and soot celebrated. Thanks to satellite technology, a worldwide audience estimated at over one billion people was also tuned in, watching the ceremonies from afar.

The place was a riot on happy gas. Policemen astride horses and wearing crowd control gear moved in formation -- multicolored lights reflecting off their helmets and shields, like technological Roman centurions. They sifted through the crowd, breaking up fights, urging people to keep moving. They were expectant, as if intuiting something bad was going to happen.

The thickening crowd was making it harder to move. Spotlights blazed white at the foot of the One Times Square, from the roof of which the New Year's Eve Ball was poised and ready to drop. The huge TV screens bolted onto the side of the building depicted fifteen foot high images of the evening's hosts, with the very same Times Square scene behind them, ad infinitum. On the stage, a band stormed through its rhythms and beats as a hip-hop duo took turns shouting out to the crowd, while a gaggle of celebrities, media notables and local leaders stood waiting for their cues from the wings.

Above it all, the digital display read, "11:45."

All of a sudden, there was a commotion in the midst of the audience standing before the stage. Flashes of fists and angry faces. Shoving and shouting. Immediately, policemen began to cut their way to the source of the conflict, tasers and riot gear held high above the crowd as they converged from all corners. Then, from the epicenter itself, a flame erupted from a gnarled wooden club held high by a desperate looking figure. His head pivoted left and right. His jaw clenched, flickering lights reflecting off his widened eyeballs. He waved the club, the flame roaring and growling as it was whipped by the winter wind, creating a space around him. On his lapel could be discerned a yellow cross.

The flame was formidable -- far larger than the club warranted. The ring of policemen closed in on the demonstrator. Someone yelled for help. Sirens could be heard in the distance.

The lunatic figure pointed the burning club at the stage and yelled, "Blaspheming bastards! Charlatans! You will all burn in hell!"

With that, the madman conjured a 3D printed firearm and began firing at the stage. Instantly, the crowd panicked.

The Tower clock read, "11:52."

A helicopter abruptly appeared above the heads of the crowd, startling everyone and whipping wind at people's faces and clothing. Hot lights shown down from above.

"You'll never get me! I'm already gone, you pigs, and tonight you'll die too!" bellowed the torch bearer. He touched himself with the burning club and set himself ablaze. His clothing ignited at once.

At the same time, other burning torches appeared throughout the throng. The torch-bearers proceeded to touch those around them with the burning pyres, before setting themselves on fire. The reaction was instant and violent. Those who found themselves in the uncomfortable vicinity of the firebrands tried to climb over each other, screaming, in an effort to get away. The first burning demonstrator lurched heavily to and fro, unabated in his hurling of slurs and diatribes of doom. He swung his torch again infecting more people with the flames. In moments dozens of people were shouting for help as the flames enveloped them. The police closed in.

A megaphone barked, "Stay where you are. Help is on the way. Throw yourselves on the ground and roll! For God's sake he's setting them all on fire..."

The megaphone was snatched away.

The lunatic, crumpling under the demands of his burning body, spat out his final words. "Repent or you will burn in hell!" With that, he let out a blood curdling scream and hurled the club into the crowd before collapsing to the ground.

The Tower clock patiently changed its display to: "11:56."

The club arced through the air, creating another epicenter of fire as it landed on an unsuspecting fur-clad woman, immolating her and those around her as she spun and grabbed anyone within reach in a blind clutch for help. The chorus of screams grew louder. People tried to run but found themselves crashing into each other. The crowd was simply too thick, the flames too hot. Anything the fires touched immediately caught fire.

The clock read "11:58."

The ball began its inexorable descent.

The police waded through the chaos of burning victims, but there was nothing they could do. The heat of the flames and the pure panic of the people around them deterred their progress. The stink of seared flesh, singed hair, scorched fur, and melted synthetic fibers clotted the cold air.

The clock, indifferent to the danger, changed its display to "11:59." The ball was halfway down its predetermined path.

Times Square was now a chaos of flames and burning bodies, while mere blocks away, set against incongruous laughter, noise makers, fireworks and strains of "Auld Lang Sine", emanated from the First Night tents, where the revelers were as yet unsuspecting. Despite the magnitude of the disaster, the crowd was so big in New York City, that for many, the calamity went unnoticed.

And above it all, the clock read, "12:00."

The New Year had begun.

Holy Name Rectory, Chicago, New Year's Day, 2020

The woman's fur coat burned like a sparkler as Thomas lay in the bed watching the small screen, still awake. He rubbed at his neck and listened to the talking head at the foot of his bed.

"Times Square was a crisis center last night, as terrorists set themselves on fire in the midst of the 2020 New Year's festivities. Hundreds have been injured or killed. Police and ambulance crews are still on the scene looking for survivors. Local hospitals are struggling to absorb the influx of trauma victims. Several anonymous callers to The New York Times and other local papers have claimed responsibility for the attack. Police officials suspect the group calling itself The Brethren may be the instigators of last night's tragedy, following at least a half dozen similarly spectacular disasters attributed to them so far this year, however no definite connection has yet been made to any particular individuals or organized groups at this time".

Mocking his wakefulness, the nightstand clock's alarm suddenly sounded off, causing Thomas to start. He was tired. All over the world a madness had prevailed in the long, final night of 2019, affecting population centers all over the world. Father Thomas Prisciotti had watched it all -- one newsflash after another.

Thomas assessed himself. His mouth tasted sour and metallic. His eyes stung. He could smell his clothing on himself. He concluded he was in a sorry state. "But so is the world," he whispered at the walls. The earth was a burning house of clowns and criminals falling off a cliff.

The night had been a vigil that he had felt compelled to undertake. The escalating tensions in the Middle East during the tumultuous past year had ignited the superstitions of the Judeo-Christian world, and talk of prophecies fulfilled and apocalypses imminent were on the rise with a fervor not seen since 2000 A.D. – but this time with one important difference; the disintegrating world of the 21st century was now in a crisis coincident with his own. The one inside of him.

As he developed material for his seminars, a growing discomfort had begun to grow inside of Thomas. It had taken seed many years before, when he was a student, but then it had been only a minor facet amongst the multi-planed prism of his growing world views. Now it had become an erosion that ate at his mind, sapping his inspiration and draining his faith.

I need sleep. He rubbed at his bristled face and tired eyes, pushing back the wetness. He sighed and sat up from his prone position. The room spun slightly and Thomas wondered at the accompanying swirls of thought that comprised his doubt.

Those who knew Father Thomas Prisciotti would not have suspected his discomfort. He was outwardly engaging and confident, occasionally brooding, sometimes self-mocking, but generally an appealing fellow. He made a conscious effort to participate in his parishioners' lives, and had been heard to say that the last place for clergymen to be was inside their stained glass fortresses. Thomas had a knack for bringing esoteric ideas down to the level of the layman. He liked to delve behind the canon; to talk about the *intent* of God's words. This made for stimulating discourse at the pulpit.

His pastoral seminars, part of the Vatican Central Committee's mandate to its far flung dioceses to provide spiritual guidance to the world's congregations in answer to the increasing fears stemming from the uncontrolled chaos in the Middle East, had been well attended.

Eventually the Vatican took note of this, acknowledging the provocative spin of Thomas' dissertations but recognizing the faith inspiring content of his writings and utterances, and granted a *nihil obstat* for the continuing public dissemination of his work. In due course, the Chicago Diocese entered into an agreement with the Trinity Broadcasting Network Faith and Family Channel and Thomas' seminar series, entitled, *Behind the Word, with Father Tom*, became a regularly televised event.

As a result of this modest exposure, Thomas was a local favorite of journalists and was often solicited for commentary on events relating to matters of Christian belief. Thomas was bemused by all this, for he considered himself to be foremost a scholar, rather than a public figure.

The sun suddenly burst through the Venetian slats and cast rays of dusty light into Thomas' room. It stung his eyes and motivated him out of bed over to the small sink set in the wall. He splashed cold water on his face and rubbed the tension out of his temples. He examined his dripping features. He was a large man, with soulful, brown eyes, which unblinkingly stared back from beneath heavy black brows, like cliffs over his dark pupils. *More like a pirate than a priest.* A wide mouth and a slightly crooked nose added to his roguish image. After toweling dry, he raised his arms upwards to stretch his tired muscles. Small cracks and pops could be heard throughout his 48 year old body. He touched his toes a few times and with that, he felt himself sufficiently ready for the day's first challenge.

Just before opening the door, to set off for the showers at the end of the hall, he bent toward the foot of the bed to turn off the small television set. As his hand reached for the chrome knob, a replay of the night's events in Times Square was again unraveling on the screen -- a camera image direct from the CNN chopper as it hovered far above the crowd. Dutifully, the invisible cameraman had recorded the surreal events on videotape. From this vantage point, high above the maelstrom, it seemed to Thomas that the chain reaction of flaming bodies and frightened people were like tongues of fire spreading across the landscape, in a portent of things to come.

Athos, Greece - Eight Years Prior

Yordon looked down upon the Aegean far below him, glistening in the Mediterranean sun, as he methodically cast stones from his high vantage point. Each stone plunked satisfyingly into the water, and formed a circle of waves that travelled outward in patient arcs.

Squinting, he looked into the distance and saw rainclouds running parallel with the shoreline, into the distance. Bursting through them, at the end of the peninsula, was the single, angular peak of Mount Athos, for which this entire outcropping of rough coasts and Byzantine structures had been named. Admiring the mountain, he wiped his brow, feeling the heat and humidity of the Greek climate. Despite the uncomfortable warmth, he wore his black robes, but being alone in these ancient caves, he allowed himself the removal of his *Skoufia*, the traditional cap of the Eastern Orthodox Monks of Athos.

He moved his lips in silent prayer, as was the custom of the monks, but this was not only for the purpose of striving to become closer to God, but also to drown out the susurrations in his head. These ghostly *currents* of consciousness subsided when he mouthed the words of worship, allowing him to feel human again; a single mind in a simple body with no compulsions or desires beyond the living of his simple, contemplative life, here at the monastery.

It had not always been like this. More and more often, this cloud of multitudinous thoughts and feelings passed through his mind; and more and more with the force of personality. They were as if wraiths of varying intent, vying for his attention, threatening to take over his consciousness and identity, challenging his very sense of self, and of purpose, imploring him to surrender himself to their will.

He, like all the monks of Athos sought to isolate himself from the outside world, and to emulate the life of Christ, in search of God. It was their belief that there was no place on earth closer to heaven than here, in this haven. No women were allowed to visit, for it was said that Christ himself dedicated the entire peninsula to his mother, and therefore no other women could set foot here, so as to fully honor the Virgin Mary.

In this purest of environments, all of his brothers, as well as he, strove to commune directly with the Lord, but Yordon feared he may have succeeded too well. He had been conscious of a certain *awareness* other than his own haunting his mind, since before the time of the uprisings in the Northern regions near Chalcidice, where his father and mother had maintained a farm. And he had always been strange, and after becoming an orphan, estranged. He was alone, and yet, he seemed to need no one. It made those around him uncomfortable. Thus, it was not hard for the young Yordon, tall and thin, with a wavy mane of light brown hair tied back into a pony tail, to make the pilgrimage to the nearby Athos monasteries to offer himself into a life of quiet contemplation and spirituality. The Monks of Athos accepted him with little reluctance, and he never looked back at his prior existence.

In the long and persistent quiet that always cloaked the peninsula, with the exception of the sounds of surf and the croaks and calls of God's creatures, one sound cut through every monk's inner reveries, and that was the sound of a rhythmic tapping upon a piece of chestnut wood, which was the call to prayer. So it had been since before the time there were bells. Yordon heard the call and began to collect his things so he could make it back to the prayer hall in time for the next 8 hour long entreaty to the Creator.

But even as he hastened to meet his summoning along with the other monks of Athos, he knew, his time in this lonely, lovely place was short, for there were other, more elemental entreaties calling him, and he could not deny them for much longer.

The world would soon know about Yordon Antropos.

Holy Name Rectory, Chicago – New Year's Day, Present Day

The Rectory at Chicago's Holy Name was an austere but comfortable home for the priests, auxiliaries, orders of men and women religious, administrators and volunteers that comprised the Cathedral's retinue. The morning meal was an informal and congenial time for the staff to congregate.

Frequently, there were guests from the congregation, or officials from the Diocese or other Church jurisdictions. But today was different. Because of the holiday, many of the regulars were absent, so there was an unusual quiet to the dining room and kitchen and those who were present seemed preoccupied.

Thomas had no trouble fitting into this mood. He half-heartedly stirred his coffee and stared into the space beyond the far wall. After some minutes of this, he reached for his newspaper, still folded on the small table at which he sat. Suddenly a loud interruption startled the entire room.

"Look at all these hangovers!" bellowed Cardinal Jacob Martin Shaughnessy, as he marched confidently into the room, looking freshly washed and starched in his plain black habit with white collar, a maroon cardigan and creased black slacks.

"Hangovers are the work of the devil, you know," he joked to no one in particular as he waded through the tables.

People rallied themselves and offered pleasantries as he passed -- he was, after all, the Roman Catholic Archbishop of the diocese of Chicago.

Oh please, don't sit here -- not today, Jake, thought Thomas to himself as he tried to shrink under his newspaper -- but it was not to be. Soon, a Cardinal shaped shadow developed over the newsprint.

"Father Tom?"

Thomas looked up. The 68 year old, ruddy cheeked, senior prelate hovered over Thomas' table, a pastry and a steaming cup of coffee in hand.

"Good morning, Cardinal Shaughnessy. Do you care to sit with me?" croaked Thomas. *Oh Lord, that didn't sound too friendly.* He smiled thinly, trying to compensate.

Cardinal Shaughnessy's eyes gradually creased in amusement until he finally said with genuine kindness, "I would enjoy that, Thomas. Happy New Year! I gather from your spirits that it wasn't a good night."

"For many."

"Ah, yes. I've listened to the news this morning." Shaughnessy pulled back a chair and sat down with a soft grunt. "A cataclysmic night in America. I sense anxiety from our flock as well. Many choose not to listen to the Holy Father's appeal for sanity."

He looked around the room, revealing a split second glimmer of worry. The two sat quietly and stirred their coffee.

Shaughnessy broke the silence. "Now, now, Thomas, I just sat down. Surely we haven't exhausted the conversation already? A shekel for your thoughts?"

Shaughnessy would, of course, be able to sleep like a baby through the latest disasters of the twenty first century. And yet he didn't waste any time on frivolities either. There was no point in denying the truth of his insight. Cardinal Shaughnessy could sniff out facades like a Papal inquisitor.

"I did have trouble sleeping, Cardinal." Thomas managed a slightly sardonic smile for the Cardinal's benefit, as if to say, *but nothing I couldn't handle.*

Cardinal Shaughnessy leaned over the center of the table, gazing closely at Thomas, and said, "It doesn't surprise me. Your soul is a stirred cauldron, my son. If I may say so, I think you're too caught up in your own thoughts. Wasn't your last program entitled *"Waiting for Godot in the 21st Century?"*

Shaughnessy shook his head. "Rather self-indulgent, don't you think, Thomas?"

Thomas raised an eyebrow, considering his superior. He wasn't exactly in prime form for this discussion but he couldn't let the remark go.

"It was apt. Though nothing ever happens in *Godot*, but the audience is held rapt by the process of waiting. It's enough for everyone involved, audience and characters alike, to believe Godot will come. He never appears, but his presence permeates every line of dialog and every action. Not unlike our faith."

Shaughnessy was about to respond, but hesitated. The Cardinal Bishop cocked his head at Thomas. He wondered whether to grapple with Thomas in yet another debate. *Not today.*

Thomas also stopped himself. "Sorry Jake. I'm a wreck -- so what brings you to the Rectory this morning? Surely you can find a more engaging breakfast companion than me?"

Shaughnessy ignored the self-deprecating remark and lowered his voice. "The truth is, Father that sometimes I get tired of being surrounded by all those blasted aides and attendants. The spiritual leader of the Archdiocese of Chicago has to get out amongst his flock every now and then! Can't just hide behind the pulpit. You've said it yourself. Besides, it's lonely over there today."

He gauged Thomas for a reaction.

Thomas voiced his suspicions. "You don't get lonely."

The Cardinal Bishop burst out in laughter. "Truly we're blessed to have such a gifted and intelligent theologian as you among us, Thomas." He shifted in his seat. "In fact, I do have a little something to discuss with you. It's an opportunity."

Thomas waited patiently.

Suddenly serious, the Cardinal explained, "His Holiness, Sylvester III, has requested your services."

"What do you mean?" asked Thomas".

"He wants to reach out to the people with a message of comfort and continuity, now that the transition is over. Frances' sudden death created a void and we're not blind, despite our official dismissiveness of all the end-times hysteria of the last year. The Church needs to take a leadership role in these times, more so than ever."

"Many people think the arrival of the Lord is imminent. They don't understand why it didn't happen in 2000 or 2001, but with the advent of a nuclear armed Islam in the Middle East..." observed Thomas.

Shaughnessy nodded crisply. "For many, that has tipped the scales. Sylvester knows this and has corresponded with the Archbishops of the world Christian community to coordinate a global campaign of spiritual response to these fears."

Thomas sipped his coffee. "That's encouraging to hear. The last thirty or forty years have been tough on the faith. Lay Catholics are openly wondering if the Church is relevant anymore. The relationship between theologians and the papacy is worse today than at any time since the Reformation, and those that do retain faith are reducing canon to a cartoonish promise. For them, redemption has two faces. Perhaps it always has. One for the winners and one for the losers. "

Shaughnessy's face took on a steely cast. "Redemption will come for those who are morally correct..."

"But whose morals, Jake? Ours or God's? What if true justice doesn't serve one's ends? What if justice is *inconvenient*? Men want to be as Gods more often than not in the act of judging others only. Not through advancements or enlightenment."

Thomas abruptly drank from his cold cup. Shaughnessy waited, expressionless. He needed Thomas to be calm. *Best to let it lie.* Thomas could as easily have been an opponent of the Church as an ally with that burning mind of his. He realized Thomas was waiting for him to say more.

"Yes, yes. You're quite the pundit, there is no doubt. And you'll have your chance to make your ideas known rather soon.

Thomas raised his eyebrows. "Oh?"

Shaughnessy cocked his head, looking bemused, then seemingly from out of nowhere, he conjured a thick stocked, cream colored envelope, sealed with wax bearing the imprint of the Papal ring. Looking Thomas directly in the eye, he continued, "I have a letter from the Pope himself, addressed directly to you, Thomas, given to me by the Prefect of the Papal Household."

"You're kidding", said Thomas, unsure of what to think.

Shaughnessy suddenly turned deadly serious. "Thomas, listen to me. You have been selected by our new Pope, following my recommendation, to join a kind of task force."

Thomas stuttered, eyeing the envelope in Shaughnessy's hand, "A task force? What exactly, is the task?"

"Read the letter, my son, but suffice to say, I was asked by Sylvester to provide the names of promising theologians of my diocese who have established themselves as positive ideologues and models for the church. I thought of you, of course."

"Thank you, Cardinal Shaughnessy", said Thomas, not knowing what else to say.

Shaughnessy nodded in acknowledgement, "You are to meet with him when he comes to America on a planned world tour later this year."

Thomas squinted, still digesting the news.

Shaughnessy continued, non-plussed, "Prefect Cerrano will make all the arrangements."

Thomas thought back to all the ideological arguments he had been engaged in through the years. Some had almost turned into brawls. "But I'll undoubtedly offend him! What about Ernesto? He's articulate…"

Shaughnessy shook his head. "But he doesn't have your background. You were educated in Rome. At one time you were being considered for service in the Curia."

"But I was disqualified."

"I think you rather disqualified yourself, my son. Then you specifically requested my diocese for service. What more need be said?"

Thomas grunted. He had indeed done that, rejecting the politicized existence of a life in the Curia, in favor of parish work.

Shaughnessy saw that he had made his point.

"You're serious?"

Shaughnessy nodded slowly.

Thomas adjusted himself in his chair, looking for signs of duplicity in his superior.

"Such meetings are planned years in advance, aren't they?"

"Not this time. Sylvester was only elected a few months ago, as you know. He also has a rather, shall we say, spontaneous style. Very unusual."

"He barely won the vote, as I recall."

Shaughnessy answered, thin-lipped. "But the Conclave wanted a strong follow-up to Francis, who was counter to many of our core intransigencies, shall we say, but also won many hearts. They want to win more hearts."

Thomas smiled, believing. "Sylvester is a philosopher by training, did you know? He wrote extensively when he was an instructor in Florence."

The Cardinal Bishop grinned. "Yes, I thought you'd like that. He likes you too. He was pleased with my recommendation. He's watched recordings of your program, and read some of your treatises. He remembers you from your university days when you interned at the Secretariat. Oh, he wonders about your more radical musings -- like all of us, heh heh -- but I'm told he is nonetheless intrigued by your views."

Thomas smiled distractedly at the comment. His mind raced ahead, envisioning the eventual meeting.

"Cardinal, I've got a lot of preparation to do. I'll have to review Sylvester's past writings…"

The ruddy Cardinal Bishop shook his head and patted Thomas' arm to restrain him. "Not so fast. There are a number of constraints I wish to impart upon to you. This is the Pope; mind you, the Apostolic Prince of Rome himself, not some rock star or politician. He's truly concerned about his obligation to provide responsible direction to our people."

Thomas tried to hide his impatience. "Yes, of course."

"The Church speaks for the ages. We don't respond to fads. Our decisions must last for centuries. We have to be careful and measured in our approach."

"I understand your concern, but you don't have to worry about me, Cardinal."

"I think I do, Thomas. Don't put the shepherd before the sheep. Sylvester is considering you for an important task, but only if you two see eye to eye. I think he plans to challenge your ideas, and you must show respect. He needs you. The Church needs you. But you must be responsible!"

Thomas' eyes narrowed. "You mean, I've got to be willing to tow the line."

"Possibly", said the Cardinal, finally handing over the envelope. Thomas accepted it and thumbed the wax seal, deciding not to open it until later, in private.

Shaughnessy understood, and continued, with sudden warmth, "Sylvester is different from his predecessors in many ways, not the least of which is his love of fresh ideas. His interest is in keeping the Catholic Church relevant to its followers. If your ideas help fulfill that ideal, there's no reason to think he wouldn't incorporate them into his liturgy. I think you two may indeed discover you have a lot in common."

☐

Georgia, near the Azerbaijan border

The lowlands south of Tbilisi and north of Tobuz and the Kura River were a fertile but featureless expanse of agricultural plantations and barbed wire. This was the border between the Islamic republic of Azerbaijan and the war-torn, Christian nation of Georgia. A movement, which called itself the Azerbaijan Popular Front, had gained strength in recent years, recruiting heavily from the semi-autonomous Western territories of Russia, the fledgling Slavic nations splintered off during the 1990's from the long extinct Soviet Union, and the more recently created autonomous regions of war ravaged Afghanistan, Iraq and Iran. From this vast swath of disaffected peoples, the APF had forged a multi-national Islamic alliance under the command of the previously unknown guerrilla leader, Eli Tubasi.

Tubasi, a former petroleum worker and a minor official in the Azerbaijan capital city of Baku, had risen to power with the overthrow of the dictator, Ali Surat Mutaliyov. He was now the primary spokesman and leader of the APF, though this movement was now extended far beyond its original borders. In the years following the dissolution of the Soviet Union, Georgia had been hard pressed to remain intact. In addition to the pressures placed upon it by the APF, there were several autonomous regions within its borders, all of which were engaged in constant struggles for expansion and military gain against the former parent nation.

Georgia was also the site of numerous stockpiles of H.E.U., or highly enriched uranium -- an uncomfortable legacy from the days of the U.S.S.R. Securing these stockpiles during this period of military conflict and unpaid salaries was a challenge that was, frankly, not being met. In the last decade, several individuals peddling nuclear material stolen from the former Soviet Union, had been arrested in Europe and the Middle East, but so far there had been no confirmed cases of countries or terrorist groups obtaining the ingredients for making a bomb through such thefts. It was only a matter of time before such a thing would come to pass.

"The reactor guards work in 24 hour shifts, al-Sayyab." said General Julian Serbenko, a veteran of the former Soviet Union's security force.

"Shhhh! They'll hear you!" whispered Ibn al-Sayyab, clad in robes, a camouflage parka and a weapons belt, his breath a vapor, as he crouched behind a soot smudged brick wall, alongside the bedraggled and unshaven Russian General. The weather beaten building which they regarded in the moonless darkness was not one hour from the capital city of Tbilisi but they may as well have been in Siberia for all the life that could be discerned here. It was also only a short drive to the border. This amazed al-Sayyab. Leave it to the Russians to build a nuclear power plant less than one half hour from the frontier. But then again, in the old days, it wasn't the frontier.

One lonely spotlight illuminated the rusting metal doorway. It was a decrepit monument to the lost heyday of Soviet science. The entrance to the storage compound of Georgia's largest -- and fully non-operational -- nuclear reactor.

The General ignored al-Sayyab's comment. "At precisely 1:17 AM both guards will be at the opposite side of the building engaged in a weapons sale. It is a ruse entirely for your benefit."

"A clever plan, General Serbenko. Who would expect one illegal activity to camouflage another?" The Persian nodded approvingly. "Tubasi will be pleased."

"*Da*, perhaps he will. And you have the payment?"

"My men, beyond the ridge, have the package. After we have the H.E.U. you will receive it."

17

"*Otlichno*. We begin in five minutes. Signal your men."

al-Sayyab turned, and hurled a few stones over the ridge behind them. He was answered with a faint, short whistle. Shortly thereafter another camouflage clad figure appeared.

"Ah, Herif. Good," nodded al-Sayyab as he was handed something. al-Sayyab and Herif exchanged whispers. Serbenko checked his weapon, his back against the brick wall. Herif ran off.

"Two minutes," growled the General softly, his voice like gravel in the darkness.

They were an unlikely pairing. Tubasi's APF machinations had thrown them together for this raid -- and each had much to gain -- but afterwards they would return to their usual condition of mistrust and mutual hatred. They waited, barely breathing.

From the other side of the building could be heard the rumble of an approaching truck. The crunching sound of the guard's footfalls quickly followed.

Serbenko poked the Persian hard with his finger, "The ruse has begun. Go!"

al-Sayyab ran in a low crouch to the base of the storage compound's doorway. He extracted a small package from the confines of his robe. Looking back for an instant, he spotted the General peering around the brick wall ready to provide cover if it was needed. al-Sayyab hoped it was not. These Russians were the worst kind of infidel traitors. They would sell their mothers.

He worked the plasticized PETN compound into the door frame and around the locking mechanism, and then embedded a radio controlled blasting cap into the plastic around the lock. Satisfied with his work he ran back to the protection of the brick wall.

"Ready, Comrade Serbenko."

"GENERAL Serbenko."

"EX-General Serbenko."

Serbenko smiled coldly. "I should kill you now and leave your worthless body here for the locals to find, you overzealous camel dropping."

"Poetic, comrade, but much as I might enjoy trading insults with you, the time has come for action."

And with that, al-Sayyab pressed the button on the radio detonator he exposed from under his robes.

FOOM!

The door shuddered and blew inwards in a cloud of dust and noise.

"The explosive works well, *vida?*" commented the General proudly.

"*Chraa*," al-Sayyab grunted, disinterested, and waved his associates on. Like wraiths they rose from their hiding places and cautiously made their way toward the entrance.

As they approached the storage facility, the two guards who should have been guarding the doorway suddenly came charging forth from opposite corners of the building with their guns blazing. The racket was curtailed abruptly by the "thup thup" of semi-automatic, silenced weapons blasting holes in the two hapless sentries. They fell face first into the dirt in a simultaneous stumbling motion, and lay inert.

"*Idioty,*" muttered the General.

al-Sayyab beckoned his man forward. The raiding party entered the facility.

"Ah, vintage fifties Empire. What an antique," remarked Serbenko, looking around disgustedly, as they scanned the gloomy interior.

"*Yala!*" shouted al-Sayyab to his men and gestured at an interior vault door.

Several of the raiders converged on the doorway and began to don radiation suits from a nearby rack.

When they were ready, three of the raiders entered the room, carrying a very large, long duffel bag. They opened the bag to reveal a lead-lined, carbon

19

graphite casing with a shaped interior exactly matching the dimensions of a nuclear fuel rod.

Following their training, which Serbenko had provided, the three raiders set about working the winch controls within the vault room to lift out one of several nuclear fuel assemblies which lay submerged in the deuterium filled containment pool. Once they had one of the assemblies positioned over a graphite palette, they extracted one of the rods and quickly placed it inside the portable casing they had brought. They worked rapidly and soon the casing was back in the duffel bag and they were out of the vault.

As soon as they had shed the heavy protective garments and re-donned their winter gear, six APF men lifted the duffel bag and, with a signal from al-Sayyab, proceeded out of the containment building into the cold, Georgian winter. Ahead, a convoy of shuttered headlights abruptly blazed into brightness, as more of al-Sayyab's troupe came forward to assist their comrades.

al-Sayyab and Serbenko stood watching for a few moments. Then they turned toward each other.

"Mission accomplished, comrade," said al-Sayyab with a bow. As he came up from his bent position, he revealed a small automatic weapon.

Serbenko raised an eyebrow and coolly assessed the weapon that was aimed at his heart. "A 9x18 Makarov. Probably Bulgarian from the looks of it. Very impressive, camel herder."

"You will cease calling me that, infidel."

"*Idioty!* Didn't you think I would expect this from the sorry likes of you?" sneered Serbenko as he slashed his arm in a wide arc. A long blade emerged from his sleeve, propelled by centrifugal force, and sliced its way through the air where al-Sayyab's neck formerly occupied space.

al-Sayyab was on the ground a few feet away, "I did indeed expect that much of you, EX-General. Now you will be more than EX, you will be altogether

EX-tinct!" al-Sayyab fired his pistol from the ground and the Russian crumpled like a heavy pillar to the ground, as he spat out a curse.

"*Chort!*"

That was his last word.

As al-Sayyab stood, he could hear distant sirens and shouting voices. *As usual, the Russian Calvary -- far too late -- probably Serbenko's fail-safe backup*, he thought to himself.

"*Ilaa l-liqaa', sharmute,*" he said with a grim laugh to the General's corpse, bidding his leave, and walking calmly toward the waiting convoy of trucks.

"To the frontier," he ordered quietly to his driver, feeling extraordinarily calm. Soon the *Jihad* would have its flaming sword to wield against the Zionists and imperialist infidels. Soon the everlasting struggle between Ishmael and Isaac, the sons of Abraham, would come to a culmination and justice would be done once and for all time. He would receive his blessing from Tubasi back in Baku. Then there would be only one more gesture to make.

Hyde Park area, Chicago

A wash of sleet splattered against the steady thump thump sound of the windshield wipers as Thomas steered one of the Rectory's cars down Michigan Avenue. He was having trouble keeping the windshield defogged and had to resort to using the sleeve of his tunic again and again.

The streets were deserted, washed clean of humanity by the heavy rain and the torpor that usually permeated New Year's day, as people nursed their hangovers and slept off the prior night's revelry.

The few cars that were out drifted morosely down the flooded streets. Thomas turned onto Garfield Boulevard. The University of Chicago was not far off. Thomas had called ahead and had not been surprised to find Professor Karin Ferguson at her desk, but that was so Karin; working away at a lecture or an article, and considering the solitude advantageous.

Karin Ferguson was a Professor of Humanities, and an Associate Instructor of Near Eastern Studies at the University of Chicago where she was studying early Christianity. She was a rising star on the faculty, producing a steady stream of incisive investigative works. Thomas' interest in the dynamics of the various competing early Christian sects intersected him directly with her. She was also a valuable source of research and anecdotal (if ancient historical tidbits could be called anecdotal) information for Thomas' televised series.

They had met at an exhibition of illuminated texts at the Art Institute one snowy evening and barely spoken to anyone else, once she discovered his knowledge of the early Christians. Now they were fast friends -- enjoying each other's dark humor, exchanging arcane historical research in a kind of scholarly brinkmanship, and flirting obliquely.

He remembered the phone call.

"What keeps you at the grist mill on such a miserable day, Dr. Karin?"

"Research, of course, Father Tom. Research is life."

"Naturally. And who is being researched this time?"

"You make me sound so nosy. Mark."

"The gospel? What new twist can you be extracting from that?"

"Oh, there are more twists and turns in the old Gospels than a Jewish ghetto. Take your pick."

"Alright. If I had to guess I would say..."

"The ending," she burst out.

"Hmm. There is an unfinished feel to it."

"Exactly! Unlike the other Gospels, it ends with an empty tomb and a mystery. Very melodramatic. And subject to misinterpretation."

"Oh, really?" had answered Thomas, intrigued.

"Oh yes, silly boy. It's simple. You see, Mark is an insider's tome. It's from a time when vocal traditions were much stronger. Mark expects the reader to participate in remembering the story of Jesus. It's meant to resonate with the folklore about Christ that was being passed down by word of mouth by people with a common secret -- frequently operating covertly to avoid persecution. It was written right after the destruction of the Second Temple in Jerusalem by the Romans, when the Hebrew and proto-Christian peoples were trying to reconcile their expectations of retribution with the grim reality of their lives. The darkness of the ending is a reflection of the darkness felt by these parties at the time. This is different from the other three Gospels of the official, Church anointed New Testament, which came much later in time."

Thomas answered appreciatively, "You're a laser beam in a room of mists."

They had said nothing for a moment or two, feeling the connection of their chemistry across the ether, each listening to the undercurrent of digital whirrs and whispers that carried their voices over their wireless link.

Then, almost impatiently, Karin had asked, "Well, what is it?"

"What is what?"

"What is it you need me to do for you?"

He laughed at himself. "Of course, why else would I call on New Year's Day? Certainly not to wish you a Happy New Year!"

Then as always, he privately enjoyed the sound of her deep laugh as she heard this. He loved her throaty, exuberant voice. He imagined her cheek, showing a hint of dimple as she laughed.

"I need to talk."

"To talk. On New Year's Day. Sure. Drop by and pull up a couch."

Thomas pulled up to the University's stone gates and waved to the dozing guard. Slowly, he navigated the old Chevy toward the Oriental Institute, an imposing art deco structure, and parked. Not bothering with an umbrella, he cast a look around as he made his way to the entrance. Not a soul to be found. The place was in remission, soggy and gray. Litter from last night's bacchanalian escapades dotted the grounds. He pushed open the heavy wooden doors and strode down the darkened hallway.

Long before he got to Karin's office he could hear the tap tap of her keyboard echoing against the quiet. The door was ajar and as he entered, his first impression was one of warmth and chaos. The entire circumference of the room from floor to ceiling was lined in books set in heavy, wooden shelves – with the exception of two gaps allowing for windows. Her desk, positioned in the center of the crowded space, was buried in papers, artifacts, office paraphernalia, a laptop -- and holding sway over the entire affair – Karin. She whirled at the sound of his entrance.

"Aaah, you made it I see. Take off your coat -- throw it on that table -- no, better yet, here's a hanger."

She produced a hanger from a drawer. Thomas accepted it and looked around for a place to hook it. Eventually he settled on the doorknob.

Karin rose to greet him. Thomas paused to admire her. Despite her careless outfit, she radiated a certain elegance. Then, as if by signal, they approached each other and embraced briefly.

"Tea, Thomas? -- sit."

"Thanks. Whatever you're drinking, Doctor."

He moved papers aside and sat on the couch with a soft grunt. She made their tea at a small table by one of the windows and returned to the couch. She sat right on whatever papers were positioned there, then, reluctantly raised herself again and pushed them aside.

"There, that's better." She examined Thomas with fond amusement, cocking her head to one side, and asked, "Can I guess?"

Thomas sipped his tea. The hot brew felt good. He nodded wordlessly.

"It's about the Pope?"

Thomas was truly shocked. "Yes! How in the name of the Pearly Gates did you know?"

She chuckled and put her teacup down on a book precariously balanced on the arm of the sofa. "Well, it's common enough knowledge that he's looking for spokespersons. You're almost famous, and no doubt, Cardinal Shaughnessy will try to exploit that -- just a hunch, really."

"More like a prophecy. He wrote me a letter."

She blinked and waited, returning to her tea.

"He's asking me join a kind of task force."

Karin almost spit out her swallow of tea in response, "You mean like, a secret mission?"

Thomas shifted uncomfortably, "No, it's not like that. It's more like a... well, okay; maybe it is like a mission."

Karin's face broke into a broad dimpled, smile, in amusement.

"But the mission is to figure out ways to re-energize the Church's message."

"You mean, like an explanation for why the world didn't end in 2001, or 2011 or 2013?"

He glanced at her in mock disparagement. "Stop. You know the Church doesn't subscribe to such claims."

"No matter." she continued, "2021 is the place to be for souls that want to be saved, according to some Bible scholars. Most of the loonies whom we thought had disappeared following the last few end-dates, are back, spreading their froth flecked rhetoric across the planet. And anyway, who needs the Church's approval? One way or another, most cultures have an apocalyptic prediction up their sleeves: 2021, 2048, 2053, 2239. The next one, just around the corner, affects at least 1,800,000,000 people and at least three major belief systems." She slurped tea nonchalantly and glanced up at Thomas, "It's a numbers game."

Thomas ignored her attempts to provoke him. "Be that as it may, Karin, Sylvester needs to show strength and composure to the congregations of the world."

"And he wants you to help him construct a communications strategy. You should be honored."

"I wonder."

"What do you think the messaging should be?"

"I don't…"

"You gotta give Sylvester an angle. Something fresh," she said abruptly. "Men have evolved tremendously in their understanding of the universe in the past two millennia but spiritual understanding remains where it was two thousand years ago; unchanged, even regressed. Let's face it, we, as a species, are metaphysical louts."

"Well, not exactly –", said Thomas.

"You know what I mean," said Karin, waving his protest away.

Thomas nodded in silence, pondering her point.

Karin sipped more tea and continued, "Religion should be giving us enlightenment, but instead it demands our faith. Platitudes and pre-packaged precepts are not focused with reality. We need to wake up and do a little thinking for ourselves. Christians may be God's flock but I don't think he would want us to be mindless sheep. The church should provide people with knowledge, empowerment, enlightenment, not dogma. That's what you have to bring to the table."

"Karin, that sounds a good deal more Eastern than Western."

"Perhaps it is," she nodded, "All Western religions have a mystical variant lurking in the wings. In the case of Christianity, it's the Gnostics."

Thomas raised an eyebrow at her.

"Oh don't get all indignant. You've said it yourself on your TV show many times. Something like, 'All we have to do is look into our hearts, to find the chrysalis of inner being'."

"I didn't say that."

"You did. You've been walking on thin ice for years, Tom. If I were the Pope I would have you watched."

Thomas deadpanned, "How do you think I got this assignment?"

Athos, Greece – Eight Years Prior

"*Credo in unum Deum, Patrem omnipotentem, factorem coeli et terrae, visibilium omnium et invisibilium…*" sang the lead *protopsalti* as the three monks that comprised the chorus held the dominant tones of the chanted melody. They were positioned before the altar, hoods removed, heads bowed, hands brought together in a position of prayer with their backs to the pews. It was evening vespers. The droning chant reverberated throughout the interior as the *protopsalti* crooned his complex, lead melody and let it dance over the chorus like a bell within the Church.

Philo Berith sat in his pew and enjoyed the music. He found it thrilling to hear time after time, and that was a multitude of times. Since he had been a young boy, Philo had climbed the chiseled steps and walked the meandering paths to the Philotheou Monastery to provide the resident monks with their simple supplies, like his father Yorgo, and his grandfather, Old Philo, before him.

Philotheou was one of the many Coenobite and Idiorrythmic monasteries that dotted the flanks of Mount Athos and the Halkidiki peninsula in Northern Greece. Each monastery housed extensive libraries of ancient writings and literature dating as far back as the tenth century, and considerable collections of Byzantine art and music. But more important than being untainted repositories

27

of Christian history, these isolated monasteries represented the highest form of spiritual life known in the Orthodox and possibly the entire Christian world.

The monks within fascinated Philo. As little as Philo himself had in the way of possessions, the monks were entirely bereft of earthly comforts and concerns, and yet they all seemed so much happier than many of the villagers around him. They had no interest in the multi-ethnic politics of the region, or in economics. They had none of the fierce pride or righteous morality that was characteristic of the local people. Though they were alternately ridiculed and revered by the townsfolk living in the vicinity of the monasteries, it was of no import to them.

The monks seemed to exist in another plain and see a different day than Philo did, many times appearing to find his mundane queries as to their needs to be hilarious, but politely suppressing their mirth while surreptitiously exchanging glances among themselves. But despite these discomforts, he loved them. They were of such purity that he sensed they knew God; that they had touched him and seen him to be real.

He was himself a religious man, a devout Orthodox Greek of Macedonian descent who aspired to a life free of sin but who lived in the practical world, as difficult as that sometimes was. He had never married, but he was a well-regarded fixture of the community. People liked Philo and he in turn liked them, but he reserved his love for the monks. And of all the monks in the monastery, he loved Yordon Antropos above all. The tall stranger, the orphan, the one with the visions.

They had met on the flanks of the Holy Mountain itself, Athos, a few years prior. It had been an early morning in spring. Located at the southernmost tip of the Halkidiki arm, the symmetrical cone of Athos dominated the scenery, seeming to hold the sun at its apex, and watch over the waters of the blue Aegean.

Philo had been wandering along the southern flanks of the mountain, a barren place despite the spectacular view, called the desert of Athos, enjoying an exhilarating hike and the opportunity for a measure of time alone. He had come to an area of *hesychasteria*, simple huts and caves in the cliff, to which monks often retired in search of isolation. Picking his way along the rocks and scrabble with the aid of a walking stick, Philo had heard the sound of pebbles being thrown into the distant water from one of the caves. Finding that curious behavior for a monk and thinking it might be boys from one of the villages playing pranks, he headed toward the cave mouth from which the pebbles came, fully expecting to have to scold some youngster.

As he entered the darkness of the cave he could hear a low murmuring voice reciting Greek chant. A pebble flew past his ear out into the sky. He let out a cry of surprise which induced a similar exclamation from the unknown occupant.

"Forgive me, brother. I was in deep meditation and I did not expect a visitor. But you are welcome," said a calm, resonant voice. A young man, perhaps in his twenties, emerged from the darkness. He was tall and thin, with strong, even features. His light brown hair was tied back and he was dressed in simple rough robes. But most striking were his eyes, which were a penetrating, translucent hazel. They seemed to seep to the core of anyone who gazed into them.

Philo tried not to show his admiration of the man's beauty.

Philo bowed theatrically, partially to hide his awe, and said, "It is I who must beg forgiveness, young sir, for intruding upon you, but I thought it was unusual to see rocks flying out of a cave's mouth."

Yordon smiled gently, "Yes, it is unusual behavior for a monk."

A monk? Philo squinted at him, not knowing what to say.

The young man seemed to understand Philo's discomfort. He gestured toward the floor. "Sit, brother, and talk with me a while. You look tired. I have water in the back." He glanced at Philo questioningly. Philo finally nodded his assent.

Returning with a clay jug, the tall ascetic sat down and handed it to Philo. He picked up another loose pebble and threw it toward the water. Without looking at Philo he answered his unspoken question. "The pebbles are a metaphor."

"Hmm?" said Philo still engaged in his drought of water from the jug. He wiped his lips on his sleeve and returned it to his mysterious host, who gazed at him unblinkingly.

St. Andrew's whiskers, what a strange fellow! "I see. Which monastery are you from?"

"Philotheou. Like your name."

"What? How did you know my name?" asked Philo, unnerved by the trick. The young hermit shrugged and looked at him playfully out of the corner of his eye. Philo eyed him back but decided to let it go. Miracles in this holy place were common enough.

"And what is your name?"

"I am called Yordon, Yordon Antropos of Philippi, a son of Panayote Antropos."

Philo responded in kind. "My family name is Berith. I provision the monks of Philotheou, as it happens, with what they can't prepare for themselves," Then after a pause, "Beriths have always served the monks."

"I am grateful then for your generations of service," said Yordon.

Philo wondered if the remark had been sarcastic but found it hard to believe from this sincere stranger. He decided to probe a little.

"I have never seen you on the grounds before. Are you recently arrived?"

"No. I have been here a long time, Philo. I tend to keep to myself."

Noting Yordon's hesitation, Philo changed his tact. "So why is the pebble a - - metaphor did you say?"

Yordon picked up another stone and rolled it between his thumb and forefinger. "Because it represents our condition, Philo. Here in Athos, we Coenobite monks seek to unshackle ourselves from all that is material and worldly. We strive for a higher consciousness through our actions and our constant inner prayer. But I am haunted by the isolation we force upon ourselves. "

Philo was surprised to hear a monk speak this way. He examined Yordon with increasing interest. "My father used to say that a man's worth is not defined by what he possesses or by what others think of him, but by what does NOT possess him."

"Hmm. And what do you think your father meant by those words, Philo?" asked Yordon.

Philo grew thoughtful. "That life is a journey. And that the passage to heaven lies within."

"Yes. But the people of God exist all around us. We monks are living outside the world. In a sense, we have abandoned it. We are like the rocks strewn along the face of this mountain. Forgotten fragments of a geological past. Only when a rock or a pebble escapes from the side of the mountain and plummets down to the sea is there any notice of its existence. Only then does it affect the world, like the ripples that travel away from a pebble after it has entered the waters. That is how it is with me. Only by plunging in can I share my experience, my discoveries, with others."

Discoveries? "Why would you do this? The world would be deaf to you, a monk. And we already have the Church."

Yordon turned to Philo and let the lines of his face betray him for an instant. Then his features relaxed again. Philo was surprised to see what could have been nothing else but anger on the man's face. Though he felt that had just

31

glimpsed the soul of this monk, he did not feel he knew this man well enough to explore further.

Groaning, Philo struggled upright. "Well, Yordon, thank you for the water and the conversation. I will leave you now and resume my walk. When you return to Philotheou, we can talk again, yes? When will you return?"

"In time," was Yordon's deadpan response as he threw another pebble into the Aegean.

And so they had met. And meet again they did. And talk again they did. Yordon grew to like Philo very much and frequently asked him to stay awhile on the occasion of his visits to the monastery. It seemed to Philo that he rapidly became a counterweight to Yordon. While Philo was pragmatic and irreverent, Yordon was an idealistic thinker and a surprisingly good orator. They fed off each other, each learning much from the other's ways. In this way, Philo came to learn about Yordon's life and how he came to be at the monastery.

He was born in 1988, the son of a farmer in Philippi, on the occasion of a great meteor shower. His family was poor but hard working. He had no brothers or sisters. His mother, an enigmatic woman, had been barren for years until one day her husband visited her in the night and they conceived their only child. Despite the aggressive efforts of the old couple, they were never successful again. But they were grateful. Both his mother and father believed that their conception of Yordon had been a gift from God himself -- an acknowledgment of their faith. Yordon's father, Panayote, henceforth gave every extra cent to the church -- often at the expense of the family. Nonetheless, it was a hard but good life that Yordon led.

His mother and father were killed during the economic revolts of the late 1980's, when Greece was in global default, not for the first or the last time. Yordon was strangely calm following their tragic deaths, many thought. He was also instantly rendered an orphan, for there were no other family members for him to fall back on. He was cared for by the local church missionaries for a short period but was soon thereafter shipped to Athos -- as an acolyte of the Monks of Philotheou.

Each of these monks had an interesting past, Philo was sure; though many did not care to share it. But Yordon yearned for it, as if telling someone about himself helped to substantiate him, make him more real. It seemed to Philo that he hungered for this.

As the Philotheou monks finished their Byzantine chant inside the monastery's Church, Philo returned to the present and observed Yordon, the *protopsalti* at tonight's Vespers, descend the worn rock steps from the altar, head bowed, and process back to his cell along with his fellow monks. His face was lost in contemplation as he passed. *There'll be no talk today*, thought Philo to himself. Yordon's contemplative states could border on the delusional. He sighed and faced toward the altar to cross himself, as he genuflected in the aisle before leaving.

Outside the little church, the monks processed out of the little stone church into the cold air of the mountains. Yordon blindly followed the footfalls of the monk directly in front of him and let the ghostly whispers swirl in his mind. He knew none of the others heard them. The visions were the worst part, and they were intense at this moment, threatening to blot out the scenery.

As he walked, a part of Yordon's mind thought back to his early days as an acolyte. He would lie there, helpless, in his small bed inside the monastery, trying to quiet the wordless currents of feelings and intuitions that ran through him. It was like a subliminal delirium, ready to burst through the skin of his perception at any moment. He felt it like this. A continuum of marvels beneath the surface of his ordinary life. He felt he had to release them somehow so that others could understand, but how? What were the right words? It was as if there was a secret his body was keeping from him, waiting for the right moment to reveal itself and change his life forever.

As he grew older, and was eventually accepted into the order of the Philotheou monks, he learned to control the wordless tide and gradually, through the power of constant prayer, and by way of that control, there would be moments when he felt himself brought fully into that domain beneath his everyday reality. The wall between his mind and the outside world would dissipate and he would meld into a place beyond language and culture, beyond the strobe-like flicker of passing days and human events. All things were one in there and when he was allowed in, he was one with all. He became intimate with every object, every sound, every light, every breath. It was joy and it was a deep knowledge of all things. The insights would leave him exhausted and sweating once the trance was broken. He would lie there breathing shallowly and feel panic at the prospect of forgetting this knowledge, even as he realized he had somehow always known it, even as he recognized that it must be shared.

After months of struggling with his growing convictions, he had resolved to do something about it. The memory of the pebbles came back, as if in confirmation of his musings, and locked in his resolve. At last, Yordon believed he was ready for his mission in this life.

☐

Chapter Two: The Gloaming Hour

Starkenville, Missouri - Eight Years Prior

The first of Mary Maccabe's significant religious experiences had been as a child during a visit to the Shrine of Our Lady of Sorrows, an apparition site in Starkenville, Missouri. The claim had been that the Blessed Virgin Mary was making regular appearances to five local children. The youngsters stated that they had been able to "see" and "hear" the Virgin every day for a year and a half.

The Vatican was undecided on the phenomena. Critics warned that popular devotion was being manipulated by hucksters and radical right Catholic activists. The local pastor had initially favored the five children's claims until one day he had inexplicably changed his mind and reported to the press that the apparitions were nothing more than a case of collective hallucination.

But the believing public had not cared a flicker. If anything, the controversy had further fueled the interest of the faithful and drawn hundreds to the site. Mary's mother and her three sisters loaded up their '72 Chevy Nova and chugged the many miles to Starkenville from Arkansas.

"What are we gonna see when we get there, Mama? A ghost?" her youngest sister asked.

"Well, honey, some people say it's a bright light. Other folks say you can see the Virgin Mary's face clearly. I don't know for sure. But I do know this -" her mother had leaned back and turned to look at them for an instant, "and all of you should listen up now -- what you see when we get there is dependent on your faith in God. You've got to go in believin' or you won't see nothin'."

Mary leaned forward and rested her chin on the front seat cushion and asked, "But isn't it the other way around, Mama? Don't you have to see something before you can believe in it?"

35

"You shush up, Mary!"

That was how it had been it those days. Following her mother like a wet feathered duckling no matter where she went. Mary sighed and contemplated her reflection in the window glass. The disparaging countenance that stared back beneath straight brows was contrasted by a smattering of brown freckles. *Just another Arkansas face*, she thought.

When they arrived at the parish church outside Starkenville, there was already a considerable crowd. The five youngsters who claimed to be able to see the apparition were positioned outside the shrine building, rosaries in hand. A large gazebo had been set up with a band playing old country songs for the crowd. There were rows and rows of folding metal chairs covering the open field in front of the church, almost all of them filled with ranks of the faithful. The place had the air of a carnival.

The Maccabe clan spilled out of their vehicle and grabbed the first seats they could find that afforded them a reasonable view. They were about 200 feet away from the shrine. Soon the band ceased playing and a murmur rose among the spectators. Without preamble, the five children began to recite their rosaries, and the crowd chanted along. As they arrived at the last prayer, they entered the shrine together, praying a bit louder so the crowd could still hear them. Then, suddenly, they stopped praying and knelt simultaneously.

Mary couldn't see anything. Once the youngsters had entered the darkness of the shrine, nothing could be discerned this far back. She had sat in that sticky back seat for almost a day and a half and she wasn't in the mood to be disappointed. And anyway she didn't want to hear any vague fabrications from her mother later -- to be used as a disciplinary lever whenever she wanted to coerce Mary. Mary was determined to see this with her own eyes. Abruptly she got up and dashed to the front of the crowd.

"Mary!" whispered her mother harshly, "You get your skinny little butt back here this instant! What you're doing is a sin! Come back!"

But Mary wasn't having it. She ran faster. No one paid her any mind. The entire field of people was focused on the events inside the shrine. She approached it, crouching low.

Inside, the children, three boys and two girls of varying ages, were on their knees, looking upward, their faces frozen in tranquil expressions. Their lips moved as if they were speaking, but they made no sound. From the movement of their lips it seemed as if they were mouthing the same words in unison. Their glances converged on the same point in space. *What were they seeing?*

Mary took a deep breath and dashed inside the shrine. There was a collective gasp from the crowd, Her mother's voice could be heard above the noise -- she was in pursuit.

"Mary! Mary Maccabe, you disobedient little creature! Get out of there at once -- you're committing sacrilege! God forgive her!"

Mary had to wait a few precious seconds for her eyes to adjust to the relative darkness. The interior was illuminated by a handful of grimy candles, which produced a minimal, flickering light. Her mother could be heard approaching, accompanied by several clucking church officials, who were venting their consternation at Mary's mother. Mary would surely pay dearly for that later. No matter. She looked up at the point in space where the five children, completely oblivious to Mary's presence, were staring -- each with a look of rapture. She stared too. Nothing. She tried to conjure up a feeling a faith -- she had always imagined it as a soft, cottony, vaguely joyful feeling. She blinked. There was only darkness. The candles wavered as if a wind had gusted but there was no wind. She could hear the scuttling of road gravel as her mother darkened the entrance with her bulk. She was grabbed by the shoulders.

"Get out here this instant, you little monster!" shrieked her mother.

Just then, the five children turned around to face her simultaneously, and all five spoke together and directly to her in a high contralto monotone -- clearly not their own voices but five iterations of an other-worldly voice -- and they said,

> *"Know that you will soon witness war and despair. See*
> *that you are not frightened, for these things must take place.*
> *It is not the end, but the beginning. You will come to know*
> *who is the Son of Man."*

Mary's heart stopped. The five children stopped speaking and approached her, stepping in unison. The oldest of the girls reached out her hand and touched Mary. The room suddenly glowed and Mary's head was filled with a rush of actinic energy and a euphoria unlike any she had ever experienced in her young life before. Mary realized the glow was coming from her, even as she succumbed to the thrill of it that caused her to fall to the ground.

The children then turned their backs to her and continued their silent prayers, oblivious to her now, as she was physically dragged from the building by two dour church prelates.

"Did you see that? Did you hear?" she said in a panicky voice, as she struggled to regain her wits and tried to understand what had just happened to her.

"What, what do you mean? Do you realize what you almost did?" yelled one of the men.

"The voice...."

"What voice? Did one of the children speak to you?" pressed her assailant, calming himself at the prospect of another miracle.

She shook her head and tried to stand but the grip on her shoulder kept her off balance. She realized she was no longer glowing. Suddenly her mother appeared out of the shadows and slapped Mary viciously across the cheek.

"Devil child!"

"Mama, don't!"

She was yanked away by her mother.

None of her siblings or her mother spoke much to her for the rest of the visit, which was meaningless since they did not see or hear anything and only came away with souvenir thimbles depicting a glowing Virgin Mary floating above the heads of five cherubic children kneeling before the Shrine of Our Lady of Sorrows. They glowered at her for the duration of the interminable ride back home. But Mary paid them back in the same coin and didn't say a word about her experience inside the shrine. It had been so strange. That high ungendered voice, coming from five mouths and five expressionless faces. And the message. How did they know her name? What did it mean? Mary knew at least one thing that it meant above all others: Whatever was appearing inside that Church, Virgin Mary or not, was real. Something big and terrible was going to happen in her lifetime. Mary shuddered. She believed.

From that day forward, Mary became obsessed with anything having to do with Spiritualism, surprising and even embarrassing her mother as the years unwound. As for her secret message, she nursed it in the privacy of her mind; waiting for the day when it would be needed.

Oval Office, The White House, Washington D.C., February 2020

President Robert Becker stood before his circle of advisers and appointees and heard the bad news.

"The Palestinians are in a broil over Avrahami's latest provocations, Mr. President. Mazir was practically jumping on his desk demanding retribution," reported Theodore Baskin, the U.S Ambassador to the United Nations.

"This could require American intervention, Bob," offered Wesley Van Ness, the National Security Adviser.

"I recommend we scramble some Hornets off the *Truman* Carrier Group, Mr. President, and put some E-2 recon birds on high alert," said Admiral James "Javelin" Farrow, the silver haired, Texas born, Head of the Joint Chiefs of Staff. "We should be ready for the worst." He squinted as he spoke, and incongruously displayed a smile that was all clenched teeth, slightly parted.

"Do you think it could deteriorate into all-out war, Admiral?" asked Kent Hanover, the Secretary of Defense.

Farrow worked his mustache as he gave his drawled reply, "This one definitely crosses the line in the sand, Mr. Hanover."

"Okay! Okay! Everybody back in your seats!" ordered the President, waving everyone down. "Try to calm yourselves, for crying out loud! We've had Middle East crisis before and more than our fair share in this administration alone. Why is it always the Middle East that bogs down? We won the Cold War, turned South America around, re-established diplomatic relations with Cuba, contained the Chinese, high-tailed it out of Africa, put aside from the drug war, hell, we've even put up a one thousand mile long wall separating Mexico from the U.S.A., but the Middle East remains the only perennially uncontrollable geopolitical situation. None of my predecessors, despite periods of progress, has ever had any luck making headway with these guys."

The President paused and began to pace back and forth at the front of the room. Pausing halfway along his course, he resumed his train of thought, "The lesson is that nothing ever really changes over there and to try and force change only results in chaos."

There was silence in the room. For a few minutes no one knew what to say.

Admiral Farrow broke the impasse by clearing his throat. "So if I'm hearing you correctly, Mr. President, you're saying, sir, that you don't think that

Avrahami's latest decision to deny access to the Old City to all Arabs in the region for the rest of the year in retribution for the killing of Rabbi Moscowitz right at the Western Wall, poses a real and present danger to the United States of America? That an escalation of hostilities is not likely?"

Becker shook his head and waved Farrow's words away as he replied, "I didn't say that. I'm trying to inject a little perspective into your thinking. This country is too jumpy about that region, in my opinion. Both Arabs and Israelis have held this nation in political shackles for decades. Our alliances cross their borders – despite our strategic errors over the last thirty years, we've still got friends on both sides of that line in the sand you mentioned -- and we can't police the region for them. That stratagem only succeeded in hobbling this country with a bottomless deficit, a never ending turnstile of warring regimes, splintered and still splintering nations, stateless radicalism, dead Americans by the thousands and wildly fluctuating prices for a barrel of oil. We used to have to wear sweaters in the White House to save on fuel."

"Until we figured out fracking and how to drill the Artic", said Farrow.

Becker slapped the surface of his desk, "Exactly, Admiral! Maybe we don't have to put up with their saber rattlings quite as delicately anymore."

The Admiral stroked his mustache and nodded slightly. The others stared, wide eyed, at the President.

Becker finished, "Those days are over, at least while I sit in this chair."

"You want to stonewall the Middle East, sir?" worried Baskin. He looked pale.

"It's risky, sir." Hanover was rubbing his hands.

"All I'm proposing here, Kent, is that we drag our feet a little bit. Let them sort it out. Allow a little silence from this side of the Atlantic. Let them rant and rave. Then we can jump in with the usual platitudes. Can you handle it, Max?"

Max Ravessi, the U.S. Special Envoy to the Middle East, didn't look confident as he replied, "If that is to be our strategy, you may be surprised to hear that doing nothing is the hardest action of all. This will be difficult, Mr. President."

"What do you mean, Maxie? You get to stay home for a change. Bounce the kids on your knee instead of bouncing your knees against the fold-down tray!"

The room shared a brief chuckle. Becker was always quick to dismantle a tense situation with a little irreverence. Perhaps too quick.

3 Kaplan St., Jerusalem

Prime Minister Moshe Avrahami looked out the window of his office, his hands stuffed in his pockets, as was his habit and the bane of his public relations adviser. He felt tense. And very tired. His shortness of breath was getting worse. Outside, he could see a column of Hassidim in 18th century *kapotas* and *shteimels* -- despite the broiling heat of the desert -- making their way through a crowd of pedestrians. Just ahead of them, a Muslim *imam* in *tarboosh* and *galabiyah*, with a group of placard carrying students in tow, walked in the direction of the Hassidim. Avrahami winced as the two groups intersected. In the bustling crowd, one of the Hassidim accidentally shoved one of the Muslims and instantly a shouting match ensued. Police came running.

The country was up in arms. Half the Knesset wanted him out at once, the other half considered him a national hero. Never had an Israeli Prime Minister ordered the Old City cordoned off to all Arabs. They had gone so far as to forcefully expel entire families who had lived within its boundaries and had moved them to tent camps within the Palestinian Autonomous Zone.

"You are committing a grave political mistake, Moshe," said the Minister of Foreign Affairs, Natan Silver. "The Palestinians' retributions will be severe. They can't do anything less."

"And do you think it's any different for us, Natan? The violation was severe. Those unwashed bastards know no bounds, so now we have bounds and they are clearly marked with soldiers and checkpoints."

Silver looked pale at this. "Do you forget that the Hamas are the Government now – they have been for years -- and they have vowed to kill you?"

Avrahami pondered this for a moment, then sighed, "*An davar.* Let them. Then I can at least rest."

Silver shook his head in exasperation and approached the Prime Minister so that they were standing face to face. Avrahami wouldn't look at him. Silver grabbed him by the shoulders.

"Moshe, it is possible that the Palestinians and their allies, the Jordanians and Syrians, could threaten us with an armed response over this. Do you want another Six Day War? And the Americans are strangely silent. Usually they are such hand wringers."

Avrahami looked up, "A conspiracy?"

Silver un-expectedly laughed, "Ha! Hasn't it always been? No, I don't think so. Or if so, it's unwitting. Their new President is somewhat thick-skulled. He may be showing his dislike for us by 'letting us stew in our own juices' as they would say."

Avrahami shrugged, "*Kaka kaka.*"

He sat down and grabbed a fig from a fruit bowl. Biting in the ripe fruit, he said through the fruity flesh, "Perhaps it's better like this, eh, Natan? They're such bunglers anyway. This way it's pure."

TBN Studios, Aurora, Chicago

Thomas was leaving the local cable affiliate's studios, after having completed the filming of another "*Behind the Word*", when he spotted a knot of reporters and cameramen coming toward him.

Britta Braxton, the well-known lead on many a field report from the *Newsline 2020* news program, approached Thomas with a determined smile. Thomas was accustomed to the attention, but he was apprehensive about his supposed assignment to the Pope's task force, of which he knew little still. He half worried that the journalists of the major media outlets, or even some well-connected blogger out there in the ether, might get word of his assignment and threaten its integrity, injecting it with rumor and conjecture, before it even got off the ground.

Braxton stepped right up to Thomas and extended her microphone toward him. The cameramen shuffled into position and several boom mikes appeared as if out of nowhere to hover over Thomas. Of a sudden, he was the epicenter of a pool of reporters. Braxton smiled at him glowingly and said, "Cameras are rolling, Father."

Thomas blinked, dumbfounded at the swiftness of it all.

Lights came on, making him squint slightly, despite the broad daylight, and Braxton turned to face the camera.

"Good evening viewers. Today we're standing in front of Trinity Broadcasting Network's state of the art Studio complex and I have with me, Father Thomas Prisciotti, whom many of you may know as the host of the popular *"Behind the Word"* seminar series, in which Father Tom reads between the lines of the Bible. Hello Father."

"Uh, hello, Ms. Braxton. It's not quite that simple…"

"Father, can you comment on the recent developments in Israel?"

"Developments? Are you referring to…?"

Braxton knifed in, "This week's forcible expulsion of all Arabs from the Old City in Jerusalem by the Avrahami Government. How does this fit in with Biblical end times writings that many are quoting as predicting this very week's events?"

Thomas shook his head, in frustration, "Where is that written? There is no correlation, that's all a bunch of hok…"

"Not in the public eye, Father. The Israeli government's actions come amid a steadily rising wave of public apprehension and rising belief in the coming of the end times, as demonstrated by recent polls, New York Times and Amazon.com bestseller lists, and your own program's rising ratings!"

"Britta, hysteria and hearsay are not news events…"

"But Father Tom, the Palestinian President has declared the Israeli move a declaration of war!"

"That is unfortunate, he has a responsibility…" said Thomas, grimly, fighting the urge to push through the circle of reporters and escape.

"And The Iranian Iman Khameini this morning publicly approved the Palestinian proposal of arming the West Bank and calling its people to action against Israel!"

Thomas fumbled for words, wanting to rebut Braxton's blatant attempts to infuse her viewers with more fear and hysteria. He felt a wave of hopelessness overtake him, and yet he could not leave Braxton's line of argument un-answered, un-countered. He had to say something rational!

He allowed his gaze to wander as he searched for words, when looking above the heads of the surrounding journalists, he noticed a long, black car gliding toward the studio entranceway. He recognized it as one of the Rectory's. He immediately knew it was coming for him. He wondered why.

Realizing this was his escape and he had only seconds, he looked Braxton in the eye and said, "End Times predictions are as old as written history, and if there's one thing they all have in common it's that they have all been wrong."

"But Father,"

"No, Britta, let me finish. The Catholic Church believes in the eventual return of Christ, but it is not blinded by the fallibility of human events and does not subscribe to the efforts of the news-as-entertainment industry to scare people."

Braxton's eye's glowed with either admiration or anger, Thomas could not tell in the moment, but enough was said and he suddenly pressed through the crowd, repeating the mantra of, "No comment", to any and all further questions.

The passenger door of the Rectory car opened as Thomas approached and he quickly inserted himself into its dark comfort. Instantly, the car drove away, leaving a phalanx of journalists and camera lights behind. Thomas hoped against hope that his rebuttal was enough to neutralize any "news" that might be garnered from *Newsline 2020's* brief encounter with him, but he knew they would spin his remarks into even more controversy in some way.

The car accelerated away from the crowd, sure with power, and proceeded toward the highway, back to the Rectory.

"What's the special occasion, Wyatt?" Thomas asked the driver, a Church volunteer, but a long standing one.

Wyatt only answered, "For you", handing Thomas a cell phone. It was already connected.

Thomas saw the prefix numbers displayed on the cell phone: 39 06 698. He realized it was a direct call from Italy. He put the phone to his ear.

"Hello?"

The voice on the other end of the call, the signal clean and crisp, was gravelly, and yet graced with a practiced unctuousness, but beneath it all, kind, "I have been looking forward to making your acquaintance, my son."

Sylvester. Thomas's heart jumped and he croaked, "Thank you, Holy Father. I've have been looking forward to speaking with you ever since receiving your letter."

"Yes, the letter. Forgive me, my son," said Pope Sylvester III, "I try to instill each conversation with a personal stamp of intimacy, but the Catholic Church, even in this time of crisis, is a globe spanning enterprise; a business, as well as a faith and a calling. There is not much time for the little things."

Hardly a little thing. "I understand, your Holiness. There is no need to explain."

Sylvester grunted softly, and continued, "I am glad to be speaking with you now, Father Prisciotti. I know that you are a vigorous theologian and thinker in the Diocese."

"Please call me Thomas. Thank you, Your Holiness."

"Your public persona is a valuable addition to the mouth of the Church."

"It has sometimes been considered controversial," said Thomas.

"And it is, from time to time, Thomas. I have listened to several of your... podcasts."

Thomas couldn't help but smile at the thought of the Apostolic Delegate to the lineage of Christ listening to a podcast, perhaps on headphones.

Sylvester talked on, interrupting Thomas' reverie, "But your voice is needed now. There have been many disturbances in our continuum."

"An interesting way to phrase it, Holiness."

"Not just in the politics, but also the terrorist acts."

"Times Square."

"Yes."

"The Brethren of the Free Spirit."

"The names do not matter."

"Nonetheless," countered Thomas, "they believe that this is the year of the Lord's coming, via some bizarre calculation comprising Jewish holidays, mysticism, the biblical 360 day length of a year, and something they call "Biblical astronomy".

47

Sylvester answered gravely, "Theirs is a difficult fantasy to counter. It seems to attract by virtue of its extremism."

"People seem to almost yearn for it", answered Thomas.

"Yes, for myriad reasons," the Pontiff agreed, then, "But one could also say that your interpretation of canon is close to the periphery."

"Holiness, it's completely different…"

"Still, I am intrigued by your ideas and I wish to know from what fountain they spring."

Thomas took a deep breath and allowed his thoughts to emerge for the Pontiff's benefit.

"Holy Father, my television program isn't just about paying homage to Biblical text, as so many of the other programs on TBN are. It's about the Holy Word in the context of the modern world."

"Yes, it is interesting. I would even say constructive, my son, and therefore, we allow it to persist."

Thomas paused. He had, at times, wondered why that was, and now, finally, the curtain was parting. There was so much intransigence on the Christian Ultra-Right and they had a large influence on the channel, but evidently, the Vatican had more.

"I am glad for it," answered Thomas, watching the city roll by as Wyatt silently drove them back to the Rectory, "More moderate voices are needed. Someone has to forge a path for modern day Christians that allows them to advance with the changing times while simultaneously preserving the essence of God's Word – and by that I mean, understanding and pursuing His *intent*."

Sylvester spoke softly in response. "Thomas, you are passionate. And you are sincere in your love of God. This I know. But some would say you endanger your pledge. Is it effective to fight radicalism and intolerance with what could be described as relativism?"

Thomas answered quickly, "Supreme Father, that word is often used as a synonym for weakness. But it is not that. It is resilience. I believe both the material and spiritual aspects of our existence must evolve together, as a cohesive whole. I believe that is God's intent. It's not the layman who is at fault for this failing. It's we who are at fault, the clergy. We're in danger of being nothing more than archivists!"

Sylvester paused to contemplate Thomas' words, then responded, "I am intrigued by your views, Thomas. It cannot be denied that Christian values are being challenged today as never before. I agree that we must do something besides issue protests and platitudes. We must provide a more intellectual, kinder, introspective spiritualism to our people. We must reveal new meaning in His Gospel and new resonance in His message."

Thomas could not believe his ears, "Yes, yes. That's it. Exactly."

Sylvester continued, "But this is not a canonical view. What we are discussing could easily be regarded as heretical, if not framed properly and introduced in the right way. The old and the new must be interwoven. The new grows out of the old and the old finds fuller expression in the new. Our fellow defenders of the faith may not be ready to hear such things. I also cannot say with certainty that I share all of your views, my son. You are challenging age old beliefs and I have a responsibility in my role as Pastor of the whole Church that ultimately must transcend my own ideals."

Thomas nodded silently, understanding the Pontiff's need for balance, for caution, and yet amazed to be speaking directly with him about such a raw topic. He finally responded, "Holy Father, of course, I understand."

Sylvester could be heard whispering in Italian to someone else who must have been in the room the entire time. Thomas felt a twinge of surprise, wondering if he would have chosen the exact words he had said had he known this from the start. *Who had also been listening?*

Sylvester spoke, "Having said that, the Church must nonetheless make extraordinary efforts to reverse the marginalization of our faith around the world. Thomas, I have discussed my intentions with Cardinal Shaughnessy, and with Cardinal Tatian, and they are in consent with what I am about to say.

Intriguing. Tatian, the Prefect of the Congregation for the Doctrine of the Faith, founded to defend the Church from heresy, was a conservative power within Vatican circles of considerable heft. Thomas could not wait to hear what Sylvester had in mind that would mesh with what they had just discussed and still be palatable to someone like Tatian!

"Thomas, the Vatican would like you to become an agent of the Curia,"

"But I am already in your service..."

"...working on our behalf as a kind of spokesperson for the Vatican within the American Church. Your cable program is an excellent starting point. We also wish to take a larger part in the creation of content for your cable program."

Thomas wasn't sure he liked the sound of that, especially with Tatian involved, "Your Holiness, that I am not sure I can agree to. I love my church and my faith but I do not want to become a mouthpiece."

Sylvester pressed on, "It won't be so drastic a change, Thomas. Your ideas will still be conveyed. I cannot force inspiration."

Thomas worked his jaw, exuding doubt.

Sylvester did not wait for a reply, "Help me pave a path of reconciliation between the Word of God and the demands of this age. Will you help me accomplish it, Father Prisciotti? You must quell your passions in the name of the greater good. In the name of the Magisterium. Your religious consecration is calling you to greater service of the people of God."

Thomas felt the pressure of the direct entreaty from the leader of the Holy Roman Catholic Church and the fact that he could not escape the moment. He could not say, *let me think about it.* He had to reply with a yes or a no. Either reply would change his course and career as a cleric irreparably, he knew.

Finally, he said, feeling a hot rush of blood to his face and hands, "I will do what my superiors request of me. I will honor my vows."

Greek Countryside - Five Years Prior

"Relations with the Phanar at Constantinople are at all-time low," observed Yordon, as he let the newspaper drop onto the chipped café table. "The Ecumenical Patriarchate and the Holy Mountain are at odds once again."

"You mean about the non-Greek monks, yes?" asked Philo.

Yordon nodded, "And me. Primarily me, Philo."

"Of course," said Philo, also nodding as he watched a group of old men in their fezzes playing with their worry beads and sitting solemnly outside the dilapidated coffee house.

"According to this, Patriarch Dorotheos, numerous representatives of the Holy Community, and members of the civil government are all convening in Philotheou next month to hold a 'trial'."

"What do you think will come of it?" asked Philo, knowing the answer already.

"Expulsion. A demand for me to 'preserve unadulterated the authentic monastic character of Philotheou' in my words and actions, or face dismissal from the Order and, ultimately, the Orthodox Church."

"Which you won't heed."

Yordon looked back at Philo through hooded eyes and, smoothing his long brown beard first, sipped his Turkish coffee.

For nearly a decade, Yordon had been a thorn in the side of the holy community of Athos. His decision to leave the confines of the monastery and embark on a traveling hermitage had been controversial. The Abbot had approved his proposal to the surprise of many, believing Yordon would simply disappear, but instead Yordon had become well known throughout the hinterlands of Greece. He and Philo had wandered the country on foot, from the plains of Thessaly and Thrace, to the western alpine mountains of Macedonia, to the northern forests of the Balkans, and as far south as Parnassus and Delphi.

When Yordon had originally spoken of it, Philo had resisted the monk's proposal to take up a pilgrimage together. He was attached to his life on Athos. He was sure that if he followed Yordon, he would never return home. But Yordon kept talking of his visions. He spoke of a knowledge that ran deeper and was more universal than that of any culture or theology. He constantly tried to explain this to Philo but the words failed again and again. Still Philo had a hint of the revelations that haunted Yordon. And he felt himself drawn to the adventure of it.

Then one day, Yordon had simply decided that their journey should begin. He gave no thought to preparation or supplies or contacts along the way and the ever practical Philo was forced to try to rein in the determined monk.

"We must prepare! You can't just walk away from here. The Abbot must give his approval, yes?"

"He already has. We are prepared Philo. All that we need is the will to undertake the journey. We have that too."

"But what about food and drink? What about money?"

"We will not want," was all he would say.

Still, Philo hesitated.

Try as he might, Philo nonetheless knew that Yordon could not be stopped. On one particularly sunny morning, Philo wandered up to the monastery feeling nervous. His apprehension was heightened when he realized he could not find Yordon anywhere on the grounds. He climbed to the highest vantage point of the monastery and searched the landscape. From this high point he saw that Yordon was walking north along the mountain trails toward the next monastery. Usually he went south, toward the caves. It could only mean one thing. Philo scrambled down and hastily made to catch up. When he was within earshot he called after Yordon but the monk only turned and cheerily waved. Philo cursed aloud in Greek and closed in. When he reached Yordon he pulled at him to stop.

"You're crazy. You're leaving here forever aren't you?"

"I see no point in planning that far ahead, Philo."

"But where will we sleep, what will we eat?"

"Wherever we are at the time we feel fatigued. Whatever there is to eat at the time that we are hungry. Nature will protect us. This I know. We are part of it and it is part of us."

"That sounds wonderful, but what about the cold? What about the wolves? Yordon! We can't begin the pilgrimage yet!"

"Yet here we are on it. Come, my friend. Don't waste your energies worrying."

"But I haven't said goodbye!"

"To whom? You have no family here. Your friends in the village will still be your friends should you return. Your things? Write them a letter," and with that, Yordon turned and continued down the path.

And so they had begun their wanderings, with no preparation of any kind and with no particular course in mind. The first few nights had been harsh. They had slept outside in the cold mountain air with not a blanket between them. Yordon had been exhilarated by it all and refused to consider Philo's entreaties to call upon their brother monks from the neighboring monasteries for supplies, or at least a meal and a roof for the night.

"This is our baptism, Philo," he had said as they sat together high on the mountain's slope regarding the moon and its rippling reflection on the dark water. "In taking this journey together into the wilderness you and I are born again. Which requires that you and I must also die. You and I must forget the material concerns and the expectations of our pasts, Philo. Forget all that is behind you and live the moment."

"But what about…?"

Yordon didn't let him finish. "Why should you hesitate, my friend? Are your past experiences really so important to your life? Are they really so imbued with significance? Or is it the day to day living of your life that really sustains you and defines you?"

Philo pondered that between shivers. "My father used to say that a man is both the sum of his experiences and the decisions that he makes from moment to moment."

Yordon shook his head from side to side. "As venerable as your father may have been, Philo, that view is only partially correct. The past does not really deserve the authority and credibility that you give it. In fact, the importance that you imbue the past with is at the expense of the present. Be preoccupied with the experience of this moment, instead. Put all your attention into the here and now. "

"In that case, my attention is pointing out to me that I'm cold."

Yordon laughed. "Very well, you're cold. That is important -- for the moment. But you unwittingly make an important observation. One that I have come to know well, and it is this: you are what your attention demands. In fact, you *are* your attention -- that is my point -- and God is the force behind that attention within you. He is the source of that attention. Do you see? You are the spirit dancing in the clay and God is that animator of that spirit. When your attention is fully in the present moment then you are in the presence of God and God is vital and present within you."

Philo regarded his mysterious friend and considered his words. He shrugged, and suppressed another shiver. "So be it. Have it your way. Tonight we freeze to death and tomorrow we are born anew."

Yordon laughed quietly, patting the villager's knee, "Clear your head of old thoughts and ideas, my friend. There is great change in store for us."

Eventually Philo conspired to obtain some measure of basic supplies for them by virtue of the charity of those they encountered. But their reception was not always benign. In those early days, they were chased out of towns as often as they were welcomed. Yordon's words were a challenge to traditional beliefs, and they had quite a few scrapes with the inflexible minds and easily stirred passions of the rural Greeks. But Yordon was immune to it all, continuing to speak with perfect strangers and sharing his philosophy when the subject matter drifted in that direction. And it did often. Yordon continued to wear his monk's robes, and combined with his wild hair and long beard, he looked every bit the traveling Byzantine deacon. People naturally drifted toward him and sought to disclose their problems and worries to him. Guilelessly he offered his own brand of preternatural advice, which would sometimes inspire, but often times anger those to whom he explained his ideas.

After some weeks of continuous exposure to Yordon, Philo began to notice more and more things about him. Most notably, his visions returned at random intervals and relentlessly tormented him. While Yordon had lived at Philotheou, he had kept these episodes hidden from others but now Philo was witness. When Yordon had these interludes he would wander off alone, even in the pitch of night, and talk to himself -- arguing, pleading, laughing, sobbing profusely – but many a time, Philo would secretly follow and watch, in silent amazement.

Philo learned to accept the visions and their effect as Yordon's gift; a small price to pay for the abilities and insights he received in return. His ideas seemed to come from another place in the scheme of creation. Philo also noticed that

Yordon harbored additional powers that he used sparingly; even unwittingly. Once or twice they had averted accidents and natural disasters by what seemed to be sheer prescience on Yordon's part. He would simply want to wait where they were for no apparent reason or he would abruptly choose to go in a different direction, even if it was more circuitous or treacherous. Later Philo would learn of some calamity that they had avoided by taking another path or choosing another time.

In the Greek countryside, over the course of the decade that followed, Yordon's popularity quickly grew and flourished. For the majority of traditional Greeks, the Orthodox faith -- heavily steeped in mysticism -- was a way of life and, as such, the miraculous and wondrous were closer at hand than in other Christian traditions. This was especially true away from the cities. Stories abounded in the countryside about people who had been 'illuminated' by saints and were able to tell the future or heal the sick. Yordon fit perfectly into this cultural landscape and, with his long mane of brown hair, tamed by his *Skoufia*, the traditional high round hat of Orthodox priests and monks, and wild beard set against his simple white cassock, made himself a distinct figure in the minds of the people. It was inevitable that fame and notoriety would soon follow.

Chapter Three: The First Debacle

Baku, Azerbaijan, March 2020 - Present Day

"Judgment Day is at hand. The Zionists will soon be licked by the hot flames of nuclear conflagration!" growled Eli Tubasi to his men.

They were collected inside a dimly lit warehouse near the docks of Baku; a cold, dank place which smelled of sawdust, brine and sewer gas. This was one of the several meeting places and strongholds of the APF organization. The surly band of men stood in a circle around the erect encasement containing the nuclear fissionable material that Ibn al-Sayyab had successfully stolen from the Russian storage facility. Tubasi beamed as he raised his arms to pantomime an embrace of the gray, Cyrillic marked cylinder. He was very happy. The men grinned back. They regarded their prize with a certain reverence as they talked and smoked around it.

"Time for action. Prepare the tanker!" ordered Tubasi. "Let's get this uranium to Iran as quickly as possible. Soon we will have the *Jihad*-bomb, my friends."

The men went to work. Tubasi scanned the faces in the gloomy circle of light until he located al-Sayyab. He approached him, offering a sly smile.

"So you had no trouble toppling Serbenko, eh?"

"It was a pleasure. He talked too much," said al-Sayyab, blowing out a plume of smoke and offering a cigarette to his leader. Tubasi accepted and tapped the cigarette against his wrist.

Tubasi laughed, then said more seriously, "He had to die. There could be no trail."

"Agreed."

"You've done well, Ibn al-Sayyab. You're a hero to the cause of the *Jihad*."

al-Sayyab bowed theatrically. "Thank you, Eli. I couldn't have achieved this great feat without your leadership. We are unstoppable!"

"Perhaps we are, al-Sayyab, but the real feats lie ahead."

"*Alhamdu lillah*," said al-Sayyab with a deferential nod. "You're the leader we've needed for too long, Eli. The P.L.O., Hamas, Hezbollah, The G.U.P., The Intefada, they've all failed to unite the Arab peoples. But now the *Jihad* is at hand. We are finally united under one man."

Tubasi shrugged with a careless wave of his cigarette, "The circumstance has been waiting for someone to fill the vacuum. So I have filled it."

al-Sayyab answered, "You have done more than that. You've united the *Dar al Islam* under your command. You've managed to bring us this unity without raising the alarm of the Western Empires -- at least not too much."

Tubasi grinned at that. "The idiocy of the West astounds the mind, does it not?"

They shared a look, and burst into laughter. The other men looked on curiously.

Tubasi eventually mastered himself and, grabbing al-Sayyab by the shoulder, said to him conspiratorially, "The funniest part of this, Ibn al-Sayyab, is that we are the saviors they expect and they don't see it."

"We are. We will destroy the infidel."

"We will expose the Zionist conspiracy -- better than that, we will just erase it."

They both turned to gaze at the gray cylinder of fissionable material standing inert under the bare light bulb.

Outside a barge bellowed its somber note as it splashed its way through the oily water of the port, as if to lament the tribulations that were to come.

3 Kaplan St., Jerusalem

"We can put you through, Mr. Prime Minister."

Avrahami looked up from his pile of Knesset briefings; his spectacles hanging on the tip of his nose. "Eh? *Tov meod.* I'll take it here, Hershel. Call Natan and arrange for him to monitor the conversation."

Despite the powerful air conditioning system his office provided, the desert heat still managed to seep through. He wiped his face with a handkerchief. He had been examining the various motions for a crisis of confidence vote against him in the Knesset. He alternated these with the increasingly violent incident reports from the Jerusalem army posts. The situation in the Old City was approaching white hot and there was great pressure for him to beseech the Americans, but Moshe Avrahami was too proud for that. They had turned their backs and he would be damned if he were to show weakness now. The Americans had more at stake than he did. And he didn't need them; they were arrogant bunglers who tried to solve everything with money. Becker might be unresponsive now, but if push came to shove he could be forced to play his part. Becker was a pawn of the Jewish Special Interests groups in America and he didn't know it.

He looked forward to reviewing the upcoming chat with his Foreign Relations Minister, Natan Silver. Dutifully, he picked up the handset.

"*Haloh.*"

"Moshe. Are you there? It's Bob Becker, speaking to you on a secure line."

"Ah, President Becker."

"Just Bob, Moshe."

Avrahami hated this habit of the Americans.

"Very well, …Bob. Thank you calling upon me at this difficult time. My apologies not being available when you first called. As you know, the affairs of state always intervene."

He had deliberately pretended to be elsewhere the first time Becker had called just to keep him waiting and to show his own nonchalance. Now, by calling back a few hours later, he established control over the conversation to be, with the added feeling of doing the Americans a favor.

"That's alright, Moshe. I understand the situation with the Palestinians is becoming increasingly more difficult to control. It must take a great deal of your available time and energy just to keep the lid on. Given that, I am doubly grateful to get a few minutes of your time."

In one sentence, the sly dog had managed to turn Avrahami's delayed response to his telephone call into a sign of weakness. Ah well, it would only show more weakness to debate it. Let him think what he chooses.

"Not at all. The Arabs are reigned in. As usual, they are posturing with their hard line and rattling their sabers in the air, but nothing will come of it."

"Meaning?"

Avrahami bit down his ire at Becker's presumptuousness. "What do you wish to know, Mr. President?"

Becker's gravelly laugh piped tinnily through the earpiece. Avrahami imagined him sitting alone in his stately office within the elegant edifice of the White House, tie loosened, jacket off -- perhaps with his feet thrown up on the desk, in the grand American style of irreverence. Or was it the opposite? Was he sitting tensely at his Oval Office desk trying his best to sound casual, surrounded by aides and advisors, all tapped into the conversation and gesturing at him with frantic hand signals? Avrahami suddenly had the intuition that it was the second scenario. He was speaking to an audience.

Becker continued, "Look, Moshe, there's no need to feel defensive. The United States is your staunchest ally. We stand ready to take extraordinary measures to support you."

So long as we do things your way, Avrahami thought to himself, but his mouth said. "That is generous of you. It gives us strength to know we have such resources at our disposal, should the need arise."

"So I take it the situation is poised to defuse?"

"Our position remains the same, in that it depends entirely on the Arabs. The desecration of the Haaguda Lenihul Batei Haknesset Haspharadim Temple was a serious attack on Jews around the world, not just here in Israel. You can't expect us to just, as you say, 'forget it'!"

A pause. "No, I suppose not. But what will it take to *forgive* it?"

For a few minutes only the static and faint warbles of the encryption routines on the line could be heard as both parties considered their next remarks. To forgive? And what about the next incident and what about the one before? Are all those to be forgiven too? Then what does that make of the Jews? No, there could be no forgiveness; that was an entirely Christian idea and there was no place for it in this conversation. Despite his nonchalance and his country's false indifference to the crisis, he was calling because ultimately, he wanted to be comforted. Well, the Americans, like those motherless scorpions surrounding the Holy Land, would have no comfort from Moshe Avrahami.

"Mr. President, to forgive it would require erasing the memories of every Jew on Earth and the bleaching of every page of written Jewish history and testament. Nothing can forgive it. Do not mention it again."

Becker suddenly sounded impatient. "Someone has to blink, Moshe. The Palestinians are every bit as unyielding as yourselves. It can't go on like this."

"Bah. We can afford to wait. Time is on our side – and so is God."

"You'd better hope so."

"And if not God, there is the IDF."

"Okay, Moshe. Okay", Becker could be heard to sigh over the line.

"I'll do the blinking. I'll send Ravessi back -- but he needs a concession from you before he can approach the Palestinians."

"What did you have in mind?" asked Avrahami. He spat out the last words of the sentence. *Always concessions.* Always giving ground, stone by stone. Suddenly something snapped inside Avrahami. The pattern had to be broken.

"Let the Palestinians back into their homes in the Old City," said Becker, easily.

Avrahami's response was instantaneous. "No. I regret to inform you Mr. President -- and I do not care to call you Bob -- that there will be no flexibility. They are evicted until the Palestinians are ready to make the concessions, not Israel."

"But that's an untenable….!"

"Enough. Goodbye, Mr. President." Avrahami dropped the phone back into its cradle and waited for Natan to come running. Soon not just Natan, but the entire world would come running.

The White House, Washington D.C

The line of polished limousines slowly moved forward, into the White House compound. 1600 Pennsylvania Avenue was glittering in the winter night as music floated out into the cold evening air. Every window was illuminated. White gloved Presidential Guards stood at attention at every entrance and in every corner of the stately mansion.

At the main doors, dignitaries and luminaries of the global arena bowed to each other and shook hands as they were escorted into the State Dining Room by the President's ushers. It was the first State Dinner of the new year. Within, President Becker, a beacon of smiles and good humor, waited with his wife and offered personal greetings to each of his guests. Unlike his predecessors, Becker preferred to greet his guests as they arrived rather than entering last, to the consternation of his security staff. The President was far too cavalier about security concerns, in their opinion.

Once everyone was collected in the State room, the President stood up and raised his glass to call for a toast. "Here here, Ladies and Gentlemen, if I may have your attention for a few minutes."

He waited for the room to settle down. When he had everyone's attention he continued, "It is a momentous occasion whenever the leaders of the free world are gathered together at an event such as this. It gives me great honor to be your host tonight. It is my country's hope that the camaraderie and family feeling we share tonight can set a precedent for the world agenda in the 21st century. The future is now. The people in this room have the ability to shape it. Let's shape a future that is forward thinking, without competitive or vindictive actions. Let's advance mankind to the next evolutionary step -- one of global awareness and cooperation, instead of remaining entrenched in tribal hatreds and colloquial viewpoints. America stands ready to support every peaceful initiative."

"He's always been good at stuffing the stockings!" said the Secretary of State, J. Stephen Waite III, whispering into the ear of his attractive companion. Waite looked around the room. It was a who's who of movers and shakers. Cabinet members, Senators and a platoon of Washington officialdom, a smattering of celebrities, some of the Joint Chiefs and other high ranking officers from the various armed forces, and half the planet's rulers.

The President finished his speech and with a broad, winning smile raised his glass high. Suddenly, the doors that led to the kitchen area swung open violently and sixteen men dressed in the white coats and embroidery of the White House kitchen staff, burst into the room, each holding what appeared to be an automatic weapon. Each carried additional weaponry and equipment on their backs. On their lapels they each wore a yellow cross. As they silently fanned out to cover the room, Waite glimpsed the inside of the kitchen and saw wafting veins of thin blue smoke, prone bodies, and conspicuous tracts of red. *The weapons must be silenced.* Waite felt the prickle of fear sweat under his armpits and quietly put his knife and fork down. The others at his table were in various states of astonishment.

"Thank you, Mr. President Becker, sir. You can sit down now," said one of the sixteen in a mocking tone, as he aimed his gun directly at the President's head. "If anyone else moves, he dies", barked the man. Looking around the room he spotted the President's bodyguards and ordered, "You Secret Service men in the room -- all of you move to the corner now!"

Once the agents were collected in the corner by his associates, the evident leader waved the gun so it brushed Becker's ear. The President flinched but his face was grim stone.

The leader was tall and muscular under the loose jacket, with a tense, square jaw and close cropped, blonde hair. He grinned arrogantly and cavalierly asked the air, "So just who the hell are we?"

One of the women at a rear table fainted and fell to the ground with a crash of silverware and glass. No one moved to help her.

The terrorist leader snapped into the silence, "I want all hands extended out in front of you, palms up, and all of you to look at the ceiling. Don't look anywhere else or I'll kill you where you sit. DO IT NOW!"

He fired a silenced burst from his weapon and raked the chandelier above, dimming the room and spattering the floor with broken crystal. It was enough noise to alert the Marine Honor Guard standing outside the banquet hall. They could be heard trying the locked door.

"We have only a few minutes, before your security forces explode into this room with, no doubt, enough firepower to take a small nation. Of course, we have some spectacular hostages, so they may not be as brash as that but the situation is bound to get interesting, don't you think, Mr. President Becker? Who will win, eh?"

Becker, hands extended and face pointed upwards said, "Who do you represent? What do you want?"

Waite found this strangely funny, as for all intents and purposes it seemed as if Becker was imploring God with his questions rather than the lunatic standing in the middle of the room.

The group's leader was also amused. "Very good, Mr. President. You are quite obedient when a gun is pointed at you. My name is John Swint and we are...", he gestured vaguely behind him without taking his eyes off the President, "...the Brethren of the Free Spirit."

"The ones from Times Square!" said someone.

"Yes, yes. Very good. I see we have notoriety."

Admiral James Farrow suddenly dropped his hands and looked directly at Swint. Pointing an accusing finger, he demanded, "How did you get in here? Security is air-tight within these walls. Everyone has deep background checks conducted..."

Immediately a gun was pointed directly at the Admiral.

Swint retorted, "Put your hands back out in front of you and I'll answer your question. Do it or we'll shoot them off."

"I'm an Admiral."

"You're an idiot, if this is what you call airtight security. Do you want to know how we penetrated the inner sanctum? It was easy. It just takes patience. The Secret Service has no defense against patience. We've been planning this for years. We've had ceramic weapons hidden within the kitchen's walls for years. Undetectable! They were brought into the White House disguised as kitchen gadgets. And deep covers. It may discomfort you to know that the Russians have had deep covers within these walls for years too. Some for decades. Perfect backgrounds. 100% red-blooded, freedom-loving Americans who want nothing more than to topple the current system of government in this country. And with the collapse of the Soviet Union ten years ago, many of these 'sleeper' agents became orphans looking for a cause. We are that cause.

The Brethren of the Free Spirit. It just takes patience, Admiral. That, and some selective recruiting, and a little plastic surgery."

Waite was amazed. Security was always designed to tackle the expected hazards. That was its inherent weakness. It was hard to guard against the unexpected.

President Becker spoke again, "Impressive, but what is it you want, Swint? To topple the government? It's going to take more than killing me to do it. The American system of government is a way of life ingrained into the hearts, minds and souls of most Americans. You'd have to kill them all."

Swint answered wearing a deadly smile, "You're quite correct. This is a nation of insolent dolts; resistant to change. The Brethren stands for a new world order. Your eloquent toast suggests some of the ideas we stand for but you don't really mean it. It's only so much posturing to you. Meanwhile, people are killing the planet and each other. The Brethren are charged with preparing the way for the second coming of the Lord. We are the advance guard of the coming change."

"And how do you propose to bring about that change?" asked Farrow warily, trying to buy time.

The other Free Spirit terrorists were looking antsy as footsteps could be heard charging toward the entrance. Shadows flickered past the windows. The place was undoubtedly surrounded by a small army by now. The President's security forces would storm the banquet hall at any moment. Swint also realized this and hastened his pace as he answered the Admiral.

"Why it's alarmingly simple, Admiral. We're going to change things by killing you all -- the leaders of the planet -- right now. We're going to take the planet from your governments and give it to the back to the people." He gave them all one last look before yelling, "KILL THEM!" Without hesitation he then aimed straight at the President and squeezed the trigger of his ceramic gun.

Waite had almost expected this, why else attempt what could only be suicidal? To try and pull off a hostage situation in the White House was sheer madness. They must have known they were going to die, which could only mean everyone else in the room was going to die too. He really didn't know why he did it -- he had always felt that his own sense of self-preservation would override all other concerns. In the end he realized that, despite his years of self-serving, back room maneuvering, despite the relentless politicking for power and influence, in the final analysis he was a patriot.

Waite jumped up on the table and lunged over the heads of his fellow guests at Swint. This caused Swint to swerve his aim away from the President just as he squeezed the trigger and instead cut a row of holes across Stephen Waite's midriff. Waite landed like a broken rag doll on the polished wood floor and slid a few inches before coming to a halt, a crumpled lump, at Swint's feet. Swint did not waste a second. He callously kicked at the body and then casually sprayed the entire length of the banquet table with hot lead. People bled, screamed and tripped over each other in a desperate effort to escape. Many died. Many ducked under the tables. Immediately, the doors and windows of the hall shattered in a rain of glass. Government agents stormed in amidst the heavy automatic weapons gunfire. Wave after wave of security men jumped into the room and began to methodically kill the terrorists.

Strangely, the terrorists made no effort to defend themselves, but instead focused on killing as many of the guests as possible. World leaders fell like cornered prey, braying the whole way down. The terrorists' bodies were buffeted by the impact of bullets but they did not fall easily.

Swint, crouched low behind the tabletops, scanned the room. It was immersed in a cloud of flying shrapnel, china and plaster. He quickly identified a particular huddle of people trying to escape the room as being the President's entourage. With a yell, he jumped up to a standing position and let loose a fiery barrage right at the group and, like layers of an onion, people fell away. The

Secret Service men surrounding the President shot back at the terrorist leader with abandon, emptying their weapons at Swint. Amazingly, he survived the blasts, though he staggered with the force of the impacts. Soon his white kitchen jacket fell away to reveal heavy duty Kevlar wrappings. Finally the last layer of the onion fell away to reveal only Robert Becker, exposed and afraid.

Through blood soaked eyes, Swint sneered and pointed his weapon right at the President's head. Between heaving breaths, he said, "Goodbye, Mr. President. The world is really dying for a change, don't you agree?"

Becker looked confused, then suddenly stood up straight and faced the terrorist head on. Though his eyes shone with fear, he growled back, "To hell with you, you cold blooded…"

Swint shot him right through the forehead before he could finish. Becker fell backwards heavily against the wall and slid to the ground. The terrorist dropped his arm and stared. It was enough. In moments he was tackled to the ground by six men.

"He's killed the President!" someone shouted.

Suddenly the mound of Government agents pressing down on the terrorist leader billowed backwards, screaming, as the center of the pile glowed bright yellow and then erupted into a ball of flame. The other surviving terrorists took this as a cue and each pulled at a small black string hanging at the bottom of their Kevlar jackets. Each one erupted into a ball of hot fire.

As they burst into flames they yelled, "My spirit is free!"

When it was all over, the State Dining Room was a charred ruin. People lay dead everywhere. The sounds of the injured could be heard intermingled with the crackling exchange of voices piped through communications equipment as investigators combed the room for clues. Security men, businesslike once again, ushered the survivors out of the room and quietly sealed it behind them. A single photographer was allowed entry.

Amazingly, Admiral James Farrow had survived the encounter, and quickly took command of the situation. He was deeply shaken and bleeding from a wound, but the American Government had to lurch forward and someone had to resume the chain of command. He compelled himself into action on the force of that thought. Time for horror and regrets later.

"Contact the Vice President," growled Farrow to an aide. "Tell him the shit's hit the fan -- hard."

Holy Name Rectory, Chicago

Thomas, bereft of his collar and tunic, and wearing only a white t-shirt and the traditional black slacks of a cleric, paced the floor of his quarters at the Rectory, occasionally stopping to look out the window. The tree branches were glazed with ice. People walked hurriedly across the lawn, their shoulders hunched against the relentless Lake Michigan winds. He shivered involuntarily, despite the warmth of his room. The President of the United States had just been assassinated, along with a legion of other world leaders. He imagined that Kennedy's assassination must have provoked the same feelings of outrage and desolation that Becker's death had wrought upon him and all those around him. The present day world was different, of course, and the United States a far more cynical place. Still, it was a disaster of the highest order. There was knock on the door to his room.

"Come."

The door creaked open and there stood the statuesque outline of Dr. Karin Ferguson, in her winter parka, which extended to her knees, and a furry hat.

"Karin! What in the heavens?"

"I had to come." she said, inching into the room, looking uncertain.

Thomas, struck at how happy he actually was to see her, strode toward her, urging her into his humble quarters and closing the door behind her.

"Take off your coat," he said, resisting the impulse to remove it himself. "Sit. Can I get you some coffee or tea?"

Karin didn't seem to notice and looked around, finally choosing to sit on his bed, a rumpled pile of sheets on a twin sized mattress, and slowly removed her layers of winter outerwear, to reveal a turtleneck and plaid wool skirt over dark stockings and boots.

"No, it's alright, I don't want you to have to run downstairs to the Rectory kitchen or anything."

"It's fine, Karin." he said, making toward the desk chair where his tunic lay.

"Stop." she said, reaching out to grab his hand. He slowed, feeling the need for human contact, and turned to face her once more.

"It's frightening, I know." said Karin.

"It's a heavy hurt," answered Thomas, through plaintive eyes. "Difficult to write messages of hope for the Pope while things like this happen."

That's all Karin needed. She began to cry.

Thomas squeezed her hands and instinctively moved to hug her. Karin stood up and melted into his embrace, shedding tears quietly. After a few minutes of this, Thomas slowly eased her away and steadied her.

Karin sighed and reached down into her bag, finding a tissue, and cleaned herself up. Once she was calmer, she turned to face Thomas and cupped his hands in hers.

"It's a terrible tragedy," she said quietly. Then she noticed how tired Thomas looked. She put her hands on his shoulders and shook him slightly, speaking more assertively, "You have to stop staying awake entire evenings in front of that little TV set of yours, Tom. You look like crap."

"I feel like crap." he answered, morosely, and offered a wan smile.

The two of them sat back down, side by side, on the bed, heads hung. Finally, Thomas said, "It didn't help matters that the claimed assassins are using religion as their pretext."

Karin turned to Thomas and replied, "The Brethren of the Free Spirit is a fringe group. I don't think the Catholic Church is in any danger of being equated with them."

Thomas thought about that, and about his Vatican controlled cable program, and finally nodded his agreement, "You're right. They're probably of limited significance". He realized he had never gotten around to telling Karin about his pact with Sylvester. "It's what comes next that I worry about."

"What do you mean?"

"The new President."

Karin's mouth became thin-lipped, understanding. "Clement."

Thomas nodded, "He's an ultra-right Christian Evangelist, and now…"

"He's the President," continued Karin. "At last, they've got their man in the Oval Office."

Karin stopped short upon hearing herself say this. "You don't suppose…?"

Thomas thought about his assignment from the Pope, and felt deep concern, but he masked his feelings.

"…that they orchestrated the assassination?"

Thomas answered, "No, no, no. It would damage them beyond repair if it ever came out. I doubt they have the wit for it."

Karin accepted this, and answered, "Nonetheless, whatever the means, the reality is that we are now governed by a President sympathetic to the Christian ultra-right."

Thomas suddenly felt a new urgency. "I must contact the Vatican to discuss this. They need to get someone into the Oval Office right away to gain access to Clement's ear."

Karin looked at Thomas, and in a seemingly innocent act of clairvoyance, said, "I think that someone may be turn out to be you, Thomas."

Meteora, Greece - Five Years Prior

"The people are feverish with the millennium," declared Philo Berith, as he swatted flies. He and Yordon, the former monk -- for Yordon had indeed been removed from the Philotheou order in the prior year, as had been threatened -- were traveling through the region south of Macedonia and west of Olympus, in the northern central highlands of Greece, on their ways toward Meteora. It was a territory rich with history and dotted with ruins dating back to the time of Alexander. They had just left Kalambaka, a medium sized town which served as a crossroads of the area.

"People ask me if you may not be the *Messiah*," said Philo, sounding incredulous at his own words.

Yordon looked around, bemused. "It does appear that we've turned into a major attraction, my friend." There was a significant knot of people walking with them.

"It's not good. This is not good at all," worried Philo, looking back at the crowd.

Of late, Yordon had begun to attract an entourage of followers, which was growing more overtly adoring. The millennium year had affected people of faith far and wide. Nothing had happened in 2000 or 2001 or even 2012, but people were expectant again. The Brethren had seen to that. At first, Yordon had resisted this firmly -- many a time he and Philo had slipped away from sleeping camps in the middle of the night -- but recently Yordon had become circumspect about the phenomena.

As they walked, Philo beseeched his tall friend. "Yordon, you're telling these people that they don't need the icons of the Church, but don't you see that you're turning into an icon? People no longer see you. They see what they want to see. They don't hear your words any longer."

Yordon raised his eyebrow at the remark but dismissed it. "They do, Philo. It's not as bad as you make it out to be."

"Not yet."

"Hmm. Time will tell."

"Time will tell what? That you were blind? You're about to be excommunicated from the Church. You're already expelled from the monastic order!"

"Yes, the Patriarch is greatly disturbed with this 'movement' that has grown around me."

"St. Andrew's whiskers! What are you going to do about it, then?" Philo almost yelled.

Yordon looked at his friend with an impalpable expression and said, almost sadly, "There's nothing I can do, Philo, except continue doing what I must do. I cannot stop. I'm on a path from which I cannot be diverted."

Philo seemed about to burst with frustration upon hearing this but instead released a sigh and shook his head. Silently, the pair moved on.

From Kalambaka it had not been far to Meteora. Here the Pinios River emerged from the deep canyons of the Pindus range and into the Thessalian plain. There were dizzying abysses, deep woods, gorges and breathtakingly beautiful, village dotted plains. It was an area well known for its bygone monasteries built atop naturally formed spires of rock -- some long abandoned, a few still vital, all dating back to at least to the thirteenth century and all built by hand, a basketful of clay and stone at a time.

In an effort to dispel the string of self-proclaimed followers, and at Philo's insistence, the two had arrived in the early dawn hours when the mist, clinging low to the ground, made it seem as if these high structures were disconnected from the earth, floating on air. They had climbed the circular flight of torturous steps, chiseled right out of the bedrock that led to the monastery of Ayia Tríatha to spend a day and a night. There was someone Yordon wanted to meet here.

When they had neared the top of the climb, a shaven head peaked over the precipice and shouted, *"Yá sou! Kalós ilthateh."* It was one of the monks. "Welcome, Welcome!"

"Ef haristó," replied Yordon between breaths, offering thanks for the warm welcome.

"Yes, hello pilgrims. What brings you to Meteora today? let me offer you water."

The sack-clothed bald monk helped them up the last few steps and led them to a large wooden basin in the shadow of the main building situated at the top of the pinnacle. Once there, he doled out wooden cups of cool water. Philo and Yordon drank greedily.

The cheerful monk waited patiently. Yordon returned the cup and answered the monk's pending question. "We've come to meet the monk Joasaph. To speak to him of his visions."

The monk sank his forearms into the opposing sleeves of his crude garment and raised his eyebrows.

"Oh, I see. Well then, I fear you may have come for naught, for that is impossible. Joasaph does not enjoy speaking of them. They are a personal matter."

He shook his head sadly, then looking at his visitors for a reaction and seeing none, he continued, "But you are deserving of consolation for the effort of your pilgrimage. May I offer you a tour of the grounds instead?"

The travelers assented to the tour and so were taken around the grounds. During their stroll about the grounds Yordon and their monk guide chatted.

"How did you learn of Joasaph's affliction, my brother?" asked the monk politely.

"I was once a monk. In many ways I still am."

"But what happened? Did you abandon the Order? To which Order did you belong, if it is not too prying of me?"

"Philotheou."

"Philotheou? Then are you…?"

Yordon nodded with half lidded eyes. "Yordon Antropos. The exiled monk. It's true. You know of me."

The monk stopped in his tracks and considered Yordon anew upon hearing this. "I am amazed at your honesty, my brother. Many would not welcome you, upon hearing this news."

"I am aware of this. It is occasionally inconvenient. But I have committed no sin in the eyes of God."

"You seem certain. How do you know this?"

Yordon assessed his guide briefly before speaking, as if to gauge the reaction to his next words. "I hear him. Like Joasaph."

The monk raised an eyebrow. "How provocative. I would think we should ask Joasaph to join us then."

"Yes, that would be opportune."

"Then it is done."

They both stood there waiting.

Philo exchanged looks with Yordon. He shrugged. Yordon finally asked their guide. "When will he come?"

"Why he's already here, friends."

"Do you mean you…?" began Yordon.

"That I am Joasaph," acknowledged the monk, gaily. "That's two surprises in one day!" He turned pink with laughter and grasped Yordon's hands in his. "I have heard much about you, my brother, and it thrills me to meet you at last."

Yordon's face darkened at the ruse but he quickly recovered and embraced Joasaph in return.

The monk released himself from Yordon's hold and gazed up at the taller man. "Come, let us talk in the meeting hall."

Once seated, Joasaph took it upon himself to go to the larder, behind a wooden door at the back of the large room, and bring out warm bread and olive oil for his guests.

Philo was grateful, as they had not had much to eat for days. Yordon restrained himself, despite the good, warm smell, preferring to listen to Joasaph's discourse.

"You must understand my caution, Yordon. There are many who would make me into a spectacle."

"I am familiar with the problem."

Joasaph continued matter of factly, "I am fortunate to have my life of isolation here at Tríatha. The pinnacle discourages many, but not enough. I must conceal my identity often."

"It's only self-defense. We have done it as well," Philo demurred.

Joasaph regarded them anew. He was plainly enjoying the prospect of sharing knowledge with someone who had had similar experiences. Suddenly he seemed to come to a decision and stood up, bracing his arms on the table. "Well, let us take some rest. There's time for talk later. You are tired travelers and you have arrived at your destination. Please accept the hospitality of the Tríatha monks and stay with us tonight."

"You are kind," answered Yordon.

Joasaph showed them to a modest cell fitted out with wooden bunks, shuttered to keep out the light. They were tired from many weeks on the road. Sleep came easily after the Tríatha monk took leave of them.

Later that day, Philo awoke in the darkened chamber and realized at once that Yordon was gone. Grabbing his things, he quietly left the cell and padded down the stone corridor until he heard voices coming from a doorway that led to the grounds outside. Through the doorway he could see that day had turned into a deeply tinted, turquoise night adorned by a glowing moon and a phalanx of silver clouds. A beautiful, cool evening. He slipped on his shoes and made for the door. As he approached, he could discern that the voices he had heard were Yordon and Joasaph conversing in the darkness.

They were standing a few feet away from the building with their backs to it, staring up at the sky. There was no one else about. Joasaph was speaking quietly.

"So, let us talk of the visions, Yordon. Without further delay, let me hear of your experience and I shall speak of mine."

"Very well, but where to begin, brother Joasaph? How to speak of such things to one another?"

Joasaph waved the objection away. "Know this. When I am stricken with the voices from heaven which I hear, they do not speak in words. Their communication is a current of meaning and sensations. I *feel* their message."

Yordon nodded vigorously. "Yes, yes, precisely. It's a thing beyond words. Words are unable to describe the rich dimension of it -- the wonder of it."

The two men talked on, oblivious of Philo. He quietly sat at the doorway, listening to their exchange.

"I have met the source of our minds, Yordon. I have seen that our intelligence flows from a common source. Our individualism is an illusion. As people, we are blind. Our human history -- what we are so proud of -- is but a prolonged stumble in the darkness. Our traditions are blind, and…"

"Our religions are blind. Say it, Joasaph. If you've really touched the same thing as I during your episodes, then you know what I know."

Joasaph caught his breath.

Philo privately echoed this reaction. Is this what Yordon really thought? That religion was blind; a mistake? Philo struggled with this. The morals and principles of his own beliefs were integral to the way he conducted his life. He had always understood Yordon's missteps with the Monastery and the Church to be an issue of interpretation. But to maintain that all faith was *blind?*

"We are not merely creatures of clay imbued with souls by God," continued Yordon, "We each have God within us. We are extensions of his mind, manifestations of his will; each of us written in the thoughts of the incomprehensible Father. We are precipitates of his attention, as is everything around us. We are Gods, in a vital way. This goes beyond the teachings of the Church."

"So it does," answered Joasaph belatedly. He was shaking slightly, Philo noticed -- perhaps induced by the cold of the night. Suddenly the monk's eyes rolled up into his head and he fell to his knees, uttering a choked cry. Yordon stepped back.

Joasaph looked up at the sky as he harshly whispered, "He hears us, and he has come. I feel it coming. Oh wonders of heaven and earth."

Yordon got on his knees as well, alongside Joasaph, as the wind picked up. Philo looked up at the sky. The clouds were increasing and the deep blue tint of the night was becoming darker, richer.

Yordon spoke into Joasaph's ear, "I feel it too, Joasaph. Be brave. The heavens have intent tonight and you are their receptacle. This much I can sense."

Joasaph shut his eyes and silently nodded. His hands were clenched fists. His face was taut and pale. He doubled over and tried to hold his head above the dirt with his extended arms but they collapsed. He rolled out of Yordon's grip and into the dirt, coming to rest facing upwards and gazing at the sky. Yordon lay down next to him. Joasaph spoke.

"The Creator... He... It is here," he sucked in a shaky breath and look upwards with eyes like glass orbs. "It is a palpable thrill inside of me. It is a vast hum of perfect tone. The pure light that has weight and has thought. And He knows you. You... you... Yordon. There's something about you. I can feel it. You're connected to the heavens in a very special way. Look at the link! It's like a tether coming out of you and going straight up. I see it." Joasaph gasped.

"You must be his Son. My God! You must be the Christ, the incarnate Son of God! Why have you disguised yourself?"

Joasaph gasped and put his knuckles to his lips, staring at Yordon with a look that could have been fear. "Are you Jesus? No. You're not. You are not. What are you then? Another son? *Another* Son of God!"

Yordon stood up and slowly backed away. His lips were moving but Philo could not hear him over Joasaph's rantings and the whisper of the evening wind. Philo strained to make out what he was saying. Frustrated and concerned, he left the doorway and headed toward Yordon.

As he stepped closer he was amazed to feel a change in the air surrounding Yordon and Joasaph. It felt colder. There was also a presence in the air, like an electric charge. The air was close, as if the barometric pressure was somehow higher in this one spot. And the sound. There was a subsonic susurration that seemed to rise from the earth. And above it an ambient harmonic tone; a hint of voices in the wind. Philo could sense there was an *intelligence* here; something that the surrounding fabric of nature could barely contain. The world around him suddenly seemed frangible and brittle, ready to shatter at the slightest sound. Philo willed himself forward. He had to get to Yordon. This was unprecedented. Yordon had had visions and episodes but never like this. Could it be the combined powers of Joasaph and Yordon that were causing this?

As he came closer he saw that something was happening to Yordon. Yordon suddenly went stiff. He then fell to his knees and toppled to the ground. He rolled to and fro until he was staring straight up at the sky. His eyes became glassy, like Joasaph's, and he began to shiver. Philo slowed his approach. Suddenly Yordon sprang upright as if he had been lifted by an invisible hand. White fisted, he yelled up at the sky, spittle flying all around him.

"WHAT IS THE TRUTH?!!!!"

Joasaph was also yanked upright in one smooth motion, seemingly by an invisible force. He turned to Yordon, speaking to him earnestly.

"Listen to me. You are the Second Son. You are the new Messiah."

He suddenly went limp. After a few moments, he slowly shook himself awake and looked at Yordon with human eyes again. Dropping to his knees, he clasped his hands together in an attitude of prayer before Yordon. "I am your servant. Ask me for any function, any service and I am yours to command. I am in the service of the Lord and you are his beloved Son. Welcome, Yordon, Son of God. We have waited long for you."

Yordon looked stunned as he watched Joasaph do this. He took a step backwards. He raised his hands in supplication and looked upward. This time, softly, he asked the heavens, "Is this my purpose?"

His expression changed again to one of fear. He looked left and right desperately, spotting Philo standing a few feet away. This seemed to bring him back to solid ground. He locked eyes with his companion and stepped toward him. His countenance grew angry and he turned back to shout at Joasaph.

"No. It's a lie. I'm just a man, like you. You've been deceived, Joasaph."

Joasaph struggled to his feet and chased after Yordon, impervious to his protest. Yordon grabbed Philo's arm and gestured for him to follow. He made for the steps leading downward from the monastery.

Joasaph pursued, imploring, "You don't know your true nature. You haven't woken up to see yourself for what you are. But you will. You can't run away from your purpose. You saw what I saw tonight. You felt it too. Now you must understand it."

"No! Get away! Your visions have driven you insane," answered Yordon. He walked faster, scattering stones in the silvery blue blackness.

Philo tugged at him, "Yordon! We can't leave in the dark!"

Joasaph beseeched from behind, "You may yet not know the truth but it is in you! We have both seen it. And soon you will believe it too, Yordon. Soon it will overtake you and you will be like a puppet before it. You will take your place on the throne of the faithful. It is you who will lead us into the new age of peace and salvation. The thousand year reign of Christ on earth. You must go to Israel and proclaim your arrival!"

"We're leaving," said Yordon curtly, angrily. He yanked himself loose from Philo's hold and made for the precipice of the Tríatha pinnacle. The stars twinkled carelessly above them. Philo ran as fast as he could to keep up with Yordon, who was running at a dead clip. Joasaph receded behind them, calling to Yordon until he could no longer be heard. Philo looked back and saw the monk had stopped his pursuit. Joasaph stood where he was, looking tiny and sad in the moonlight. Finally he turned away and reluctantly made his way back to the monastery.

Yordon was already a good 50 feet down the steps and determinedly making his way in the gloom.

"This is madness, Yordon! Of course, you can't be the Savior -- you're too crazy!" yelled Philo from behind.

To his surprise, Yordon stopped dead in his tracks and looked up at Philo upon hearing this. Philo felt a wave of uneasiness wash over him which threatened to loosen his bowels. He was forced to sit down in order to regain control of himself. Yordon broke his stare and continued down the steps.

Philo breathed relief. "Or maybe I'm the one who is mad," he muttered to himself, as he rose and followed Yordon into the darkness.

Arkadelphia, Arkansas - Five Years Prior

Mary Maccabe snuck back into her house in the dark of night and wondered where to start. She had resolved that tonight would be her last night spent in the thrall of her myopic, devout, wacko mother.

At age 17, she felt as if she had lived under the weight of her Mother's strict oversight for centuries. She was tired of living a lie, of telling lies, of listening to lies where the liars were too dense to even know they were spouting nonsense. It was all nonsense. Literal interpretation of the Bible, when it was clearly not a literal text, was just dumb. So crazy. It disgusted her. Even as her mother and her friends obsessed over the words in that old book, they blithely and blindly lived out their lives in a state of high hypocrisy - all of them were racists, and death penalty supporters, just for starters. They never seemed to understand that what they sought did not reside in the differences, but in the underlying commonalities. Why was she was the only one among her forlorn family that could see this?

Bradley was right. There was no hope for her mother and her den of old biddies; claustrophobic, gossipy, dying, living away their days in a haze of 1950s nostalgia and Fox News-induced paranoia, while the local police harassed the young who were only looking for diversion, and the meth lab at the edge of town produced poison for those not clever enough to leave. There was no future here and this was no place for her. The future lay elsewhere. Whether it was with the Millenarians, with Bradley, or with some other radical sect proselytizing their own version of truth, the only way forward for her would be to venture out in search of her own epiphany, whatever, whenever, wherever that might be.

She didn't need much, just a few personal items: her diary, the thimble from Starkenville (strangely enough it had been her and not her mother who had imparted it with significance over the years), a few items for personal hygiene, some clothing, a handful of books, some photographs. She would bring her cell phone, not wanting to leave anything that could be used to derive her whereabouts. Bradley said he could "brick" it for her once they were on their way, after which they would dump it in the river. She thought briefly of the music, texts and the pictures on that phone that would also be lost and felt a twinge of regret over losing these. Bradley had made her delete everything from her iCloud account as well, so there would be no chance of retrieval once the phone was dead and drowned.

As she threw these items into a backpack and turned to look at her room one last time, she heard a small sob from the adjoining room. Unable to resist, she tiptoed over to her youngest sister's room and cracked the door. After a few moments of allowing her eyes to adjust to the cobalt gloom, she could make out the prone form of her little sister, and could more prominently hear the soft crying coming from within the room. She crept inside and knelt beside the bed, and softly stroked her sister's hair.

"You can't go, Mary," pleaded her sister forlornly. Mary felt her throat thicken. Of all her siblings, Elisa was the one she loved best. Elisa was the only one who listened to Mary when she mused about her longings or vented her frustrations. Mary, in turn, was the only one who would comfort Elisa when she was the target of their mother's random strictures and bouts of religious rigidity.

"I have to. You know I do."

Elisa's eyes just stared at her, two points of faint light in the dark. Mary stuttered, "I'll come back for you when I figure stuff out."

"Will you?"

"I'll try."

"You're not coming back, I can see it in your eyes."

Mary bowed her head, letting her hair hang over her face. "I don't know, Elisa." Then, looking up and leaning forward, "I love you."

Elisa didn't seem to hear. "I'll find you, somehow, someday."

Mary found herself unable to speak, and instead kissed her sister on the cheek roughly. She made her way out of the room and down the stairs to the first floor of their little house. She tiptoed as quietly as she could but the house was ramshackle and the floorboards creaked, inevitably. She paused for long moments at every wooden complaint her footfalls produced, listening for any rustling, but she heard none.

Eventually she was at the front door. Slowly she turned the knob and pulled the door open. It emitted a faint whistle of ungreased hinge against metal, causing her to grimace. She took one last look back at the inside of the house in which she had grown up, and spotted a silhouette in the darkness of the TV den in the back behind the living room area. She thought it might be her mother, probably having fallen asleep in front of the TV and too lazy to move once she had turned it off. She waited, frozen. The silhouette did not move. Finally, the silhouette receded into the darkness and all was still. Despite all her resentment and anger at her mother, accumulated across the years, the retreat she just witnessed stabbed at her feelings and she blinked back tears.

Plainly, she was not the only one letting go.

The National Mall, Washington D.C., March 2020 - Present Day

The crowd hunched inside their coats and held onto their hats, standing fast against the March winds that raced down the length of the Mall. At the top of the broad steps, in the shadow of the Capitol, Adam Clement, a jowlish bulldog of a man, raised his right hand and repeated the Oath of Office as read to him by the Chief Justice of the Supreme Court of the United States of America.

In the wash of applause that followed, Clement observed the crowd and the expanse of white tents covering the lawns from the steps of the Capitol building to the Washington Monument. He felt his heart race. He was the President of the United States of America. He was the leader of the free world. And now he was a prime target for madmen and terrorists. *But you'll soon be my prime target, you bastards.* His wife, Marcia, and their two sons, Franklin and Winston, gazed back at him proudly.

Adam Clement felt great sadness at President Becker's fate. He considered himself lucky to have been 'otherwise engaged' at the time of the State dinner.

Surely he would have died at the hands of those Free Spirit lunatics as well, had he not been hospitalized following his hunting accident. The twinge of sadness expanded in his chest. He had not always agreed with Becker but he had respected the man. The party and the country had looked to him to keep it hanging together despite the worldwide frenzy taking place around them.

And what of me? His constituency, a broad swath of Christian denominations that together called themselves the religious right of America, was expecting him to act on his beliefs. He was the President, with no Robert Becker to temper his intentions. Many among his supporters considered Becker's death an act of God; a message to get on track right away or else. *But politics isn't that simple, is it?*

President Clement sighed and manufactured a smile for his wife, who noticed his sad eyes and knew his inner disconsolation. He tried to brighten his countenance for the sake of the cameras.

On an impulse he took two steps toward his wife and his sons and grasping their hands, raised them high toward the crowd and yelled, "God bless America! Our great nation will prevail! Together, we will weather the storm!"

The crowd picked up on it right away. "We will weather the storm! We will weather the storm!…"

"Nice one, sir," whispered Kent Hanover from behind into his ear. Clement frowned at the remark as Hanover backed away and melted into the crowd. To people like Hanover, this was all a game. But the time for games, Clement knew, was long past.

Chapter Four: Into the Abyss

The Iraq/Jordan Border, April 2020

The Jordanian supply convoy rumbled past the dusty border station between Jordan and Iraq with a casual wave from the Jordanian guards stationed there, ostensibly on its way to Amman. al-Sayyab waved back, flashing a sardonic grin, as he steered the vehicle forward, and looked over at his passenger.

"Soon you shall be in Heaven, Marif."

"Praise Allah, al-Sayyab. I'm happy to do this."

"The Children of Stone shall rise once again."

al-Sayyab turned the heavy steering wheel and guided the rumbling vehicle southeastward toward the West Bank.

Smuggling the suitcase nuke through the Iran-Iraq border had been relatively easy, given the continuing sectarian chaos in Iraq, corrupt nature of the border police, and the hatred for the Jewish state felt by so many Arabs. It was a perfect port of entry for the Jihad-bomb, thought al-Sayyab. The only real challenge lay in penetrating the Israel-Jordan border. Although the border was relatively lax these days, operating under an "Open-Bridges" policy intended to promote trade between Jordan and the numerous West Bank Palestinian towns, the recent closing off of the holy city from Arabs and Muslims had heightened tensions considerably. There could be problems.

"Remember, Marif, to say that we are proceeding on to Jericho to pick up a shipment of tires for our return trip."

"I will," answered al-Sayyab's skinny companion.

"At the junction of Highway 90 and the Dead Sea coast road, we veer off to the pre-arranged site, to prepare our gift. Then it's on to the coast."

"Soon the Zionists shall know our wrath," said Marif with a nod and the smallest of smiles.

"Praise Mohammed," answered al-Sayyab, thinking about the terrible package that lay hidden under the pile of wooden crates in the back of truck, encased in a false rubber covering intended to look like a spare tire.

Aegean Greek Coast - Five Years Prior

Philo and Yordon were seated at a small, unsteady table by the water, after a long trek through the rocky countryside. They were in a fishing village along the beachside slope of the Mount Pélion range; a region of sleepy beach towns, creamy sand, turquoise waters and hidden coves.

Wiping his brow with a rag, Philo joked breathlessly, "At this rate, my friend, we will have walked the entire country!"

"If that is what God wants, Philo."

"What about what *we* want?"

"Hmm? What could we want? We are simple men."

"Well I, for one, would like a jeep with a full tank of petrol! Or at least a pair of new shoes!"

Yordon did not laugh, which worried Philo. He had stopped laughing of late. Formerly, his serious friend was penetrable with a little good natured jibing, and could be made to laugh.

"Ah, the food at last," Philo observed, noticing the *kaffaneia's* owner coming toward them.

"*Singnómi!* Sorry to keep you waiting, Masters Antropos and Berith. Please accept this meal as a gift from my wife and myself! It is our dearest pleasure to serve you," announced the grizzled proprietor as he backed away, almost knocking over an unsuspecting waitress.

Yordon was a well-known character in the Greek countryside by now. The rumor that he was also the Messiah had gotten out of control in the last few years, following their encounter with the monk Joasaph. Joasaph unceasingly proclaimed that he had met the Son of God and that the time of tribulations was at hand. Numerous sensationalist periodicals had picked up on the story, causing a surge in visitors to the Tríatha monastery. This greatly upset the monks of the order, though the village locals took full advantage of the increased tourism and quickly found ways to exploit the public's interest.

Philo had heard that it was possible to witness night-time re-enactments of the fabled meeting of Joasaph and the Messiah and to obtain taped transcripts of Joasaph describing the night of the visions in which the truth was revealed to him. Joasaph was eventually removed from the monastery at the order of the Patriarch and put into 'retirement' in Istanbul, where he quietly disappeared.

Yordon, in turn, had been ordered by the Ecumenical Patriarch himself to desist and deny such talk or face an excommunication. But Yordon had not changed his behavior in the slightest. In the end it was inevitable that he would be officially denounced and expulsed from the faith. The Church simply could not have one of its own walking around claiming to be the Messiah, even if he wasn't saying any such thing. The truth of the matter was that it was becoming increasingly dangerous for Yordon to wander freely through the land.

Yordon was pensive, oblivious to the theatrics of the proprietor. He had grown increasingly distracted and erratic since the incident at Tríatha, two years prior. Philo considered this and sighed. Putting one of his thick, stolid hands on Yordon's shoulder, Philo beseeched his friend.

"You seem more restless than usual these days, Yordon. Why not confide in an old friend, yes? Are you still obsessed with Tríatha? Is it love?"

Yordon chuckled softly, "Love, Philo? It would break your heart."

"Ah, my heart's been broken before. You would still need me anyway. Who else would explain you to your wife?"

Yordon barked a good laugh at that one and relaxed. Philo quietly waited, legs crossed under the table, picking at his yogurt.

"You're right again, Philo. I've been thinking about Joasaph," said Yordon.

"And the vision you shared?"

"I've had more like that. And they've become more intense. Ever since Tríatha. I thought I had grown accustomed to them, but they're becoming impossible to control. I'm afraid of what they hint is to come. And yet they've always been precious to me. I *feel* God through them."

"So you have said to me many times."

"So I have. Are you telling me I'm boring?"

"Ha! At last a joke from the soursop himself! You? Boring? Never. Only the burning core of the Sun is less compelling."

Yordon crossed his arms behind his head and smiled, leaning back in his chair a little, and closed his eyes.

Philo almost whispered, "And what is to come, Yordon?"

Softly, Yordon spoke, as if in a trance. "A great change, Philo. A time of trials and tribulations. And I think I'm inextricably involved in that change. I've begun to understand the source of these visions a little better in these last few months. I feel closer to Him, to It. He's trying to tell me something. I begin to understand what that something is," he sighed. "How can I explain? This source, this pure intelligence, is omniscient. He can focus on many things at once. He knows what's transpired and what's to come. He knows our thoughts. He is our thoughts."

Philo said nothing, not sure what to think, even feeling afraid to think, for fear the heavens could tap his mind and disapprove at what they found there.

Yordon suddenly sat up and fixed Philo with his eyes. "I have come to recognize eternity's thoughts as my own. Philo. I begin to see my purpose more clearly."

Philo's eyes widened in response. *Now this was a change in the wind, indeed.* Were Joasaph's assertions true? Or was this Messiah talk getting to Yordon?

"But what are you to do with that head full of eternity's thoughts, Yordon?" he asked. "Why are you so blessed -- or cursed?"

"It must be… it has to be, because I am the vessel which is to deliver this knowledge." Yordon straightened in his chair upon hearing himself say this. "I am to deliver the Word. Everything we've done so far has been preparation."

Philo grunted, feeling a sudden urge to move on. "Well, let's get back on the road and find some shelter for the night, for the short term. You can worry about all mortal men later, yes?"

Yordon looked at Philo sadly -- or was it pityingly? -- and eventually nodded.

They finished their repast and Philo dropped a few coins on the table as they made to leave the *kaffaneia*.

As they wandered down the village road, Yordon swung toward Philo and grabbed him by his shoulders, stopping them both in their tracks. "I've made a decision."

"Just now?"

"I want to leave Greece."

Philo shook his head incredulously, "Are you serious? Not enough trouble for you here at home?"

Yordon waved Philo's words away. "My mission, my destiny is far larger than the here and now. It's far more than a conflict of interests between me and the Byzantine Eastern Orthodox Church. The possibility of our capture and relegation to insignificance at the hands of bureaucrats burns away my doubts. Perhaps Joasaph was right. I know what I must do next. I know it with conviction."

"Conviction?" parroted Philo dumbly.

"Yes. We must go to Israel, Philo. To Jerusalem. It is time."

Philo frowned at this but held his words.

Yordon shook him slightly.

Philo kicked at a stone and shrugged himself free of Yordon's grasp. "Why do you wish to do this to yourself? Jerusalem won't welcome you or your ideas. People will say you're just another crazy."

Yordon shook his head emphatically. His eyes softened. "I have no choice."

Philo fanned away the words like flies. He worried. His thoughts returned to that night in Meteora and Joasaph's stark pronouncement. Philo found himself wondering exactly who this man was that he had spent so many years with.

He gazed at the fishing boats and attendant men busy with their nets, just off the road. The sharp smell of mud, brine and fish commingled with the rich aroma of Turkish coffee brewing inside the nearby *kaffaneia*. The forlorn cry of seagulls and the playful sounds of water slapping against the hulls of the moored vessels made him smile. His nostrils quivered in the salty air. *Ah, sweet and pungent Hellas.* This simple life lived in unaffected harmony with nature was a thing that he never wanted to trade away.

But he would have to leave it now, perhaps never to return. He didn't agree with Yordon's desire to journey to such a distant and foreign place but, realizing its inevitability, he calmed himself and began the process of accepting it. He was Yordon's only friend, he knew, and he suspected Yordon would be needing a friend for what was to come.

He took a deep, exasperated breath and said, "We'll need passports."

Tel Aviv, Israel - Present Day

Tel Aviv-Jaffa, "the Hill of Spring". The fathers of modern day Israel named it so to symbolize their hope for a new future, built over the accumulated debris of the past. Today, it was a seaside city of hot metal, dirty white concrete and sand, roasting mercilessly in the sun. The crowds that roamed its broad, tree lined boulevards, pressed together in the muggy heat by virtue of their sheer numbers, wore both traditional and cosmopolitan clothing.

This was a metropolis that lay at the crossroads of a people's history. Outwardly, it was a city of the 21st century, but the people that lived in it were ancient, as were their beliefs, their feuds, and their traditions. An embattled history and deep religious conviction coursed beneath the dusty streets and concrete foundations of the city like a nest of reptiles hiding under a desert stone, waiting for an unsuspecting bare ankle.

al-Sayyab and Marif drove their truck slowly down Sheinkin Street, squinting in the bright light and feeling the palpitations of their hearts intermingle with the clashing of the gears. Every bump in the road brought them closer to their goal. The exhilaration caused by this knowledge made it hard for them to speak. They could only stare ahead looking at the dusty street signs, the names of which they had memorized in the prior weeks.

"Left, there, al-Sayyab."

"Ah, yes. Get out of the way!" al-Sayyab shouted out the window, blasting the horn at the unheeding crowds. Traffic slowed to a crawl as they approached a triangle shaped area of elegant Bauhaus-era homes and businesses in the Lev Tel Aviv neighborhood, considered by many to be the heart of the city. It was the eve of Passover and the streets were jammed with package-burdened mothers and grandmothers busily shopping or haggling over goods for the first Passover meal.

Marif found himself remembering the legend of the plague brought down by Moses on the Pharaoh, which tonight's festivities commemorated. "This time the plague of the first born sons will not pass them over, eh al-Sayyab?" he joked, as they passed under a huge blue and white banner announcing an organized pilgrimage to Jerusalem in honor of the event.

"Nor their daughters nor their fathers or mothers. Let's put the truck over there." al-Sayyab pointed at a bus that was just leaving. This area was used to discharge groups of tourists. There were statues to the left and right of it and a solid wall of stone behind it. It would be a good spot for their grand gift to the Jewish nation.

At the Station House overlooking the triangle, Duty Sergeant Yad Cohen, sitting at the electronic surveillance station, could not believe his eyes. He turned the dials of the ultra-sensitive Geiger counter embedded in the control panel and rubbed at his sockets. He felt a cold trickle of panic-sweat amble down the small of his back and became acutely aware of the ache in his toes from his unyielding service boots. Taking a deep breath, he turned and ran to the communications center.

"Contact Captain Emek at once. Go!" barked the Duty Sergeant at his colleague, looking pale and incredulous.

"What's wrong, sir?" asked the communications officer of the Tel Aviv Metropolitan Police force, even as he riffled through his contact book for the number.

"Tell him… we have an isotope reading."

"A what? You don't mean?"

"*Nahon*, man! Get him, now!"

The communications officer dialed the special number that rang in the private reading room of the Emek residence, which was at this time filled with guests and relatives. Captain Emek himself was feeling warm and relaxed after a glass of wine and the jovial camaraderie of his two sons, whom he had not seen in many months.

"Papa, it's the reading room phone for you!" yelled his youngest daughter, popping her head into the salon and gesturing toward the particular phone in the reading room. She discretely did not call it by its true name or purpose.

"Eh? A moment, boys," Emek grunted as he rose, despite his lean build, and made for the room, feeling only slight worry. *No doubt, a nervous novice fretting over ham radio traffic.* He would get a piece of Emek's mind. Closing the door behind him, he sat in his creaky leather chair and picked up the receiver.

"It better be good."

"Isotope reading in the Lev Tel Aviv area," was all the serious, frightened voice on the other end said.

"What did you say?" breathed Emek, his euphoria immediately supplanted by a hard pulsing in his temples, as he felt the weight of the words descend upon him.

"Forgive me Captain, but we have detected the emissions of a fissionable substance in the Triangle. What are your orders, sir?"

Emek absorbed this in an instant and his mouth moved in reflex, though his head felt like it was rolling off his neck into a corner of the dark room. "Listen. Mobilize the IDF and tell them to deploy the Containment Team at once! Inform the Mayor, I'll call the Prime Minister."

"At once, Captain Emek."

Emek was about to slam down the phone and make for the door when he realized something. "Wait."

"Yes, sir?" said the tinny voice of the Comms officer.

"At what time did you first detect the emissions?"

"Minutes ago, sir, It was Cohen. I…"

"Good God! We might nab them then! Send a broadcast to every officer on duty in the city and order them to surround the Triangle immediately. Discretion to the wind! I'll take full responsibility! No-one leaves or enters the area, do you hear? No one or I'll personally tear you in two!"

Marif sat in the driver's seat nervously eyeing the people wandering about the Triangle as he listened to al-Sayyab rustling in the back. The truck swayed slightly. Marif felt himself going mad with anticipation.

"Are you finished back there?" he asked, unable to control himself.

"Almost. I've set the timer. We've got 12 hours to leave Israel. I've got the panic button, just in case," He winked at Marif, but seeing the cold sweat on his cohort's brow, he changed tactics. He was not exactly calm himself but the actual execution of the plan always helped him regain his composure. It was the waiting between the moments of action which he always found difficult. But Marif -- he was really looking brittle. "Here's your new clothes. Quick, come back here and change."

Marif hesitated, then clumsily climbed over the seat to the back.

After a few minutes they were both ready. Tubasi had obtained sharp looking, light weight suits and dark glasses for both of them and had ordered them to shave before leaving the truck. The soft fabrics and close, tailored fit of the expensive suits felt strange to al-Sayyab but he smiled at himself as he observed the transformation as best he could in the rear view mirror.

"We look like gigolos!" he joked.

"Stop your preening and let's be gone!" hissed Marif.

"Yes, yes. Now quickly and quietly. *Yala.*"

al-Sayyab turned the latch of the rear panel doors of the truck. White hot sunlight poured into the interior, threatening to blind them were it not for the shade of the facing stone wall, and their dark glasses. Marif leapt out first and brushed himself off. al-Sayyab followed and closed the doors of the truck. As planned, they went down opposite sides of the vehicle and moved away from it as inconspicuously as possible.

al-Sayyab put his hands in his pockets and fished out a pack of cigarettes. He lit up, barely slowing down and not looking back for Marif. They were each on their own now. But al-Sayyab had the panic button device. Tubasi trusted only al-Sayyab with this and he could clearly see how wise his leader had been in this. Marif had looked like he was going to shit in his pants when they had parted ways. He laughed at the thought.

He abruptly stopped laughing when he spotted the knots of policemen waiting straight ahead. He slowed down and surreptitiously scanned the area. He heart shriveled in his throat as he quickly realized that the entire triangular area was surrounded by police. *Why? Could they know? How could they possibly know?* The device was shielded. The truck, perfectly innocent. They had even sent a decoy in weeks earlier to test the plan. Could it be a leak within the APF?

He turned around to gaze back at Marif and saw that his partner was far less calm about the situation and al-Sayyab would hardly call himself calm at this moment. Marif was standing in the middle of the Triangle, frantically turning to and fro in an open pantomime of someone seeking escape. Two policemen nudged each other, pointing at Marif, and walked toward him.

Noam Zuck wiped the sweat off his brow and listened to the police frequency as the mayoral limousine raced toward the crisis point in Lev Tel Aviv.

"Faster," he growled, and his driver, nodding wordlessly, put more weight on both the accelerator pedal and the automobile's horn. People leapt out of their path as they careened through the crowded streets.

"The entire Triangle area is contained, Noam," said his deputy, Chaim Kiryat, who sat alongside Zuck.

The mayor nodded, holding onto a strap against the swaying of the vehicle. "Impressive. An impressive display of mobilization. We Israelis' are always on the alert, as if we had any choice. But this is not a stray dog we're talking about, Chaim. This is a thermonuclear explosive device, quite possibly. We can't simply 'contain' it, I would think."

"True, it's a tiger in our midst, but you can catch a tiger by its tail."

Noam shot a surprised glance at his sometimes annoying assistant and released a low chuckle, despite himself.

"We have no choice but to think that. Well, we know the nature of the tiger but do we know who the 'tail' is yet?"

"No clue as yet. It could be anyone -- Hamas, Hezbollah, Intefada..." responded Kiryat.

"No matter, the response is the same for us."

al-Sayyab quickened his pace in an attempt to get to Marif before the policemen but it was no use. Marif started to run -- the idiot! -- and the policemen automatically gave chase, signaling to their associates. They surrounded Marif, closing in on him in a tightening circle. al-Sayyab, seeing there was no hope for his associate, padded toward the parked cars along the nearest wall, trying hard to look like a passerby and nothing more. People began to scurry away from the developing confrontation.

Marif searched the clearing for his companion, but al-Sayyab had anticipated this stupid move and had already ducked behind the parked cars. He watched from a crouch through the windows of one of the parked vehicles as a policeman tapped Marif on the shoulder. Marif swung around as if he had been stung by a wasp and shoved the policeman's hand off his shoulder. No sooner had he done this, than another policeman grabbed his other arm and forced it around behind his back.

"Nooooo!!!! Allah's wrath upon you!!!" yelled Marif as he struggled. Then he did the unthinkable. He pulled a gun from his jacket and shot the policeman attempting to restrain him at point blank range. There were screams from a few people who witnessed the blunt act. They ran in all directions. The back of the man's head blew off in a rain of blood and brains. al-Sayyab heard the splattering of the man's brain tissue against the flagstones as it echoed lightly against the walls of the surrounding buildings of the Triangle. There was a moment of silence and hanging gunpowder smoke.

That was all the other policemen needed. The second policeman threw himself away from Marif as nearly a dozen of his fellow officers cocked their guns and rifles and simultaneously emptied their magazines into Marif's twitching body. He died a dancing rag doll. Once it was done, his riddled body fell to the ground, leaking its fluids into the cracks of the stones.

al-Sayyab realized his knees were shouting pain in the ensuing pause and made to stand up when an iron-vise of a hand gripped him by his biceps and pulled him upright. He was pivoted around forcefully and found himself face to face with an expressionless, visored member of the Tel Aviv police force.

"Friend of yours?" questioned the policeman silkily.

"No! No! I was only watching! Is he… was he a terrorist?"

"The question is what are you, friend? You seem to have the same tailor as that scoundrel who is staining the pavement. Come with me."

al-Sayyab paled at the realization of this. How monumentally half-witted. He weakly croaked his protest.

"No. I'm innocent."

"Then you have nothing to fear. Let's go."

al-Sayyab went limp as his mind raced. He let himself be drawn out into the clearing of the Triangle area by the insistent policeman. As they approached the inert mass of Marif, something inside of him quickened and adrenaline juiced back into his arms and legs. He reflexively jerked himself away from the policeman's grip. Even as his mind sought the reason, he was already committed to a course of action. He remembered Tubasi's words.

If the remote detonator for the bomb is found, all will be lost.'

"Stop or I'll shoot you down like a dog! Stop!" yelled his ex-captor.

So this is how my life ends, thought al-Sayyab with wooden realization. He felt sadness, then a reconciled joy. His entire life was devoted to this cause and defined by this struggle; and he realized that every moment of it, from his first sucklings of his mother's sweet olive breast in their family's desert tent, to this moment where his soft leather shoes slapped the hard stones of Lev Tel Aviv in a futile attempt to escape -- all of it was incandescently etched into the stars themselves to lead him to this destiny. He knew it as he had never known anything else in his life. God was with him in this moment. *Praise Allah that it is in his service that I die.*

A warning shot dug into the stones along his path.

He slid to a halt and whirled, raising his arms up to show what he held in his left hand.

"Don't shoot or everybody dies! There is a thermonuclear device in this clearing which I have set to explode as soon as I send the signal with this device. Do you understand? You cannot shoot me fast enough to stop me from exploding this bomb."

The policeman who had grabbed al-Sayyab hesitated, then slowly lowered his service weapon. He waved his hand, signaling his associates to do the same.

"The Mayor is on the way!" someone yelled, holding a walkie-talkie to his ear.

This visibly relaxed the policeman. He could wait.

"Don't move, Arab pig, or I'll shoot you anyway. What do you want?" he asked.

"That megaphone behind you."

al-Sayyab realized he had time. He would die, but he could define his death to these fools. This would help Tubasi and the APF -- give them notoriety and strength. The media was already arriving -- he could see the news vans and boom microphones positioning themselves at the periphery of the clearing.

The megaphone skidded to a halt at his feet. He locked eyes with the policeman as he crouched down to pick it up. He pressed the speaker button and put it to his lips.

"I am a member of the Azerbaijan Popular Front. Eli Tubasi, our leader, is the modern messenger of Allah. He is ordered by the Infinite One to unite the Muslim peoples of the world and mobilize for action."

Noam Zuck's black car screeched to halt at the northeast entrance to the Triangle. Both he and Kiryat bolted out of the car and made for the command post which had been set up behind several police cars and vans. Captain Emek waved them over. He was looking at several portable television monitors which had been hastily set up. Zuck and Kiryat joined him.

"That's the lunatic right there. The one that won't shut up," he pointed at the monitors.

"Those Arab bastards like to hear themselves talk," sneered Kiryat, zeroing in on the flickering image of al-Sayyab standing alone in the clearing of the Triangle. "Why don't you kill him where he stands?"

Emek and Zuck exchanged glances.

Zuck, almost gently, looked at his hot-tempered deputy and said, "Information, Chaim. We wait."

"Shhhh! He's talking again," said Emek.

They leaned down toward the monitors to hear better.

"The Muslim nation will strive against you, disbelievers and blasphemers, with our hands and our tongues and our feet and our sweat until you are expunged from the land. These are the words of the *Q'uran*. You will not remain here for much longer, nor will you prevail for long against the inevitable coming of the *Jihad*."

He hefted the detonator in his hands and gazed at it lovingly. Returning to the megaphone, he continued. "The *Jihad* begins at this hour. Allah has pronounced your retribution and the *Ummah* shall observe joy and gladness today. This is our land. This is Canaan, not Israel. We will not rest until it is returned to the *Dar al Islam*."

He stopped speaking, amazed at the strength in his trembling voice. The detonator was a hot brand that seemed to have fused with the skin of his palm. He felt he could not let go of it even if he desired. The Israeli police, a battalion of IDF soldiers, and the recently arrived anti-terrorist squad surrounded the Triangle. There was no escape for al-Sayyab. Except the one, the holy, the fated.

"He wants to die, Noam. Listen to him. He has no demands we can satisfy." insisted Kiryat, "He is the ultimate suicide bomber."

"We await your orders, sir," said the police Captain; his expression unreadable behind the riot helmet's dark visor.

"Kill him!" hissed Kiryat.

"Wait!" barked Zuck. At this moment he wondered who he hated more. Was it stupid Kiryat with his territorial hatreds as vicious and cowardly as the sweating Arab out there in the square? Or was it Prime Minister Avrahami and his hard line posturing for letting it come to this? Or maybe it was himself that he hated, for still trying to find peace even as the fires of destruction stood poised to strike? It was futile. *Endless.* Why not let it all burn and go to hell? These people so full of poison for each other deserved no less. But they were his people. The Jews. The bloody, desperate, endlessly persecuted and paranoid Jews. But also the blessed, beautiful Jews in search of God, in need of a home. The Chosen People. And Tel Aviv was the political capital of their land. It could not die.

He turned his head slowly toward the Captain Emek. "Do you think he'll detonate the bomb?"

Emek somehow managed to convey his fear despite the dark glass of the helmet's visor. "In moments, sir."

Zuck sucked in his breath slowly. "Can you kill him before he presses the button?"

Emek looked up at the rooftops. His best men were stationed up there. They all had the same stakes in this. They were the best anti-terrorist force in the world.

Emek steeled himself and faced Zuck. He removed his helmet and squinted at the Mayor.

"I know it."

Zuck nodded. "Tell the snipers to shoot to kill. Simultaneous barrage."

"Yes!" shouted Kiryat.

The captain spoke the order into his walkie talkie.

al-Sayyab heard Kiryat's cry and understood.

He released the button as the hot lead of automatic weapons fire ripped him open. It had been a dead man's switch.

Several hundred feet away the tactical nuclear device received its electronic signal, commencing the mechanical process by which two masses of weapons grade uranium isotopes were made to collide and form a supercritical mass which resulted in an instant nuclear fission chain reaction of tremendous explosive force. The blast of heat, expulsive force and sun-white light obliterated everything and everyone in its immediate vicinity in an instant. In the one and a half seconds before Mayor Noam Zuck melted into the ground and became his shadow, which itself burned into dust an instant later, he thought to himself, "Forgive me God. For I have turned the land of milk and honey into a land of blood and tears."

The explosion killed thousands, knocked down buildings in a radius of over a mile, burning everything in its path, even the very air, as a miniature mushroom cloud rose to the heavens, and spread out in all directions. The radiation poisoning spread much farther.

Cheyenne Mountain Complex, Colorado

"The Joint Chiefs are ready, Mr. Under-Secretary."

"Thank you. And the Vice President?"

"Airborne, sir. So is backup C-cubed."

"Good. Please tell the President we will commence at once."

The War Room inside Cheyenne Mountain was all business. Military personnel stoically worked their computer consoles and communications equipment. Above them, digitized maps and satellite images depicted the world situation on the floor to ceiling screens which covered the forward wall of the bunker in a raised semi-circle.

The place was crowded. The Joint Chiefs of Staff were all there, as were the National Security Council's senior members and key members of the Cabinet. There were also a phalanx of advisers, cabinet secretaries, appointees and deputies. The President's family had been put in the guest chambers on another level. An illuminated, pulsating sign on the wall beside the wall screens silently announced, "DEFCON 3".

The heavy, reinforced steel and concrete doors that led into the room suddenly swung open. In walked the recently sworn in President of the United States, Adam Clement III. Nodding to all those present he went directly to the illuminated, real-time map table where the Joint Chiefs, the Security Council members and the Secretaries of the Navy, Army, Air Force and Marine Corps were assembled.

"At ease, everyone. Let's get right to business. Admiral Farrow, why don't you brief us on the situation so far."

Farrow, who was near the head of the table and closest to the President, straightened his uniform jacket and stood at attention as he spoke. "Very well, sir." He turned to face the length of the table. "The detonation appears to have been produced by a backpack nuke somewhere within the boundaries of Tel Aviv. It may have been manually detonated to avoid the detection of any trajectories or transmissions associated with the bomb."

"So it was a suicide," stated Kent Hanover, half asking, half stating the obvious.

Farrow barked a laugh and said, "Hell, it was whole lot more than that!" He turned back to face the President, "The footprint was at least a mile, perhaps more. That city now hosts a radioactive crater, sir."

"Casualties?"

"Hundreds of thousands. Including Americans."

Clement cleared his throat. His Adam's apple bobbed inside his neck. "Go on, Admiral."

Farrow looked over to Wesley Van Ness, who with a curt nod, took his cue and continued the briefing.

"The major powers are scrambled, Mr. President. This situation is critical. White hot. You must contact the Russian President at once and forestall any impulses on his part to over-react -- you know what a firebrand he is -- then the Chinese Prime Minister, then..."

"Enough!" said Clement, looking overwhelmed for an instant. "Get me Ikomikov on the hot line right away! What's the situation in Israel?" Van Ness responded, "We have done everything possible to dampen down the Israeli response but time is running out. The GW BAT carrier group was fortuitously on a port visit in Haifa and General Farrow has ordered it to set sail and take a position 11 miles off the coast of Israel."

Farrow added, "That's right, sir. We've also got Hornets and Tomcats scrambled and patrolling the airspace. Our E-2 Hawkeyes are deployed and feeding us SIGINT as we speak." He pressed a few controls on the map table and surface glowed into a satellite image of the Middle East with Israeli airbases and nuclear weapons depots highlighted.

Van Ness continued, "We've made it clear to Avrahami and Co. that any action taken without prior consultation with us will be most gravely regarded. The Israeli government is nonetheless determined to respond with a nuclear attack of their own. Or, they want us to do it. And they want to do it now."

Clement rubbed his brow, "Are they out of their minds? We can't allow that. The coin would drop for all of us, dammit!"

Kent Hanover chimed in, "They don't see our perspective that well, sir. They're pretty much wrapped up in their own requirements."

Clement absorbed this and whirled to face his Generals. "What is their nuclear capability, and who do they plan to strike against first and what can we do about it?"

"Israeli nuclear strike capability is limited to tacticals and a small fleet of short range ballistic missiles," answered General Hugh Bonhoeffer, the Army Chief, "But it's more than enough. They can wipe out the region at the press of a button, sir." He looked unhappy.

"Well that's just a dandelion, isn't it?" Clement spat sarcastically.

General R.R. Pearson, the Air Force Chief, answered, "Mr. President, the Israelis have exceptionally good intelligence, as you know, and they have pre-established counterstrike plans against all of their known enemies. The problem with the current situation is that the culprits are a relatively new development in world politics."

"So we know who did it?" asked Clement.

Van Ness answered, "Intel has established the identity of the bomber through photographs taken of him during the encounter with the Tel Aviv police force prior to the detonation. Fortunately, the Tel Aviv police were proactive and, even as they had their showdown, transmitted images of his face via satellite to various intelligence networks around the world. His name is, or was, Ibn al-Sayyab, an Afghani Shiite who was associated with the APF."

"That's the Azerbaijan Popular Front, Mr. President. A recent phenomena headed by Eli Tubasi," added General Augustus "Plain Truth" Plain, of the Marine Corps.

"Have the Israelis also identified him?" asked Clement.

"Yes, sir. They have," said Van Ness.

"Can we stop them from launching?"

Pearson answered, "Mr. President. Speaking from a strictly military point of view, it's possible for us to launch a pre-emptive counterstrike against all their known points of delivery. We can have a fleet of Stealths scrambled and in the air in a matter of hours. Since they need no escort and are radar resistant they will provide us with our maximum chance for a surprise move."

Farrow didn't agree with Pearson. "But that assumes our intelligence is one hundred percent accurate, Rex. We can't be sure we know every location. Those Israelis can keep a secret. What's more, our Stealth fighters have limited payload capability. We might not have enough of them to catch all the targets in the first go round."

"Now hold it right there, Jav…," protested Pearson.

Unperturbed, Farrow went on more earnestly, "Also, let's not forget that those Israeli pilots are good, damn good; possibly better than our own. I know that's a hard pill for you to swallow, Rex, but the fact is, they're in the air and fighting all the time. They're water walkers."

"So who are they targeting?" asked Clement, dismissing the topic for the moment.

"Well, that's the rub, sir," said Van Ness. "They're not certain who to target so they are entertaining two possible options."

"Well, spit it out!"

"Option One is to launch against Afghanistan, where they think Tubasi is based, and also to launch against several western provinces of the former Soviet Union, to be sure they get him."

"What? Launch nuclear missiles into the territory of the former Soviet Union? That's sheer, shit shucking madness!" growled Plain, scanning the faces around the table for agreement.

"You got that right, Augie. So far I hate it," said Clement simply, "What's Option Two?"

"To launch against the entire Middle East. *Blitzkrieg*, for want of a better word," said Van Ness quietly, realizing the irony of his choice of language, and throwing his pencil down on the hard glass surface.

"Apocalypse, Mr. Van Ness, not Blitzkrieg. It's called apocalypse," said the President darkly.

University of Chicago Campus, Hyde Park, Chicago

"Apocalypse, Tom, it all points to apocalypse," said Karin as she and Thomas walked together on one of the many paths traversing the Main Quadrangle of the campus. Thomas had been visiting quite a lot more frequently, as world events became steadily more alarming, almost as if seeking safety, or perhaps, solace.

Thomas bent to pick up a flyer that had been discarded on the ground, and examined it.

Are you ready to be judged?
Will you be saved?

He showed Karin the flyer then crumpled it into a ball and put it in his pocket. Looking at Karin, he said, "The kooks are out in force. And people are listening."

"No surprise there," answered Karin, "a nuclear explosion in Israel will do that. And even without the convenience of a catalyst, people have a primal need for this stuff."

"So you are fond of saying, said Thomas, looking directly at her as they strolled.

Karin blessed him with a look of impatience, "Now now, Thomas. You make me sound like another kook. This is obvious stuff! End times prophecies are basically an accounting. They're viewed by those who believe in them as a coming of justice; a retribution against all those who followed the wrong path, and a happy ending for those who flew straight."

They came to a fork in the path. Thomas gently grasped Karin's arm and pulled her to the right, as she continued talking.

"A nice thing to hope for, but when it threatens to become reality, it turns out to be highly inconvenient and scary. An end-times reckoning is not just a judgement of those that have committed transgressions, it also amounts to an end to each person's former way of life. For a lot of people, that might really suck, Thomas! And even if you don't care about that aspect of it, no one's a saint. Not even you." Karin's eyes cast Thomas a fleeting but challenging look, which was not lost on him.

Karin felt the faint warmth of the early Spring sunlight and drank in the beauty of the campus. *Hard to believe that a major city had just been deeply damaged, with thousands dead and more wounded, by a suitcase nuke on the other side of globe.* She saw that Thomas was also lost in thought, for the moment. They walked in silence for a time.

Finally, she turned to Thomas and asked, "Are you planning to say anything about current events in your next installment of *Behind the Word?*"

Karin did not yet know about Thomas' pact with Sylvester to script the show with content provided by the Vatican. He felt embarrassed and perhaps even a little ashamed of having agreed to the arrangement, and yet, he had the ear of the Pope, and that was quite an achievement.

He had tried to temper the change by editing the scripts to more evenly match the messaging of his own writings, which caused some friction with the Vatican functionaries who were handling the passing of content to Thomas, but so far they had managed to walk a line. Thomas had not received any scripted content regarding current events and wondered if he should proceed on his own. There was much he could say, but would anyone be listening?

"Hmm? No, I'm thinking about putting the show on hiatus. I need to take time off to work with Sylvester. I think they want me to travel a bit. He also wants me to meet Clement."

"He does? But why? He already has a delegate for that."

"I think it's because he wants an American representative of the Church there too. Paoli is old school Curia. No chemistry."

"Yeah, he's definitely a stuffed cassock", said Karin with a grin.

The last time Thomas has spoken with anyone from the Vatican, it had been Bishop Paoli himself, who served as the Pro-Nuncio to the U.S. Government. Paoli had explained that Sylvester wanted Thomas to meet Clement as soon as possible, to establish a relationship with the President. Thomas thought it was too provocative a move, given his liberal leanings, and that the Pro-Nuncio served well enough in the function of liaison to the U.S.A."

"Rome has made inquiries to the White House, but so far we've heard nothing back. Clement is, no doubt, otherwise engaged with current events."

Karin shoved at Thomas, as they walked, "Well call them back or something."

Thomas found himself smiling, despite his prevailing mood, at Karin's taunts. "No, you have to understand how the Vatican works. The whole thing works more like a medieval *bassadance*. Any public actions or policy decisions require a certain vetting and pacing. Even if God was coming to dinner there would still be committees to decide what to feed him."

Karin smirked, "Well, if they take too long, God may find his dinner date has gone up in smoke."

☐

Israeli Crisis Center, Jerusalem

In Jerusalem, the dust and radiation from nearby Tel Aviv had not yet affected the area, thanks to prevailing westward winds, but panic was widespread. The available members of the Knesset were on their way to meet with Prime Minister Avrahami, who had been en route to Tel Aviv to visit his brother's family. That would now be impossible. They lived, or had lived, within the blast radius of the explosion. Avrahami had to push the horror of what had occurred out his mind. He could not think about the ashes that lay in the place of his neglected brother's bungalow. He could not contemplate what they must have felt, what they must have thought in those last moments before they were incinerated.

The electromagnetic pulse of the explosion had severely disrupted communications in the region. This, the public panic, and the Passover holiday resulted in many of the Knesset members being unavailable. As much of the plenum as could be found had to convene and decisions had to be made. In the meantime, Avrahami was severely challenged to keep the Army and Air Force generals from launching an immediate counterstrike. His chief argument was that they were not certain who to retaliate against. The APF was a stateless organization whose cells and strongholds were still not fully known. If they did launch into the general region suspected to be Tubasi's neighborhood, that would mean launching into Western Asia which would involve the Russians. What's more, many of those former provinces of the Soviet Union had their own nuclear arsenals. A nuclear counterstrike would undoubtedly send the planet sliding down a track to utter incineration. Lastly, the Americans were in his face; uncompromising in their own threat to do anything in their power to snuff the Israeli counterstrike.

"A message of sympathy from the Islamic mufti of Jerusalem, Kahlil Salahi, Prime Minister Avrahami," said Hershel Katz as he entered the Crisis Center, many hundreds of meters below the Knesset building. He handed a sealed envelope to the Prime Minister.

Avrahami and a small group of ministers were huddled around a long conference table as they scanned situation reports and the tactical display screens along the wall. He glanced at the envelope for half a moment and let it fall to the desk.

"The Jordanians are on full alert and have scrambled F18s and AWACS units from Sakarta. Our own K'firs and F16s roar above the desert countering every approach of Arab jets but so far there are no engagements. American planes have taken off from their bases in Turkey and Saudi Arabia and fly above our skies but so far they only watch and wait," reported the hawkish Minister of Defense, Ariel Engel, as he paced the area by the door.

David Chalutz, the spindly Minister of National Infrastructure, added, "I have reports that Arab demonstrators have taken to the streets in actual celebration of the destruction of Tel Aviv! Intelligence also shows that several Arab leaders are considering mobilizing a combined invasion force to take advantage of the chaos."

"We should at least mobilize our conventional forces and amass our strength at the borders to the North and to the East, Prime Minister!" demanded Engel.

"No!" retorted Natan Silver. "That would only provoke an equal reaction from the Jordanians or the Syrians and push them over the edge. They're looking for an excuse. We would lose control of the situation!"

"Bah! We've already lost control," spat the highly agitated Engel. "This is no time for apologist politics, Natan! We don't have the territorial depth to play cat and mouse. We must be prepared to take the battle into their territory immediately or risk being pushed into the ocean!"

"It's Avrahami's hard line stance that led us to this," accused Chalutz. He turned toward Avrahami. "What do you propose we do, Mr. Prime Minister? You are responsible for this mess!"

Avrahami looked up, wearing a stricken expression. His chest felt constricted by the excitement, making it difficult for him to breath.

Just as he was about to answer, the gravelly voiced Minister of Science and Technology, Dr. Schmuel Ephrat, interrupted the argument. "You're wasting time with your bickering. We all agreed to the Prime Minister's policies at the time so we're all to blame. We must find our way out together. Time is of the essence and so are the facts. We need facts. All we have is conjecture and emotion. We must endeavor to obtain whatever facts can be discovered from the explosion site itself. Moshe has achieved a tense balance of terror among our enemies and so-called allies for the moment. The swords hover over our heads but they cut both ways. That knowledge holds our enemies at bay but it won't last. We should use the time to obtain information from the epicenter."

The group of ministers was quieted by this, intrigued by the suggestion.

"What are you proposing, Schmuel?" asked Chalutz, looking nervous and impatient.

There was a beep and a flashing light on the conference phone.

Katz picked up the phone and listened, nodding.

"Mr. Prime Minister, two more plenum members have been located and escorted to the Crisis Center. They are waiting outside."

"Let them come," said Avrahami, nodding curtly. He wiped at his brow with a handkerchief.

Two tremendous metal doors slid open with a hiss of hydraulics and in marched the darkly dressed, fully bearded figures of the Sephardi Chief Rabbi, Yoram Chet, and the Ashkenazi Chief, Rabbi Lechaim Weizman.

They nodded at everyone and joined the group around the conference table.

Ephrat rolled his eyes. He had succeeded in capturing the attention of his contentious audience and now these fomenters had chosen that key moment to enter the room. He silently cursed the air.

Ephrat tried to return to his point once again. "As I was saying, research is needed to help determine the source and nature of the bomb. That will help us."

"The nature of the bomb is very clear, my esteemed Doctor Ephrat," interjected Rabbi Weizman with iron politeness.

Rabbi Chet nodded gravely in agreement.

"What are you getting at, Lechaim?" asked the Prime Minister from the head of the conference table. They turned to face him. He cleaned his glasses with his handkerchief as he pointedly stared down the length of the curving table at the Rabbi.

Rabbi Weizman gazed back defiantly at the Prime Minister. "You know exactly what I mean. It's the hour of vindication. This is the beginning."

Silver barked out a laugh. "The hour of what? The hour of vindication? You sound just like Engel." He looked around the table for support. No one laughed.

Rabbi Chet joined in, defending Weizman. "He means the return of God, you idiot. It starts with fire; a great disaster. The Prophetical books foretell how out of an immense cosmic catastrophe shall arise a new Palestine which shall be like a new Eden for all Jews to come home to. Today there is the day of God's wrath but tomorrow is the day of deliverance!"

Avrahami donned his spectacles and regarded the mix of personalities vying for his attention. They sat around the table like conspirators and yet they stood kilometers apart in priority and doctrine. Such different views of the world. Such different beliefs of what it means to be a Jew. It was truly a wonder that this nation got anything done at all. He felt annoyance at the religious fanaticism introduced into the discussion by the two Rabbis, but he knew it couldn't be avoided. He turned his attention to Weizman.

"And how will Eden be made out of these ashes, Rabbi Weizman? And while we wait for this miracle, what is your prescription for a course of action that we; mere mortal men whose feet hurt and who cannot foresee the future should undertake?"

The Rabbi's lips moved but no sound came out.

Rabbi Chet ran interference and retorted quickly. "You don't respect the words of the *Torah*, Avrahami. You never have. You hate Arabs as much as any of us in this room but you are more of an Israeli than a Jew. You use God like a stick to beat your enemies with but you yourself have no hope that the Day of Redemption will come. You think this is purely a geo-political problem."

Engel interjected, "Well, I have news for you, Rabbi Chet. Until *Yahweh* himself comes down from the sky, it *is* a purely geo-political problem. More Jews will die in the streets if we do not decide on a defensive posture soon. Palestine may belong to the Palestinians by the time the day of deliverance arrives, if we sit idly fingering our prayer books, waiting for God to come."

"We should take this time to evacuate the population," suggested David Chalutz.

"Evacuate?" gasped several of the other ministers at once. Chalutz shrank in his seat.

Avrahami waved them all to silence. "*Maspeek!* This is going nowhere. Ephrat is the soberest voice among you. As he tried to say before, we need facts. Who did this? Was it the APF? How did they get away with it? Where are they now?" He extended his hand toward the Science Minister who looked surprised. "Well Doctor, you have the floor. How do suppose we should get those facts?"

"We should send an expedition to Ground Zero."

Somewhere near Devil's Lake, North Dakota

"The War of Gog and Magog is taking place before our eyes!" declared Mary's companion, a card carrying member of the Disciples of Gabriel. He determinedly steered the light blue pickup through the brush. "Magog is Russia and Gog is Ikomikov! They're supposed to attack Israel in cooperation with the Arabs and Persians. Where do you think that Tubasi and his crew got a nuke from?"

Mary tried to read the small type of the book in her hands despite the shaking of the truck. "But Doug, no one knows for certain where Magog is or if all these prophecies refer to a real war."

Doug veered the vehicle violently to avoid a large ditch.

"Doug Oakes! You're not listening!"

Doug swung his head to face her and said, "It's you that's not listening, Mary."

"Doug."

He drove grimly on.

"Doug!"

The truck hit a rock and bounced straight up into the air. They landed with a loud crash and, impossibly, kept moving forward.

"DOUG OAKES STOP THE CAR!!!" shouted Mary, clutching at the steering wheel.

"Okay, Okay." He slapped the steering wheel and went slack against the driver's seat. The pickup wandered to a halt. Metal popped and tinked as the overheated engine cooled. The seats creaked quietly. They both stared out of the grimy windshield at the North Dakota prairie land.

"We're doing the wrong thing. This is stupid."

Doug grabbed the old, dog-eared Bible she was holding from her and flipped pages frantically as he spoke, "In Ezekiel 37, it says right here that the prophet was shown a valley full of bones in the land of Israel. How would you describe the aftermath of the Tel Aviv bombing, Mary? The false prophet is supposed to bring down fire from the skies, as recorded in Revelation 13, in imitation of the real Elijah's actions in Kings II! What would you call a nuclear detonation if not fire from the skies? Who is that bastard Eli Tubasi if not the false Elijah?"

"But we're running away, Doug. I don't want to run away. I want to face my judgment day. And if it really is judgement day, you can't really hide from it, can you? No one can."

Doug took her hand, his sparse blond beard hiding the gaunt lines of his face. She could see the edge of panic in his eyes.

Doug took a deep breath and calmed himself down a little. "Mary, we can't go back. Everyone's white-eyed back in Grand Forks. We had to leave. It was getting dangerous."

"You're looking pretty dangerous yourself." said Mary, trying to slow down her breathing. "Get a grip, Doug. We've gotta relax and think this through. What we're doing is no less insane than those people rioting in the streets back there."

Doug admonished, "At least we're trying to keep our skins intact, Mary."

She spat a grim laugh in response. "Listen to you. What kind of a Disciple of Gabriel are you? You're no better than any other religious nut-job I've ever met."

Doug frowned, "What are you talking about?"

Mary stared out into the barren terrain, "It's all gimmicks, Doug, don't you see? People can't tell good from bad anymore."

Doug said nothing. In the ensuing silence, Mary turned back to face him, "You know, it may not actually be a bad thing that's happening here."

Doug looked incredulous. "How can you say that?"

She remembered the five children and their words. "Can't explain it more than that. I just think good things are coming from behind these dark clouds."

"That doesn't give me a lot to go on. Just take it on faith, eh?"

Mary laughed again, "That shouldn't be hard for someone like you. Maybe."

Mary examined Doug's fear lined face, sighed and ran her fingers through her hair. It had grown long over the years. *This was hopeless.*

"Doug, let's not run. Let's stop for the night. We're pretty much in the middle of nowhere already."

He squinted at her, "You mean sleep here? In the brush?"

She touched his hand. "No, in a motel."

Doug's eyebrows shot up and he gave Mary an unreadable, blank look for long minutes. She couldn't tell if he was contemplating leaving her in the middle of the Dakota prairie and continuing to run on his own, or if he was weighing the prospect of sharing a bed with her. Maybe both. She fidgeted.

"Okay. Okay. We'll stop. Maybe you're right. And I guess we've driven far enough. We'll turn onto the first road we find and go until we hit a fleabag."

They bumped along in the dimming light until they encountered the road to Devil's Lake. Turning onto the road and driving into the violet embers of the day's end they eventually came upon an outpost of ramshackle buildings flanking the road, and at the end of the small collection of buildings, a roadside motel, *Enoch's Comfort Inn*.

"Looks like our only option," said Doug.

Mary tried to sound cheery. "It's not the Hilton, but then again I've never been inside a Hilton."

They both laughed, feeling more relaxed at the evident continuity of civilization – such as it was -- and the prospect of a mattress and sleep.

"Leave your car and your keys here. It's motel policy," drawled the proprietor, a wrinkled, rheumy eyed veteran. "Room 117 at the end of the parking lot. Check out at 11 AM. We check the room before you get your keys back."

Their footfalls crunched gravel as the rising moon revealed the parking lot devoid of other vehicles. The specter of the nuclear explosion in Tel Aviv crept back into their minds and neither spoke as they neared the cracked, stained door of room 117.

"It's probably always like this out here, Mare," said Doug with false casualness.

"Sure. Let's go inside and turn on the TV."

Once inside the darkened room, Doug went directly to the old set that was facing the foot of the bed but Mary grabbed his wrist and stopped him.

"No. On second thought, let's not. Let's just get some sleep."

Doug plopped down on the bed and lay still.

Mary whispered into his ear, "It's going to be alright, Doug. You're scared and you're tired, I know."

After a time Mary heard Doug's breathing relax into the rhythmic pattern of sleep. But sleep eluded her.

Seeing the easy chair and lamp table in the corner of the room for the first time, she went to it and flicked on the lamp. The glare was blinding.

This won't do at all.

Taking a pillowcase, she covered the lamp shade and turned on the light, producing a dim red glow. Now more certain that Doug's sleep would not be disturbed, she settled into the easy chair and began to riffle through the local literature. She read the advertisements crowded into the brochures and came across one that instantly commanded her attention.

The Son of Man Alive Today?

Come to the Branford Young Crusader's Hostel next Sunday night at 9 P.M. and learn about the man from Athos, Greece, named **Yordon Antropos**. Many claim he is the Son of God made incarnate. The word is spreading fast. Could it be true? **The Monk Joasaph** from the famous Ayia Tríatha monastery in Meteora talks about his encounter with the so-called 'Son of Man' in a taped interview. Discussion with a panel of experts to follow. **Free refreshments.**

The Son of Man. The words wavered on the leaflet. Mary turned the phrase over in her mind and remembered the five voices, so many years ago back in Starkenville, speaking in unison. *You will come to know who is the Son of Man.* And the glow that had shone out from her own body upon being touched by them. *Who was this Antropos?*

Mary felt a pull, a tremor from deep within herself. *Could he be?* She let the leaflet fall to the table and wondered.

After a time, Mary knew what she had to do, come morning. She turned from the window, switched off the lamp, and padded quietly back to the bed.

Chapter Five: The Stranger in the Desert

Ground Zero, Tel Aviv, May 2020

Zachary Jobson felt itchy inside the radiation suit and wished to hell he could discard it and scrabble around in the ruins unencumbered, as his archeologist's instincts begged. But it would be certain death. The Roentgen readings promised it. If the radiation didn't kill you then you'd slowly choke from breathing the heavy, irradiated dust that hung in the air. The entire "Ground Zero", mile wide sector of Tel Aviv had been turned into piles of rubble and hardened slag. But the damage done, to the lives of thousands of Israelis, and the economic well-being of the country, was far worse. The entire city had been evacuated in panic and fear of the radiation and the possibility of more explosions. The formerly teeming metropolis was now a ghost town, except for Zachary's team and their encampment. Only because of the utter chaos following the explosion, the Israeli Cabinet's Science Minister's unexpected support, and his personal stature as a leading Archeo-forensics specialist from UCLA, had Zachary been able to mobilize this team in so short a period of time, even beating out the Negev team. And only here on the outskirts of the explosion radius were the effects of the suitcase nuke conflagration sufficiently attenuated to allow some forensic exploration to take place.

The building he was currently exploring had once been a typical family house. He bent down, feeling the ache in his 62 year old bones. Using the lead lined tongs, he picked up the charred object that had reflected the light of his lantern from inside the crumbling dwelling. Examining the object more closely, he realized what it was and thought to himself that a less experienced person might have dropped it in revulsion. But Jobson was too old and too experienced at his specialty to be so alarmed. He turned the object in his gloved hands in fascination.

It was the hand of a child holding a glass bottle -- almost unrecognizable due to the charred, blackened skin. The five fingers were intact, and fused into the glass along with the palm. Except for this hand, this child had literally melted into the ground. Jobson felt sadness. Such widespread horror was easy to regard empirically, but when an individual life was singled out in this way, it brought the tragedy home for him. The detached scientist within reminded him that empathizing with the dead through their fossilized remains was, in fact, a requirement of his profession.

"Dr. Jobson?" questioned the intercom inside his helmet.

Jobson was startled out of his reverie by the voice on the intercom and the shadow that appeared at the doorway. He tried to make out the face inside the radiation suit's helmet.

"Eh? Ahh, Yasu, it's you. Yes, what is it?"

The young Japanese-American intern gingerly made his way into the crumbling stone and brick dwelling. Jobson stored the glass hand in the lead case he carried with him. Better to reveal the finding later, under the cold light of the lab. Yasu looked around, especially at the ceiling beams, gauging the risk of being inside the building.

"Dr. Jobson, are you sure you wanna be in here?"

"Come come, young man. It's sufficiently stable for our purposes. What is it?"

"There's a group of refugees heading this way".

"You mean survivors?" he said, fascinated by the prospect of interviewing actual, modern day survivors of a fission explosion.

Yasu nodded quietly.

They exchanged looks, realizing they were both thinking the same thing. These people would be afflicted with terminal radiation sickness. They were undoubtedly mutilated in unspeakable ways. There would be no hope for them… Yet they were heading this way because they hoped that Jobson's team could help them.

Jobson put a gloved hand on the shoulder of his student. *A bright lad with brighter prospects.* He would always remember this day in his long career. Jobson realized the importance of his own conduct in the next few moments.

"You're a scientist, Yasu. You must be dispassionate, but also compassionate. This is a difficult balance to achieve at times. And I won't dally with you, lad. This is one of those times."

Yasu stared, wide eyed, at the Doctor.

"Deal with the present as pragmatically as you can. Process the emotions later. Be assured that this is the best disposition you can adopt right now. And one more thing."

"Yes, sir?"

"You must be prepared to lie to these people, Yasu. They may not know they're as good as dead. Telling them may not be a good idea, though some might welcome it."

Together, the two archeologists made their way out of the building and squinted through their helmets into the particle occluded light, trying to discern the stragglers more clearly.

A small group of people could be seen moving toward the base camp that Zachary and his team had set up along the edge of the blast zone, in what must have once been a parking lot.

Some were dragging themselves, evidently crippled to the point of not being able to walk. Voices could be heard, carried by an incongruous breeze. Moans of pain and cries for help.

"Get the food and water and bring it out here right away!" ordered Jobson. "Jean, bring out the med kit and tell Manuel to contact the local Red Cross facility. Tell them we have located survivors."

"Right away!" answered the stout brunette, sounding robotic over the intercom's cheap speaker, as she dashed toward the supplies tent at the perimeter base camp.

His team galvanized into action.

The survivors, seeing the strangely suited team, stopped short and showed signs of panic, but then one of them took the lead, realizing he was looking at people, and beckoned the ragtag group forward.

Jobson switched on the small external speaker installed in his helmet and yelled, "Don't be afraid! We have medical supplies and water. How did you survive the explosion?"

He continued asking questions in a business-like fashion to keep the man who seemed to be the leader engaged. He ushered the man, who almost fell into his arms, toward the supply tent.

The man gasped his response, "We were underground, working construction. At least some of us. We've gained a few here, lost a few there. The incredible heat and vibrations! It's a miracle we weren't crushed! But who are you? What are you doing here?"

The man looked Jobson up and down, taking in his strange costume and accepting water from one of Jobson's staff. The other survivors came forward. A few men from Jobson's team blocked the entrance to the supply tent.

Jobson looked back and ordered, "Give them everything they want, for God's sake!"

"But our instruments, Doctor?" protested Yasu.

Jobson realized his point. "Yes, of course. Then pass out the water at once -- as quickly as you can."

"Instruments?" questioned the survivor's leader. "What are you doing? Did you cause that explosion?" He was suddenly angry.

Jobson took a step back and raised his hands defensively. "What? No, no. Don't be ridiculous. We're scientists. We're measuring the," he realized his mistake, but it was too late, "radioactivity."

"Radio... what do you mean? Was that a *nuke* we felt?"

"Tel Aviv has had a so called "suitcase" nuke detonated within its boundaries, young man," answered Jobson sadly. One of the women among the survivors began to sob. Her skin was sloughing off her arm and she was trying to slide it back into place.

"But why? Who? You bastards!!" The man jumped at Jobson. Yasu was there and the two fell to the ground, raising dust and sending small rocks and pebbles scuffling.

"Sedate him!" ordered Jobson as he went to help the others.

Soon a tent had been emptied and cots crowded into it for the survivors. They were quiet for the moment, intent on feeding themselves and having their wounds tended. Many of them showed signs of dementia and panic. Jobson feared they could easily have a control problem, despite the grave condition of most of these people.

One of the UCLA team members approached him. It was Jean. "We have to leave soon, Doctor. Our air supplies are running out. What should we do about the survivors?"

Jobson gazed at the setting sun. The human, compassionate side of him struggled with the dispassionate scientist. These people were doomed. The opportunity for discovery was unique, at the same time. The survey expedition had to continue for as long as it could. Their mission was not medical relief. And yet these were human beings who needed his help.

He declared, "Leave everything for them. We'll abandon the camp before dark. We'll have to leave discretely, though, to avoid a panic. That's a problem. They'll hear our vehicles. When are the Red Cross trucks coming?"

Jean looked uncomfortable, even through her glass helmet. "I don't know, sir. There's no one who can tell me with any certainty."

Jobson and Jean watched the survivors swaying and hugging themselves on their cots. Misery glowed from them. *This is what hate does. Human hate.* Jobson shook himself to escape the thoughts.

Yasu came running toward them. "Doctor! There's another group of survivors heading this way!" Jobson felt panic. It was getting dark. The team had to leave. The survivors in the tent would try to overwhelm them if they realized they were abandoning the camp. They would also not share their windfall of beds and supplies gracefully with the second group of survivors, if he knew human nature. Chaos was minutes away.

Thinking quickly, Jobson snapped orders at Yasu and Jean. "Get the others, right away. Tell them to start up the trucks. We've got to intercept the new arrivals and use them as a diversion. Maybe we can avoid a confrontation."

"What do you plan to do?" asked Yasu, his breath audible over the intercom speaker. Jean was already on her way to tell the others.

"We'll send a couple of our people out to meet the new group of survivors and the rest of you are going to drive back to Rehovot. In the confusion most of us should be able to get away without much trouble. Those of us that stay behind will guide these people to the tents and hope for the best. Let's go -- no time to waste, son. Make haste!"

Jobson and Yasu, accompanied by Jean and Manuel, made their way through the rubble toward the approaching group. As they drew closer, Jobson noticed, even in the fading light, that this group was unlike their predecessors. They walked upright; and with a discernible aura of purpose. At their apex was a tall man with long flowing hair, held down by high round hat, and wearing what appeared to be a white cassock. Close behind him walked a shorter man of stocky build wearing robes and a vest. The two were talking and pointed at Jobson's entourage. The shorter man yelled something to the rest of the people that were with them. The entire group stopped in its tracks and waited for Jobson's team to approach.

Jobson, in the lead, stopped not ten yards from them. He waited for Yasu to catch up, then the two scientists strode together toward the apparent leader. Manuel and Jean waited a few yards back. Jobson almost stopped when he heard the distinct click of an automatic weapon's safety being released behind him. Manuel had come prepared for the worst. Ahead, the tall man raised his hand in a gesture of peace and spoke as soon as Jobson and Yasu were within earshot.

"Greetings. You're dressed strangely. Are you from another planet?"

Yasu chuckled over the helmet intercom at this. Jobson switched on his external helmet speaker.

"Well, at least your sense of humor is intact. No, we're scientists. This region is dangerous without protection."

"You mean the radiation. Yes, we know."

Jobson felt a tingling sensation at the back of his neck, as if something was terribly wrong about this. He felt off-balance, unprepared for this exchange. Nonetheless, he pressed on.

"Yes, the radiation. It will kill you."

"Do we appear to be dying?" asked the man nonchalantly.

Jobson scanned the group and felt bewilderment. "No."

Jobson took a step closer, gesturing to Yasu to follow, and extended his gloved hand.

"I'm Jobson. Doctor Zachary Jobson. And this is Yasu Makazawa, my assistant. We're scientists. We're collecting evidence."

"How lucky for you that a nuclear explosion just happened here!" said the stout companion, with a gruff laugh.

"Philo…" said the tall man, waving the shorter man to silence. He looked Jobson directly in the eye and said, "My name is Yordon Antropos. This is my traveling companion, Philo Berith. Forgive his sarcasm. He becomes rude when he's tired. We've been walking all day. We've collected a few survivors along the way."

"All day? In this? Do you need any assistance, Mr. Antropos?" asked Yasu, examining the people who were standing behind Yordon.

"No, young man. We are not sick. In fact, we're here to help others. There are many who need help."

"So we've seen. There's a group of people in one of the tents back there, at our camp," answered Yasu, pointing behind him with his thumb but not looking away from Yordon.

They all turned toward the camp in time to see the UCLA convoy departing.

"Looks like they're on their own now," said Philo.

"You don't understand," protested Yasu. Manual watched the retreat through binoculars, while Jean kept an eye on the newcomers.

Jobson interjected. "Look, we didn't expect to encounter survivors. This city is supposed to be entirely evacuated. Even so, we've given these people all of our supplies. But we must leave the area. We can't survive here without these radiation suits and we have to replenish the air supplies, which brings me to ask how you can look so healthy if you've been walking this area all day, as you claim. It's not physically possible."

"And yet here I stand before you, Dr. Jobson."

Someone from the group of people with Yordon spoke up. "He can heal the sick. He's a miracle worker."

Jobson waited for Yordon to answer the question, ignoring the remark. Someone else corroborated the first person's comment. "It's true."

Jobson waited still. Manuel's voice crackled over the helmet intercom. "Everything okay, Doc?"

Yordon looked toward the distant tent containing the sickly survivors. "Why don't you show me to those people back at your camp? Let me help them."

"But how?" asked Yasu. "You're just a man wandering the ruins. Are you a doctor too?"

Jobson interrupted, feeling a sudden impatience. "Enough talk. Time is running out. Let's take them back to the tents and get ourselves to Rehovot before our air runs out."

Yasu looked put upon but obeyed quickly enough, waving Manuel and Jean to return to the camp. Yordon and his party followed suit.

The inside of the refugee tent was dark, now that the sun had waned and was dipping below the horizon. Yasu, Jobson, Yordon and Philo entered quietly so as not to disturb the survivors within. Jobson had sent Manuel and Jean onwards, overriding their protests.

"We've got about an hour's worth of air left, Doctor Jobson. We've really gotta go," said Yasu. He was looking nervous.

Jobson felt a growing apprehension as well, but he also felt that there was something left to do here. *Something to see. Something to say.* It was purely instinctual, a feeling he had learned to respect over the years.

The victims lay on the ground or on cots, mostly unconscious. As Jobson watched, Yordon walked among them, touching them on their heads as he passed. Amazingly, each person he touched underwent a metamorphosis. Jobson watched incredulously as clouded eyes became clear, labored breathing became easy, and skin lesions were healed before his and Yasu's eyes.

Yordon circulated through the tent, arousing the people within. They spoke together, expressing their amazement. He made his way to the entrance of the tent, where Jobson waited, and turned to face the people he had touched.

"My name is Yordon Antropos. I am from Athos, in Greece. I've traveled to Israel because the spirit of God is upon me. He has commanded me to bring

127

good tidings to the afflicted. He has sent me to bind your wounds and liberate you from your afflictions. This is a gift from God. This power comes from God himself. I am his instrument, nothing more. You will not fall ill again, though I advise you to leave this area soon. Remember that God is within all of you, the same way he is within me. I am only more aware of it. I must go now, for there are many who need my help. Use your good fortune to help others too. And remember that God is within you. He is you. You are but a prism for the heavenly light. Goodbye."

Yordon gestured to Philo, and the two made to leave. Jobson tried to shake himself to alertness and exchanged looks with Yasu, whose mouth hung open in amazement. Yasu stared at the departing Yordon, then back inside the tent at the now healthy individuals.

"Did you see that, Doctor Jobson?" he stammered.

"We've got to get these people out of here or they'll get sick again," declared Jobson in a thick voice, feeling disoriented.

"They won't," said Yordon matter of factly from the tent flap. "You're running out of air, Zachary."

It hit him like a cold knife. Yordon was right. They were in trouble. They had barely 20 minutes of air left and the drive to the neighboring city of Rehovot, 27 clicks away, was going to take a bit longer than that. They were going to have to shed the suits before they were back at the bunker in Rehovot.

"Yasu, let's go, time for questions later."

Yasu nodded emphatically and they headed for the jeep. As they made their way past Yordon and Philo, Jobson slowed just long enough to ask Yordon, "Where can I find you? There's much I'd like to know."

"And there is much you will learn, I have no doubt, and still you will not know." said Yordon above the rumble of the jeep's engine. Jobson clambered aboard and signaled to Yasu. The jeep leapt away, and as the figure of Yordon receded in the dust, he waved to them, a smile on his face.

Jobson bobbed absently in the jeep as it careened down the empty streets of Tel Aviv. It was getting dark and the air was still hazy with dust from the explosion, making it hard to see. The headlights of the jeep carved tunnels in the grimy gloom. The particulate matter in the air was, for some reason, denser at this hour. *Perhaps the cooling air allows the detritus in the atmosphere to descend back to earth at this time of day,* he automatically mused.

"Doctor Jobson, who was that guy?" Yasu asked, needing an explanation and trying to distract himself from the air gauge on his wrist, which hovered a hair above zero. He didn't want to have to breathe this poison.

Jobson returned to alertness and grabbed the dashboard. He steadied himself enough to turn slightly toward Yasu. "A wild card, Yasu. Something strange and unexpected. Watch for those overturned vehicles ahead. The highway is not far now."

"He was like a God or something. Only Gods can do that stuff, right?"

Jobson smiled tiredly. "And men, Yasu. Men can perform miracles too. I hesitate to jump to conclusions."

"But didn't you see with your own eyes?"

Jobson shook his head. "There's no room for the supernatural in my world, Yasu. I've lived my entire life in pursuit of facts and explanations. I've studied many an ancient civilization and dissected their mysteries and superstitions in the hard light of science. And I've learned this basic truth clearly and fully. The universe operates under one set of rules and laws and there's no room for miracles in it. To me, it's far more likely that Antropos is an alien from another world than some kind of miracle-wielding angel, or a devil in disguise," he smiled fleetingly at Yasu, but it was lost behind the visor.

Jobson returned to a normal sitting position. Up ahead he could see the single strip of road that led to the town.

Yasu looked angry for a moment but then visibly relaxed. He sighed. "Okay, Doc. Have it your way. Oh shit! I'm out of air. Gotta pull off this helmet."

They had reached the Ayalon Highway, which led to Rehovot.

"But the radioactive particles! Don't Yasu! We can share my hose," protested Jobson.

Yasu looked panicked behind the glass of his helmet then, suddenly, his eyes widened in a private realization. He relaxed and calmly steered the jeep onto the blacktop. Stopping the jeep, he removed his helmet and shook his long, straight hair free. "No worries, Doc. There's a cure now and his name is Antropos, remember?"

Yasu calmly put the helmet down on the seat between them and shifted the jeep back into gear.

Jobson realized that, despite his outspoken skepticism, he too believed that statement. However this Mr. Antropos had achieved his feat of healing, it was undeniable that it had occurred -- Jobson had witnessed it with his own eyes.

The air in his helmet was thick and stale. He reached for the release catch and hesitated. Yasu was staring at him in quick glances, alternating with the road.

"Ten minutes to Rehovot, Doc. Can you make it?"

Jobson sucked in the hot wind that substituted for air inside his helmet. He was getting light headed. His hands were frozen on the release catch. Gradually he lost consciousness, but the helmet stayed on.

To the people of Rehovot, it was a strange sight indeed to witness the dusty jeep barreling through the gate, driven by a crazed looking, young Japanese man with long hair flowing out behind him, and seated to his right, a man wearing a full radiation suit and helmet. It looked to them as if they were witnessing two characters from entirely different stories that, by a strange happenstance of the imagination, had accidentally been placed in the same moment, in the same vehicle.

Ground Zero, Tel Aviv – the next day

The Israeli Defense Force's expeditionary squad and the team from the Negev Nuclear Research Center stood at the perimeter of the blast crater in the midst of the abandoned cityscape. The chaos of twisted metal and rubble that lay strewn within glowed slightly in the dim light. Toxic gas and dust floated in the air and a reddish haze hung over the entire area. This section of the city had been erased, a vision of hell left in its place.

Under the protective escort of the IDF group, the Negev scientists had set up their equipment in the same base camp area as Jobson's team, near the rim of the blast crater. Wrapped inside their radiation suits it was hard to discern any hint of emotion or humanity. The scene was a cold epilogue to what had been a crime of utmost passion.

"More visitors," said Yordon from inside one of the survivor tents.

Philo peaked out through the flaps of the tent and scanned the terrain around them. Closing the flap he turned toward Yordon, "Should we hide?"

Yordon answered by emerging from the tent and waving to the soldiers who instantly began trotting their way.

Philo sighed and came forward too.

The captain of the IDF squad marched to within inches of Yordon and over her helmet's intercom demanded, "What is God's name are you doing out here? This area is HOT! Who are you?"

The other soldiers moved to surround the two travelers and raised their weapons.

"I am Yordon Antropos. This is Philo Berith. We're here to help. Please don't be afraid."

The helmeted figures turned toward each other, exchanging glances.

131

The captain spoke again. "It's you that needs help, whoever you are. And fast. Come with us. Yitzhak! Fetch one of the jeeps. David, are there any extra suits?"

"Don't move," coughed the transistorized voice of one of the remaining soldiers.

"Please don't shoot. I want to show you something. I won't hurt anyone," said Yordon.

Philo held his breath as Yordon walked a few paces away so that he was standing alone on a patch of clearing overlooking the ruins of the blast crater. The soldiers waited expectantly.

Yordon raised his arms and the wind picked up. The conjured gust orbited around them like a small whirlwind. Philo could see the dust on the ground following the pattern of the wind. Above, the sky began to change.

Puffs of cumulous appeared and began to spin rapidly. They collected into larger accumulations until the sky was pulsating with fat, white, churning billows. Yordon, with his arms still raised, turned slowly, in concert with the phenomena. The soldiers looked up, dumbfounded. Some fell to their knees. The wind gained in velocity. The Negev scientists gestured excitedly at the sky and scrambled to aim their recording instrumentation at the phenomena. Several of the soldiers made to run away, but paused upon seeing that the clouds covered the sky to the horizon in all directions.

Yordon closed his eyes and the sky began to change again. The ceiling of boiling cumulous began to darken and grow thick. The particle occluded air grew dimmer as the cloud layer above turned gray. They were in the center of a cylinder of madly rushing air.

Philo's eyes were stalks on his head. He felt the barometric pressure drop, changing the pitch of the air around him and causing perspiration to pinprick on his skin. The humidity rose precipitously.

"What is he doing? How is it possible?" asked the IDF captain.

Slowly, a mist rose. Philo felt the cool moisture dancing around him. It grew in density until a discernible fog formed around them.

"A fog in Tel Aviv. It is amazing," said another soldier.

Several members of the Negev team made their way toward Yordon, deducing that he was somehow instrumental to this phenomenon. They carried a variety of instruments which they clumsily pointed both at the sky and Yordon. There was also a cameraman and someone wielding a microphone.

The moisture in the air was almost unbearable. When it seemed the air would burst with wetness, Yordon whispered, "Rain."

Lightning crackled across the sky in long, jagged shafts that lit the grayness with a cold blue cast. A deep thunder rumbled in the distance and pealed ominously toward them. Philo felt his teeth rattling in his skull. He gazed upon his companion of years with new wonder.

Then, it rained. It poured. The sky opened upon them in vast sheets of unceasing torrent. Water flooded the crater area and ran in rivers and rivulets down the empty streets and gutters of the forlorn city. It bounced off cars and low lying structures in thick droplets and coursed down the sloped city streets toward the ocean. The soldiers and scientists could not see two feet in front of them. Philo could only make out watery blurs behind curtain-like sheets of falling water. He could just discern the cameraman busily trying to record the event while at the same time attempting to protect his camera from the incredible rain.

Then the rain began to subside. In the distance, the ocean frothed, and rose in answer to the rain to fill the streets of Tel Aviv like a monsoon thirsty for its hot and dusty surfaces.

Philo realized Yordon was standing alongside of him, looking tired. The scientists and soldiers stared at him. The rain became a drizzle. The wind died down. The waters receded. The captain of the IDF squad slowly approached him and said, "It would appear that you did this, but what, exactly, have you done?"

Yordon answered, "Ask your scientists to read their instruments."

"Captain, come quickly! Something incredible!" called one of soldiers from the base camp. The captain looked over, startled. The solder who had called her had removed his helmet. The other soldiers around him were doing the same. Above, the clouds were dissipating rapidly.

The scientists were visibly excited by what their instruments revealed. Slowly, all of them were removing their helmets and cautiously breathing the air. Yordon and Philo went with the group surrounding them back to where the rest of the team waited. It was getting hot. The clouds were thinning and sunlight was peeking through -- not the reddish light of the post nuclear pollution, but a bright, yellow, warm light; the light of the desert, returned in full glory and baking the land in spots all around them. A fresh breeze picked up, ruffling their hair. Philo breathed it all in and felt pure joy.

"You did this," he whispered, looking at Yordon.

The familiar baritone voice answered, "Yes. I did."

"But how?"

Yordon looked frail just then, the skin on his face was taut and pale, the bones beneath pronounced. He seemed to be looking within; searching for an answer to Philo's question. He placed a hand on Philo's shoulder and looked at him with great warmth.

"I don't know how -- and yet somehow I can."

The chief scientist of the Negev team -- still in his radiation suit from the neck down -- came forward to grasp Yordon by his upper arms. He was a grizzled, older man with a creased and square jawed face.

"You're responsible for this effect, this... miracle?"

Yordon merely nodded.

The scientist continued, "The radiation. It's gone. Completely. I'm not sure how it's possible or how you managed it, but the readings are incontestable. No isotopes are present in the air. All particulate matter in the atmosphere has been washed away. That rain did it. Something in that rain. We've got samples but so far it's just showing up as water. The ground too. Just dirt, sand, concrete, tar. No clicks on the Geiger counter. How did you do it?"

Yordon answered, "I did it by willing it to happen."

"*Oof*, but that's impossible," snorted the chief scientist in disdain.

"And yet it happened", said Yordon, tiredly.

"But why? Why did you perform this act?" demanded the chief scientist.

Yordon looked the man straight in the eye and said, "Know this. I've done this because I wish to make myself known to the world. I am the beginning of something wonderful. I am a messenger. Men have committed a great sin here. They have poisoned the land of Israel with their weapons of destruction. Ignorance and hate have wrought madness in the minds of men. I am here to save you."

"To save us?" parroted the scientist, his eyelids heavy with suspicion, unbelieving.

The IDF captain shouldered her way to the forefront. "Do you know how ridiculous that sounds?" She looked at the scientists and soldiers surrounding Yordon and Philo, and finally looked at the two of them directly. "It's a trick," she spat, "I'm willing to bet there's a couple of radiation suits hidden behind the tent where we first spotted you,"

Yordon answered, "There are no radiation suits hidden anywhere. I am not lying. We will leave now. Remember my words."

He pushed his way through the ring of challengers and walked in the direction of the waterfront. Philo followed, looking back at the group. The captain yelled at them to stop but Yordon ignored her. She ordered several soldiers to intercept Yordon but none of them moved. The captain prepared to voice her consternation but suddenly found that she had lost the will to pursue the matter. She watched the stranger and his companion make their way toward the shore, and inexplicably felt a thrill course through her. Looking up she saw that all of her men were smiling like children who had been told a wonderful secret.

Israeli Crisis Center, Jerusalem

Moshe Avrahami clicked off the small TV and swiveled in his chair to face his companion.

"Well, what do you make of that?" asked Natan Silver with a lopsided grin. He put his feet up on the square meeting room table and let the chair lean backwards against the wall of the underground bunker. It was just the two of them for the moment. They had just watched a hastily prepared documentary showing the miraculous rain at Tel Aviv and the stranger named Antropos. It was playing on every major television network in the world. They also had the readings and reports from the Negev expedition.

Tiredly, Avrahami responded, "Perversely -- *both* Dr. Ephrat and Rabbi Weizman may have been right! There were pivotal facts to be learned from the epicenter -- though I don't think these are the kind of facts Schmuel had in mind."

Silver grinned at this. "No – I'm sure he didn't expect to find 'God's messenger' performing miracles."

Avrahami responded, "Clearly it's a deception."

"Clearly," echoed Silver, growing pensive.

The Prime Minister rose from his chair and shoved his hands in his pockets. He began a methodical pacing of the length of the room. His voice echoed hollowly in the empty chamber. "And yet, here we are; two Jews in Israel, rulers of a nation that has been waiting for this day for millennia and now that it's possibly here, we don't believe it. We're pathetic."

Silver nodded in agreement, "*Tov meod*, what if we're wrong to be skeptical? What if it's true then, Moshe? What happens to us then? Is there any need for an Israeli Parliament if God has returned?"

Avrahami raised his eyebrows at his compatriot's musings and turned to face him, "Hmmm. A very human thought, my friend. But let's not get ahead of ourselves. First we must determine what Mr. Antropos is. We must meet him, bring him into our house and feed him. Talk to him. Even if he isn't what he says he is, he could be very, very useful."

Avrahami pulled at his face as his thoughts raced.

Silver groaned himself upright, intrigued. "What are you thinking, Moshe?"

"What I mean is this. What better way to defuse the crisis of the moment than with an equally compelling distraction? Even if Antropos is a fraud, so long as he thinks he is what he claims, he could be used as a pacifying force in the area, don't you see, Natan? All of us -- Arabs, Jews, Christians -- are expecting the Messiah, implicitly or explicitly – it's all the same in the end. And here he is, dressed in white robes and wearing sandals, just as we imagined him -- and he has performed miracles. He is convincing, *nahon*?"

Silver frowned and shook his head. "He would also cause a panic. People like Weizman and Chet will froth at the mouth and race through the streets thinking it's the End Time."

"Not if he tells them otherwise. Not if he directs them to do something else."

"Such as what?" Silver demanded.

"Such as make peace with their neighbors. Such as command the Arabs to stand down! They're Islamic, are they not? They believe in a Messiah. He could go to the Temple Mount and speak to them there!"

"Impossible. Even if God himself asks." Silver's frown deepened.

"You would be surprised, I think, Natan. Jerusalem is the capital of contradictions."

Silver was not impressed. "You assume he'll do what you ask. He's not a member of your Party, Moshe. If he is what he claims, it's *we* who will be the puppets, not him."

Upon hearing this, Avrahami stopped his pacing and straightened himself. "Enough speculation. We must meet this man."

He punched the intercom. "Hershel?"

"Here," answered the device.

"I have an assignment for you."

Motza, Judea, Israel

Avrahami nodded to Hershel to open the door of the safe house. The Prime Minister's Cabinet members had protested his plan to leave the safety of the subterranean command center but he had ignored all objections. It was more discrete this way. They were some miles outside of Jerusalem, in the village of Motza, a small hamlet of several thousand citizens nestled in the Judean foothills.

Hershel swung open the door, allowing the desert brightness to flood the room. From out of this blinding light and into the curtained room entered a tall, lanky man in his thirties. He was traveling with another but the associate remained outside. Avrahami regarded the tall man, squinting against the blinding light. The man had the ambience of a traveler. He smelled of desert sand and wind. His face was strong and serious, yet frank and open. Alert. His eyes beneath a high forehead were sharp and piercing. He wore white robes, something like that worn by Orthodox priests and monks, except for the fact that his uniform was entirely white. The visitor approached the Prime Minister with a friendly expression and extended his hand.

"*Shalom*, Prime Minister. I am Yordon Antropos." said Yordon, speaking English with a Greek accent.

Avrahami grasped Yordon's hand. A strong, warm grip.

He greeted Yordon in his own, accented English. "*Shalom.* I'm pleased to meet you. Hershel says he found you traveling the land on foot, laying hands on people and curing them."

"Your nation is crippled and your people suffer greatly, Prime Minister. I've come to help."

Avrahami considered his visitor, thin-lipped, and after a moment, gestured to a seat by the coffee table. Yordon sat.

"May I offer you some refreshment? Coffee, Tea? Water?"

"A glass of water would be welcomed," answered Yordon.

Avrahami gestured to Herschel, who nodded briskly and disappeared into the next room.

"You're Greek. A former minister of the Greek Orthodox faith?"

"I was once aligned with the Greek Orthodox Church."

"You're excommunicated."

"You've been studying me."

"I do what's necessary for the well-being of the people of Israel. I – we need to learn about you." Avrahami settled into his chair and looked Yordon over, rubbing at his chin, "What motivates your incredible feats? What do you want, cleric? Why are you here?"

Hershel reappeared at this moment with a cold glass of water and handed it to Yordon, who nodded in gratitude. He took a sip and held the glass to his forehead for a moment, before settling it onto the coffee table that lay between himself and Avrahami. Turning back to Avrahami, Yordon answered the Prime Minister's question, "I wish to spread a message. A directive from God, to all the races and all peoples that comprise the human race."

Avrahami frowned, "You make it sound as if you've been talking to God himself."

Yordon regarded him calmly, then, "You find it hard to believe, I am sure."

Avrahami paused. Could this man be another religious lunatic; only different by degrees from the devil who brought destruction to Tel Aviv and Moshe's family; his brother, his nephew and nieces? He fought down a sudden rush of anger.

Trying as hard as he could to keep the emotion out of his voice, he responded. "Of course I do. And why is it hard to believe? Why is the sudden appearance of a man who can seemingly make rain and reverse the effects of a nuclear explosion hard to believe? I should ask this, don't you think? I should wonder who this man is? I should meet this man. And here you are. And you still haven't answered my question."

"I'm just a man," answered Yordon softly, then with more force, "But a man who has a gift. And that gift is an awareness of the invisible; of the motive force behind the world's curtain. It is an *intelligence*, Prime Minister."

Avrahami squinted at the lanky cleric, exuding skepticism, yet he waited, wanting to hear the rest.

Yordon continued, "It isn't so much that I can talk to this force. It's more that I can *hear* this force, this God. I begin to believe that I am his instrument and I am here to convey His word."

Avrahami responded, "Are you saying you think you are God's messenger? Like Jesus Christ?"

Yordon pondered this, as if trying on the idea, then, "Perhaps. He was also a messenger."

Avrahami dismissed this with wave of his hand. "Jews don't believe in Jesus."

Yordon sighed. "You are so full of what you think to be the truth that you can't see what's in front of you."

140

Avrahami only stared back, jaw working.

"I don't fit into your preconceptions, nor do I wish to."

"Whether we like it or not." replied the Prime Minister.

Yordon's expression hardened a fraction, but then he seemed to think twice of it and hesitantly answered, "No. It's not like that. I must make you understand…"

Avrahami pounced, "Understand what?"

"That a time of great change is upon us."

"And what is this change?"

Yordon's eyes brightened, "The end of nations, the end of hatred, the end of ignorance. The raising of human awareness of the cosmos and our place and purpose in it."

A complete meshugina, thought Avrahami, *but possibly a useful one, as I suspected.* "I see. And what's our say in this? Nothing I suppose."

Yordon's voice suddenly became steely, "Those who ignore or defy the coming change will be trampled by the onrush of events to come – as has always been the case in human history."

Avrahami saw at that instant that beneath this man's calm exterior and benevolent manner lay a formidable determination. He might be a crazy but he also had a rapidly developing following. This was familiar ground. *I might not know what to do with Gods or their messengers, but I can deal with delusionals and devils.*

Avrahami responded, "I don't believe any of it. Here you are, a man alone; dressed in robes, and you claim the end of life as we know it is imminent. And you expect me to simply believe this drivel?" Avrahami impaled Yordon with a hard stare. "I think you're a preacher with a few tricks up your sleeve and a delusion of significant magnitude ingrained in your head. I would have you arrested but I don't think you're much of a threat. You might even do some small measure of good performing your medical tricks in the countryside. Leave me now."

Yordon's eyebrows rose, "Wait. I realize my words sound fantastic but if you think about it, isn't it your reaction that's more fantastic? You are a Jew, are you not?"

"What else could I be?" replied Avrahami with a show of impatience.

"And, as a Jew you believe the words of the TANAKH, don't you?"

"I believe in Jewish history, Mr. Antropos, and whatever of it is represented in those books I regard as the truth."

"And what of the *destiny* of the Jewish people, even if you are a pragmatist?" pressed Yordon, "What do you believe of that?"

Avrahami considered this. While he was not a religious fanatic, and often regarded the religious zealots in his Parliament to be obstructionists to progress rather than patriotic Jews he, like them, nonetheless held a *belief* in the ultimate vindication of the Jewish peoples by one means or another; political or miraculous. Perhaps it was true of Jews everywhere on the planet.

Yordon continued, "Whether you believe the Christians or not, whether you believe there was a son of God that walked the earth – don't you believe your people's prophecies? Don't you believe in eventual redemption?"

Avrahami found himself nodding.

"So when it comes, when the redeemer is here at last with evidence to support his claims, when your country is in need and the redeemer comes before you and announces himself – you don't believe it? What more must be done to convince you, then, Moshe Avrahami? Don't you want your day of vindication?"

"Vindication," echoed Avrahami, almost involuntarily. The word was like chocolate covered with gold. All his life he had fought for exactly this. *Vindication.* His hatred of the Arabs was deep -- too deep to admit to anyone. And if Yordon was who he claimed? The cordoning off of the Old City would be the tiniest of gestures by comparison to what would be possible. God would truly be part of his army. *Vindication.* And if Yordon was false, what was the worst? Only reality; the status quo played out to its logical conclusion. Yordon ridiculed and disgraced; shoved aside in the march of history. No damage, if handled correctly. The situation before him had the potential for maximum gain and minimum loss; a politician's dream. Avrahami looked up at the waiting Yordon, whose face was a wave of changing expression, as if he rode the current of the Prime Minister's thoughts along with him. *Yordon Antropos could be useful indeed.*

He answered. "Yes, vindication. It's what all of Israel wants. And peace, Yordon. We want peace and secure borders. And an end to persecution."

"This is coming to all men, not just Israel. But we begin here. I am the messenger. I am the *signet* of man's redemption…"

Avrahami ignored the provocation, "What do you require of the Government of Israel?"

Yordon answered, "Nothing. Leave me to my work and I will heal your people and your land, though I cannot bring back Tel Aviv."

"And once you've accomplished this? What next?"

"Jerusalem. I will speak to the Christians, Jews and Muslims of that city together and announce the Good News."

Avrahami snorted his skepticism, "*Mah?* Your talk of great change and an end to nations? That would cause nothing short of a riot!"

"That depends on the words chosen to deliver the message."

Avrahami bit his lip. What Yordon proposed was suicide. And yet Moshe had argued with Natan that this very avenue being proposed by the desert cleric might be a good one for defusing the current geopolitical situation. One step at a time.

He made a decision.

"You said support. Agreed. We will provide you with an escort, a means of travel, supplies, communications equipment. It's the least we can do; to facilitate your mission. Please come see me once you arrive in Jerusalem."

Yordon bowed his head slightly in appreciation of the offer. "I only require your passive support, Prime Minister. There's no need to trouble yourself…"

"I will trouble myself anyway I choose to." Avrahami's voice was iron.

Yordon gazed at Avrahami curiously. His countenance was hard set. The two men faced each other unwaveringly for several moments.

"As you wish, Prime Minister."

Philo was startled to alertness when the heavy wooden door opened to release the squinting Yordon. He turned back toward the inside of the house and shook hands with Avrahami. It was all very cordial. The aide who had brought them came from around the side of the house, accompanied by several soldiers. Yordon looked at his friend with an expression of bemusement and said, "Well, Philo, it looks like you're going to get your jeep."

Amman, Jordan

The streets of Amman wavered beneath the heat and the cloud of smoke from Eli Tubasi's cigarette. He gazed out the window of the dilapidated apartment and listened to his associate's report.

"…and within minutes the radiation effects were totally erased from the area, *Imam*, according to our contact from Negev. "

"Don't call me that," sneered Tubasi. He hated the tendency of so many of these Arabs to grovel. "And what of the city?"

"Damaged, but habitable again."

"Hmm. And who exactly is this Antropos? Where does he come from?"

Silence.

Eli turned to face his informant; one of the dozens of youthful malcontents he had picked up in his travels – like so many of them, clad in an eclectic conjunction of Western and Eastern dress. The young man's usually fervent features were cast in an expression of doubt. He looked embarrassed.

Eli blew smoke at him. "Well what is it?"

"Many are saying he is the Son of God."

"The what?"

"Because of the miracle."

"The what?" Eli realized he was repeating himself and felt annoyance. The fool must mean the incident of the rain. *This was too much.*

The callow young man continued, "He has also met with the Israeli Prime Minister and rumor has it that they are working together. He is reported to travel with a small contingent of IDF soldiers and vehicles."

"You believe this?" asked Eli, snubbing out his cigarette and wiping his lips with the back of his hand.

The informant wrung his hands together. "No, but…"

"But you're ready to believe it at the slightest nudge, aren't you?" said Eli accusingly. He turned away in disgust. "Get out before I kill you, you gullible shit." This was the danger of so many angry, uneducated minds always in search of vindication. *Vindication.* They would follow any fool's cause if there was a hope of vindication.

The young man waited, feeling shamed; wanting to make amends.

In a flash, Eli pulled out his pistol and cocked the safety off. The young man made to disappear. Suddenly Eli had an idea.

"Wait."

The young man turned back slowly, sweat visible on his brow.

"You said Tel Aviv is again habitable."

The young man nodded hesitantly, "Slowly people are returning…"

"In that case, I think it's time for the APF to make another demonstration. We still have some of the isotope in storage, and the makings of a second bomb in the lab. We need to undo this Yordon's 'miracle' before these rumors gain any more ground. We must get the *Jihad* back on track before our allies are affected by these gossips or, *Allah* forbid, the Zionists get any ideas of surviving our wrath. Send a message to the APF communications center in Baku. Inform them that I wish to speak with the leaders of all command cells as soon as possible."

The young informant quickly left the apartment. Nodding to the two burly men acting as guards, he hurried down the rickety stairs to the streets of Amman. Shouldering his way through the unruly crowd, he headed toward the nearest alley where, once he felt sufficiently concealed, he pulled out a battered cell phone. He quickly dialed a long sequence of numbers.

"Please go ahead," said the pleasant female voice at the other end. She spoke in Hebrew.

"This is Galgalatz. I am reporting a red flag. I repeat, red flag," whispered the young man, also in Hebrew.

"One moment. I'll connect you." said the voice.

The young man listened to the blips and warbles on the link as the call was encrypted, scrambled and redirected via several relay stations so that its origin could not easily be discerned. At last there was an open hiss. He waited a few seconds more.

"MOSSAD Intelligence Operations. Report, Agent Galgalatz," said the firm, clipped voice.

Knesset Building, Jerusalem

The area around the Knesset in West Jerusalem was deserted and quiet, as it had been for weeks, since the destruction of Tel Aviv. Only the Old City, surrounded by Suleyman's ancient ramparts, and rising from the center of the more modern metropolis, showed any evidence of life. The wavering air held a feeling of suspense, like the sustained note of violin. The city lay in wait.

Natan Silver ran his hand through his sparse hair in a surreptitious moment and made himself a cup of tea at the sideboard. They had grown tired of the Crisis Center's basement accommodations and were now convened in the

Bureau Office of the Prime Minister on the second floor of the Knesset building. Sipping at his cup, he surveyed his colleagues seated at the round, highly polished, wooden table.

Present in the room were Science Minister Ephrat, Defense Minister Ariel Engel, David Chalutz, Avrahami's perennially attendant aide Katz, and the Rabbis Chet and Weizman. Avrahami had also managed to locate the Secretary General, Elisheva Rosenthal, and the Knesset Speaker, Avi Grinker, ensuring that this meeting would be procedurally onerous and interminable. He shook himself out of his cynicism and returned his attention to the table.

Engel was speaking with great earnestness.

"We have confirmation from one of our deep covers that the APF dog, Tubasi, is behind the Tel Aviv nuke and is planning to release another. He is currently hiding in Jordan. We've also learned from another of our sources that the first bomb was smuggled into the country through Jordan."

He let the words sink in.

The grizzled Knesset Speaker, Avi Grinker spoke. "So much for our supposed, emerging ally."

"Abdullah is no Hussein," agreed Secretary General Rosenthal.

Engel slapped the table. "The Arabs won't rest until the Jewish state is no more. They've shown their true colors. Treaties and talks – it was all a waste of time. Now is the time for action! Time for us to stop bickering and worrying about each other's interpretation of prophecy or what walls we are allowed to piss on! We have to focus on this problem. We must mobilize our forces immediately."

Avrahami waved him down, wiping his pale face with a handkerchief. He was not feeling well. "There can be little doubt what Tubasi's next target is. We have no idea how much time we have. I'm afraid Ariel is right this time. There can be no further delay. Tubasi is currently in Amman. I propose that we move against him at once."

"I second the Prime Minister's motion," said Engel, barely able to restrain himself.

"Ariel, deploy your teams and capture him. Don't kill him. We need to find out the location of the other bomb."

Engel's eyes shone and the lines around his eyes tightened in anticipation of things to come.

Rabbi Weizman was about to say something, when David Chalutz interrupted, "What about Jordan?"

"Are you worried we'll anger them?" asked Rosenthal, trying to keep derision out of his voice.

Chalutz ignored the dig, "Shouldn't Jordan itself be punished for the Tel Aviv horror? Isn't it an accomplice?"

Avrahami shook his head gravely. "As much as I'd like to extract our revenge from them, we don't know that for certain. Their cooperation might have been passive."

"Bah! It's the same thing," spat Engel. "Those that choose to look away might as well be plunging the knife in themselves. Chalutz is right, Prime Minister. Why not let me move an armed column across the border zone? Or at least allow us to shell their positions. We have considerable forces positioned near Jericho…"

"*Lo!*" shouted Avrahami. He was getting irritable and his hands shook. Katz looked at him worriedly. Avrahami wiped his face again, and paused to catch his breath. After a few moments, he answered hoarsely, "You fools want to start the war of Armageddon."

"It's inevitable," lamented Rabbi Chet to no one in particular.

"We will win such a war, Prime Minister. God is on the side of the Jews," stated Rabbi Weizman, more soberly.

Grinker looked at the Prime Minister accusingly. "Isn't it true you met with Antropos, the miracle worker, recently? Rumor has it that he proved to you that he is the Son of God, the Messiah."

Avrahami looked at the Speaker with an odd expression of sadness and vitriol. Grinker held his stare, unabashed, wordlessly insisting on a response from the Prime Minister.

"I met a wandering crazy who claims to be sent by God, and because of this we should attack Jordan? Then it's we who are the wandering crazies." Avrahami laughed dejectedly at his own words.

"They bombed Tel Aviv! That's half a million Jews affected by their actions, Moshe!" replied Rosenthal impatiently, jowls shaking.

Engel stood again, looking restless and driven. He faced the Prime Minister.

"A crazy this Antropos may be and yet you supplied him with soldiers and equipment." He turned to face the rest of participants in the room. He had their attention.

"For your information, Antropos travels in an IDF jeep with IDF personnel as his guards. Is he so crazy then, Prime Minister? Is the Son of God enlisted in our army?"

The group erupted into loud debate upon hearing this news. Natan feared Moshe had lost control of the meeting when he suddenly rose from his seat and barked, *"Maspeek!"*

Everyone turned to face the Prime Minister.

"Son of God or Son of Sand, Yordon Antropos is a wild card in the game of Middle East politics. He has the attention of the world. He needs to be watched. The situation is extremely delicate at this time – I don't think I have to explain that. We are like a plate of glass before a mob bearing stones. Surely you can all see that? What choice did I have?"

"He's a potentially useful ally," added Silver.

Avrahami gave everybody in the room a long look, staring them down, daring them to argue further.

Seeing that he had agreement, however tenuous, Avrahami closed the meeting. "Engel, you may alert our divisions at Jericho to stand ready for mobilization – in case it comes to that – but no action, do you hear? No action without my direct order."

Engel stood up from his seat and answered in a crisp, clipped voice. "*Hevanti.* Your orders are clear. And I will personally go to Jericho." He made to leave the meeting room.

"And Ariel, bring us Tubasi – alive," croaked the Prime Minister. Engel paused his stride for a second but did not look back as he left the room.

The Allenby Bridge, border of Jordan and Israel

Ensconced in an oasis in the midst of the barren West Bank countryside, Jericho, so important in centuries past, was today a sleepy town of some 7,000 people pursuing a quiet agricultural existence. It was a place of fruit and vegetable markets, and dusty cafes where old men played backgammon and sipped coffee. Heading east, the terrain became a no man's land between enemy territories, punctuated by Israeli military checkpoints along the solitary road that led to the only crossing for miles in either direction.

The Allenby bridge, once an antiquated wooden relic, but now a modern concrete structure, arched across the Jordan Rift into the sands of the Hashemite Kingdom of Jordan. It was crowded with travelers heading to and from Amman, 30 miles to the East. Israeli soldiers peered suspiciously at everyone, poking the muzzles of their machine guns into the sacks, parcels and personal belongings of passers-by. On the other side of the valley, the Jordanian Border Guard held station and checked parcels too, though not with the same fervor as their Israeli counterparts.

There was also a small contingent of the Palestinian Guard on the Israeli side, in acknowledgment of the fact that the West Bank territories had been turned into a semi-autonomous zone several years prior, but this was mostly symbolic. Tensions between the Palestinians and Israelis had frayed so badly in the last years, that any control the Palestinians had over this strip of land was pure artifice. The tension was a constant electricity in the air, made worse by the heat, which was a solid wall to be climbed with every step.

General Ariel Engel paced back and forth along the dirt path by the side of the road. He had ordered the capture of Tubasi hours before. His agents had been poised to strike the apartment in Amman and still there was no word. Finally he could stand it no longer.

"Take me to passport control now!" he snapped at one of the soldiers. He climbed into a jeep and they sped toward the bridge. They came to an abrupt stop in front of the large white building on the Israeli side of the bridge. Engel went inside to the communications desk and rang the listening post back at Jericho.

"Any word?"

"None, sir. But it's unlikely that they would…"

"I know, I know." Engel marched outside and peered over the heads of the crowd into the territory beyond. Somewhere out there were his agents. The plan was for them to sedate Tubasi then whisk him across the border inside an empty produce truck. But they were late.

Engel wiped at the sweat which beaded his brow as he paced in the white hot light of the desert. Sun burnt and supple, Engel was a Sabra, a native born Israeli, who like the cactus fruit for which they are named, was outwardly as prickly and tough as they came. He was strong, loud and argumentative, it was true, but it stemmed from deep emotions and feelings of pride in his Jewishness. He had been raised in the homeland in a time after the Holocaust and after the initial battles for a toehold in Palestine, following the Second

World War. He was proud of his Jewish heritage and was part of an unselfconscious majority – something not seen among Jews since the times of King David.

There was a shout from the opposite side. Engel could discern a commotion on the far side.

He snapped orders. "You two, march down there right now and find out what's going on."

Two IDF soldiers nodded briskly and trotted down the bridge road. Engel turned to one of the guards standing by the entrance to the passport building.

"Sergeant, alert the men, there may be a need for action. If a truck makes a break for this side, do not oppose it. Do you understand? You are to warn away anyone who tries to obstruct it. If you must, shoot them. If you can, wait for my signal."

"As you command, sir."

On the Jordanian side, there was indeed a truck, surrounded by several Palestinian men. One of them was shouting excitedly. He had evidently been trailing the truck in his own vehicle. Whatever he was saying was causing those around him to become agitated. Engel could see the two soldiers he had sent over jump onto the running boards of the truck and shove men away with the butts of their rifles and their boots. The one on the driver's side tapped the arm of the driver and waved him forward with the muzzle of his machine gun. The truck lurched forward and the sea of traffic traversing the bridge parted reluctantly. The crowd of Palestinians that had surrounded the truck followed on foot, yelling obscenities the whole way. As they came close, Engel caught scraps of their diatribes.

"By Allah! Eli is in there!"

"The bastards have Tubasi!"

"Eli is captured!"

Engel could see they were getting ready to do something stupid. He turned to the Sergeant on Duty.

"Order your squad to fire their weapons into the air. Now!"

The man barked orders into his walkie-talkie. In seconds there was the sharp crack of automatic weapons fire. Everyone on the bridge ducked for cover. The Jordanian soldiers on the other side raised their weapons. Engel caught the eye of the IDF soldier riding shotgun on the truck's driver side and urgently waved him forward. Other IDF troops shouted to the civilians to stay calm and keep down. He could see one of his men talking to the commanding officer across the rift. The Jordanians held their fire.

Engel trotted onto the road to meet the truck, pistol drawn. He jumped onto the rear as it passed him and climbed inside. He gave his eyes time to adjust to the relative darkness and, after a minute or so, examined the faces within. Most were Israeli agents dressed to look like Palestinian merchants and traders. They nodded grimly at him. All except one.

Tubasi still felt groggy from the injection they had stabbed him with but he clearly understood that he was looking into the eyes of the man who had ordered his abduction.

"You think you have slain the jackal, don't you? Israel is again safe for tourism." Tubasi laughed weakly.

Engel said nothing. What was the point? The murderer was as good as dead – he would never be free again. He might even be sentenced to death, whatever the political cost. But most of all, he didn't dare. Tel Aviv was lost forever and many loved ones with it. He could not engage this man in conversation without showing his passionate hatred – and he wouldn't give him that. No. Tubasi would die before a sea of stony faces.

Tubasi seemed to sense his thoughts and taunted him. "It's not over, Zionist. The *Jihad* is a bomb that has been ignited, like the one I sent to Tel

Aviv, but once this fuse is lit, it can't be stopped. Soon you will be expulsed from this land."

Engel forced a laugh and shook his head. He jumped out of the truck, as it passed passport control. He tried to ignore the shaking of his hands and the throbbing of his pulse. He marched inside to the communications desk and spoke into the handset that was immediately handed to him.

"Tell Jericho Command, to prepare for our guest. Mission accomplished."

Engel returned to the bridge. The pedestrians on the bridge began moving again, though more slowly than before. Engel could feel their anger. He knew they felt themselves to be the victims despite the fact that it was one of them, one of their kind, who had damaged Israel's second city and the lives of approximately half a million Jews with it.

"Lousy Jew bastards. I wish I had delivered the bomb myself," said an anonymous voice from a few feet away.

Engel spun around but no one was looking his way.

"It's you Jews who are the terrorists."

Engel spun again in time to see one of his own men turning red with indignation at this taunt. Before Engel could order him to silence, the man had spit back his response.

"You lie! The Holy Land is too good for you. You'll never be allowed back now that you've done this."

This raised a ruckus among the crowd. Several men wearing turbans stopped in their tracks and veered toward the soldier. One of them shouted a retort.

"Allah will see to your eternal damnation, Jew, and while you're on Earth, we'll be your tormentors. Jerusalem will burn before you can have her. Tubasi will be avenged."

The soldier became visibly enraged upon hearing this. He aimed his gun at one of the taunters.

Engel shouted, "No! Idiot!"

But it was too late.

In immediate reaction to the belligerent gesture of the IDF soldier, one of the men reached within his robes and produced a small 9mm semi-automatic handgun.

Both Engel and the soldier stared at the blunt weapon in stunned silence. Engel later believed that in that split second of pause, the events that followed could have been stopped had they the foresight and reflexes, but the moment was too short and he was too slow. Before anyone could say anything further, the Arab squeezed the trigger. A flash of light and a loud report shattered the air and the head of the witless IDF soldier. His tall body folded and fell face first into the dirt. The passing crowd of civilians instantly panicked, scattering in all directions.

Engel took a few steps in the dead man's direction, then stopped himself. He looked up. The attacker was looking at him through narrowed eyes, a snake poised to strike in the midst of the boiling throng of people. His gun wavered in the air, as if sniffing for a new target. Several of the IDF soldier's compatriots charged forward, cocking their weapons and aiming at the civilians on the road. This caused an even wilder panic. There were screams as people were trampled. Someone blew a whistle from the bridge itself.

Out of the corner of his eye, Engel could see a knot of Jordanian border guards trotting toward him. Palestinian guards from his own side of the border were approaching from behind as well. He felt a twinge in his spine as he realized the situation was turning mercurial. The assailant took advantage of the momentary confusion and made a dash toward the Jordanian side. An IDF soldier fired a single round at the man, hitting him in the neck. The man barked once, in agony, and fell.

Engel spun to face his men and raised his hand in a silent order for restraint. The soldiers glared back angrily and lowered their weapons, but only slightly. The Palestinian guards were kept back by his men.

"Remove him from the road. Now!" snapped Engel, gesturing at the fallen Arab. He turned back to the approaching Jordanians and Palestinians, not waiting to see his order obeyed.

A grizzled, broken toothed man in a Jordanian captain's uniform walked up to him and demanded, "What's happened here? Are you the Commanding Officer?"

"I am. Engel. General Engel."

The Jordanian was unimpressed, if anything, more belligerent. "A General, eh? Captain Shakir. Now General, help me understand what I am seeing. I see a dead Palestinian man with an Israeli bullet in him."

Engel shot back, "And I see a dead Israeli soldier with a Palestinian bullet in him not 20 yards away. Return to your side immediately. This is an Israeli matter and you would serve your country best to stay out of it, Captain."

The captain did not move. "Justice is done then, is it? An eye for an eye?"

Engel looked straight at the Captain. He saw glassy hatred staring back. He swallowed his own ire. Avrahami was relying on him to be steady right now. As calmly as he could, he almost whispered his answer. "My men did not start this, Captain."

Shakir seemed to think that over. Engel took that moment to realize they were surrounded -- IDF men at his back, instinctively protecting him, and a phalanx of Palestinian and Jordanian guards standing behind Shakir.

Shakir exchanged glances with his men, then his face broke into a leer. "Oh, but you did. You have Tubasi."

Engel locked himself down. It was stunning that they could forget the destruction in Tel Aviv so easily. As much as he wanted to jump down the throat of this self-important thug in a soldier's uniform, he had to control himself, or the situation would surely melt down. His next words would steer events toward a border conflict or back to the reluctant status quo.

"Tubasi is a terrorist. We have apprehended a murderer. Are you speaking for your King? Is the Hashemite kingdom Tubasi's ally?"

Shakir worked his jaw and thought that over.

One of the soldiers standing behind Shakir spat his thoughts. "Tubasi is Allah's messenger. You defy the will of the Infinite."

"Silence! Not another word!" commanded Shakir, glaring at the young soldier. He returned his attention to Engel.

Engel pressed his momentary advantage. "Return to your side of the border, Captain, before this turns into an incident. I think none of us want that, at least not without the approval of our leaders?" He allowed himself a predator's humorless grin upon saying this.

Shakir slitted his eyes at Engel, doing his best to control his own desire to shoot Engel where he stood. Engel held his ground. At last, he relented and barked a series of commands at his men. The majority of them begrudgingly disbanded and made their way back to the bridge, muttering their disapproval of the outcome. A squad of soldiers stayed behind at Shakir's signal. Engel ordered his own men to back off. Shakir and Engel still stood before each other.

Shakir sighed deeply and rubbed at his eyes. He looked at the General and spoke again, more quietly, revealing a world weariness. "You and I are only soldiers, General. Even you, with your high rank. I'm sure you killed many Arabs to get it. But, even for Generals, in the end we soldiers are doomed to follow the orders of our political leaders. That's our duty."

Shakir gauged Engel's reaction. Seeing a glimmer of agreement in Engel's eyes, he went on. "I grow tired of all the politics, General. But I do not tire of hating you and your stinking people. You've usurped our land. You've barred us from Al Aqsa, in the Holy City. You've taken our spiritual leaders and imprisoned them. You shoot our people and expect us to stand idly by. It's an unjust world, General. And an unjust world demands justice. One day there will be justice."

Shakir backed away and signaled to the waiting squad of his men. To Engel he said, "We'll take the imbecile who shot your man."

"Of course, Captain," said Engel, stunned to brevity at the momentary eloquence of his adversary. To his men, "Bring him!"

"This is not over, General," warned Shakir as he left.

"That's the only thing we can be sure of, Captain. It never is," answered Engel.

He started back up the road toward the barracks, ignoring the stares of his own men.

He was not 50 paces from the confrontation when he heard the distinctive hiss of rockets and the whistle of artillery heading toward him. *That half-wit!* He threw himself to the ground instinctively as the ordinance exploded all around him. Rubble and metal shards sang by his head. Struggling back to his feet he sprinted away from the bridge and toward the passport control building, simultaneously pulling out his handgun, removing the safety, and shouting orders at his men, ahead.

"Prepare to return fire! Mobilize the 11th Artillery and launch batteries at once. Get me IDF Headquarters on the wire! We need air support!"

Engel watched in horror as incoming Jordanian missiles found their targets and reduced the Israeli border structures to ruins, and yet his heart thrilled his veins with adrenaline. He breathed in the sights and sounds of battle. Soldiers ran everywhere, shouting to each other. Machine guns chattered in concert, punctuated by gut rattling explosions. Men lay wounded on the ground. The peppery smell of gunpowder, blood and dust. Sirens in the distance. *Police? Ambulances from Jericho?*

He looked toward the bridge. Jordanian troops were advancing, led by a phalanx of Scorpion tanks. *Incredible.* He shouted at his officers, ordering their own tanks into position. *What to do?* An immediate counterstrike and deep penetration into their territory was called for. Take the battle onto their ground as soon as possible. He looked again toward the approaching sirens and spotted two men clad in robes, riding in an IDF jeep toward the battle. He didn't have time to wonder about them further as he was shoved to the ground in time to avoid the rain of shrapnel from a nearby explosion.

Engel watched a column of Israeli M-48's rumble forward to meet the Scorpions. One tank lay capsized in the roadside ditch, its turret sheered open by some internal explosion. On the other side, he could see more tanks and troops approaching the bridge. He was reminded of the Six Day War. What a glorious victory that must have been. He smiled fleetingly. A small voice inside his head shouted at him. *You've lost control of the situation!* Another part of his brain responded. *What's done is done – you always wanted this. Now to make the best of it.*

An aide came scrabbling through the dirt. He shouted, "Sir! Sir! A message from Jerusalem. You are ordered to cease fire at once, sir! The orders are from Prime Minister Avrahami himself. You are ordered to return to Jerusalem immediately."

Engel looked at the man as if he were diseased. "Are you insane, man? Do you think I can flick a switch and turn off what's been started? Tell Avrahami it's too late for that. The only way to end this battle is to win it. Now get out of my way."

He marched away from the messenger. Part of him could not believe his own words but he knew it was his heart speaking its convictions and he shook with the fire of it. He was about to yell orders at the artillery Captain when he spotted the robed man and his companion approaching him. None of his men seemed to notice and none moved to block their approach. The man came right up to Engel.

"General, you must stop this battle. You have the power to do it. Please do it now."

Engel looked into the man's hazel eyes, prepared to lambaste the stranger, but instead found himself muted. He recognized Yordon Antropos from the video broadcasts. Engel found himself intrigued and impressed by the calm power in his eyes but the soldier in him awoke once again and protested.

"Out of the question! What right do you have...?"

"If you don't stop this, I will."

Engel barked back, "Leave or I'll have you arrested."

"You know who I am," said Yordon with infinite calm, despite the chaos and noise.

Engel was unnerved but he responded with anger. "Enough. Oh yes, I know your face. And I know what you've done and what you've said. But what you *are* remains to be seen. Right now I've no time to find out. Guards! You men over there! Take this man and his companion away. Put them in one of the trucks."

"No!" shouted Yordon in a voice that seemed to reverberate in the air above the noise. He raised an arm as if to block the approaching soldiers. They stopped, looking puzzled. Yordon moved without restraint toward the bridge. Missiles sailed in from the Jordanian side and exploded around him, but no shrapnel touched him. Philo tried to follow but Engel restrained him.

To the amazement of the combatants, Yordon walked onto the Allenby bridge and crossed its length without hindrance until he was at its center. The soldiers didn't seem to see him and fought their battle around him. No bullet or explosive harmed him. He raised his arms. A wind began to swirl around him. He raised his arms higher and faced upwards. The wind became stronger, raising currents of sand and dust that formed a whirlwind around him that grew in circumference, rising higher and higher into the atmosphere. The armies on either side found themselves unable to continue the battle as visibility dropped to nearly zero.

Engel was face down in the dirt, clutching a handkerchief to his face to avoid being blinded by the onslaught of sand and dust. He could barely make out Yordon, still standing on the bridge. To his right, he observed Philo, crouched low against the storm. Engel watched Yordon shake his arms in the air, as if commanding the phenomena. The sandstorm, to his amazement, responded by doubling in intensity. It was impossible to move from his prone position. Dimly, he heard the confused shouts of his men. He could barely breathe, let alone move his head to see what was going on around him. Dust and sand stung his bare skin. The air was a howl combined with a crunching sound, like a rain of marbles hitting metal.

The wind ceased. The barrage of flying particles stopped in mid-trajectory, falling to the ground with sudden disinterest.

For many moments no one moved. There was not a sound from anywhere on either side of the Jordan. As Engel's ears stopped ringing and his body stopped shouting pain at him, he began to hear small ticks and scrabbling noises as rocks fell off of vehicles and his men began to move. Engel groaned and struggled erect, brushing himself off. Philo approached him, arching an eyebrow.

"Impressive, yes?"

Engel was flabbergasted. He almost laughed but chose to conceal his amazement and sternly retorted, "Exactly what did we just experience? You sound like you knew this was going to happen."

Philo brushed off the accusation. "Not exactly. I never know what Yordon is going to do. But I begin to know what he is capable of doing."

"He did this?" exclaimed a nearby soldier. Engel shushed him with a stern look.

Philo nodded and shrugged. Yordon, in the distance, had lowered his arms and was walking toward the Jordanian side of the border.

Philo was about to elaborate when one of Engel's men came running over.

"Sir! Sir! Something's happened to the weapons!"

Engel sprang forward. Philo followed in his wake.

They ran toward a knot of soldiers standing near one of the tanks. Their weapons had been thrown into a pile and they were distraught.

Engel looked at the weapons. They seemed normal enough, though discolored by the dust of the incredible sandstorm.

"Pick one up, sir," said one soldier quietly.

He crouched and took hold of a DROR light machine gun minus its ammo belt. He tried to brush off the dust but found it unyielding. It also felt unusually light. He tried to work the firing mechanism but it resisted. He tried again more forcefully but, to his astonishment, the gun fell apart in his hands, crumbling into rocks and dirt between his fingers. Taking in the pile of weapons with new eyes, he quickly realized all the weapons were similarly discolored.

"All of them, sir," said the same soldier, who had been watching, as Engel locked gazes with him.

Engel crouched down and sifted through the weapons. He flung one and watched it explode into a cloud of dust as it landed in the middle of the road. He kicked the pile in frustration and it crumbled easily.

"How is this possible? A chemical weapon?" breathed Engel to no one in particular.

Philo pointed. "Look across the river."

Engel looked into the haze and saw the white clad figure of Yordon walking back toward the Israeli side. Jordanian soldiers followed. Shakir was among them.

"What in blazes is going on?" Engel shouted. No one offered a response. He spotted an M-48 parked nearby and snapped his fingers at some of his men. "You. And you. We'll ride the tank to the foot of the bridge…"

"We can't, sir," said one of the men, almost timidly.

"Eh?"

"It's not a tank anymore."

Engel felt himself teetering between disbelief and ire. He could barely say the words, "It's not a…? Then what is it?"

"A stone monument," said Philo as he picked up what was formerly a rifle, walked up to the tank and smashed it against the fender. The rifle and fender fell to rubble.

He turned to face Engel. "I would guess that every weapon, every tank, every instrument for making war has been turned to sandstone and lime, General."

Engel stared at the ruined fender for only a minute before he started determinedly walking toward the bridge with several men in his wake. Philo matched strides with him. Engel looked livid. He broke into a jog as they neared the bridge. Philo followed, as did Engel's men.

Engel turned to Philo and between clenched teeth said, "It's a disaster, you fool. Not a miracle. We're helpless now. The Jordanians…"

"Are also unarmed," interrupted Yordon from the foot of the bridge.

Engel trotted right up to him and seemed intent on bumping Yordon out of the way but he stopped just short of actually colliding with him. He was slightly shorter than the ex-monk, which he didn't like, and he had to resist the urge to stand on his toes.

"Explain yourself. Do you have something to do with this?"

"I do."

Engel seethed with impatience. "Talk or I'll arrest you myself and you'll not see sunlight for a very long time. What did you do?"

"I took away their weapons, as I did yours."

Engel stopped short. Did he believe that? *It was crazy!* And yet the weapons had been transmutated. He looked at the people standing behind Yordon. There stood Captain Shakir. He saw Engel staring at him. He spoke.

"We are also disarmed, General. Listen to him."

Engel couldn't believe this sycophant was the same belligerent army captain he had exchanged ultimatums with not one hour ago. *What had Yordon said to them?*

Yordon took his cue. "Listen to me. There is a great change come upon you. No longer will you attack and slander your brothers, who are like you, sons of Abraham."

Engel shook his head in disbelief, "Do you think it's that simple? These Arab dogs have hated us and persecuted us from the day we sailed to these shores as the flotsam and jetsam of the Second World War. Jerusalem is our holy place, our capital city, from time immemorial."

Yordon stopped him, "It is their holy place too. And of the Gentiles. All of you are sons of Abraham and all of you believe in the same Creator. Jerusalem is a cradle to you all. It is the navel of the world."

"They do not follow the laws of the Torah!" protested a nearby IDF soldier.

Yordon answered, "It is irrelevant. True service of God doesn't consist of following rituals and recitations. Those are only outward symbols of religious awareness. God is a matter of the heart, the mind, and the soul. God is a matter of *ishan.*"

Upon hearing this, a murmur swept through the throng of Jordanians and Palestinians standing just behind Yordon. He turned to them. Abruptly one of them shouted, "By the 99 names of God, he is the prophet! The final prophet who comes before the Last Day." The man then prostrated himself before

Yordon and began to chant. *"Ash-shadu an la ilaha illallahu was Yordonur rasulullah!"*

One by one the chant spread from person to person and rose in volume until it soon seemed that every Arab in the area was shouting it.

"What are they saying?" asked Engel of no one in particular.

An Israeli soldier standing nearby answered, "There is no God but Allah and Yordon is his genuine messenger."

As the spectacle spread outwards, Engel realized he was exhausted. He looked toward his own troops. They were slack jawed.

Yordon let it continue for some minutes before speaking. "My brothers, know this. The heavens envelop the earth equally. The night displays all stars equally. By God's decree the sun shines with the same splendor on rich and poor, for all things good and bad alike. The rain falls and the wind blows for all. Similarly God has bestowed sight on all of us without distinction or discrimination, to be enjoyed equally. And food grows from the earth for all to share.

"It is the divine law that all things should be shared equally and that there should be no divisions between men and woman. But man-made laws have undermined the divine law and destroyed the communal order in which it was expressed. I am come to you now to reinstate the divine law.

"It is not a matter of turning your allegiances to the East or to the West, or subscribing to one religion or another. Politics and Religion are the true despots, I tell you. If you are going to fight, fight against the real oppressors, the systems of colliding beliefs that have kept you at each other's throats for centuries. That is what must be destroyed.

"It is your belief in God and in the words of his messengers that will guide you to your salvation. You must become messengers of peace and deliverers of reconciliation. You must act and think as one people if you are to bring about change. God says in the *Q'uran*, 'Allah will not change the state of the people until they change what is in themselves.' The change must come from within.

"You must realize that there is no sin in the world. There are only those who make sin. You must reach out to your brothers and sisters, even your adversaries, regardless of their origin or religion, and forget your competitions and vendettas. Such are the people who believe in God. Are you these people?"

The mob looked at each other, some of them frowning, some of them smiling, some of them ambivalent, but slowly and inexorably, some began to clap, then more joined in until very soon, almost the entire contingent of Jordanian and Palestinian soldiers and civilians were clapping and soon thereafter, cheering their acknowledgement.

Philo was taken aback with the clarity of Yordon's words. He seemed to be emerging, at last, as a clear agent of change. No longer was he the strange monk preaching enlightenment. He was turning into an outright revolutionary. Philo wondered if Yordon had thought through the consequences of his undeniable miracles and revolutionary ideas mixing together. Where would this *Jihad* against religion itself take them?

* * *

The word spread. The movement grew. Yordon continued to travel the frontier and made forays into Jordan, Syria, Egypt and the Bedouin camps in the desert, appearing in places far removed from each other from day to day, despite his transportation consisting of only an IDF jeep and some soldiers. Like quicksilver, his ideas and influence spread throughout the lands of the Middle East.

The World Muslim League, the World Sufi Council, The Islamic Council of Europe, the World Islamic Mission, The Muslim League, the American States Islamic Mission, and the Islamic Cultural Center soon declared their allegiance to Yordon, believing him to be a new Prophet, much like Jesus and Mohammed himself, returned to deliver new revelations from the lips of Allah. Of the almost 75 countries on the planet who considered themselves to be part of the house of Islam, a full two thirds of them declared their allegiance to Yordon as the new messenger of God come to Earth to lead his followers to heaven. The remaining outlaw nations and rebel movements were either more concerned with their earthly power struggles, or they were recalcitrantly watching events for further evidence of divine intervention.

The APF aligned nations, under the former leadership of the captured Eli Tubasi, were already pre-disposed for unification. Many saw Tubasi as the foreteller of Yordon's arrival, like a prophet preparing the way for the arrival of the true Messiah. As a result, many former followers of Tubasi came to consider the two movements to be one and the same, and looked to Yordon to fill the power vacuum left by Tubasi's capture.

News and speculation about Yordon was soon on every internet blog, wire service and video network on the planet. Yordon quickly became a regular presence on the front pages and television screens of every household. Inevitably, he had to come to America.

Oval Office, The White House, Washington D.C.

The headline read:

Clement to meet with Antropos at White House.

"Now how in hell's back alleys are we going to arrange this meeting!?" yelled Adam Clement at Max Ravessi, as he threw the newspaper down. ""And who let this leak out before arrangements could be made?"

Max Ravessi sat on the Oval Office sofa and calmly drew smoke from his cigarette. "It's *being* arranged, Mr. President."

Clement's U.S. Special Envoy to the Middle East was the best man to represent American interests in that black hole and he knew it. He had kept him on during the turn of Administrations, along with several others, but he didn't trust him. Ravessi was too Machiavellian for Clement's tastes. *Likes to play both sides against the middle.*

"Who do we have to pay to make it happen, Max?"

Ravessi stubbed out his cigarette. "Let's not be crass, Mr. President. It could be that Mr. Antropos wants to meet you as much as you want to meet him. His agenda is unknown. Give us a little time. A day or two."

"But the god-deuced *Washington Post* has already announced the visit! How in the hell did that happen? Now we're forced to play catch-up."

"We'll put the Press Secretary on it right away, sir."

"Damn right you will. And get that Antropos character over here!"

* * *

The three men waiting on the White House lawn instinctively ducked as the Air Force helicopter gracefully descended. It touched down smoothly and as soon as the hatch opened, one of them rushed forward.

"Welcome to the United States of America, Mr. Antropos!" yelled Max Ravessi above the din of the helicopter's blades as he approached the hatch, hand extended. Yordon stepped down from the helicopter deck and grasped Ravessi's hand, showing no fear of the slicing blades inches above his head. Philo followed close behind.

"Thank you for inviting me," he said, somehow penetrating the noise without shouting. "It's an honor to be invited to meet with the leader of the free world."

"I'm Max Ravessi."

Yordon nodded in recognition. "The Special Envoy. I read the briefing materials on the plane. You wear the weight of your role, Mr. Ravessi."

"Max, Mr. Antropos."

"Yordon."

They both nodded.

"This is my traveling companion, Philo Berith."

Philo nodded gruffly. He didn't understand why Yordon had agreed to fly to America now. When Yordon had received the message, he had agreed to be ferried to a transport plane at once. He had left his followers behind without a second glance, saying only that he would return and that this trip was necessary. Philo looked up suspiciously at the White House, which loomed ahead in stately grandeur.

Ravessi ignored Philo and continued unperturbed, as he led the way toward his waiting entourage. "May I introduce Arthur Blaine, our Secretary of State."

Blaine, as dour faced as Philo, shook hands with Yordon, then with Philo. "Welcome to the United States, gentlemen."

Ravessi gestured to the second man who had been waiting with him. "And this is the National Security Adviser, Wesley Van Ness."

"Pleased to meet you," said Van Ness with a professional grin.

"Hello. Am I considered a security risk, Mr. Van Ness?"

Van Ness chortled at this as they clasped hands. "You don't look like one. But they frequently don't."

Ravessi quickly led the small party toward the Executive Wing of the White House where, after a prolonged security check which Yordon smiled through patiently, they proceeded directly to the Oval Office.

As they entered, Clement came gliding around his desk, hand extended, a big, toothy smile on display.

"Welcome to the U.S.A., Mr. Antropos, and… Mr. Berith, isn't it?", Clement looked to Philo.

Philo bowed his head slightly, feeling disarmed by the importance of the man before them.

"Come in, gentlemen. Come in. Can we offer you something to drink? Coffee? Tea? Water? Soft drink?"

Yordon silently declined the offer with a shake of his head. He regarded the generous sofa for an instant, then folded himself into it with ease. Despite his evident comfort, he looked incongruous in the setting. Philo sat upright at the edge. The large sofa made him feel short. So did all these tall people in the room. As he scanned the room, Clement resumed speaking. Blaine and Van Ness seemed to take this as a cue and moved to sit as well.

"Mr. Antropos. May I call you Yordon?" asked Clement.

"Please do."

"And you may call me Philo," said Philo sternly.

President Clement gave Philo a split second of callous regard before returning to Yordon. Yordon's eyes twinkled at Philo. A couple of the security men fixed their attention on Philo permanently.

Clement continued his overtures, "Yordon. First of all thank you very much for accepting my invitation to visit our great country. I've been looking forward to meeting you personally for some time."

"It is an honor to meet you as well, Mr. President."

"I thought we could speak about some of your recent activities in the Middle East."

The phone at the end table by Ravessi rang. He picked it up and listened for a moment, then answered, "Send them in," and hung up. "Mr. President?" Ravessi inclined his head toward the white door opposite the one they had entered by.

Clement nodded his assent, "Forgive me, gentlemen. I am neglectful of our other guests."

Everyone turned toward the door opposite the one they had entered by. A security man opened it, passed through and shortly returned with Thomas Prisciotti and Karin Ferguson in his wake. The two of them fixed their attention on Yordon as they walked in. Clement, still standing, made introductions.

"Yordon, Philo, this is Father Thomas Prisciotti, of the Chicago Archdiocese and this is Karin Ferguson, Professor of Humanities and Near Eastern Studies at the University of Chicago."

"Hello," said Thomas simply.

"Pleased to meet you, at last," said Karin, shaking Yordon's hand vigorously, studying his face. She also shook hands with Philo, examining him like a lab specimen in the brief moment of their contact. Philo grimaced back.

As Thomas and Karin were seated, Van Ness filled the momentary silence. "Gentlemen, President Clement thought it would be useful to have 'experts', if you will, present to help, shall we say, 'illuminate' our conversation."

Clement glared at the National Security Advisor but was silent. Van Ness, unperturbed, crisply continued, "The Pope's Pro-Nuncio declined to attend, given your somewhat 'unofficial' status, but he has most helpfully suggested Father Prisciotti in his stead. Father Prisciotti has also been highly recommended by Archbishop Shaughnessy of the Chicago Archdiocese. Father Prisciotti traveled and worked with the Pontiff, during his abbreviated American tour earlier this year."

Thomas nodded deferentially.

Van Ness continued, "Father Prisciotti has been a stateside spokesperson for the Church for several years now. He hosts a televised seminar, and has written and spoken extensively on church issues."

"It keeps me out of trouble," said Thomas.

"Except when it gets you into it," retorted Karin.

"I'm honored," answered Thomas, ignoring Karin but smiling slightly at her jibe.

Yordon inclined his head slightly in acknowledgement of their introductions.

Van Ness drawled on. "Father Prisciotti was also kind enough to recommend Professor Ferguson, as a secular expert on the civilizations and cultures of the Middle East."

"Actually, the region's *ancient* civilizations, cultures and beliefs, Mr. Van Ness," corrected Karin. "I'm quite keen on origins. How beliefs are formed over the ages. How they reflect their societies, and so forth."

Yordon turned to the President. "Judging from the backgrounds of your other guests, Mr. President, it appears you invited me here today to discuss my religious and historical significance."

"You're danged right. Hard to know where to begin," responded Clement, pointing a finger at Yordon.

"Perhaps we should start with your motives," suggested Yordon. "Why did you think it necessary to fly me to the United States?"

"Isn't it obvious?" asked Karin.

Yordon and Philo turned to her as one, their eyes expectant.

"People think you're the Messiah. Some even say you're the Son of God."

Silence. Yordon fixed his eyes on Karin. Her face danced with alertness.

Blaine rubbed at his ear and squinted as if someone had just said something impolitic. Clement waited pensively, arms crossed. Van Ness watched both Yordon and Karin, fascinated, while Ravessi slowly panned all the faces in the room.

Thomas cleared his throat to interrupt the sudden quiet, "Mr. Antropos. Please forgive us. Such assertions aren't made lightly and I don't think anyone here can claim to believe these stories."

"However, the Church acknowledges the possibility of miracles, does it not?" asked Yordon of Thomas.

Thomas paused a moment, searching for words, "Yes, but a great deal of verification and proof is needed."

Yordon turned his gaze toward the President. "Is that why you brought me here, Mr. President? To see for yourself?"

Clement waved off the accusation and answered, "Whether I personally believe you're the ever-lovin' Son of God or not is unimportant. What is important is that many people do believe it and the country is in a twitch over it. The truth is, the country has been in turmoil ever since the assassination of Becker and his guests by those Free Spirit Brethren locos. And now there's you."

Van Ness added, "And it's not just us. The entire world is in a white knuckled panic, following the explosion in Tel Aviv, as I am sure you can easily imagine. Many see this as a sure sign of the coming end. The Big Eight economies are all train wrecks. The nations of the Middle East are losing their territorial cohesion. Oil prices are through the roof. The Third World is in terminal meltdown."

"What is it that you want then, Mr. President?", asked Yordon.

Clement hesitated, then, "Well, to put it plainly, we want to know your agenda."

"What is it that you're trying to accomplish?" added Arthur Blaine, joining the President.

Yordon seemed amused as he responded, "It's very simple, gentlemen. I am spreading the word of God."

Thomas took that as a cue, "And what do you think that word is?"

Yordon's eyes turned to Thomas, "It's an order, Father Prisciotti. To reawaken men to their natures. To put things right."

"God is 'ordering' us to do this?" asked Thomas.

Yordon nodded, "Yes. He is real and I am his instrument."

Blaine, Ravessi, Van Ness and the President all exchanged sour looks and shifted uncomfortably. Yordon noticed this. "Don't you gentlemen believe in God?"

Clement's jaw hung slackly open for an instant. Karin took advantage of the President's loss of words and said, "The world has many belief systems."

"But God underlies all of them," answered Yordon.

Karin retorted, "But what we're having trouble *believing* right now, is how you, a single man, expects to change anything at all? And once the world is changed, what's your role in it? Explain 'put things right'."

Yordon hardened slightly as he replied, "You say I am but a single man, yet you are threatened by me. Why is that? Perhaps you think of me as another terrorist leader?"

"Not necessarily," answered the President, composed again. "Look, Yordon. We could be very helpful to each other. We invited you here to find out what you're after. What makes you tick. Perhaps we can make common cause."

"Well then, we're back to the beginning. What do you want of me?"

Clement answered crisply this time, "Look, Yordon, today in America, we have polarization. We have civil disobedience. We have chaos. We have fear. But is it just because of external events? Or is it something more? America has been a lifeboat to the world for centuries. People immigrate here in huge numbers, seeking religious and political freedom, with the result that today we suffer from too many voices. We're caught in a relentless onslaught of what is benignly called multi-culturalism. In reality it's increasing moral ambiguity. Your arrival on the world stage has further galvanized the situation to the point that these trends threaten to destroy our nation's political heritage."

"That's one viewpoint, Mr. President," said Thomas.

Clement spat back, "It's called the Plain Truth. When the founding fathers wrote the Declaration of Independence, they understood that democratic rule and the principles of justice and freedom depended on a population with a fixed moral compass. They believed the nation would always have a common ethical center and consistent moral basis." Clement turned his attention to Yordon, "That's where you come in, Yordon. Most of us get our notions of morality and ethics -- our sense of right and wrong -- from our religious and cultural beliefs. Isn't that true?"

Some of the attendees nodded in tentative agreement.

Clement continued, "American culture and our Christian heritage are under siege, Yordon. There is no longer an absolute standard of morality, and there's no way to make people accountable to society except by litigation or coercion. This nation is drowning in laws and violence!"

Clement looked to Blaine, who seemed to take a cue. He straightened himself on the sofa and picked up the President's thread. "The President is correct. The 21st century has not been kind to America. The disputed Presidential election of 2000, the terrorist attack in New York City on September 11th of 2001, the Great Recession of 2008, the rise of home grown terrorism, all of it exacerbated by the uncontrolled flow of information and disinformation across the Internet, has led to growing polarization and discomfort in this country. We have talk of secession in Texas."

"You're serious? Again?", exclaimed Karin.

"Deadly." answered Clement.

Blaine resumed, "If this trend is left unchecked, the freedom we enjoy will be replaced by something resembling a police state."

Yordon was intrigued, "And what would you wish me to do to assist your campaign against 'moral ambiguity', Mr. President?"

"Be a moral compass for America. Help me 'set things right', as you say. America needs a charismatic figure like you to act as a lightning rod for its beliefs and priorities."

Yordon stroked at his beard and thought about this. Philo wondered how he would respond to this man's offer. This Clement president was single minded and silver tongued.

Clement tempted Yordon further, "The fact is you're an important religious leader, Yordon. You've taken the world by storm. People openly wonder if you're the Messiah. Whatever the hell you are, you can help us restore the peace."

"You mean, help *you*, Mr. President. You mean help you turn this country into your vision of what it should be."

Clement's eyes softened at this, "It's a thoroughly Christian vision, Yordon. The Bible's way."

"You mean the religious right's way."

"Well, yes," answered Clement, iron defensively returning to his voice.

"That is a highly intolerant view of things, Mr. President. You are wrong to assume I share that view."

Thomas' eyebrow's shot up at this.

Clement looked as if he had been slapped. "Am I hearing that right? How can you call yourself an instrument of God and not support the Catholic Church?"

Clement looked at Thomas accusingly, scolding him with his eyes for not speaking up as well. Thomas said nothing though he felt about to explode with questions.

Yordon's eyes spat fire. "You have a very colloquial view of things, Mr. President."

Max Ravessi uncrossed his legs. Leaning forward, he flatly asked, "And what is your view of things, Mr. Antropos?"

Yordon answered, "A view that is not tainted by politics or false morality." He shot a glance at Clement. "Man's relationship to God is, at best, crudely approximated by your religions. God cares nothing for these, or nationality or politics. Each man must find God uniquely and personally."

"Are you saying that organized religions are a waste of time?" asked Thomas. *How fascinating.* He would have liked to sit and chat with this man in a non-confrontational setting.

Before Yordon could answer, Clement barked, "That's utter cow cud. You can't mean that, Antropos. You're advocating chaos!"

"It's already here, Mr. President," noted Blaine dryly.

"Yes, it is, Mr. Blaine. Precisely," said Yordon. "But that chaos represents change. Change is underway. I am only a part of it. The end result will be a new order. You wish to preserve the old order. I cannot help you with this."

Clement narrowed his eyes and answered tersely. "So I see."

The smoldering anger in his stare gradually turned to something else. He suddenly looked very tired.

The President slowly walked to his desk and looked out the bay windows for a moment, then sat heavily and steepled his fingers in thought. The room waited silently. Finally, with a creak of leather, he leaned his elbows on the famous desk and stared through hooded brows at Yordon.

In a crackling, wooden voice he dismissed his guests. "Then this meeting is over."

Foggy Bottom, Washington, D.C.

After the meeting was adjourned, Clement asked Wesley Van Ness to act as tour guide for Yordon and Philo and to ensure they made it safely back to the airport. Plainly, he wanted close tabs kept on his guests, and no deviations from the planned itinerary. Thomas and Karin were also asked to join the group, most likely as an additional means of finding out more about Yordon.

Riding through Potomac Park on their way to the Tidal Basin, Karin and Thomas tried to be friendly to Yordon. They sat in the spacious rear section of the White House limousine, and watched the groomed parkland roll by.

"Well, you certainly succeeded in alienating the entire room back there," said Karin, lightly. "Hard to believe you're the same person who has mesmerized entire armies."

Yordon unexpectedly laughed, "Your irreverence is refreshing, Professor."

"Irrepressible is more like it," said Thomas, deadpan.

Karin shrugged. "Can't help it. Pompous asses bring it out in me."

"Thanks," said Thomas dryly.

Karin pursed her lips and looked at Thomas with a mischievous glint. "Not you, Thomas," then looking back to Yordon, "Call me Karin, please."

"Your President is certainly imperious," answered Yordon.

They shared a laugh. Van Ness tried hard not to hear.

For several minutes the five some sat in silence, watching the world glide past through the heavily tinted glass. The Washington Monument glowed ruddily in the late day, copper tinted sunlight, casting a long reflection of itself onto the waters of the Tidal Basin.

"You are an expert on ancient cultural beliefs," said Yordon as he turned to Karin.

She nodded, "Correct. My Doctorate focused on the Zoroastrian roots of the three modern day apocalyptic religions.

Yordon's eyes took in Karin's face. Plainly, he liked her and respected her.

"What do you believe of all this?" he asked.

"Hmm?"

"As a scholar, you're obliged to be objective. You study the histories and roots of people's faith with dispassion. You lend empiricism to the mystical. Perhaps it's all a puzzle to you that patiently awaits your solution."

"It's a little like that," she mused.

"Is this another puzzle, then?"

She pondered that, "Yes, I suppose. It's all the same puzzle really. One big mystery. And you're the latest piece of it." She paused, then with sudden impatience, she asked, "Yordon, are you a modern day Jesus Christ?"

He answered, unblinking. "No."

Karin frowned, "OK then, how about this? Do you see yourself as the prophesied Messiah? The second Son of God, as people have called you?"

"Many say that I am. But the meaning your belief systems infuse that label with is a distortion I would rather do without."

"Believe it or not, I almost understand that," answered Karin. "How about this? Are you sent from 'up there'?" She rolled her eyes upward, "from 'heaven'?"

Yordon shrugged. "I don't know. I had a mother and father, like you, though I didn't know them well. And yet, there is a difference. There is a power within me which steadily grows. It has volition. It has purpose." Yordon's face darkened upon saying this but he shook himself free of whatever demons lurked behind those words and returned his attention to Karin and her companions. "I am God's messenger. That's how I can best explain it."

Karin shifted in her seat to face Yordon more directly. She shot a look at Thomas, before continuing, "Why not allow us to collect empirical evidence of this power, Yordon? Let us examine you in a medical lab. It would be fascinating for all of us, including you, I think."

"Evidence? And what will *that* give you? Erudition? And what will that give you? Another book for your bookshelf? Experimental results aren't going to provide you with proof of God's existence. God is unknowable. The truth is so awesome and so foreign that there's nothing I can say to you that could describe it in a manner comprehensible to you. It wouldn't mean anything to you. Words can't contain the image. God is primary revelation. He is superior to all superlatives. He isn't something which exists, but another thing, before existence. He is unfathomable and yet he is self-comprehending. Knowledge of God can only come through an acquired intuition of the structure and intelligence that lies beyond this physical plane. It's all reflected rather crudely in your primitive mythologies. You should look there for some inkling of the truth."

Karin's eyes shone with interest. "Our primitive mythologies? Tell me more about that."

Yordon sighed. "You want creation *explained* to you. That can't be done. You have to take a leap. True understanding requires a certain *faith*, Professor."

Thomas recognized the leap of faith Yordon was talking about as the leap beyond the books and traditions to a place beyond words. He wondered if he would ever achieve it.

"A leap of faith," echoed Karin. "Just take it on faith?" she laughed and turned to gaze out the window at the passing streets.

Yordon spoke again. "You asked me if I was Jesus Christ. Does that mean you hold out the possibility that a Savior will come?"

Karin turned back from the window. Her face was an ambivalent mask. "I'm not sure. It seems fantastic. I find it hard to believe."

"What is your religion, Karin?"

She hesitated. "I'm Methodist."

"Then you must believe in eventual redemption, isn't that right?"

"Well, yes, but…"

"Then why is it so fantastic when it finally happens?"

She answered quickly, "Because you're so human. You're sitting here in the back of a Presidential limo with me and Thomas and Mr. Van Ness and Mr. Berith…"

"Philo," said Philo.

"Yes, Philo – and you have a beard and a smell, and you wear simple clothes, and it's possible to anger you. You're so, well, physical, dammit!"

They were quiet for a while, as the government car rolled smoothly toward the Potomac, past the Lincoln Memorial, and into the Foggy Bottom area. Thomas was a storm of thoughts. Yordon implied so much with his words. They were tantalizing wraiths. Were they also Yordon's secret to commanding so many followers? Were his words rendered so vaporously that all who listened shaped them into the answers they wanted? Or was it blind acceptance of the miracle events that had swayed so many? He had viewed the footage of the miracles but without having seen them firsthand, he felt unsure. He was a pragmatist as much as a theologian. He lived in a world of special effects and man-made, fantastic achievements. He was still unconvinced.

They turned a corner and drove down a street lined with hotels. Ahead, just across from the Hotel Lombardy, there was a sudden commotion. Gunshots rang through the air, capturing everyone's attention.

The driver turned to Van Ness. "Should we drive through, sir?"

Van Ness leaned over the front seat to gaze out the windshield. "Stop the car," he ordered.

Two men erupted from a storefront and began hopping over cars in a frantic attempt to escape the scene. They shoved passers-by out of the way and made for an alley.

Someone shouted from the store's doorway, "Stop them! They've killed the owner!"

Two policemen came sprinting from one of the surrounding hotels and made chase. Another police car arrived on the scene as the occupants of the limo watched and spilled out more police onto the scene. More gunfire. One of the policemen spotted one of the gunmen hiding behind a parked delivery van and shouted his discovery. The gunman threw himself into the oncoming traffic. A car swerved to avoid the wild-eyed thug. The driver lost control of his vehicle and rammed headlong into a woman and her two daughters at full momentum. They were crushed like stick figures by the runaway vehicle, which barreled over them and continued to roll down the sidewalk until it crashed against a lamp-post, erupting into flames. People ran in all directions. Policemen waded through the chaos in vain pursuit of the thieves.

Thomas was the first to exit the limo, making straight for the injured woman and her children. The springtime air blended incongruously with the smell of burnt rubber and gunpowder. The crowd melted out of his way at the sight of his clerical collar and soon he was kneeling before them.

The mother was still breathing but unable to move. *A broken back?* She moaned and opened her eyes. As soon as saw Thomas she clutched at his shirt and mouthed words. He knelt close and felt her dying breaths against his ear.

"My girls…?"

Thomas looked over at the two crumpled bodies. One girl's head was crushed to a pulp. The other's neck lay at a strange angle, giving no doubt to her lifelessness. He returned to the woman. She was not looking at him. He followed her gaze and met the face of Yordon. Yordon touched her and her eyes closed in repose. Thomas stood and backed away.

"She will rest for now," he said. Thomas looked into his eyes and was taken aback by the feeling of power that seemed to mist from them.

Yordon's attention turned to the children. He knelt by the girl with the broken neck and touched her. Amazingly, the bruises around the collar subsided but she did not stir.

"You have healing powers," gasped Thomas. He knelt beside Yordon, who still had his hand on the dead girl. He seemed to be concentrating.

"What are you doing?" asked Thomas.

Yordon replied, "I am trying to restore her."

Karin was out of the car and kneeling by Thomas. Philo too, looking at Yordon with some concern. Van Ness was conferring with the police and was successfully gaining their cooperation in keeping the crowd back.

Yordon placed his other hand on the girl's body and raised his face to the sky. Suddenly the air took on a crisp quality. Philo found it familiar. Then he realized where he had felt that subsonic sharpness before. *Tríatha*. It was a feeling – no, more fundamental -- that there was an intelligence present in the air itself. A huge, terrible *cognizance*. He looked at the priest and could see that he felt it too. And the professor. The crowd was backing away, looking around in confusion for the source of this added element.

Thomas shuddered as the quickening air made his bowels thrill. *What is this effect?* He saw that Yordon was in what seemed to be a deep trance. Yordon clutched at the girl and spoke to her. His voice took on a hollow quality. His eyes were hazel orbs that radiated power.

Yordon lifted the girl by the shoulders so that she was sitting upright and embraced the body. He looked upwards again and with sudden ire yelled into the sky, "I want to do this!"

The thrumming of the air changed in tone. It became a perfect, crystalline vibration. It was almost unbearable. Thomas didn't know whether to cry in joy or scream in terror. Karin did scream – but only a short, confused exclamation. She knelt on the pavement and clutched at her head, as did many others on the street. Philo held Karin by the shoulders, as much to hold himself upright as to comfort her. Yordon's body quaked with the effort of what he was trying to do. The skin on his face took on the quality of parchment; the bones beneath clearly outlined. His eyes burned the air like hot jewels. His voice whispered directly into everyone's ears, no matter where they stood.

"Awaken, child."

The child stirred.

The crowd gasped as one.

"It's a miracle! He did it, yes?" yelled Philo in delight.

One of the crowd, a member of the Latter Reign Ministry of Ducasy, Virginia, heard this, and put her hand to her heart to still it. She realized she

183

must tell her friends about this at once. They should all have the chance to meet the one and only Yordon Antropos. He was here and he was performing a miracle before her eyes. She collected herself and rushed into the Hotel Lombardy.

The Lombardy was filled with the followers of the Right Reverend Story Bouvier that day. They were congregated in the Nation's Capital for the entire week to hear their favorite theologians, spiritualists, channelers, celebrities and notable authorities speak about the latest thinking in modern Revisionist Christian Theology.

Mary Maccabe sat in the back of the Banquet Hall, listening to Bouvier speak. She had wandered for weeks following her night at the motel with Doug, eventually ending up in D.C. and drifting into this conference, not quite sure why she was here. She had not yet found a place to stay. Feeling her weariness, she was gratified to have a place to sit for a while and rest, at the very least.

Bouvier's booming delivery had diminished to a hushed whisper. He brought the microphone close to his lips. "My friends, you have never heard this word preached anywhere. It is hot, it is sacred, it is profound, it is deep! Something great is about to happen to all of us! It is being released into the world as new wine, bringing joy and laughter to the nations. It is part of what I call, the Laughing Revival, for those that directly hear this revelation of God are subject to uncontrollable joy. My friends, I'm getting ready to laugh and I'm getting ready to roar, and I tell you this whole world is going to feel the shaking of that laughter and the power of that roar. Let's release our joy together in this room and join in laughter. Haaa ha ha hahahahaha! OH yes! HA HAAA HAHAHAHA."

One by one, the people in the room began to laugh. At first timidly, then with more and more abandon, as they observed others joining in their laughter.

Mary had to admit it was infectious. She found herself unable to suppress a chuckle. A woman sitting beside her slapped her on the back, displaying a potato chip flaked open mouthed countenance for all to see. Mary laughed back. The entire room was soon laughing with gusto. The noise was incredible. Mary looked around, covering her own mouth as she laughed -- not sure if she was feeling happiness or a giddy fascination at the amazing sight and sound of all these people prone with laughter. She bent over laughing, tears streaming down her face. She felt that she could no longer control her emotions. Incongruously, she began to cry.

Just then the conference moderator came running from one side of the stage and approached Bouvier, who had been standing in silence, eyes gleaming, as he observed the gleeful chaos he had provoked.

Bouvier listened for a few seconds and then as if prodded by an electric barb, sprang back into action. He put his microphone to his lips as he gestured to the stage technician to turn up the lights.

"Ladies and gentlemen, ladies and gentlemen, I have wonderful news. A true miracle – a true sign of coming new age has occurred right outside the doors of this hotel. A child has been revived from death! And do you know who is responsible for this? Can you guess the marvelous truth of it?"

Some of the laughing crowd were drying their tears and trying to listen but most of the audience was still drunk with uncontrollable laughing. Bouvier abandoned the theatrics.

"It's Yordon! He's just outside on this very street and he's waiting for you! This is a coincidence that can only have been orchestrated by God himself!"

At this, Bouvier threw his microphone behind him and made for the doorway. The audience followed.

Mary was a helpless mote in a rushing tide of laughing acolytes. The entire banquet hall emptied through the wide, double doors of the hall, carrying Mary with it. She stopped crying or laughing or whatever it was she was doing – she couldn't tell anymore -- and abandoned herself to the tide. Like a survivor clutching at fistfuls of foam in a whitewater current, Mary was moved helplessly down the carpeted corridors of the Lombardy, surrounded by a moving, bouncing river of laughing people. They were like mad, gleeful children, despite their suits and dresses and wigs and bellies and balding heads. Other guests of the hotel, as well as hotel personnel, stared wide-eyed and tried frantically to get out of the way of the rushing bulwark of mirth-inflicted humanity, led by the jester-happy Bouvier.

They burst out onto the chaos of the crime scene, which was still unfolding, before the Lombardy's entrance, and scattered in all directions, searching for Yordon.

Yordon was crumpling onto the pavement, even as the young girl stood shakily and loosened herself from his collapsing grip. Karin rushed up to grab her. Police and medical personnel had also arrived on the scene and were shouldering their way through the surrounding crowd.

Thomas stepped back and tried to take it all in. The scene seemed to spin around him. The child alive. *Fantastic.* Karin holding her. Van Ness looking bewildered by it all, searching for the limo. Uniformed personnel swimming upstream to get to the eye of the whirlpool, where he stood. Yordon crouched on the ground and absently waving over his companion, Philo. He appeared to be greatly weakened by his efforts.

A sea of people suddenly poured out of the Lombardy. Many of them were shouting for Yordon.

"We've got to get him back to the car!" declared Van Ness, suddenly decisive at the sight of the coming crowd. Thomas agreed and moved forward to help.

But it was too late. Even as Van Ness commanded a small cadre of policemen to help him usher Yordon to the car, the laughing hordes from the hotel overtook the smaller group surrounding Yordon. Total chaos ensued.

The small clearing around Yordon's entourage was compressed to a bare minimum. Fighting erupted all around them as the people around Yordon instinctively resisted the shoving and hysteria of the laughing newcomers. Van Ness was shoved away from the group and was soon lost in a swirling miasma of angry and laughing faces. Thomas struggled toward Karin and grabbed her by the arm. She turned to face him and tried to blink back the fear she knew was in her eyes. Thomas held her close and felt his concern for her course through him. She looked at him wide eyed and thin-lipped and seemed more helpless than he had ever seen her. His heart reached out to her in silence but he forced himself to focus on the situation around them.

Mary Maccabe was lifted, more so than stumbled, down the steps of the Hotel onto the street. Someone spotted Yordon, recognizing him from the infamous Tel Aviv video, and rallied those around him to follow. Mary was carried toward Yordon. Her group quickly encountered the crowd surrounding Yordon and tried to pry through by their sheer weight of numbers. The people they shoved, shoved back. Insults were traded. Blows were exchanged It all deteriorated quickly into a morass of fighting, and, of course, laughing. Mary was conveyed through it all, miraculously avoiding injury, except for a large scratch across her palm.

Suddenly she was forcefully shoved against a tall, fair haired, bearded man with intense hazel eyes. In her struggle to regain her balance, she inadvertently touched him. A light burst forth from her, leaving her breathless, and enveloped both her and the stranger. It turned her knees to jelly and she felt herself grow faint. She clutched at him to keep herself upright.

Yordon seemed to grow stronger at her touch. He tried to rouse himself. Beside him, supporting him, stood a gray haired, smaller man with a bulbous nose and a very concerned face. He tried to shove her away from Yordon, though he was making no attempt to escape through the crowd, which was like a pack of wild cats all around them. Yordon locked onto Mary's face and, releasing her grip, shook himself to alertness.

"Let me speak to this woman, Philo."

She knew it was him. All these months Mary had wondered what she would say to Yordon if she were to successfully meet him, but in the hot flash of the present, with her nose inches from his chest, and her mind swirling into darkness, she found that could only croak her most elemental thought.

"Save me."

As Mary and Yordon regarded each other's questioning faces, the entire street scene faded, and the air around them grew quiet. All Mary could see and hear was Yordon. Despite his exhaustion and confusion he exuded a corrosive vitality that invaded her and lifted her.

"No it is you who have saved *me*," he replied. He helped her stand. The glow between them had forced a clearing around them. Slowly the glow subsided as the two of them gained strength.

"Who are you?" he asked.

"Someone who's been searching for you. All my life."

She felt like reaching out to touch his face but the crowd once again threatened to burst into the clearing. She feared to move, wishing to preserve the moment for as long as possible.

He looked at her searchingly. "Your name is..."

"Mary."

"Your touch gave me strength. How did you do it?" He paused, examining her face further.

"I don't know. I just know that at last I've found you," then with a sudden explosion of self-realization she blurted, "and I love you."

Yordon's face softened at this and he brushed at her hair.

"I can feel that."

She didn't know what to say to this. He could read minds. It was frightening. She clutched at her chest uncomfortably.

Yordon suddenly seemed to realize their moment was about to be broken. He took her hands in his, "Come with me now."

Thomas heard this from a few feet away, his arm still holding Karin protectively. He glanced at her, and saw that she had also heard the exchange. She turned to face Thomas and raised her eyebrows, questioningly. Thomas returned her gaze, feeling her fear, her emotion. Without knowing quite what he was doing, he pulled her closer and she willingly allowed herself to be cocooned by his strong embrace. She placed her palm flat on Thomas' chest and looked right into his eyes.

"Thomas, I…"

Philo suddenly grabbed Thomas by the shoulder, and said, "We must go, priest." He looked to and fro, casting about for an escape. The crowd was about to completely overtake their small clearing.

Yordon held Mary's hand tightly, as they were led by policemen to the waiting limousine, cutting a rough swath through the milling throng. Philo followed closely behind Yordon and Mary. Thomas ushered Karin forward too, using the policemen's wake to get through to the car. Van Ness was already there, holding the door open. They all fell in and the limo raced away, leaving tire marks on the tar and fishtailing slightly in its haste to get away.

Inside the limo, Van Ness spoke crisply to the driver, as he dialed numbers on his cell phone.

"Take us to Andrews right away. The President said to make sure Mr. Antropos makes it back to airport and to Israel as soon as our tour was completed. I think we can say the tour is over."

Mary huddled in the corner position of the back seat, buried in Yordon's robes. She felt him breathing hard. She felt exhausted and confused. She turned to look out the rear window of the limo. The surging crowd could be seen vainly pursuing the vehicle.

She was distracted by a strange tingling sensation in the fingers of her hand. She looked down to examine them and was stunned to discover that the wound on her palm was gone. And not only that. That age old scar on her fingertip from the time she had caught it in a door as a child was utterly erased. She stared in fascination and fought down a storm of mixed emotions: wonder, horror, violation, helplessness, love, curiosity.

But knifing through the torrents of feeling was one clear thought which ultimately willed her to calm: she had met Yordon at long last and now she was here, with him, *the Son of Man*. She would become his intimate, his confidant, his solace and his refuge. And she would learn everything she could about him.

☐

Chapter Six: With the Rod of His Mouth

University of Chicago, Hyde Park, Chicago, June 2020

Karin clicked off the television set and dropped back into the large leather sofa in the professor's lounge. Thomas languorously stretched his large frame and glanced sideways at her, in silent comment on the panel show they had just watched.

It had been a debate about the nature of Yordon Antropos. On the panel had been a UFOlogist, defending the opinion that Yordon was an alien; a televangelist, claiming that Yordon was Jesus Christ; an eschatologist, offering the view that the Yordon was the sure sign of the coming end of the world; and Dr. Zachary Jobson, who had actually met Yordon at the Tel Aviv site and who, despite this, believed him to be all too mortal.

"High drama on the airwaves," quipped Karin.

Thomas grinned. He enjoyed their exchanges. They had been spending a lot of time together in the last few weeks, both in D.C. and now back in Chicago. He was reminded once again that Karin was one of the few people who really understood him.

President Clement quickly came to consider Thomas and Karin to be his "Yordon" experts, as he put it, and constantly called upon them for advice and comment. Shaughnessy was all too glad to have Thomas as a fixture in the Clement Administration and encouraged his cooperation.

But Thomas didn't need a lot of encouragement to fixate on Yordon. On that indelible day in Foggy Bottom, he had *felt* a cognizance in the air and had seen a dead girl re-animated. For all his lifetime of faith, Thomas had never felt such a thing before. It had had *intent*. And more than that, it had been *alien*. Thomas had to try and make sense of it. He shook his head recollecting the debate they had just watched. People were clueless. He realized Karin was waiting for him to respond.

191

"It was ridiculous. Both Harglow and Coathing performed a huge disservice to the Faith. All that eschatological mumbo-jumbo! And those other crackpots! Sometimes I think the human race is nothing but a knuckle dragging mob."

"I wouldn't give the human race even that much credit!" laughed Karin.

Thomas grunted. Walking over to the soda machine, he dropped a few coins in and retrieved a can of Coca Cola.

"About the only sober voice in the entire room was that Dr. Jobson, Zachary, wasn't it?"

"Yes. Zach. He must be dying," said Karin with a grin.

"You're acquainted?"

"He knew my father. He's been an inspiration to me – kind of a mentor. Other times he's a pest. Like you. I'm surprised you two haven't crossed paths yet."

Thomas ignored her playful jibe. "I wonder why he agreed to be interviewed on that show?"

"Oh, he's always giving people too much benefit of the doubt. And he's such a skeptic at the same time. People are complicated, Thomas. No doubt, Zach had no idea what he was getting into."

Thomas smiled absently, and grew quiet.

Karin leaned closer, reaching for Thomas' arm, "What is it?"

"I was thinking that Jobson has personally met Yordon. That's a very exclusive club."

Karin nodded, seeing where Thomas was headed. "We should get together with Zachary. Exchange notes. As it happens, he's due to visit Cornell next week as a guest lecturer. I could probably convince him to stop over in Chicago for the night."

"Serendipitous, Doctor", answered Thomas.

"He's a brilliant deductive investigator. You'll like him."

192

Edgewater Area, North Chicago

The restaurant was crowded and festive. Jazzy Ethiopian music wafted through the air, mingling with the spicy aromas of the food.

"I don't get out enough," said Thomas, looking around, visibly relaxing, even as he perched his large frame precariously on one of the brightly painted wooden pedestals that served as seats in the dimly lit restaurant.

"Shameful really – and it's much closer to your environs than to mine – there he is. Zachary!"

An older, gray whiskered gentleman approached the table. He was grinning broadly. "Ah, Karin, and Father Thomas Prisciotti, I take it."

Thomas extended his hand. "The pleasure is all mine, to meet a renowned member of the Institute for Antiquity and Christianity."

Jobson nodded, in acknowledgment of the compliment, as Karin looked on. Then in unwitting unison, both he and Thomas said, "I've heard a lot about you."

They blinked, still grasping hands and looked to Karin, again in perfectly mirrored pantomime.

Thomas spoke next. "We rehearsed that."

Karin laughed. "Ha! Guilty. I guess I talk about my friends a lot – to my friends, that is."

Thomas recovered himself and gestured to an unoccupied stool. "Please, sit, Doctor.'

"Thanks. Long trip. Hard to find this establishment."

"Karin likes to root out obscure restaurants as much as rare tractates."

Jobson put his things on the ground by the table. "Evidently you two have been spending some time together." He gave Thomas a lingering stare.

"Call me Zachary," said Jobson, breaking into a smile, softening the odd moment.

"Tom," said Thomas, feeling a certain relief.

"Very well."

Karin had watched the exchange and gave them both a warm smile. "Well, now that we're all friends, why don't you take a look at the menu, Zachary? Good heavens, you haven't even ordered a drink…"

"Here comes the waitress," said Thomas.

"Anything. Karin, you know my preferences."

"Sorry, but there's nothing with mayonnaise on the menu, Zachary."

"Ah, but you're a rake, my dear." Jobson focused his attention on her. He rubbed at his whiskers, crinkling his eyes appreciatively, and smiled. "It's good to see you again."

"Try the Doroh Wot. It has egg."

They ordered and, after the waitress left, Karin resumed, "I'll have you know, my friends, that besides being acquainted with the good Doctor Karin Ferguson, and the fact that you've both met Yordon, you and Thomas have another great thing in common."

"You mean the studies?" Jobson turned to Thomas. "I've read some of your treatises on Christian Origins."

"I'm flattered."

Karin interjected, "No, not that. I mean you're both television celebrities!"

Jobson grimaced. "Oh, that. I should've guessed."

Karin laughed. "You must be breaking a blood vessel over the *Viewpoint* interview."

"Embarrassed is more like it. What a charade."

"An unfortunate reflection of the world we live in," noted Thomas.

Jobson considered Thomas. "Hmm. Can't argue."

"The world's a bar-room brawl," said Karin. "I thought that Harglow character was going to jump down your throat and pull out the devil himself by his goatee."

"You should have seen him after the camera cut. He had to be wrestled off the stage."

They laughed.

"You always have had a way of inspiring people, Zachary," continued Karin.

"You think so? I was asked to leave by way of the loading dock! They thought I was reckless. Just another crackpot."

"How terrible," Karin breathed.

"The truth is up for grabs," said Thomas.

"It's seems to be increasingly whatever people choose to believe," said Jobson.

"Like Yordon Antropos is the Son of God," replied Karin, directing the conversation as she sipped wine from her glass.

Jobson answered, "That belief is shallow in the extreme. I admit it's difficult to explain Yordon's acts -- modifying the weather, curing the incurable, inducing acts of nature, all without any apparent power source or technological trickery. Yet there must be a mechanism."

"But no evidence of such is available," countered Karin. "You've allegedly seen Yordon heal the sick with your own eyes. What more do you need?"

"Oh, come now, my dear. Even if I had evidence, more than mere evidence is needed. The problem is that we have a model of the universe that is empirical and physical. Supernatural beings are not part of that model. It's like asking us to believe in magic because someone can conjure a rabbit from a hat. Even if there is a God, he must fit into the universe we know. Even if he is powerful, he must fit into the laws of nature while he operates within our sphere."

"But didn't God create the universe?" insisted Karin, "Didn't he invent the laws of nature? As the Creator, what is to prevent him -- or his Son -- from making up his own laws and doing whatever he pleases?"

"Nothing." said Jobson.

"Then what's the problem?"

"The laws themselves. Nothing would prevent a God from making up his own laws and doing as he pleases but if he did so, it couldn't be within our universe. If there is a God who made this universe, even he must operate within its laws or it would be destroyed! A theoretical Creator can conjure up any universe he chooses, but once it exists, in order for him to interact with it, he would have to enter it and thereby be subject to it. If he wanted to use different laws, he could, but it would have to be outside of the universe in question. He would either be making up a new universe or operating outside of the current physical plane. Do you see the point?"

"Completely," said Thomas.

"It's a very simple point, really. I'm amazed more people don't see it."

"It's because they don't read, Zachary."

"Exactly!," exclaimed Jobson, not realizing the taunt, "Doesn't it disturb you that so many people in this country are Bible obsessed and yet have never read the Bible?

Thomas responded, "But that's not the sum of Christian faith. There's morality, and love. There's charity, kindness, forgiveness, tolerance…"

Jobson laughed at this. "Tolerance? I can think of several moments in history where the Catholic Church was anything but tolerant."

Karin raised her voice. "Now, you two. Calm yourselves. We didn't come here to draw lines in the sand. We came here to talk about Yordon. What does he mean to us? To the world. Remember?"

Jobson bowed his head. "Sorry, my dear," he turned to Thomas, "My apologies. Perhaps I will have some of that wine."

Thomas poured Jobson a glass. "Not to worry."

Satisfied, Karin said, "The fact is, gentlemen, that no matter what doubts you may cast, the masses *believe*. And they are legion. That makes it real."

"She's right," said Thomas. "There are 60 million Catholics in America alone. At least 10 million of them are among those fundamentalists who are taking Yordon very seriously."

"You have to wonder where all this is heading." said Karin.

Before anyone could answer, the food arrived.

"Tell us about Tel Aviv," Karin finally asked of Jobson through a mouthful of food.

"Hard to put it into words." Jobson paused, collecting his thoughts. "It was the pit of death. Devastation beyond words. Desert heat, ashes and rubble." He shook his head. "Forgive me. I was at odds with myself during the entire expedition. First, in the sense that I was exploiting a holocaust to advance our research of the Ancient Near East, then in light of my encounter with Mr. Antropos."

"Tell us how you met him," urged Karin.

"An incredible episode. In the midst of dealing with a group of survivors, he showed up. Just strolled over to our campsite, no protection whatsoever."

"No symptoms?"

"None."

"Amazing," breathed Karin.

Jobson nodded and lowered his voice. "He healed them. He touched them and they healed before our eyes."

"What did he say to you?"

"He said a great many things. But what I remember most distinctly are his final words to me."

Karin waited, then impatiently, "Well, what?"

"He said there is much I will learn and still I will not know."

Her eyes lit up. "He did? Wow. He's like a living fortune cookie!"

Thomas smiled at this, and dabbed at his mouth with his napkin.

"And what about your own encounter with him?" asked Jobson in return, unperturbed by the wisecrack.

"Also incredible, Zachary," answered Karin, "We were with him on a tour of D.C. when there was a hit and run. A mother and two girls were injured."

"And then?" asked Jobson.

"Zachary – while we watched, he brought the little girl back from the dead. He healed her, then he revived her."

Thomas added, "And there was some kind of energy field. It gave off a feeling of… a feeling of *awareness*."

"Like a living presence," said Karin, "and then there was that young woman. And the glow. She touched Yordon and there was a glow."

"Who was the woman?" asked Jobson, enthralled.

"I don't know." Karin adjusted her seat, as she recalled the event. "But Yordon was quite taken with her, from the looks of it. She escaped with us and left with him." She gestured at their barely touched meal.

"Eat. You must be hungry."

"What? Ah yes, of course." Jobson made an attempt to scoop up some of his dinner into a handful of dough, as he had seen Karin do.

They ate in silence for several seconds.

Wiping at his lips, Jobson resumed the conversation. "The whole thing's fantastic. Despite all the eyewitnesses, I still find it hard to believe."

"Are you sure that's not simply your refusal to believe in anything miraculous?" challenged Karin.

"Oh it is that indeed, Karin. Quite. It just doesn't fit our framework."

"Or our understanding of the universe is incorrect or incomplete and, in fact, Yordon fits perfectly," said Thomas.

Jobson looked surprised at that remark. "Perhaps you have something there, Father."

Somewhere over the Atlantic Ocean

The military transport thrummed its way over the gray-blue carpet of the Atlantic Ocean as Yordon and Philo were taken back to Israel.

"It was madness for you to think they would just let her get on this plane, without knowing anything about her," said Philo, as he laid a comforting hand on his increasingly erratic friend.

"She will come," croaked Yordon, rubbing at his temples.

"Yes, I have no doubt that she will," sighed Philo, "As soon as she can get a passport, a tourist visa and a plane ticket, she will come to Israel, or wherever your impulses decide we should travel next -- of this, I have no doubt," answered Philo, wishing it wasn't inevitable, but he knew it was. Yordon had connected with that woman in some fundamental way.

The two companions were alone in the cabin, which Philo found fortunate. Something else had changed in Yordon as a result of resuscitating that little girl. He had tapped some additional well of power within himself in order to accomplish that incredible feat. It was a power which, after performing its miracle, had turned on him and was taking him like a devouring demon. Now he was hunched in his seat, lost in a fog, talking to himself a little, and looking feeble again.

He suddenly turned to his longtime companion, "Philo, please get me some water. I'm thirsty. So thirsty."

Philo went to see about the water, shaking his head the entire way.

Yordon rubbed hard at his arms with his hands, trying to keep himself in the present moment by focusing on the tactile sensations of his skin being roughly abraded. His mind was awhirl with visions and voices. They were louder and more present than they had ever been before. And more importantly, they were discernible voices now, with words and demands, and there was more than one. Never before had the voices coalesced into discrete streams of consciousness like this. That intangible presence that had floated like a glowing jewel in the back of his consciousness throughout his life had precipitated and taken purchase within the precincts of his mind, like a great corpuscle that pulsated with rival thoughts and urges. Yordon felt panic and deep disorientation at this. He wondered if he had perhaps crossed a boundary that he might come to regret. But even as he thought these thoughts, alternate currents of consciousness shoved his trepidation into a corner and enveloped him with their own confidence. Yordon teetered between confusion and conviction, disdain and determination. He was afraid he might be losing his mind.

Several hours later, they were flying over the Mediterranean and close to the end of their journey. Yordon had gradually emerged from his febrile state and was looking much better, though the set of his face was hard. He was gazing out of the small window and examining the rolling coast line with intent.

"We have much to do, Philo, once we land," said Yordon, showing a sudden stridency.

Philo replied, "Please forgive this simple villager for asking such a half-witted question, but what exactly are we... you... trying to do? Each time I think I understand, you change direction and again I am confused."

Yordon regarded his friend thoughtfully and relaxed a little, becoming more his old self for a moment, "The same as ever, Philo. We are spreading the word of God to the world of men."

"By flying to America to argue with that, how do they say? 'Good Old Boy'?"

Yordon smiled at the barb, "I've barely begun, Philo. At Philotheou, my communion was secret and personal. Then I became a traveler, and I spread my insights. Then, as a healer, I gained the notice of the world. I now have the attention of the world. Now I must be a leader."

Philo tried to keep his voice level, "A leader usually wants something from his followers."

"No, not from. *For*," said Yordon.

"And what would that be?" asked Philo, trying not to sound skeptical.

"Liberation, Philo. I am going to *liberate* people from their warring belief systems and help them discover a new and truer one."

"Is that God's will? Or yours?" asked Philo.

For an instant, Yordon's face was darkened by a shadow of puzzlement.

"I'm not sure. I'm scaring you, aren't I?"

Philo stared back at Yordon, blankly, then shrugged.

Yordon sighed, "Philo, can you imagine what it is like to one day realize that the voice inside your head is not fully yours? Can you fathom the horror of discovering that you do not know yourself after a lifetime?"

"Are you saying you're possessed?"

Yordon's eyes lost focus for a moment, "I don't know. In a sense, I am in thrall to a greater power. If only you could know the immensity of that power."

"But you can resist this!"

Yordon shook his head, resigned. "No. This is my destiny, old friend."

Philo searched the face of the man sitting beside him and tried to find his friend.

Yordon became intense. "The situation is different now. I'm different now. There will be days when you look at me and you won't find me, Philo."

Philo was slightly taken aback at having his thoughts read, but replied steadily. "But how will you do what you say?"

"With words, as always. To set the stage properly."

"And then?"

"With force. In the end there will be force."

Philo shook his head. "You mean death." Now it was Philo's turn to sigh. "This is not good, no, not at all. At Jericho you said that killing for religious beliefs was wrong; that religion should never be forced on someone. And now you propose this very thing. I do not understand."

Yordon answered, "No, Philo. Haven't you heard any of my words throughout all these years together? Beliefs are the inventions of men. God is not a belief. He simply *is*, and people have to wake up to his presence. There's no politics, religion, or oppression in the act of waking up. It's liberation, not oppression. I am simply an agent of change. I am no tyrant."

Philo tried to keep the skepticism from his face. "It sounds to me like you are. Or will be."

Yordon turned toward the window and looked down at the waves washing up on the shore miles below and said, "For some, I will be."

La Via Dolorosa, Jerusalem

The city was joyous at the arrival of the Pope. Accompanied by the usual entourage, Sylvester made a tour of the fourteen stations of the cross, along the arched galleries of the narrow, winding Via Dolorosa, traversing both the Moslem and Christian quarters of the Old City. Thousands came out to hear him and observe the spectacle. He was a beacon of hope and stability in a time of deep uncertainty.

He had taken up residence in the tower apartments above the Church of the Holy Sepulcher. It was here that he met with his various visitors, primarily the local heads of the various church bodies that inhabited the physical and ideological landscape of Israel.

Sylvester signed several letters while he heard his schedule read to him by the domestic prelate. He carried on like this for several hours until the time of the meeting they had all been waiting for.

"Santissimo Padre, the one who calls himself the, eh… Messenger of God, awaits your audience in the foyer," pronounced Cardinal Dvorni, the Papal Chamberlain, head bowed slightly. "He has not come alone, your Holiness."

Sylvester exchanged looks with Tatian, who sat to his left. Cardinal Tatian emanated an authority once common in Church officials of several hundred years before but now rare indeed. He held sway over much of the Vatican's political landscape and was a close advisor to the Pope, though they did not always agree on policy and dictum. Archbishop Giancarlo Agostini, the Latin Patriarch of Jerusalem, was also present, looking uncertain.

"I see, "said Sylvester, "*Buono*. Show only him into the chambers. The others must wait. Offer them refreshments."

"At once, your Holiness."

Dvorni whispered instructions to the waiting usher. In a few moments, there was a knock on the door and Yordon was allowed to enter. Sylvester was seated comfortably in a high backed, ornately appointed chair, befitting the Sovereign of the State of Vatican City. The rest of the entourage was seated on either side of him, in a rough semi-circle, that followed the lines of the room.

Yordon was introduced by the Chamberlain. "This gentleman, who is called Yordon Antropos, requests an audience with the Supreme Pontiff, the Archbishop and Metropolitan of the Roman Province."

"The audience is granted."

Sylvester offered his hand, bearing the fisherman's ring, but Yordon only glanced at it. He inclined his head slightly in a bow, as the only acknowledgment of his host's authority. The rustle of cloth in the room spoke volumes of the tension and disapproval felt by the others who were present. Sylvester cleared his throat and tried to gloss over the moment.

"Welcome to the Church of the Holy Sepulcher, Mr. Antropos."

"You may call me Yordon."

"And you may call me Holy Father."

Yordon paused at the note of sharpness in the Pontiff's response, then conceded, "As you wish."

"May I introduce the Dean of the College of Cardinals and Prefect of the Congregation for the Doctrine of the Faith, Cardinal Matthew Tatian."

Tatian bowed silently, his face cast in conspiring stone.

"You are the defender of the faith," noted Yordon neutrally.

"Correct," answered Tatian in silky reply.

Sylvester propelled them forward, "And the Primate of this diocese, Cardinal Agostini."

"Welcome to our humble church," said the rugged faced Cardinal.

"Thank you for receiving me."

"And the Papal Chamberlain, Cardinal Dvorni."

"God be with you," said Dvorni.

Yordon smiled slightly.

Sylvester extended a hand toward an empty chair. "Please sit and talk with us awhile."

The usher brought the wooden chair forward.

Yordon sat.

Sylvester spoke, "We are aware of your word and actions in these last few months and we are pleased to be able to speak with you about them."

"I have been looking forward to this encounter as well."

Sylvester inclined his head in acknowledgment. "You are from Athos."

"Yes. I come from Philotheou."

"Please indulge my curiosity. Why did you leave the monastery?"

Yordon looked at each of his hosts in turn before answering, as if weighing their mettle. The set of his face softened a little. "I was compelled. God called me forth from there and I obeyed."

"God?" queried the Pontiff, "Tell us more about this."

"Yes. The primal force. He has given me signs and insights which have led me from moment to moment since that time."

Tatian glanced at the Pope. Sylvester nodded imperceptibly.

Tatian asked, "If you are blessed with insights from The Most High, why was this not reported to the Vatican? It is our responsibility..."

Suddenly angry, Yordon didn't let him finish. "To do what? Denounce the visions? And if not, what then? Flocks of pilgrims overrunning a personal experience until it is trampled in sensationalism?"

"There is no need for your ire, my son."

Yordon calmed himself, then more quietly, "No. My vision was my secret for many years. And my brothers at Philotheou kept this secret with me. They understood."

Sylvester responded, "Perhaps we do as well. Communication with God is a deeply personal experience."

"Precisely. I wonder if you can understand that statement for its full implication."

"You are speaking to the Supreme Pontiff of the World Catholic Church!" protested Dvorni.

Yordon cast a critical eye at the figure of the seated Pope. "He is merely a man."

Tatian countered, locking eyes with Yordon, "As are you. However, in the case of the Holy Father, he is much more. He is the inheritor in the Apostolic succession -- invested with full, supreme and universal power over the Holy Roman Catholic Church. You will respect him."

Sylvester changed the subject. "Yordon, I am told you have been excommunicated from the Greek Orthodox Church."

Yordon answered levelly, "Dorotheos has been displeased with my actions ever since my departure from Athos."

"Thus your audience with us, rather than with the Patriarch," surmised Tatian, unctuously.

Yordon ignored the taunt. "I eventually saw it necessary to leave Greece." Yordon paused for a heartbeat. "No matter. It is you, Sylvester III, whom I wished to meet, not Dorotheos."

"Explain this," said Sylvester.

"The Christian faith stems from the Latin rite church. You are its head. Despite your divisions, you speak for all of Christianity."

Sylvester accepted this. "I should, in truth, not welcome you within these walls but I must admit my curiosity has the better of me. Tell me, Yordon, are you not concerned for your soul?"

Yordon showed surprise at this. "The excommunication is meaningless to me. And it is meaningless in the eyes of God."

"Then what *is* meaningful to God, young man?" asked Sylvester, unable to clear a note of indulgence out of his voice.

Yordon answered, unperturbed, "Personal enlightenment. Our redemption before God begins when we throw away the rituals and divisions that man-made religions impose on us and raise our eyes above day to day concerns."

"Do you mean to say we should abandon our religious traditions?" asked Tatian mockingly.

Yordon turned to face him. "Yes. Only then does your awakening begin. Then you would see that we are all part of one continuum of awareness which stems directly from God."

Dvorni cleared his throat and hesitantly asked, "So you believe that God is knowable without faith?"

Yordon nodded, "In a sense. Men do not need a clergy to guide them to God. In fact, your organization obstructs God from men by deceiving them into believing your rituals and Sermons are enough."

"This is all nonsense!" coughed Tatian. "Your words are nothing more than New Age pablum."

"Nothing could be farther from the truth," answered Yordon, raising his voice a little.

Yordon and the Cardinal Prefect exchanged cold stares again.

Tatian's next words were icy shards. "You suffer from a dangerously simplistic view of things."

Yordon answered sharply, "Do I? Or is it your view that is simplistic? God and his realm are infinitely subtle. It requires work to know him. He is not attainable by rote."

"It is not rote, it is order. It is structure," snapped Tatian.

Sylvester interjected, trying to be consoling. "The clergy brings its traditions to men in order to aid them in their reunion with God. That is called Church, my son. A church is a community to inspire faith and bring strength where there would otherwise be persecution. The church brings guidance and discipline to the masses."

Yordon answered, "And you've turned discipline into dogma. The Vatican exists for the purpose of preserving itself and its orthodoxies. It promotes men unrelenting in their view of church discipline. It is a bureaucracy filled with careerists who are out of touch with the people and their priests"

"You are speaking of us, Yordon," said Sylvester.

"That is so."

Sylvester was strangely reminded of Thomas Prisciotti, and of the phone conversation they had had before the world started tumbling down, many months and seemingly a lifetime ago. But that was quite a different discourse.

The Pontiff forced himself back to the present. "Not careerists, but people who have devoted their lives to the service of God,"

Yordon answered dismissively, "It's hypocrisy. It is a bureaucracy with all the trappings of a medieval court."

"Ridiculous. Outrageous," responded Tatian, his face reddened, "You are a dangerous and outspoken fool!"

Yordon answered angrily, "No, Cardinal Tatian. I am not. I speak an important truth. Christ wanted people to find their own path, not follow blindly in his footsteps. People are crying for change and you do not listen, defending the old guard at all costs. The Vatican is a village of washerwomen. Your dogmas are not sacred. The Apostle Paul invented this Christianity, not God. It is not God's word you defend, but men's words about God. Religion should be the living reflection of the soul of the people. Since you are not these things, you and your organization will eventually fade from history."

"I doubt that very much, Mr. Antropos," said Tatian sternly, "The truth of the Church's teachings is not gauged by how many Catholics accept it. The Church's doctrines are derived from Christ's lips. We preach His message. Even when it is distinctly unpopular. The Church has been challenged by tyrants before and prevailed."

Yordon retorted, "And now it is ruled by them. What of that, you who pretend piety?"

Tatian was momentarily taken aback, feeling the sting of Yordon's unexpected insight into his character.

The conversation had reached an impasse. Tatian was livid. The Pope was examining Yordon intently. Dvorni looked like he was about to faint. Cardinal Agostini also looked distinctly uncomfortable, as if he had come to the wrong meeting, and now found himself trapped. Finally, the rugged prelate steeled himself and asked a question.

"Mr. Antropos, in our exchange of passions, perhaps we have missed the essential point. May I, Holiness?"

Sylvester nodded.

Agostini gazed at Yordon and asked, "Why did you wish to meet with us?"

Yordon responded coldly and levelly, "To see if there is any opportunity for change here. But there is not. So instead, I am here to tell you that your end is near. This capital of rituals and rectitude will soon crumble and fall."

Tatian laughed at Yordon, but his eyes were cold steel. "I think we've heard enough of this, Holiness."

Sylvester sighed, "I am disappointed in you, Yordon. We seek to revitalize the faith. What you preach is anarchy and disrespect of the covenant God has placed in our stewardship. You are, at best, a false prophet. Go now, and may God have mercy on your soul."

Yordon looked at each of the attendees and finally said. "Very well. But we shall meet again, Artieri, and next time it might not be as comfortable."

He made to exit, but as he crossed the threshold, he turned back once more and said. "You didn't ask me about the miracles."

Then he was gone.

The four clergymen were uniformly speechless.

"How could we forget?" thought Sylvester.

Chapter Seven: Parousia

The Capitol Mall, Washington, D.C., July 2020

The procession of Antropostles, as they had dubbed themselves in the months prior, wound their way down the length of the Capitol Mall. Among them could be seen members of the Brethren of the Free Spirit, discernible by their yellow cross pins. They had recently declared Yordon to be the fulfillment of their predictions of a coming hour of judgment and had placed themselves at his beck and call. Many held signs on which was painted one word. Many were shouting the word, in unison.

Thomas and Karin watched in fascination as the demonstrators streamed by. Karin nudged Thomas and pointed to the pavement where someone had sprayed the word in bold red. Thomas looked down.

Parousia. And sprayed all around it in stencil, were the little icons of Athos that had come to represent the followers of Yordon.

From the crowd of onlookers, an elderly gentlemen in a plaid jacket approached Thomas.

"Excuse me, Father, what does it mean, Parousia?"

"Parousia?" echoed Thomas, wondering at the ancient word. "It refers to the Second Coming. The Second Coming."

The old man looked toward the crowd. "These people, they believe it's the time."

"They do."

The old man took a step closer and touched Thomas' arm. "Father, are they right?"

Thomas fought down the welt of anger he felt at the man who had merely asked him for a word of comfort. He reminded himself that he still had an obligation.

"Abide by your convictions, friend, and you will survive this."

The old man held Thomas' eyes before he looked away with an air of resignation. He started to leave but then turned his head back toward Thomas.

"What about you, Father?"

Thomas felt the words inch up his spine like cold fingers. He remembered Karin and looked to her. She was smiling gently at him. He turned back to answer the man. He was gone. He hadn't waited for Thomas to respond.

"Let's leave here," he said.

"Not our kind of party, is it?"

Grabbing his arm, Karin led Thomas away from the confusion and directed them north, then west toward Georgetown. As they walked, Karin tried to keep Thomas talking. She knew he could become dark if left alone at a time like this. She knew how much he needed to work out his thoughts and convictions in light of the changing tides. She understood the conflict of his academic underpinnings and the demands of his faith. She had always loved him for his strength of character, for his ability to balance to two halves of his mind and find a degree of harmony and purpose there. That tension gave him vitality and magnetism, which she was drawn to. But now that balance was in peril. She wanted to help him and yet she knew, if she allowed herself to reach out to him, to really reach out and give him the comfort and love he so desperately needed, she might tip him off the tightrope and cause him to betray himself in a vital way. For now, at least, she could only be his steady, and sardonic -- for he needed to be jostled -- companion on this journey.

The noise of the demonstration receded and the streets took on a semblance of normalcy.

"Whew. That's better. It's like the 60's around here lately."

Thomas grunted.

Karin asked, "Did you ever think it would happen in your lifetime, Thomas? You know, the Second Coming?"

"You believe him?"

Karin grinned and shook her head. "I'm too skeptical to believe anything. I'm asking you."

"No."

"Even though you knew you would probably be alive for the millennium?"

"Nothing happened then. End time dates are arbitrary, as you know," answered Thomas dryly.

"Yet you believe in the return of the Messiah? It's what the Bible says will happen."

Thomas didn't reply.

Kate nudged him, "Thomas. What do you believe?"

"Yes. Yes, yes, yes. I believe He will return."

"Well, what's the problem then?"

"You're taunting me. Yordon is no Messiah. The Messiah is supposed to be on our side, I mean the Church's, when he returns, for starters."

"But instead he calls a press conference in Jerusalem and denounces your entire organization and furthermore says he is the legitimate voice of God. Funny."

Thomas stopped in his tracks and faced her, "You're not helping."

Karin stared him down, until he sighed and resumed walking, "But then again, maybe you are. We say he's no Messiah. He says he is. It comes down to this: somebody is wrong."

"Yup." said Karin, "But you have to admit, Yordon said some pretty interesting things at that press conference – at least, I thought."

"Interesting? How could he say those things? It was preposterous."

Karin whirled on him. "Because they're true. And you know it. Christianity has been shaped by human history and politics since its beginnings. When Constantine was converted to Christianity, it instantly transformed the religion of a minor, persecuted sect into an instrument of social and financial gain for the senators and nobles of the Roman court. Legions of unrepentant pagans joined the Church for the sole purpose of gaining favor with the Emperor. Inevitably, their beliefs and practices were assimilated into church tradition, to make it more palatable to the masses, until the church became unrecognizable to the original Christians."

"So Yordon says."

"Come on, Thomas, you know it's academic fact."

Thomas pursed his lips as if tasting something sour. Finally he said, "You have to wonder what the church would have been like if Constantine had not converted, if it had remained pure."

"No you don't," answered Karin, "For starters, Father Prisciotti, you wouldn't be wearing that collar. In its original form, Christianity would have never resulted in a mass movement. It was simply too esoteric for most people. There was no power, and no profit, in it. It had to undergo a certain alchemy, to be changed by human ambition into a more easily acceptable shape before it could grow. The invention of the clergy, the concept of Apostolic authority, the adoption of pagan rituals – all those things were a way to give the Church leaders temporal power and make it easy for people to join up. Unfortunately, with that power came a culture of intolerance and superstition."

Thomas started to voice a defense but came up short. He felt unexpectedly exposed. As an intellectual and scholar of early Christianity, he knew these things, so why was he so moved? He was afraid to say too much one way or the other. He realized that some part of him would be betrayed no matter which stance he chose to take, and the time to choose was at hand. He closed his eyes.

"Thomas."

He had stopped walking again. Karin was looking at him impatiently. She took his hand and pulled gently.

"Keep those feet moving. Georgetown is still a hike."

Israeli Crisis Center, Jerusalem

Avrahami and his circle of ministers, grown larger since the days of the explosion, were back in the war bunker, many levels below the desert plain. The situation in Jerusalem had deteriorated considerably since Yordon's recent pronouncements against not just Christianity, but all religions, with so many religious denominations residing within its cramped confines. It was no longer safe in the government buildings. Avi Grinker, the Knesset speaker, was delivering the latest report from the field.

"He is said to have bestowed on his followers the power to heal diseases, Prime Minister. Who can resist this? Many of our own citizens believe him to be the Messiah. Tensions are running high. Several Haredim sects are waiting for his signal to begin rebuilding the Third Temple. And you know what that means."

"The destruction of the Dome of the Rock mosque to make room for it," answered Eli Rosenthal, the Secretary General.

"And then chaos!" answered Ben Zion Yaakov, the newly appointed Minister of Defense. "Utter warfare between Jews and Muslims. They do not see this! The streets would flow with blood if this were to happen."

"This is very serious. This creature must be stopped," said Rosenthal, red-faced.

Yaakov nodded tersely and looked to Avrahami. "Agreed. He is dangerous. Volatile. His followers are volatile."

"But there's no way. He's untouchable," said David Chalutz.

"And is it wise to take an antagonistic stance? Don't forget it was we who gave him support when he first came to our attention," said Silver.

"Then what do we do? Nothing? And if we do nothing?" protested Rabbi Weizman. "There will be bloodshed in Jerusalem!"

"Will there be?" asked David Chalutz, rising to Silver's defense. "Remember the Jordanian soldiers he sent to the city a few months ago. They were doves."

The Science Minister, Ephrat, shifted his weight and nodded in recollection. "He did something to them. And to poor Engel. He hasn't been the same."

"Yordon is different now too. Aggressive," added Ephrat.

Rosenthal turned to Ephrat. "Schmuel, his followers are blind. They see a promise of peace and ignore the guarantee of war."

"How so many of them would love to wage a God-sanctioned war against the Jews," added Yaakov darkly.

"This is not how it was supposed to happen," bemoaned Weizman.

"We could infiltrate his ranks," suggested Grinker, ignoring the Rabbi.

"To kill him? And what if we did manage that?" countered Ephrat. "The reaction of his followers would be violent. It would be worse."

Rosenthal pounded the tabletop. "There must be a way to stop him."

The debate came to an impasse and the circle of ministers found themselves turning to Avrahami. He looked up at them, letting the silence hang. Finally Yaakov could stand it no longer.

"What is your opinion, Prime Minister?"

Avrahami looked at Silver, who was seated beside him. He raised his eyebrows and shrugged.

Coughing, Avrahami answered, "We must do something – there is no doubt. We can't just sit here like sardines as our country tears itself to shreds above our heads. But killing Yordon is not the answer. That will only turn him into a martyr. We must do better than kill him. We must disarm him. We must *discredit* him."

"But how?" asked Rosenthal.

Avrahami let his head hang, not answering immediately, lost in thought. Silver glanced at him. Avrahami felt his appraisal and stared feebly back. Silver tried to hide his concern.

Avrahami regained himself. "I don't know. But we're running out of time and we must find a way."

Oval Office, The White House, Washington, D.C.

President Adam Clement rubbed at his cheeks and stared down at the papers on his desk as he listened to Wesley Van Ness read the Presidential Daily Briefing.

"The Houthis in the Western region of Yemen have declared their allegiance to Mr. Antropos, following his seemingly miraculous restoration of their drinking water sources. As you know, the city of Sana'a was experiencing severe drought conditions."

"It's the dammedest thing, isn't it?" growled Clement. "Go on."

"Similar rumblings are coming out of Saudi Arabia, to the great consternation of King Salman. It appears that all of Islam is inexorably turning into a camp of Antropos followers, or Antropostles, as they have been coined by the news media. The situation in the Middle East is unprecedented. Borders have become fluid."

"And American interests are deeply at risk, sir," added Arthur Blaine, who, along with Kent Hanover and Max Ravessi, had been invited to sit in on the Briefing. "We still need Saudi oil."

"Indeed," said Ravessi. "While the people who are pledging their allegiances to Mr. Antropos largely view him as a religious figure, the reality is that he is a geo-political wild card. He has the potential to upset the international balance of trade and international relations. He's a material danger to our country's economy, Mr. President."

"And to our European allies. The Germans and the French have expressed concern and are talking about calling for a special G7 Summit to discuss potential developments and countermeasures," said Blaine.

"Countermeasures?" asked Clement, "Are we talking about sanctions? How do you sanction a stateless figure like Antropos?"

They all shifted uncomfortably, until Ravessi volunteered, "It's possible that military action may be put on the table as a response to current events."

Clement sighed and leaned back in his chair, looking tired, "It seems to always come to that. The irony of the situation is that this Antropos character is actually having a pacifying effect on the entire Middle East."

"Is it *pacifying* or is it *unifying*, sir? It's a significant difference. A unified Middle East controlling the oil supply, and even possessing nuclear fuel and delivery systems would be a far more threatening development to Western interests," said Ravessi.

"The last thing our NATO allies will want to see is a competing power block that could actually sanction them, right next door to them," added Hanover.

Clement nodded, accepting the thrust of his advisor's assertions.

"Get me the German Chancellor on the horn."

The Papal Apartments, Vatican City

Pope Sylvester III was having trouble keeping his composure. The other inhabitant of the room was speaking earnestly.

"Christianity has been sufficiently challenged by the secularism and skepticism of the modern world. We don't need some modern day false prophet working the masses into a state of pandemonium," said Cardinal Tatian as he paced back and forth across the chamber.

"Not since Wycliff, not since Martin Luther, have we faced such a challenge to our authority," he fretted. "This creature is destroying the world congregation, Holiness."

Tatian's voice sounded brittle. Sylvester tried to inject his own voice with calm.

"Then we must repair it, Matthew. We must challenge *his* legitimacy. I should have done it sooner."

Tatian turned to him. "But you didn't, Holy Father. Why?"

Sylvester rubbed the tension from his face as he reflected. "Yes, why? A good question."

Tatian unclenched his fists and settled himself by a window to stare out at the complex of soot blackened buildings below. *Everything I believe in.* There was a demonstration of some kind taking place. The Swiss Guard, as well as the more plainly attired Vatican security guards were running to and fro. Sylvester spoke from behind him.

"Because I doubted."

Tatian turned his head toward the Pontiff, "He can't be real," he said, spitting out the words.

"Hmm, yes. That MUST be our position."

Tatian answered grimly. "His statements leave no room for reconciliation. He wants to destroy the church. We must act."

Sylvester sighed his agreement. "This is not an easy decision, I tell you frankly. I would have thought our people would be more resilient. They are almost eager to abandon us."

A shadow of sadness darkened the Pope's face.

Tatian made himself wait. It was time for action, not words. Unprecedented action. He felt like picking up the Pontiff and shaking him.

Sylvester seemed to read his thoughts. He straightened in his chair and proclaimed, "Matthew, the time has come for action."

"You can excommunicate him, like Bartholomaios did. Declare him a heretic," agreed Tatian.

"Yes. We must immediately denounce Mr. Antropos as a pretender. Our supremacy as the Apostolic successors cannot be challenged."

Tatian quelled his excitement and tried to control the smile that threatened to erupt on his face. "I wholeheartedly agree, Holiness. The situation also calls for a formal Council. The Code of Canon Law dictates that…"

Sylvester stopped him in mid-sentence. "To perdition with the Code of Canon Law! There is no accommodation for a situation of this ilk in any of the canon books. Expediency is required. Decisive action is demanded."

Tatian nodded, clasping his hands and pacing, "Given the expediency, Excellency, then perhaps a meeting of the College of Cardinals is the appropriate vehicle for developing our response?"

"No. What is needed is a *Synod*," replied Sylvester slowly, developing the idea in his mind as he spoke. "An *Extraordinary* Synod. The gravity of our problem transcends the Roman Catholics. I need more than just the special college."

Tatian pondered the Pope's suggestion. A Synod could be ecumenical, calling forth all Christians, regardless of doctrine or sect.

"Yes, that's it," said Sylvester. His voice took on the tenure of command, "I charge you with gaining support for this Synod, Matthew. I decree that we call an Emergency Synod at once and that the topic will be Yordon Antropos. See to it. Work with Bruni. You are dismissed."

* * *

Within days, the Petrine Office declared the extraordinary meeting, exactly as proposed by Sylvester. The order was delivered to all Christian congregations of all denominations, in dialogue or estranged, attached or unattached to the Latin church.

And they came.

The heavy wooden conference table, polished to a mirror-like finish, was positioned at the front of the room inside the Apostolic Palace. The rest of the hall was divided into rows of chairs to accommodate the large audience. Despite the lofty ceiling and great size of the meeting hall, it felt crowded and close.

At the head of the table sat Sylvester III, engaged in conversation with the adjacent attendees. A phalanx of pages waited a few steps behind the Pope, ready to answer his requests. To his left and right sat the most senior members of the College of Cardinals and other senior members of the Curia. Occupying the rest of the room were the various heads of the Curial councils and dicasteries, as well as representatives of the Western Latin rite churches and the Eastern and Orthodox Dioceses, attending as ex-officio members. Among them sat the Superiors General of the Jesuit, Franciscan and Dominican orders, as well as representatives of the Anglican, Lutheran, Reformed Church, Methodist, Disciples of Christ, and Baptist churches and the presidents of various Episcopal Conferences. Also, as had been the case in prior councils of this scope, a smattering of well-known theologians and laypeople were in attendance.

Cardinal Lorenzo Bruni, Vatican Secretary of State and Head of the Secretariat stood and ordered quiet in the room. He was technically the number two person in the Vatican hierarchy but in practical terms competed for power with Tatian in continuous and intricate ways.

"The conference will now begin. If I may ask for your attention."

The room quieted, as pages circulated about and whispered the order into the ears of the inattentive.

Sylvester accepted his reading glasses from a page and began to read from a prepared statement. "In regard to our common problem and our urgent need for collaboration, the questions before us are these. How may we respond to the accusations and claims made by Mr. Yordon Antropos? How do we prove him to be the transgressor of the true faith? How do we reclaim for the people the conviction that we are the legitimate representatives of God's will? We must seek to discover concrete ways in which we may respond, so as to save the Abrahamic faiths of the world."

"Your Holiness, surely the members of our churches will return to us if you simply present yourself before them and counter this madman's claims. You are the Pope!" offered Cardinal Broneri in a trembling, thickly accented voice. He nearly 80 years of age and easily agitated.

The Patriarch Bartholomaios, solemnly expressed his agreement. "*Kalá.* All we, as sister churches and brothers in ecumenism, have to do is echo your fundamental rebuttal of this man, Antropos. If we speak with one voice, the people will listen."

Many of the attendees murmured their agreement.

"Ha! We can barely agree on the day of the month and you want to agree on an official statement against this Antropos?" laughed the most Reverend Helmut Gerhard, a normally somewhat severe man.

"It may not be enough, anyway," interjected Shaughnessy, who had been invited as part of the American delegation. "In the United States, we've been battling dwindling congregations and revisionism for most of the 20th century. A merely verbal response will fall on deaf ears."

"Shaughnessy is right," said Cardinal Campos, the Sostituto, presiding over General Affairs at the Vatican. "Antropos is offering something intoxicating to his followers. Something different than the canonical text. Something they find personal and exciting. And he's articulate."

221

Bruni answered disdainfully. "What he preaches is so much offal. He talks in mysteries and cabalisms. Yordon merely speaks words spun into riddles, with no practical basis. For this reason, our response must be more than words."

"Well, if not words, then what? Do you expect us to dance before the doubting crowds?" retorted another Cardinal.

Cardinal Delpretti asked for permission to speak, though no one else had paid homage to the old customs so far, and after Sylvester recognized his request, he spoke in the most respectful and cordial voice he could muster.

"Supreme Father, perhaps the correct response is to ignore Mr. Antropos. Are we over-reacting? Are we too accustomed to our elected and anointed positions to accept a challenge to our legitimacy? This too, will pass, in my opinion, Holiness."

"That would be a grave mistake!" exclaimed Bruni, his voice echoing against the lacquered walls of the vast chamber. "We are talking about the most serious challenge to our legitimacy since the Reformation! How can it be wrong to defend ourselves?"

Several others in the room also voiced their protests, while other expressed agreement with Delpretti. Arguments sprouted up along the length of the room.

"Gentlemen, gentlemen. Let there be order in this hall!" yelled Sylvester. The Pope raising his voice was enough to draw everyone's attention. Order was restored, though not without a small amount of grumbling.

Sylvester regained his composure and spoke forcefully. "This is not a matter of calculation or convenience. We collaborate for our survival! For the sake of Christ! Given this, our efforts must be selfless and unprecedented; decisive and daring. In this room we shall decide the future of *all* the Abrahamic faiths, for they all believe in one God and in the Savior's return."

There was respectful silence. Many exchanged glances.

A voice from the back of the room. "Holiness, what then shall be the manner of our collaboration, if it is not words in denunciation of Antropos?" It was Cardinal Chowdhury, the Patriarch of the Malankar congregation of India.

Sylvester stood up and planted his outstretched arms, palms down, on the table. Leaning forward, like a military conspirator, he said, "We shall release a denunciation in due course, my friend. This is to be expected. But what is not expected is that we shall do more than that."

Tatian, who had enjoyed watching his peers and adversaries spar over the matter, raised an eyebrow at this. *What was Sylvester getting at?*

"*Santissimo Padre*, perhaps you could explain?" he asked unctuously.

Sylvester barely let him finish. "We must not merely denounce the pretender, but rather, we must *demonstrate* his illegitimacy beyond all doubt."

"He performs miracles and heals the sick," said Bishop Malcolm Ender of the Lutheran World Federation. "How will we disprove that?"

"The Roman Catholic Church has miracles too, and we will use them when we need them."

Tatian locked eyes with Sylvester. *What was this?*

Sylvester stared back opaquely.

"But ours is not a faith of spectacles, Brother Ender. I am proposing that we seek an alliance with selected governments and scientific bodies of the world to form a special task force whose assignment shall be the investigation of the true nature of Yordon Antropos, with the aim of discrediting this man and ultimately *disarming* him of his influence. In this manner, we will *defeat* him."

"An alliance with governments? Even with armies?" gasped Broneri. A page moved closer to him.

"Common practice in prior centuries," said Tatian dryly. "The church routinely involved itself in matters corporeal at one time."

"To the detriment of the purity of the Holy Office!" answered Broneri. "It took centuries to overcome such practices!"

"And it's exactly what Antropos accuses us of having done to the faith to corrupt it," warned Manzanero.

Sylvester interjected again, "Nonetheless, I fear there will be no church at all if we do not actively *defend* it. And this time, that means an offense."

* * *

Despite Sylvester's insistence on quick action, it took three weeks of debate and deliberation over the wording and content, before the Emergency Synod released its proclamation.

In an auditorium filled with the mitered ranks of the world's bishops, Sylvester read the Ex-Cathedra Declaration himself. In the document, Sylvester reinforced Bartholomaios' excommunication of Yordon by also excommunicating Yordon from the Christian faiths of all rites. Furthermore, any Christian known to have dealings with Yordon would also be subject to instantaneous excommunication.

The reaction of the world was, for the most part, sanguine in the West, which was distracted by events of a more geo-political nature, and antithetic in the East, which had gone over to Yordon's camp en masse in the last few months, with the notable exception of Israel. Large parts of the Middle East and the Asian Steppes were under Yordon's control now, but Jerusalem remained in the hands of the beleaguered Avrahami Administration.

* * *

"Archbishop Paoli is on the line, Prefect," said Cardinal Meinl, who was Tatian's Undersecretary of Doctrine, after reading the slip of paper that had been passed to him by one of the staff. Tatian had been in private conference with his fellow Superiors when the call came in.

"Put the Nuncio through to the white phone in the alcove," answered Tatian.

Meinl waited for the staff person to leave the small meeting room. As soon as the door clicked shut he asked, "Why does the Apartment want the American government involved in this? That's very unusual."

"So is the situation, Cardinal Meinl. Unusual methods are required. Now is a time for you to take a firm grip on your faith and follow orders without questioning their motive."

"As you are doing, Prefect?" retorted Meinl silkily. He always had been ambitious.

Tatian only glared back, then went to take the telephone call.

Folding his long frame into the stiff chair that was positioned by the telephone, he picked up the receiver. "This is Tatian."

"Ah, Prefect. I have news for his Holiness," said Paoli's voice.

"Good news, I take it?"

"Indeed. I have made overtures to President Clement as to the recent Vatican proceedings and I'm happy to report that he is receptive, as we had surmised he would be."

"Excellent."

"He proposes a secret meeting."

"His Holiness cannot travel easily at this time."

"I know this." A bit of iron in the normally obsequious pro-nuncio's voice.

Tatian let his answer be silence. Long ago he had learned what kind of claw silence could be in a verbal exchange.

Paoli continued, "I have proposed Gandolfo."

Tatian smiled to himself. "Very good, Giovanni. Excellent. The Pope will be able to move easily and secretly. I shall convey your idea to the Pope and, following his approval, we can begin to make the arrangements."

Sea of Galilee, Israel

It was approaching dusk by the western shore of the Sea of Galilee. The day's alarming heat was breathing a cool sigh of relief at last. A light breeze blew off the lake. They were a few miles outside of Tiberias, the lake's ostensible capital. All around them, their followers had set up camps and were busy preparing the evening meal. Nearby, a wooden craft made shore and was quickly met by fishermen, who helped the boat's crew unload dripping nets of fish. Incongruously, water skiers and windsurfers, basked in peachy sunlight, glided on the water's surface in the distance, closer to the town.

Mary closed her eyes and breathed the Summer air. She felt relaxed. She lazily thought back to her journey across the ocean by plane to Israel, and then once reunited with Yordon in Israel, on foot and by jeep, in his company. From the desert in the south to the plains in between to the lovely, hilly greenery of this northernmost section of Israel, Yordon had traveled and she had followed, and in that process, their searching souls had become intimate. She could hardly believe it.

Watching him talking to a knot of followers, touching a sick child, taking crutches from an old man, Mary fought down a thrill. *He could be the real thing.* This is what she had been looking for all her life; something that transgressed the parade of sycophants and pretenders that had beguiled her existence. Something that gave it all meaning. And yet, Yordon also attracted an element of miscreants and malcontents, a growing current of former rebels and insurgents from around the neighboring countries subdued by his powerful words and miracle acts. She wondered where all this was leading.

"You're happy," observed Yordon, looking down at her as he neared her.

She snapped out of her reverie and blushed a little.

"Happier than I have ever been."

Yordon bent at the knees and joined her, allowing her to lean back into the cradle of his arms. Some members of the throng stepped toward the couple but Yordon, showing a flash of impatience, waved them away. Finally alone, even if it was by dictate, they sat quietly together, enjoying the evening. Silently, Mary wondered at Yordon's ideas. They knifed through the skin of one's beliefs and penetrated into a dark and fundamental water. She sensed that the cognition that waited there was corrosive; that it would burn away all that she was and all that she knew and leave an altogether different woman standing in her place, were she to gain it. Was this what had happened, what was still happening to Yordon?

She looked up at Yordon, "You are my Savior."

"You were already saved, Mary."

"I don't understand."

"You were already the kind of person God wants us all to be. Open, searching. You are my example to others. You are my *validation*, Mary." He smiled then. "And you saved me too."

She shook her head, feeling discomfort at the role he wished to put on her.

Before he could continue, someone yelled his name in the distance. He turned to face the valley behind them and the setting sun. His unblinking eyes gleamed as he gazed at the field of people below, spreading into the foothills.

Mary guessed at his thoughts. "What are you going to do with all these people, Yordon?"

He turned to her. "What I must do. Make them like you. Aware. Enlightened. Then I will send them everywhere. Until the world is one."

She realized he was different from the man she had met in D.C., or perhaps it was that she had merely gained more insight into his personality. Despite his

227

pacifying words and show of confidence, she saw how much he was in conflict with himself, as if he was of two minds, one human and one of another species altogether.

He was a like a God; commanding an army of devoted followers and performing miracles, healing the sick, turning fallow into fertile. But he was also a man; a terribly confounded man who was in the thrall of greater forces. She could see that he was at times uncomfortable with the authority he commanded, with the press of expectation that surrounded him, and yet he was somehow driven forward, almost against his will. She had watched him suffer the inner voices he talked about and seen him struggle to control the spirits within him. Like a man possessed. She could feel in his embraces how much he needed her to acknowledge his essential humanity, to keep him anchored to the mortal plain.

She followed Yordon's gaze and saw Philo. His portly form was making its way through the crowds as he headed toward them.

He arrived breathless and excited. But it wasn't a happy exhilaration.

"I have news from Nazareth," panted Philo, wiping his brow with a rag.

"Tell me," said Yordon. He looked northward. He seemed to know what was coming.

"Pope Sylvester has issued a formal declaration against you, Yordon. He has denounced you as a false prophet. The declaration says that any Christians who follow you will be excommunicated from the Church and damned in the eyes of God for all time."

"I see."

Philo clutched at the rag, shaken by the gravity of the words he had delivered, and waited. Clearly, he had more news to deliver.

Yordon reached out and touched Philo's arm. "Be calm, old friend. Go on."

Philo took a deep breath and continued, "He is also conferring with the American President and European leaders about more actions against you. It's going to be in tomorrow's newspapers!"

To Philo and Mary's mutual surprise, Yordon laughed at this. They stared.

Yordon contained himself. "The first part of your message, Philo, is nothing. It is the sound of a balloon letting out its last indignant gasps of air. The second part, however, is of some consequence."

"I think this is so," agreed Philo, worriedly.

"We must prepare for it."

"What will you do?" asked Mary.

"What we must do," proclaimed Yordon. "We must bring the battle to them. We must go to Europe."

"But why, Yordon?" protested Mary. "You'll be apprehended."

"You'll disappear," said Philo grimly.

"And if I stay here and allow the Vatican its alliances? If I do nothing?"

"You can do much without leaving here. As you have done so far," said Philo.

Yordon answered, "The stakes are higher now, Philo. And we've reached the limits of what we can do from here. As we did back in Hellas."

They locked eyes, remembering. After a moment's pause, Philo nodded reluctantly. Mary looked from one to the other. She didn't understand.

"What are you talking about? What about your followers?"

"Those who can follow me, will. The rest will follow my words still."

"And what will we do in Europe? It's not like here. It's not as... elemental," said Mary, doubt catching her voice as she spoke. "Where will we go?"

"We will go to Italy, Mary. Rome, of course. To the pretender's lair. The Vatican," answered Yordon simply.

"And then what?" protested Mary.

Yordon's eyes glowed with intent. "We will destroy it."

Her face paled. "Why?"

"Because I must. The icons of the old order must come down."

Mary and Philo glanced at each other.

Mary spoke again. "You're talking about the Vatican. Think of the art and history that's stored there."

Yordon's eyes flashed impatience. "It's irrelevant."

Mary's voice betrayed her skepticism. "What's happening to you? You're changing. Don't you see it?" She swept her arm across the valley. "Do you think these people will just accept acts of violence in your name?"

For a moment, a veil of doubt fluttered across Yordon's face, and he looked at Mary, reaching out to touch her. She inched her arm away. Philo raised an eyebrow at this.

Yordon breathed a sigh and his face became stone. "But they will, Mary."

Her mouth dropped open and shut again. She realized he was right. The Middle East had been a hotbed of fanaticism for decades - long before they had ever heard of Yordon. And while he had quieted the unrest typical of the region with his words and miracles, he was, in fact, a match poised to ignite them again. She glared at him angrily but could not hold the stare against his unblinking expression.

"It's wrong! I can't be part of this!" She got up and stormed off.

"But you will be," answered Yordon sadly, softly, though she did not hear his response.

"'He that sows the wind reaps the whirlwind'," said Philo. "Is it really necessary to do such a thing?"

"You must believe it, Philo."

"It is difficult." said Philo and turned to leave.

Yordon regarded Philo's back as he walked away, then whispered to no one in particular, "For me, most of all, old friend."

Chapter Eight: The Papal Task Force

Castel Gandolfo, Vatican City, August 2020

"We're talking about the faith of 60 million Catholics in America alone!" shouted Clement, forgetting himself.

Admiral James "Javelin" Farrow squirmed slightly in his chair. To him the issue was strictly geo-political and he believed the President should stay similarly focused, but Clement swung hard to the right on matters religious.

"But the country has no defense agreement with the Vatican, sir," he said.

"And yet, here we are in Castel Gandolfo," quipped Max Ravessi, casting a look at the ornate appointments of the Salon room in which they sat waiting. He tapped ashes into an ashtray.

"The situation does have political implications for all of us." It was Mervyn Goss, the Deputy Minister of Foreign Affairs, European Union, and a Senior member of the Council of Europe. The American delegation had been surprised to see him there but also impressed. He had similarly been impressed with the presence of the American President. Normally the Vice President would have attended such an affair.

Robert Raith, the U.S. Ambassador to the Vatican, was also present and agreed with Goss. "What Herr Goss says is true."

"I would say Mr. Antropos is more dangerous than any terrorist threat," replied Goss evenly.

"He's one step away from controlling all of the Middle East Nations," observed Ravessi. "And if he controls the Middle East…"

"He controls the flow of Middle Eastern oil," said Farrow. They were right, and Clement needed to hear this. Looking directly at Ravessi, hoping the man would utter the clinching remark, he added, "And if he controls the oil…"

"He controls the world," finished Ravessi.

Farrow tried not to smile.

Clement looked at each of them in turn and slowly sat back in his seat. "What the hell. And he's very close to achieving this, isn't he, without so much as raising a sword!"

"At least not yet, sir," said Farrow.

"Clearly, he must be contained," said Goss with waxy calm.

"At all costs," agreed Raith.

"Danged right," exclaimed Clement. "Our robe wearing friend could topple the global status quo!"

Farrow scanned the room, taking note of the vast power controlled by those present. And yet they found themselves on the defensive. How did it happen so quickly?

Just then, the doors to the side of the room opened and the Papal entourage entered. Sylvester, wearing a plain cassock, was followed by Tatian and Bruni, and the Chamberlain, Cardinal Dvorni, who stepped forward to make introductions where they were needed.

Once they were all seated, Sylvester signaled to one of the household pages to distribute folios emblazoned with the papal seal to all the attendees. As they all sat and opened their folios, Sylvester spoke.

"Welcome to all. We are here today to discuss Yordon Antropos and to seek common cause. We of the Catholic faith seek to expose Yordon Antropos as a false messenger and break his hold over his followers. He is a grave threat to the sanctity of God's word. For some of you the Word of God may not be what is threatened by his actions, it may be your nationhood, your economics, your political base, but the goal is the same nonetheless. We must relinquish our own subjective views and pursue the common goal. "Sylvester opened his own copy of the folio and continued, "What you have in your hands is a proposal to establish a multi-disciplinary task force to investigate the background and abilities of Mr. Antropos with the goal of exposing and destroying him."

Sylvester cast a glance at Cardinal Bruni.

Bruni took his cue, "The Sostituto has put together a package of dossiers of people whom we consider to be good candidates for the task force. Please review these."

Sylvester added, "We've secured a villa on the outskirts of Rome which will serve as their meeting place and laboratory."

"A lab?" asked Clement, leafing through the photographs and resumes.

"Yes," said Tatian. "There are several scientists among the proposed personnel."

Sylvester added, "I propose a team of experts in a variety of scientific disciplines, as well as representatives of nations, theologians, intelligence agencies and international military leaders."

"That would be unprecedented, and difficult to coordinate," said Ravessi doubtfully.

"I am intrigued that you would turn to the sciences to help solve your problem," said Goss.

"Herr Goss, the light of reason and the light of revelation both emanate from a single source." responded the Pontiff levelly.

Clement read through the dossiers, "You've got a geneticist here."

Bruni answered him, "Doctor Dolores Arbolera, Mr. President. She's a member of the Pontifical Academy of Sciences."

"She teaches at the National Institute of Health in Bethesda, sir," added Farrow. "I recognize the name from some of our own short lists. She's one of the best."

"You've also got Yoon Sun Deng, from M.I.T."

"The physicist," answered Bruni. "He too, is a member of the Academy and will pursue the investigation with Christian perspectives in mind."

"This is a formidable list," noted the Admiral. I didn't realize the Vatican had such people at its disposal."

"We have a great many resources," responded Sylvester with a small smile that did not escape Tatian's notice.

Israeli Crisis Center, Jerusalem

There was a knock on the door of the Israeli Prime Minister's emergency office, inside the Crisis Center many levels below the ground.

Natan Silver opened it. An aide waited outside.

"Sir, we have a call from one of our operatives."

"We'll take it in here."

The aide nodded and hurried off to transfer the call.

The red light on the phone began to flash. Avrahami picked it up.

"Yes. Go on."

The Prime Minister listened for a few minutes. His face was quicksilver as it responded to the information being whispered into his ear. After a few minutes he hung up the phone carefully. His hand shook slightly.

"Who was it?" asked Silver from the chair opposite the desk.

"Ravessi."

Gulf of Taranto, Italy

The trawler laid anchor off the coast of the Gulf of Taranto, between the heel and the toe of the Italian peninsula.

Yordon and his followers lowered ropes off the side of the ship and boarded the skiffs that waited on the water below.

Mary looked around at the bobbing ships on the water – a mix of pleasure craft and small fishing vessels. It looked innocent enough, but she knew that hidden among the population of ships, were many who had made this journey across the Mediterranean in the wake of Yordon.

"Come, Mary." It was Philo. He offered his hand, which she accepted as she climbed down into the smaller craft.

"I've never thought I would make it to Italy," she said distractedly, as she alighted.

Philo snorted a laugh. "*Kalá.* I know what you are feeling. I've traveled more in the last year than I have in my entire life."

"Where do you think this will end?" she wondered at Philo, seeing Yordon's skiff several meters ahead, well on its way to making shore.

"It ends at the end, where else?"

She stared back silently.

Philo motioned at Yordon with his chin.

"Mary. Look at Yordon."

She looked, but saw nothing unusual. Yordon was at the shore helping people step off neighboring boats.

"He no longer blinks," said Philo in a hoarse rasp.

"What?"

He cleared his throat. "I have been watching him, wondering what it is about him that has been giving me such a feeling of dread."

"You mean other than his increasingly erratic behavior?" Mary answered with a snort.

Philo nodded, closing his eyes in acknowledgement of her concern. He realized there was a growing feeling of allegiance with this woman. Shaking off the momentary reverie, he pressed on with his point, "I finally realized it in Galilee. I do not know for how long he has been like that, but now that I have noticed it, I cannot stop. It's his eyes. It's…"

"It's inhuman."

"Yes," he stared at her, blinking rapidly, in an unintentionally comical counterpoint of Yordon. Finally he sighed and motioned for her to sit. The men assigned to row began to work the paddles and the boat glided toward the rocks.

Downtown Washington D.C

The bedside telephone rang, waking Thomas. For a moment he didn't know where he was. He expected to be in his room back at Holy Name but there were two large beds in the room, instead of his single bed, and there was a large, flat screen color TV, flashing news images at him as he blinked, rather than his tiny portable. He remembered he was in a D.C. hotel. He had done it again – an entire night watching mass demonstrations and violence erupt on the screen before him. All of it because of Yordon. The ringing was insistent. He rose and picked up the handset. Before he could croak a greeting, a merry voice warbled out of the handset speaker.

"Hello, Thomas? Good morning!"

"Jake?"

"Very good, my firebrand cleric!" laughed Shaughnessy.

Thomas rubbed at his eyes and face, forcing back alertness. Jake was back from Rome. The Synod. He was calling. He wanted something. Thomas waited, listening to Shaughnessy's breathing across the miles.

"Sylvester wants to speak with you," continued Shaughnessy, "I am to arrange a meeting between you and His Holiness."

Thomas took a deep breath. "In Rome?"

"Right again."

Immediately following the Synod. "Sounds ominous," said Thomas. "Exactly what's expected of me?"

"Participation in a special project."

"But I'm assigned to the White House."

"Not anymore."

Thomas sighed. "Are you going to tell me anything else?"

"I can't."

Thomas suppressed his impatience. "Cardinal Shaughnessy, I wish you would."

"Thomas, I know it's unsettling to be yanked from place to place on the merest threads of information, but the situation demands that you answer the call. You are needed. Think of it as an honor. You're considered a very important part of Sylvester's plan."

"So you know the plan."

A pause. "I do. What Sylvester will ask of you will be difficult, that's all I can say. My prayers are with you."

"When do I leave?"

"Tonight. Your tickets are waiting at the concierge desk."

St. Peter's Square, Vatican City

Thomas crossed the great flatness of St. Peter's Square, that place of statues and water fountains, passing the distinctive obelisk, and admired the two curved expanses of roofed columns that embraced the square, the Bernini colonnades; built around the same time as the new Basilica.

Thomas recalled that the columns were said to represent the sheltering arms of the Church. He felt appreciation for that image. The stone walls and columns gave an impression of permanence and solidity. The Vatican was a rock, as it must always have been through the dark and terrible centuries, despite external and internal attacks on its infallibility.

There were few tourists about, unlike his younger days when he had studied here. He recalled those warmer, easier times -- lines of visitors waiting in interminable, winding lines for entrance into St. Peter's, squinting in the bright sunlight, taking endless photographs of the surrounding structures and of each other, sitting at the cool bases of the closely packed columns, or watching the world go by as they nibbled at cherries sold by any of the numerous vendors about in the square. Now the passersby were largely the employees and clerical staff of the city state, moving languidly as they went about their business. The place had an air of sadness.

Arriving at the other side of the square, Thomas passed the Leonine Walls and went through the Gate of St. Anne into Vatican City, where no tourists were allowed. He was asked for his pass by three different Swiss guards as he made his way into the Apostolic Palace and upstairs to the third floor where several meeting rooms and the Papal Apartments were found.

The Prefect of the Papal Household, Bishop Cerrano, met him. They exchanged greetings politely and he was escorted by a younger cleric to one of the ornate meeting rooms, which was reserved for the Pope's private audiences.

They left him waiting a long time. Thomas went to the windows. He opened one of the panes and let in the hot summer air. As Thomas watched the blue and yellow clad Swiss Guard go about their daily exercises with slow, poetic precision, he let the sun drenched ambience of Rome well up within him. He sighed, relaxing a bit, and reminded himself that this was merely the *bella figura* – the way of doing things here. The world crisis receded in his mind.

In Italy, crisis was an everyday affair. The government dissolved and was reformed, strikes paralyzed the country routinely, telephones stopped working, mail did not get delivered for weeks sometimes months, scandal spilled its ink on the front pages of the national papers with regularity, but Rome and the day to day life of its population went somberly on. Part of it was the fact that Rome had been the capital of an ancient empire and the seat of Popes through the centuries. The ancient ruins surrounded them. The history was steeped into the ground. It gave a sense that this was the unmovable center of the world and all else was the periphery.

The clocks in the room ticked woodenly in syncopated, near precision. The rhythm carried Thomas into his own thoughts. *To believe or not believe.* He recalled one of his most cherished books, Pascal's *Pensees*, perhaps that mathematician's most famous and deeply personal work -- a treatise on human suffering and faith in God -- and its much quoted idea, Pascal's Wager. It was elemental. A game of odds from the master of probability. Belief in God is rational. If you believed in God and in the end you were proven right, you would be vindicated and paradise would be at your feet. You would gain everything. And if it turned out you were wrong you would lose nothing. The only injustice was that if you were right in believing that there was no heaven, no after life, no souls to be saved, your victory would be pyrrhic, for there would be no awareness of victory in such an end. Only dust and death.

It had always been easy to resolve his belief in God in times of doubt -- which had been many -- by reminding himself of this simple tenet. But now it was more complicated. The essential cowardice of that position was exposed. Suddenly his faith was revealed to have a Janus face. One side known and safe, the other dark and threatening, its true nature unknown.

Perhaps it was safer to believe in Yordon. His teachings were not far from Thomas' own views of Christianity. The Church *was* a bureaucracy. People didn't really have an understanding of Christ's teachings, only their volumes of canned dogma. It was safer that way. No, that wasn't the reason for believing in the Church. Faith shouldn't be safe. Faith implied strength. Faith implied courage. Faith implied danger.

And the Catholic Church was in danger now. This was the time to prove the veracity of his word, his essential integrity! He was a man of the cloth! A life of celibacy and devotion to the teachings of Christ had been his promise to God and to the Pope.

But now there was Yordon.

The white double doors suddenly swung open to reveal Pope Sylvester III, accompanied by the silkily patrician Cardinal Tatian. Sylvester's face became a warm smile upon seeing Thomas. Tatian's was a firmly worn mask. Thomas approached the pontiff and knelt to kiss his ring. As soon as Thomas had completed this gesture, Sylvester clasped his hands around Thomas' hands and pulled him to an upright position.

"Welcome to Rome, Father Prisciotti." said the Pontiff, warmly.

"Greetings, Father." said Cardinal Tatian with practiced solemnity, "It is my humble pleasure to meet you at last."

Thomas bowed his head slightly to both of his hosts in return, "I'm honored to be invited."

"And, no doubt, you are burning to know why you are here," continued Sylvester, with a glint in his eye.

Thomas smiled. He liked Sylvester. He nodded.

Sylvester gestured to Thomas to sit at one of the plushly upholstered Rococo chairs and then moved to sit in its nearest twin. Tatian followed suit. Once they were all seated, Sylvester turned toward Thomas and began to speak in a low, urgent tone.

"The Synod was only the beginning of our response to Mr. Antropos."

"Your denouncement of him was forceful and eloquent," Thomas replied.

"It was expected of us," answered Sylvester curtly.

Thomas took a chance, "But you're not done."

Sylvester responded instantly. "Should we be? Its effect was limited. Yordon still travels freely and still commands an army."

Thomas brooded over this. "I've heard rumors that Yordon's army, if it can be called that, is on its way here."

"Yes, we have also heard this from our contacts in Jerusalem," added Tatian, as he rubbed at a ring on his finger.

"What do you think his intentions are?" asked Thomas.

Sylvester answered, "Thomas, I fear to know what may come, but I know what we must do. We must retake the minds of our people if we are to avoid a calamity. We must consider unusual actions."

Thomas stared at both of his superiors, wondering what to make of this. Sylvester looked determined. Tatian merely returned Thomas' regard with an impassive mien.

"You have a plan."

Sylvester's eyes shone. "Exactly, Thomas. We have a plan, as you say. Consider this, my son. Our age is a time of scientific and technological discoveries rather than an era of saints. Yet despite all our marvels and luxuries, the human race finds itself starved. A man without a soul is not much more than an animated husk, and our flock senses this, I believe. So they grasp at any sign of guidance."

"It's a dangerous time, filled with dangerous ideas," added Tatian.

Sylvester nodded, glancing at Tatian briefly. "And Yordon Antropos has seduced his followers with such ideas. Words strung together to imply insight and profundity, but they are deceptions."

"But what of the miracles? It's not *just* words. What is he then? A devil?" asked Thomas as evenly as he could.

Tatian shifted in his chair upon hearing this. Sylvester's eyes danced in his head as he considered this. Eventually, he took a deep breath and sank back into his chair. He sighed.

"No, I think I would sense that, dear Thomas. Yordon is not a thing of that nature. But he is also not the Savior."

"Agreed," said Thomas.

"There are no saviors."

"Perhaps not. At least not yet."

"There are only saints."

Thomas cocked his head slightly, looking at both of his hosts in turn. "Meaning?"

"People like you, my son," the Pope responded, "People who are guiding lights. People who are the bedrock of our church even without the church there to defend them. People who are Christians even in the absence of Christianity. I am not talking about the self-righteous defenders of dogma and tradition."

Thomas willed himself hard to not look at Cardinal Tatian right at that moment.

"I am talking about men of enkindled spirit," continued the Pontiff.

Thomas narrowed his eyes at the Pope. He didn't like being cast in this light. Sylvester sat up again and looked him closely in the eye.

"The Church needs you, Thomas, more than it has ever needed any of its spokesmen."

Thomas closed his eyes. It was as he feared. He feared this. He steadied himself.

"What exactly do you expect of me, Holiness?"

Sylvester rose from his chair. He went to a table by the double doors and returned with several folders. One folder was marked with the seal of the Fisherman's Ring, which the Pope offered to Thomas. Thomas felt the weight and texture of the thick, cream colored stock, on which was imprinted the crown and two crossed keys insignia of the papacy. A purple ribbon was wrapped around it, fastened into place with a red wax seal of the papal ring.

Sylvester spoke, "I am giving you a special assignment. It is the most secret conclusion of the Emergency Synod. Inside this folder you will find a chirograph, written in my own hand, in which the details are explained."

Thomas looked at the Pope as if he had just spoken in tongues. Sylvester ignored his expression of amazement and went on.

"In short, a select group of individuals with unique experience are to set forth on a mission of research and discovery. You are to work with the other members of this Papal Task Force as the Vatican's Apostolic Delegate, and you are to help them find out the true nature of the creature Yordon and determine a way to discredit and if necessary, destroy him."

"To destroy him?" echoed Thomas, dumbfoundedly.

"The future of the Catholic Church and, indeed, the order of the world itself are at stake, my son. This assignment is given to you with maximum gravity."

"But how will I do this? I can't kill."

"You cannot take a life and yet you must find a way to end this creature's rampage. Combine your insights and inspiration with the special knowledge of this team…"

Thomas blurted out, "You once said to me that you can't force inspiration, and now you've given me no choice."

"The time for choices is finished, Thomas. And you are already inspired. You always have been. Since your time at the Gregorian University, the Vatican has watched you and known of you. I myself remember you as a student living at the North American College. You kept to yourself, and yet I recall that people still sought you out for your ideas. But your ideas were too radical, too disruptive for the times and the people in power. Ironically, now that everything is so profoundly disrupted, it is you who whom I choose to be our spokesman."

"But why? Why me?"

"Because this is the time that you have always been waiting for, Thomas. The moment is undefined, and you are in a sense, undefined as well. In finding the answer to our dilemma perhaps you may find the answers to your lifelong questions, and I believe this will give you the strength to prevail."

"You really believe that?"

Sylvester nodded gravely. Thomas was stunned to realize that the Pontiff knew him far more deeply than Thomas had ever suspected.

"You may leave us now, my son. Examine the documents I have bestowed upon you carefully and consider your assignment with utmost seriousness. We are counting on you. *Vai con Dio*."

After Thomas had made leave of his hosts, Tatian turned to Sylvester. "He's an interesting young man, your Holiness. Earnest, intelligent, charismatic, dark." He laughed abruptly, "A good choice."

243

"Despite his unorthodoxies?" asked Sylvester with an upturn of one eyebrow.

"Indeed," grunted Tatian.

"And do you think he possesses the spirit we require?"

Tatian answered curtly, "He will perform to the best of his abilities, Holiness. Of this I have no doubt."

"Yes, to the best of his abilities," Sylvester answered with a sadness that Tatian did not expect.

Somewhere along the Tiber riverbank, Rome

After his meeting with Sylvester, Thomas was allowed to leave the Palace until the time the other members of the group were expected to arrive. He decided to take the opportunity to wander around the city a bit and visit his old haunts. Eventually he found himself by the river. It had become dark.

He found a bench and sat. He broke the seal of the Papal folder and examined the documents and photographs within. Thomas read the roster and was both surprised and relieved to find Karin and Jobson there. It made sense. The three of them were among the few people who had the combined characteristics of significant exposure to Yordon, and strong theological or scientific grounding.

No doubt, the Pope expected him to play a big part in persuading them to join. Thomas began to see the wisdom of the Pope's choice of himself for the role of Apostolic Delegate. Sylvester gained not one, but three powerful researchers by co-opting Thomas.

Thomas wondered how they would fare working in partnership with the other members of the so called Papal Task Force. There were the members of the American government: Admiral Farrow and Max Ravessi – now there was an interesting counterbalance; perhaps President Clement had some subtlety to him after all, and Mervyn Goss, representing the European Union. Politics would play a part in their group stratagems. Thomas hoped it wouldn't be a hindrance. But these men could give them access to vast resources. There was also Yoon Sun Deng of M.I.T., and the geneticist, Dolores Arbolera. Could a divine being be examined under a microscope? – if Yordon was that. He closed the folder.

Things were happening too fast. There was much to think about. Much to clarify in his mind. What was his place in this group -- this group whose intent was to destroy Yordon? *Am I on the right side?*

He kicked a pebble into the dark, oily water and he heard it sink with a thick *plunk* sound, swallowed by the depths. He wondered if that was to be his fate as well.

As he mused in endless inward spirals, the encroaching darkness and the jet lag from the flight worked in concert and he found himself dozing off, like a retired cleric on a bench between bird feedings.

In what seemed to be only a few moments later, the temperature of the air dropped noticeably, and Thomas involuntarily rubbed at his arms. He scanned the walkways on both sides of the dark waters of the Tiber and saw no one. Then, a voice spoke from slightly behind his right ear. He jumped off the bench and whirled.

Standing on the other side of bench, dressed in Roman robes, stood a man of some 50 years. He had a deeply lined face which was framed by graying curly locks, though the top of his scalp was balding. The face contorted into a smile for Thomas. Thomas found himself smiling back. This person, strange as he seemed, exuded a sense of comfort and congeniality. He was also slightly translucent.

In a gravelly voice, heavily laced with a nuanced Italian accent, the stranger spoke to Thomas. He spoke in medieval Latin.

"*Salutem dicit*, Pater Prisciotti. Don't be afraid. I am pleased to make your acquaintance."

"You know my name," croaked Thomas, fascinated, responding haltingly in Latin as well.

"*Certo, certo,*" said the stranger, a bit impatiently.

"You have me at a disadvantage."

The stranger bowed his head slightly. "I am, or I was, called Sabellius."

Thomas' mind tingled at the mention of that name. He knew that name. *Who was that?*

The man looked at himself, in response to Thomas' gaze. "You think I am dressed strangely?"

"No, I mean yes, but it's not that."

Sabellius smiled indulgently. "Ahh, you recognize my name, but you can't quite place it, is that it? Let me help you. I am a Christian. Or, at least I was a Christian before Dionysus condemned me as a heretic. Now I am just dead."

"Dionysus? The third century Pope?" Thomas remembered the significance of the apparition's name.

Sabellius grinned, nodding. "Hmm, so this is the future." Sabellius turned to view the lights of Rome. He sighed contentedly, "So the *Caput Mundi* survives. And what of those lights! Like a million, blazing candles. Miraculous!", he paused, wrinkling his nose, "But the smell of this place. Is it Oleum?"

"You're smelling petrol. We have cars. Let me explain."

"Don't bother. It isn't important. My appearance before you tonight is. Have you recognized me yet?"

Thomas nodded as the historical facts coalesced in his mind. "You are remembered because you famously declared that the Father, Son and Holy Ghost of the Christian Holy Trinity were not distinct divine persons but three different manifestations of the one God. You and your followers were promptly condemned and expelled from the Church."

"Exactly. Impressive. I was right you, know. I know that now. But not exactly right."

Thomas' adrenaline juiced into his veins as he listened. What was this ghost saying? Was he a messenger? Was this a trick? He looked around the embankments again for signs of equipment or other people. There was no one save Sabellius, himself, and the evening mists.

Sabellius waited patiently for Thomas to settle himself. He looked curiously upwards at a passing passenger jet, as it lazily arced a path across the dome of the sky, and smiled in wonder.

Thomas asked, "What wasn't exactly right, Sabellius? Is that what you're here to tell me?"

Sabellius laughed at this. "It's tragic, really. Our obsession to try and understand the unknowable. How can we explain infinity with mere words? How can we grasp the unendurable knowledge of existence with only our flesh bound brains? God exists, my troubled friend. But he exists in many forms, often exercising their own volition, even as they are one; the *anima mundi*. And yet there is no one you can call the God. There is nothing and that nothing is the source of everything. But already I am entangled in my poor attempt to explain it. Another tragedy."

Thomas clenched his fists, hungry to know more. But what did he want to know? What should he ask this creature?

"Why are you speaking to me? Is there something I must do?"

Sabellius grew serious. "You are about to encounter great difficulties, Thomas. Your soul will be blasted by the winds of change and powerful forces will try to crush you. I cannot tell you what to do but I can tell you that you will need certainty, not doubt, when the hour of judgment is at hand. You must break through the mists, *Pater.*

"But how do I...?"

"Higher knowledge of God begins with the rational mind, as you intuit. But it cannot continue to the point of direct perception of Him solely through the intellect. It is a knowledge beyond words, a knowledge beyond mind. A knowledge requiring you to take a leap of *Faith*."

A leap of Faith. There it was again.

"That is your challenge. You must trust in yourself; your intuitions. You are essential to the events that lie ahead. But you must find yourself first."

"But what's going to happen? You know what's going to happen."

Sabellius shook his head solemnly, "Not exactly. Nothing is written in stone, but there is always the will of heaven."

"What do you know about Yordon Antropos?" asked Thomas, feeling himself grow frantic. Sabellius shrugged and backed away, fading into the moonlight until only a voice was left, carried on the wind.

"*Macte animo*, my friend. I have faith in you, even if you do not. You will prevail."

Thomas was alone again. Somehow he was sitting on the bench again. He looked at the sky, trying to imagine God watching over his creation. As he gazed upwards, the cold sky became a sheltering roof over his head and the stars no longer seemed cold and inimical; instead they were like the lights of a home town viewed from afar, familiar and companionable.

Papal Task Force Villa, Rome

"They've badged you with 'Apostolic Delegate'?" Karin laughed. "Isn't that what the church gives to people it wants to move out of the way?"

Thomas looked sheepish. "Well, yes, but I think it's a little different."

They were interrupted by the arrival of Zachary Jobson.

"Hello all," he said pleasantly, removing a handkerchief to wipe at his neck. "Devilishly hot out there."

"You get used to it," answered Thomas.

"If you're lucky enough to be a student living in a non-air-conditioned dormitory," quipped Karin, referring to Thomas' student days.

Thomas laughed, happy to see them and relieved that they had agreed to join him in this Vatican-sanctioned quest. They had been circumspect at first when he had telephoned, but in the end the prospect of deeply investigating Yordon with plenty of dollars and resources behind them had ensnared them both.

Thomas looked around the room. Max Ravessi had made himself comfortable in a chair next to the room's land line telephone and was pulling out a pack of cigarettes. Karin lounged on the couch, legs crossed, and dangled her foot, her shoe hanging half off precipitously. Next to Karin, Dr. Yoon Sung Deng waited, stiffly upright, on a chaise. Admiral Farrow had stationed himself at the central conference table, where the various monitors, pads, maps and reference materials had been collected, and appeared to be reviewing them intently. Dolores Arbolera and Mervyn Goss sat uncomfortably side by side making no conversation.

Seeing everyone was present, Jobson went directly to the head of the room where there was a large whiteboard and world map positioned opposite each other on easels. He turned to face the small group.

"We are rather the diverse collection, I daresay. Well, it comes as no surprise. Only a multi-disciplinary investigative force has a chance against our subject."

The participants appraised each other with mild interest.

"Seeing we have no elected leader, allow me to begin our proceedings."

No one protested, though Farrow looked doubtful.

Jobson continued, "The first question we must answer is who or what is our opponent? Mr. Antropos looks like an ordinary man, though one possessing uncommon charisma. Beyond that he seems to command extraordinary powers."

"Let's try to break it down," said Thomas, "What have we seen he is capable of so far?"

Karin quickly volunteered the first example. "Let's see. He cleared the Tel Aviv area of radiation with rain. He can make magic rain."

"He can turn metal into stone," said Ravessi, referring to the events at Jericho.

"I have personally observed him perform mass healings," added Jobson.

"And he's brought a dead child back to life," said Thomas, noting the pause in the room following his words. That one took the cake, hands down.

Farrow broke the silence, "So he has supernatural powers, that's established. But what about his power base? What do we know so far?"

"He's taken over the Tubasi following and made it his own," answered Goss. "He effectively controls huge tracts of land in the Middle East and parts of the former Soviet Union."

"He has armies at his disposal. Primarily Muslims in the Arab nations," added Ravessi. "But huge non-Muslim followings in other parts of the world as well."

Jobson stroked at his beard, pondering the data points, "But despite this impressive resume, Mr. Antropos appears to have limits."

Faces frowned back at him.

"What do you mean, Zachary?" asked Thomas.

"For instance, why has he not suppressed all threats before they take root? Why not make the Pope disappear with a sweep of his arm? Why allow this group to convene?"

"Maybe he knows we'll fail," suggested Karin.

"Or he could be waiting until we pose an actual threat," suggested Ravessi.

Farrow responded, "That's all a bunch of hooey. Jobson's right. Yordon is a flesh and blood human, no matter what powers he has. He sleeps, eats, shits, sweats, smells – just like us."

Ravessi said, "I agree with the Admiral. I do not so easily presume he is supernatural. He says he is a messenger of God but never more than that. We should try to expose the mechanism of his powers, whatever it may be."

Goss added, "We need an insider. A spy. Someone to gain his confidence. Or even better, someone who already has it."

"But who?" asked Dr. Arbolera.

Goss responded easily, "Perhaps we should begin by identifying the people that are close to him. The people in his inner circle. They are ordinary people, are they not? What do we know about them? Maybe they can be turned?"

Farrow stood up and approached the whiteboard. He began to write names as he spoke.

"There's very few people that we're aware of in Antropos' inner circle. But without question the primary one is a certain Mr. Philo Berith."

"He is almost always at Antropos' side," noted Ravessi.

Dr. Deng, who had been silent until now, added, "And on his other side is also always the young lady -- Miss Mary..."

"Mary Maccabe. He met her in D.C. She's key," acknowledged Karin, looking at Deng. He smiled toothily back.

They wrote down the names of a few of the other known followers of Yordon, including former APF members and former Jordanian army officers. Once the list was considered complete, Farrow stepped back and admired his handiwork.

"So what do we know about Mr. Berith?" asked Jobson, from the side.

Farrow responded, "Berith comes from Greece, just like Antropos, and in fact, knew Antropos when he was a monk. He's been his right hand man since before anyone was looking. If anyone knows the true story about Mr. Antropos, it's going to be Berith."

"I take it you have a dossier on him already?" said Jobson.

"Of course," snapped the Admiral. "After him, the most significant player is Mary Maccabe, as Dr. Deng correctly guessed. The girl is recent to the scene, but clearly important to Antropos, judging from her constant proximity to him."

"They met for the first time in D.C.," said Karin.

"Affirmative. We believe that is where they first met. Other than these two, little is known about the others. American Intelligence is doing its best to lay down some detail. We'll know more in the weeks ahead."

Goss rapidly jotted down notes. "That's very good, Admiral. Clearly his two primary confidants invite a deep background investigation. The European Intelligence agencies have already begun this and I will endeavor to share their discoveries with all of you, of course."

"I will similarly contact our friends at MOSSAD, Shin Bet and INTERPOL as well, Mssr. Goss," added Ravessi.

Goss nodded dutifully back.

There was a pause in the conversation. Jobson stepped to the center of the room. "All well and good. Our next actions should be to research each of these areas."

Farrow nodded his agreement crisply. The others also nodded, scanning the room to confirm the reactions of their new colleagues.

Jobson continued, "Let's see, the intelligence aspects we know will be handled by the Admiral, and Messrs. Goss and Ravessi."

The three men indicated their assent.

Jobson went on, "The power wielded by Yordon invites scientific investigation. Dr. Arbolera? Dr. Deng? Sounds like you have your work cut out for you."

"We'll start on the work immediately."

"As you wish."

Jobson turned to Thomas and Karin. "You'll help me do the background research on Yordon. There's much to be discovered there. Why does Yordon want to destroy the Church? What are his limits? What does scripture and prophecy say about him? Where does he fit in?"

"And more importantly," added Karin, "Where do WE, as in the human race, fit in?"

☐

Chapter Nine: The Siege of the Vatican

Vatican City, September 2020

The considerable throng that comprised Yordon's followers positioned themselves around the complex of buildings that comprised the Vatican city-state. They arrived gradually, in small, disparate groups. A great many of them had followed Yordon all the way from Israel. Many more had welcomed him at the shores of Italy. The crowd had grown as word of his arrival spread, and he made his way steadily toward Rome.

Now his following numbered in the tens of thousands and surrounded the Vatican. The municipal police force stood by watching for trouble, not really knowing what to expect. The Swiss Guard, stationed within the compound, steadfastly ignored them.

Yordon, accompanied by Mary and Philo, climbed atop one of his follower's vehicles, which was parked on the Via di Porta Angelica, directly before the colonnaded entrance to St. Peter's Square. Yordon turned to face the assemblage.

"Hear my words." His voice carried to all.

"We stand here before the seat of the Roman Catholic church, the so-called universal church which claims all of Christianity as its flock. But I tell you it is not a church at all. It is we who are the church. This is but a collection of buildings."

Mary looked up at Yordon. Despite hours of intimate conversation, he remained opaque, an enigma, perhaps even to himself. Philo said he had always been a man alone.

"The spiritual requirement for membership in the House of God has been replaced with an easily digestible and degraded dogma. It has been usurped by literal-minded interpretation of scripture, reverence of icons and allegiance to rituals. This has only succeeded in creating division amongst us. It is no replacement for the true word of Christ.

Christ's mission on Earth was not just to bring you salvation, but to teach you *enlightenment*. His words were provocative; not a set of pat answers. Through his words, he sought to inspire men and women in their search for higher knowledge. His words were meant to give you power."

Mary realized Yordon was leading the crowd up to something big. She felt a tingle of apprehension down her spine as she gazed at St. Peter's Basilica nestled at the rear of the Square behind Yordon. It was stained with age.

In a coincidence of language, Yordon seemed to pick up on her last thought. He looked down at her briefly as he spoke.

"This is a tainted place. At the behest of those who have ruled from here, it was once illegal for an ordinary man to possess a Bible! At the behest of those who have ruled from here, a privileged clergy, separate from the people, was promulgated. At the behest of those who have ruled from here, the Inquisition persecuted innocents. Indulgences were sold in exchange for money and political favor. Murder, infidelity, intolerance, ambition, avarice – it has all happened here, in this so called sacred place. Heed me when I tell you, this is no Godly place."

Yordon turned in a circle and raised his arms. Then he pointed to the Basilica.

"These structures behind me are nothing but walls; stone and marble meant to keep you out; piled higher and higher protecting a sterile, creedal religion."

Yordon bowed his head and lowered his arms.

"The walls must come down."

Mary put her fist to her mouth as she felt a subsonic disturbance, like an intestinal insurrection. It came from deep inside of her, and yet it was not -- of this she was sure, for the walls themselves vibrated from it. She grabbed Philo, and the two of them leaned against the vehicle acting as Yordon's stage for support.

Abruptly, the ground along the length of the Via di Porta Angelica collapsed downward with a loud report, forming a long and wide rift. The crowd fell to its knees, holding on to each other as the rift spread and widened all around the City, following the line of the walls. The sound was like a prolonged crack of lightning. The rumbling of the earth increased in intensity until slowly, reluctantly, the Bernini colonnades began to totter. Like dominoes, they fell against each other in thunderous ranks, raising a cloud of dust and spitting shards of stone.

Incredulous, Mary looked behind her and realized that the rest of Rome was unaffected. The earthquake seemed to have been focused on the grounds of Vatican City. The buildings outside the confines of the city-state were relatively unscathed.

"By the whiskers," whispered Philo. He helped Mary up and they looked upon the Vatican in wonder.

The seat of the Roman Catholic church had been turned into an island of rock. Its three thousand occupants were now surrounded by a moat of air, separating them from the rest of Rome. The small heliport and its lone helicopter had been crushed to mangled metal by falling stones. Yordon's army stood at the rim, and the Papal forces, such as they were, were completely trapped within.

Yordon shouted into the wind and his voice carried to all ears, "Hear me Cardinal Artieri, who calls himself Sylvester. This is only the beginning of the end. You must surrender your claim to the Apostolic succession and acknowledge that I am the one true messenger of God. Until this is acknowledged by you, and you tell your flock that this is so, you will experience misfortunes and calamities until there is no one left to surrender. Change is upon you and you're only choice is when you will accept it."

Mary could not believe her eyes or ears. Yordon jumped down off the vehicle and came to stand beside her. He scanned his handiwork once more. She stole the moment to examine his profile. His thin, straight features, his wilderness hardened skin and eyes, the gleam of light in his oddly unblinking eyes, the hard set of his lips. For an instant she saw him as a demon, very clearly, but it dispelled when he turned to look at her.

"It is done, Mary. A new day is close at hand."

She backed away from Yordon. "I don't understand. I don't understand any of this."

Philo put an arm around her, and looked at Yordon with uncomprehending eyes.

Yordon's jaw flexed but some greater motivation inside of him prevailed and his countenance relaxed. He extended his hands to them.

"This is difficult for you, I know. But you've known me long enough to know I do what I must do. It's for the best. You two, of all the people in the world, must try to believe in me." He glanced at the chasm that yawned a few feet from them.

"What I am doing here today is a minor disturbance, a necessary infraction meant to clear the way for your own salvation. If you could understand what awaits you after this is done, you would embrace me and urge me to hurry."

"Are you going to kill them inside?" asked Mary, trying to regain herself.

Yordon's face was still, but his eyes were afire. "If they die, it's because they kill themselves."

The Papal Apartments, Vatican City

"The Technical Services Department reports that the telephones, water, and electrical systems have been cut off from Rome proper," reported Cardinal Manzanero, trying to sound nonplussed but failing miserably.

"But we have several generators within the confines of the city, isn't this so? And water in the Vatican store, and the three transmitters at Vatican Radio."

"*Sì*, Padre."

"Then see to their activation at once, Nelson. We are counting on you."

Manzanero bowed and left quickly.

As soon as the door clicked shut, Tatian approached the Pope.

"Holiness, there can be no doubt. This Yordon must be the anti-Christ. He is upon us."

Sylvester seemed not to hear him. He sat in a hard wooden chair before the blazing stone fireplace and was now evidently deep in prayer, eyes pressed shut and lips moving slightly.

Tatian wished he could be struck dumb, for he could not bear to hear the nightmare of his own words. "It is prophesied that he would come in the form of a false Christ and that he would seduce the masses with soothing words and political successes -- and that then he would jab at the heart of the Christian Church. It is exactly as Ezekiel has written."

The Pope opened his eyes slowly and raised his head to look at the Cardinal Prefect. "Matthew, if Yordon Antropos is what you claim, and the final days are upon us, is this not what we have waited for through the millennia?"

Tatian retorted, "And what of the tribulation that is to come then? Men will suffer greatly. The earth will be raped and burned. Millions will die. We will die, Most Holy Father."

Sylvester nodded sadly, "*Va bene*. But at long last, after millennia of waiting, a new age of man. Apocalypse, and then salvation for all."

With that, the Pope looked up at the Cardinal. Neither man was happy. Tatian saw Sylvester distinctly. *Just a man.* He felt a cold wind in his heart. As a young prelate he had occasionally wondered if the Lord would ever return and what the chances of that happening in his lifetime might be, but as he grew in rank and responsibility the question had settled into a half forgotten musing drowned out by the worldly concerns of administering the affairs of the world spanning Catholic Church. And now that reality beat at their door with angry fists, they were cowed and afraid; hiding in the Pope's inner chambers.

Sylvester spoke. "I ask you this, Matthew, if Yordon is the beast, where is Christ?"

"I don't know. But he must be imminent."

"You believe these things and yet you are afraid."

Tatian felt the reins of his composure loosen. He had not expected this of Sylvester. They had always recognized each other's incompatibilities and had enjoyed a certain professional distance. But now they were alone together. Two men in a lifeboat.

"Forgive me, Holy Father."

Sylvester insisted, "What do you fear? If you believe in God, you will be saved."

Tatian felt himself perspiring. "Sylvester, this is difficult to say, but I must confess it. I am afraid of my own death." He bowed his head and closed his eyes.

Sylvester's face flushed. Coldly, he asked, "And what about the death of the Church?"

Tatian broke out of his contrition, hearing Sylvester's ire. "It will rise again."

"Do you BELIEVE that?" snapped Sylvester, suddenly angry and upright, inches from Tatian.

Tatian took a step back, feeling like a boy being reprimanded by his father. He searched deep inside himself. He wondered if he knew the answer to Sylvester's question. The Pope took a step closer, backing Tatian into the wall. Tatian touched the cool stucco wall and realized his hands were drenched in sweat. He fought an impulse to rip off his robes and run until he collapsed and lost consciousness. *Oh, to be at rest and without thought.*

"Cardinal Tatian. Matthew! Answer me! Or leave this structure and never return."

Tatian found himself and ventured, "Then you are without doubt in your belief? This terror will lead to salvation? The monster outside will be defeated by the Lord? If you believe it -- truly believe it -- then I will remain at your side until the coming deliverance. I will swallow my heart and don the armor of faith."

Sylvester didn't say a word. His jaw worked slowly. He stepped away from Tatian as he spoke. "You can save your noble acts for another time, Matthew. Your test of faith is yet to come."

Tatian tried to understand. "What do you mean?"

Sylvester didn't answer immediately. Instead he went back to his chair and sat. "I believe, like you, that Yordon is a terrible predator. But I do NOT believe it is the end time. You point to prophecy as proof that the creature outside is the Son of Satan. And yet we both know that there are many prophecies in the Canon that haven't come true; that contradict each other and that probably will never come true. Matthew, there have been no symbols in the sky, no rebuilt Temple in Jerusalem, no sermon on the Mount, no loud trumpets, no wars against armies of the North or Kings of the South. Only Yordon Antropos waging war against Vatican City."

"But isn't that enough? Some of the prophecies have come true."

"Matthew, Yordon is NOT the beast. It is NOT the end-time. He is NOT the Messiah. I feel it in my bones. I know it in my soul. This is something else."

"But if he is neither the beast nor the Messiah, then we will merely die here; then there is no salvation for us."

"Your soul will not die, Matthew," uttered the Pontiff in a voice like gravel.

"But you cannot defeat him. Or can you?"

Sylvester squinted hard at Tatian, his jaw working, as if keeping himself from saying something more. Abruptly, he snapped, "*Basta!* It is the will of God. Be gone, Cardinal Tatian. I will hear no more of your diatribe."

Vatican City

The array of devices hummed softly in response to Dr. Deng's manipulations.

"These are the most portable instruments of this type ever devised. It is fortunate that I have access to them," he muttered as he worked.

Dolores Arbolera interrupted her assessment of the milling crowd below and turned to the small figure of Deng crouching over his instruments.

"What do you hope to find out, Deng?" she asked, trying to sound supportive. Deng didn't answer immediately, consumed by his work. She watched him, admiring his diligence. Even though she had been hand-picked from scores of esteemed scientists affiliated with the Pontifical Academy, she felt underqualified to tackle her assignment. *To put God under a microscope?* She drifted back to observing Yordon from their rooftop vantage point. She had to admit she felt a certain awe of Yordon. He was so much like she imagined he would be, if he was what he claimed.

"I'm getting readings. Look here."

Once again she snapped herself out of her ruminations. How could Deng remain so dispassionate?

Arbolera remembered her physics training. "Is that a spectrometer?" she asked, observing the readings on the liquid crystal display.

Deng nodded enthusiastically. "A scanning probe multi-technique spectrometer to be exact — ideal for remote observation — and here alongside it, an energy ion beam analyzer and an x-ray diffractometer. A good start. My trace shows a discernible peak in the upper microwave frequencies. See? Here. And here. This is from Yordon's body."

"Hmm. Fascinating." she answered emptily. She turned away from the instrument and faced Deng. Eventually he returned her gaze, his expression a mixture of query and embarrassment.

She voiced her feelings. "Do you really think any of these tests will be able to help his Holiness?"

Deng put down the probe, took off his glasses and proceeded to polish them with his handkerchief. "If it can be measured, it can be understood. If it can be understood, it can be controlled, Dr. Arbolera. You are so doubtful. Don't you think that if we fail, the governments of the world will eventually intervene?"

Arbolera gave him a direct look. "This is their involvement, Dr. Deng. Us. To see them do more will be to see them make war."

Deng pondered this and, after a few moments thought, answered, "Then I should take more measurements."

Deng returned to his instruments and let Arbolera dwell in her thoughts. After a few more minutes, he announced, "We are too far away. I will go downstairs."

Dr. Arbolera absently nodded her assent.

From the rooftop she watched as Deng appeared on the street a few blocks away from Yordon, and proceeded to set up his equipment once again. She listened to Yordon's voice.

"Many will resist us. Many will denounce us, but none will prevail. In a matter of days we will…"

She could see Deng shaking his head and peering around the vehicle he had chosen for cover. Hurriedly he packed up his gear again and began to snake closer to Yordon's position.

Arbolera felt the urge to yell a warning to him. Deng drew closer until he was mere yards away from Yordon, in a relatively clear spot. He pointed his probe.

"…and those that think we can be defeated will be destroyed in turn. Like this." Yordon looked directly at Deng and pointed a finger at him. Out of a perfectly clear sky came a lightning bolt which struck directly at Deng's location. The lightning struck Deng with a loud report. He let out a yelp, and the electricity consumed him, and then dissipated, leaving only the probe Deng had held in his hand. It hung in the air for an instant, before falling to the pavement with a clatter. Everyone backed away from the spot.

Arbolera covered her mouth with her palm in stunned silence. The casual cruelty of it! Fighting her horror, she hurriedly made her way to the street. Pushing through the crowd that had formed around the spectrometer, she entered the circle and stared at the charred spot where Deng had once stood. Nothing but burn marks. Fighting her immediate impulse to run, she steadied herself and grabbed at the equipment. The Task Force needed these readings. Forcing herself to stand erect, she dared a glance in Yordon's direction. He was looking directly at her. So was the encircling crowd. Her heart expanded in her throat. She backed away to the circle's edge. The crowd backed away behind her, maddeningly maintaining a clearing around her.

"Go," said Yordon from his perch. "Your instruments won't help you. Nothing can help Sylvester now."

She didn't wait for further encouragement. She turned and dove into the wall of people, instruments in tow, and ran as fast as she could.

The Papal Apartments, Vatican City

"We will last approximately 30 days if we carefully ration the bottled water from the Vatican store," reported Prefect Cerrano to the Pope.

"There is no other supply?"

"All other sources are tainted or the conduits to the City have been severed by the chasm, Holiness."

"And what about the Infirmary?" asked Sylvester dolorously.

"Many are ill. Anyone who drank from the taps. The situation is grave." Cerrano looked like he was about to break down.

"Justicio, my dear fellow, take strength from your faith in your God. We will prevail. You have always been a reliable member of my household. I need you more than ever to be strong now."

"*Si*, Papa. Forgive me. It is frightening."

"It is. But you must be brave."

Cerrano bowed slightly and left the room, shutting the door carefully behind him.

Sylvester sighed and rose from his chair to take a look out the window. The dust had settled and the day was clear of smog. The chasm was a dark wound separating the Vatican from the teaming metropolis beyond. On all sides, a restless, angry crowd of Antropostles carried banners and signs calling for the demise of the Pope. Himself. It was hard to believe. How did this happen?

He observed Yordon directly across the chasm opposite the Square. He was speaking to his followers from a platform.

"*Mio Dio*," whispered Sylvester as he listened.

The church's long and circuitous history was peppered with incidents of malfeasance, it was true, but it had as much to do with the congregations as with the clergy. The clergy came directly from the population. The history of the Church was part and parcel with human history. It would be no different for Yordon.

Sylvester startled himself with that thought. It was a primal truth. Perhaps it was the germ of understanding as to why all of this was happening. What was going on out there was the reflection, wasn't it? This room festooned with artworks and furniture was not. He felt himself shiver with the cold truth of it, and wondered if any of the souls inside these walls would survive what was to come.

Papal Task Force Villa, Rome

They were alone in the salon room. Goss came and sat beside Ravessi.

"We must take independent action," he declared, his manicured breath too near.

Ravessi blew smoke at the invisible assault.

"Independent and yet together, you and I?" said Ravessi with a tight smile.

Goss didn't return the smile. "The situation demands it."

"So it does. What do you propose?"

"So far, Antropos has operated almost entirely in the European and Mediterranean theatres. Yet the Americans dominate the task force."

"Sylvester wanted them involved. They have the resources."

"That's nonsense. So do we. What is needed is stealth and intelligence. I think you would agree the Americans are relative paupers in both areas."

"I am an American, Herr Goss."

Goss grinned at Ravessi. "But we both know your allegiances."

Ravessi squinted at Goss through a veil of smoke, wordlessly. After some moments of silent impasse, he grunted his assent.

Goss took his cue. "You undoubtedly know the Israeli plan."

"I know nothing of such a plan."

Goss ignored this. "The Council of Europe also has a plan. I propose we join forces and prepare a joint maneuver, should the Americans play a heavy hand or become bogged down in their typical, poll-driven, partisan politics."

"You're very cynical, Herr Goss."

"Why, thank you."

The Lateran Palace Archives, Rome

The Librarian of the Archives at the Lateran Palace led the visitor to the reading table. He also brought with him the selected apocrypha and codices the two researchers had requested. They were deeply immersed in their readings and the pile of books and documents strewn around them had grown tall. There were limits to this and soon he would have to express his concern at having such rare materials exposed to the light for so long, and accumulated in disorderly piles. He laid the requested materials in a clear space on the table and padded away without waiting for thanks.

Jobson, the visitor, cleared his throat.

Karin and Thomas looked up with identical startled expressions.

Karin rubbed her temples. "Zachary. That hurt. You just yanked me across eleven centuries!"

"Sorry, my dear," he whispered solemnly, "But I'm afraid I've got some very bad news."

Karin blinked at him as he pulled back a chair and joined them.

"What is it?"

"It's Deng. He's gone."

"You mean dead," said Thomas.

"Dead? It can't be." breathed Karin.

"I'm afraid it can be," replied Jobson solemnly.

Thomas shook his head in disbelief. "Yordon?"

"We think so. According to Dr. Arbolera, he was vaporized by a lightning bolt as he was taking measurements of Yordon. They were working together."

"How horrible! Poor Deng," said Karin quietly, closing the text she had been examining. Her hand shook slightly.

"Yordon must have considered him a threat," croaked Thomas.

"Why do you suppose Deng's attempt to take measurements was a threat to him?" implored Karin.

"I don't know. It seems odd. Maybe it's the man we should be looking at." answered Thomas pensively.

"We've got Goss and Ravessi on that," remarked Jobson.

"I mean the man. Not the intelligence on the man."

Jobson inclined his head toward Thomas, intrigued. A few other patrons of the library looked over at their susurrating conversation disapprovingly.

"Explain."

Thomas lowered his voice to a conspiratorial whisper. "If he is anything like his predecessor, which many think he is, then he is another "Son of God" made corporeal. That means he's subject to the same weaknesses as any human."

Jobson nodded in agreement, "Even Jesus was occasionally ruled by his human urges. Jesus as a child was said to be capricious and impatient."

Thomas continued, "Indeed, Zachary. But Jesus' example to us was that his spirit was able to transcend the flaw of Adam, thereby conquering original sin and making it possible for all of us to re-enter heaven."

"Except for the fact that Yordon's not doing any transcending," finished Karin.

Thomas closed the books in front of him and pushed them aside. He gave both his friends long, appraising looks before continuing. "That may be, Karin. It's possible his corporeal side can't handle the godly power. Thus, instead of a savior, we have a raver on our hands."

"You mean a mad god?" asked Karin, fascinated.

"Perhaps. But on the other hand, Yordon, like Jesus, can be looked upon as an agent of change. That makes him unpopular with the status quo. That makes him a threat to the established church hierarchy, just as Jesus threatened the Jewish Sanhedrin and Roman governors of his day. Yordon talks about a world without nations or politics. That's terrible to the defenders of the old order, but it doesn't necessarily mean his intentions are evil."

Karin dismissed the idea. "I doubt that. He killed Deng!"

Jobson agreed, turning from Karin to Thomas, "His recent acts are definitely capricious. He may be losing control of himself. That makes him fallible. And if he is fallible, he can make mistakes."

"What if we're the mistake and Yordon's here to fix it?" asked Karin morbidly.

"I don't believe that. If anything, it may be that Yordon is the mistake," answered Thomas.

Yordon's Encampment, outside Vatican City

The Vatican City State was a disaster scene. Helicopters rumbled overhead. Television crews stood before the crowds talking into cameras. Medical personnel threaded their way through the melee.

For the moment, the City of Rome's Municipal *Polizia Locale* as well as the National *Polizia di Stato* were at a standoff with Yordon's amassed army of civilian followers and militant loyalists. Thousands of them occupied the buildings and streets immediately surrounding Vatican City. The more militaristic members of Yordon's strange flock took it upon themselves to establish perimeters and checkpoints into the encampment, seemingly overnight.

Yordon regarded all this with an air of entitlement, as far as Mary could discern, as she watched him talking to his lieutenants, before returning to their table. They were in a local café, which Yordon had commandeered as a base of operations.

Yordon sat and immediately, the café owner approached and asked him if he wished for any refreshment.

"Just water, *signore*, and thank you for accommodating us."

The cafe's proprietor bowed in deference, and perhaps a note of fear, Mary observed, as he dashed off.

"Yordon, do you see how the café owner reacts to you?" she asked, putting a hand over his. He flinched for a second, then relaxed at the touch and looked her in the eyes.

"He is a little afraid of me," answered Yordon, betraying a note of bemusement.

Mary jumped at the admission, "As are many, many people here. Or else they are enraptured with you, fanatical in their blind devotion to your cause, whatever that is."

"You know my cause," answered Yordon, quietly.

Mary shook her head, her brow crinkled in doubt. "I'm not sure, Yordon. I'm not sure I know you. Perhaps I never have."

He squeezed her hand, "You knew me the moment we touched, back in Washington, Mary. What you felt then, that is who I am. What I am."

The Son of Man? "Maybe in that moment," Mary answered, "that might have been true, but Yordon, what you're doing here, to the Vatican, to the people inside, that is not what I expected from you then. Not who I thought I met in that moment."

Yordon sighed. "Mary, this is all a necessary disturbance, so that men can free themselves from their brittle creeds and be open again, to a real connection with their creator. It's a cloud of dust before the wind. And once we're done here, we'll move to the next temple, and the next one."

Mary felt a chill travel down her spine upon hearing him speak so casually.

"You mean other centers of worship, like, like in Mecca?"

He nodded, "Yes, exactly."

Mary let go of his hand and clenched the edge of the table. "Until the whole world turns against you? Don't you realize that by upsetting people's beliefs, you're also upsetting the secular power balance? Already you virtually control the Middle East. Do you think governments are going to sit back and let that happen? Are you trying to start a world war?"

Yordon's eyes hardened, showing a hint of impatience. "Nothing they do can change the outcome."

"And why is that? Because of your powers? Are you going to knock down warplanes from the sky with a sweep of your hand? Or turn armies of men into clay? Are you going to kill people who get in your way? You already killed one scientist…"

Yordon bore holes into her eyes, seeming to grab her attention by sheer force of will. "Mary, you mustn't doubt. I am doing what I must and it is the right thing to do."

"How do you know that? Why can't you be more like that priest we met in D.C., Father Prisciotti? He enlightens people through his TV show. With words. And they're good words, like you have used to say in the past."

Yordon broke eye contact and scanned the room instead, seeming to lose interest in her diatribe, for the moment. "Words are inadequate."

Mary insisted, "You didn't used to think that. Philo has told me many stories of your time in Greece together."

Yordon turned toward her and his eyes cast inward, as if recollecting those times. "It was different then. Much has happened since then. Much has happened to me, Mary."

"Yordon, what do you mean?"

Just then, the café owner returned with the water and set it down. Yordon nodded at the man and smiled.

Mary watched the exchange and felt even more confusion. *He could be so human.*

Yordon took a sip of the water and returned his attention to her. He stared at Mary, unblinking, making her cringe at the 180 degree turn toward inhumanness, then suddenly he did blink, and a well of moisture appeared within each of his eyes. He seemed to deflate, then he took both of her hands in his and leaned forward in his chair so they were closer together, like conspirers, in the midst of the chaos of the café.

"Back in those times, on Athos, in the highlands, in the villages, I was tortured by *awarenesses*, of such power and motive, but without coherent meaning. I didn't know what to do, except escape inward. I went to Athos to hide, in some ways, and through meditation, to find the roots of those currents ravaging my mind. I felt I might even be a schizophrenic. And yet those spirits inside of me also gave me the purest of insights. I could see, in fleeting moments, through the veil of reality, but I could not comprehend the purpose of these visions."

"And then you left Athos. Why?"

"Because, Mary, I was compelled. The thoughts inside my head, not quite voices, but more like urges, pushed me outwards. To travel the land and tell of my insights to others. And it has led us to here."

"Just like that."

"Well, no. As I learned I could wield powers, supernatural powers; to heal people and alter the wind and the rain, to revive the dead, at each iteration of these acts, each one more fantastic than the one before it, the chorus of voices in my head became louder, clearer, more coherent. And as my abilities have grown, I have realized that I possess the power to bring about a fundamental change in this world that would be for the good of all mankind. And it is what God wants. That's why I am here, Mary. I am a messenger -- that I have known for some time, but I am also an agent. I am the mouth and the rod of heaven. I am a phalanx, harnessing the power of heaven to wield change upon this world."

"You're admitting there are voices in your head controlling what you do?"

Yordon sat upright, breaking the spell of his confession to Mary, and pondered this. Finally, he answered, "If I say yes, you will draw the negative conclusion you seemed determined to draw anyway. If I say no, you will think of me as denying what is obvious to you and that will furthermore convince you that I have probably lost my senses."

Then with a note of sadness, almost a pleading, he asked her very quietly, so she could barely hear it amidst the cacophony of the café, "Have I lost you, Mary?

Mary wasn't sure what to think. She had spent most of her life searching for a spiritual guide, someone with wisdom to give her clarity of purpose not unlike that which Yordon claimed to have discovered for himself. And he did have wisdom. She believed his ideas about the need to strip away religion and get back to roots. But she never suspected there would be suffering.

She turned her face upwards to look at him again. "Yordon, you stand on the edge of greatness. You don't have to do things this way. The moment you destroy something you become the enemy. What you are doing here is undermining your very purpose, don't you see that? There must be another way."

Yordon shook his head, and returned to his normal speaking voice. "There isn't. This is the only way to clear the path to the future."

"You're wrong. What you're doing here is...evil," she blurted out.

Yordon raised his eyebrows at that. His face betrayed a flush of anger, and the café actually seemed to grow warmer.

Finally, he said with an utmost calm belying the emotion on his face, "You should leave. You simply don't understand. It is to those that are worthy of my mysteries that I will reveal my mysteries."

That hurt. Mary felt the icy touch of Yordon's anger. She fell silent.

Oval Office, The White House, Washington D.C.

Clement was feeling congenial. He shook the Admiral's hand as Farrow entered the Oval Office.

"Welcome back, Jav."

"Good to be back home, where the ground's relatively solid."

"Not as solid as you might like, Admiral." said Hanover. He was seated in a button back leather wing chair across from Wesley Van Ness. Their side tables were covered in technical briefs and reports.

"The situation in Texas," Hanover began.

"Not now," barked Clement, suddenly serious. He returned his attention to the Admiral. "Thanks for flying back on such short notice, Admiral."

Farrow nodded morosely. "A huddle was definitely called for, sir. We've all read the AP news dispatch."

Clement replied, "It's not to be believed."

"The man's a menace," said Farrow, "A plague of boils inside the Vatican complex. And it's evidently the doing of that son of a gun Antropos. It's like something straight out of the Bible."

Clement patted the Admiral's shoulder and urged him forward, "Have a seat, Jav. We have a lot to talk about."

Farrow went to the sofa, where the ever dour Secretary of State, Arthur Blaine, and the distinguished but cautious U.N. Representative, Ted Baskin, were already seated.

Farrow proceeded to recount Yordon's actions and the steps the task force had taken to date. When he was done the room was quiet.

"I know it all sounds hard to believe," he added awkwardly.

"But plenty of people believe it stateside, Admiral," answered Clement.

"The American church is in total disarray," added Van Ness. "Some groups oppose Yordon's claim to legitimacy. Others support the Pope. There's fighting in the streets, much of it religiously inspired."

"And it's not just religion. It's dividing the Union," said Hanover. Clement shot him a scorching look. Hanover blinked but said nothing more.

Sighing, the President went to his desk. Rubbing at his temples, he propped his elbows on the desktop and steepled his fingers. "Jav, it's becoming increasingly clear that countermeasures are going to be needed if we want to avoid a national crisis. Direct countermeasures."

Cabinet Room, The White House, Washington D.C.

The next morning, Clement strode into the Cabinet room at a brisk pace. Seated along the length of the large conference table were his senior cabinet members, a transcriber and an aide. They all stood as he entered.

Clement took his position at the head of the table and scanned the twin rows of faces. Present were Vice President Baudet, Hanover, Blaine, Ravessi, Van Ness, and the Joint Chiefs: Generals Pearson, Bonhoeffer and Plain, and, of course, Jav. Baskin was present too, he noticed, though he couldn't remember inviting him. He let his gaze rise upward to the surrounding busts of former Presidents, situated along the mantle that girdled the room right up to the classical, white marble fireplace. *A Full House.*

He cleared his throat. "You can all sit down."

Clement began, "Okay what do we have?"

General Pearson stood up and faced the President. "Mr. President, we have been liaising with CINCEUR and our counterparts in NATO to discuss mobilization options. Here is our current tactical situation."

At his signal, the aide dimmed the lights and an enormous flat screen LCD monitor appeared from behind the wall at the head of the table as two wall panels slid apart. A map of the Middle East came into focus on the screen in vibrant color. Flags and markers dotted the map. The lower portion of Italy was highlighted in red.

"We have troops stationed here, and here, across the border in Switzerland. We can surround metropolitan Rome in a matter of days, if…"

"If what?" interrupted Baskin.

"Ambassador, General Pearson has the floor," warned General Bonhoeffer, who was seated next to Pearson and appeared to have been enjoying the presentation.

"He's speaking about a large scale mobilization of troops," said Baskin, "Against one man?"

Pearson frowned at Baskin, and countered, "But he's not just one man, Ambassador. He has a large, fanatical following."

Baskin was unconvinced. "Even so, they're not the threat. They're civilians, not soldiers. It's Antropos we want, not a military confrontation. If we want to *control* the situation we have to control him and him alone."

Clement worked his jaw as he considered Baskin's words. He cast a hard look at both Pearson and Hanover.

Baudet cleared his throat to get the President's attention and said, "Mr. President, but our government must find a way to assist the Vatican City State. They are effectively under siege."

"We have no defense treaty with the Vatican," countered Blaine, "and furthermore, Pope Sylvester hasn't asked the United States for help."

Van Ness was quick with a response. "But we are partners. Remember Gandolfo. And in fact, Sylvester has asked us for options, Arthur -- through covert channels."

Clement grunted in agreement and said, "It's true. And even if he hadn't, I can't ignore the situation. As a Catholic, as a conscientious American, on a humanitarian basis alone…"

Baskin didn't wait for him to finish. "You'd kill thousands of civilians to save the Pope? I think we are better served allowing the Papal Task Force, an enormous diplomatic achievement in and of itself, more time to devise some strategies."

"A research group?" laughed Pearson, who was still standing. "Be serious. Do you intend to bury Yordon in paper?"

Baskin glared at him.

Farrow interjected, "Gentlemen, the time has come to brief you on a plan we have been developing in secret, in conjunction with our intelligence community. It's an abduction plan."

"You are planning an abduction?" breathed Baskin, incredulous, "of whom?"

"Sit down and be quiet, Ambassador!" barked Clement, "Jav, go ahead. No point in beating around the bush."

Farrow turned to the screen and began without further ado. "So far, we know Antropos has two close associates: Philo Berith and Mary Maccabe." He signaled the aide.

The screen changed to show greatly enlarged, grainy black and white long range camera shots of Mary and Philo.

"We've been doing the background checks. We know they're both important to Yordon. We propose apprehending one of them, maybe both. The only question is 'how?' It's not going to be easy to get close to them." He let that sink in for a few moments.

"Explain that," said Clement.

Baskin answered for the Admiral, "He means Yordon can kill at a distance. Remember Deng? Yordon would, no doubt, exercise that power against anyone he perceived attempting an abduction of either one of his confidants."

"A distraction is needed then," suggested General Bonhoeffer.

Farrow responded, "I wonder if that's enough. He seems to know what's going on around him – he can read minds."

"What are our options, then?" asked Clement.

"Maybe our targets have to come to us," said Farrow suggestively.

Clement was intrigued. "Go on."

"We have an interesting bit of footage to show you." Farrow gestured to the aide.

The screen changed again to show a video of the speech given by Yordon prior to the alleged plague of boils afflicted upon Vatican City. A woman standing near him could be seen to hide her face in her hands and shake her head violently.

"Freeze the film!"

"Now zoom in on the shaking woman -- in the light colored shirt and dungarees."

The film zoomed in on the image of Mary Maccabe.

"That's Maccabe!" said Pearson.

"As you can see something's wrong with her. Advance the film at half speed."

The grainy film resumed, slowly now, and the people in the room observed Mary in a slow motion argument with Yordon, culminating with her beating Yordon's chest with her fists. Then she turned away in tears.

Clement rubbed at his temples and considered what he had observed. He fixated on Farrow.

"What do you think, Jav? You've been on the scene."

Farrow agreed, "She's upset, but I don't have confidence that she will participate in any plan to compromise him. It isn't a black and white situation."

"It never is," answered Clement, "But plainly, she's got doubts. They need to be cultivated. Exploited."

"She's turnable," agreed Farrow, working his mustache.

"Then that's our angle," concluded Clement.

"We need to infiltrate Yordon's ranks," offered Van Ness.

"Let's put all our Indians on it right away, Wes", said Clement.

"Yes, sir."

"What about the man? Berith?" asked General Plain, who had been silent until now.

The Admiral answered. "That one's tougher, Augie. He's harder to read and goes back a lot farther with Yordon. I would bet he's not there yet. But the girl, she's ripe."

"Agreed," remarked Clement. He gave a nod to Farrow. "Good work, Jav."

Farrow smirked at Clement, and said, "Your bad deed for the day, Mr. President."

"But what happens after we have her?" asked Hanover.

Clement rewarded him with a predatory smile. "We bargain, of course."

3 Kaplan St, Jerusalem

It had been a while since he had been back in his office. The Crisis Center had finally begun to seem silly. The crisis was really in Rome now – even though the danger in Jerusalem was undeniable. People were wild in the streets, expecting the last days to commence at any moment. His government was barely able to hold things in check. The IDF was a virtual police force, corralling the enraptured mobs to prevent them from attacking each other. Strangely, sometimes both sides of these confrontations claimed to be followers of Yordon. Avrahami shook his head. He tiredly moved away from the window and pulled his hands out of his pockets.

Natan Silver sat on the other side of Avrahami's desk looking morose.

"Eventually he will return here, Moshe."

"If he is who he claims," answered Avrahami as he weakly plonked down into his swivel chair. His condition, which was bronchitis, unbeknownst to most of his colleagues, was taking its toll. He feared it had become a full-fledged pneumonia.

"Even if he isn't. So long as he thinks it. So long as others think it."

"*An davar.* We need leverage." He wiped at his glasses.

The phone rang. Not the regular phone, but a black phone with no buttons, obviously meant to be answered only. Avrahami picked it up.

"Avrahami. *Haloh*."

He sat up as he listened to the voice on the other end of the line, forgetting his fatigue. He asked a few questions, then listened further. After a few minutes he softly hung up the phone and rubbed his head.

"What?" asked Silver, impatiently.

Avrahami looked up. "That was Ravessi."

"From Washington?"

Avrahami nodded, "The Americans are planning to implant a spy among Yordon's following in Rome."

Silver slouched back in his seat. "Pah. How dull."

"There's more. The spy will attempt to turn the Maccabe woman. They think she's close."

"No kidnapping? Unusually subtle for the Americans. It will take them time. A mistake."

"An opportunity."

"You mean for us?"

"I'm afraid so, Natan."

Vatican City

The next calamity Yordon brought upon the Vatican state was an attack of scorpion-like bugs which seemed to grow out of the ground. There seemed to be no escape from the creatures, as they grew from every corner. The grounds of Vatican City became inches deep in the dead carapaces of the bloated, pink insectoid horrors. No one could walk far without having to bear the sound of crunching, or the sensation of squashing the pulpy innards of the insects beneath one's feet.

"It seems we are at the end of the world, Matthew," croaked Sylvester, as he watched a page attempt to sweep away the carcasses from the Pontiff's apartments.

"*In capo del mondo*," agreed the Prefect, very quietly. He wondered how much longer they could last.

Papal Task Force Villa, Rome

Karin let out a deep sigh of exhaustion and fell onto the winged leather chair inside the sleeping quarters that had been assigned to her at the Villa. *"Dog's balls,"* she thought to herself, "*This is starting to feel futile.*"

She rubbed her eyes and tried to relax. As she stretched her neck to loosen the muscles there, she examined the books she had brought with her to read, from the Vatican archives, which lay in disorder around the room's desk.

The sight of them gave her comfort. Books were her life. Books were patient and deep, *like Thomas.* She smiled at the thought of his solidity and his presence. He was the endearing straight man to her terrible jokes. As she shook off the stray thought and scanned the pile of tomes, she was reminded of something Thomas had said to her a few weeks ago.

"*If you read the Bible as a modern novel, then God, not the Jews, becomes the main character.*"

Something about that tickled at her subconscious. After a few moments, she sat up and found a bible in the top drawer of the night table.

She read into the night.

As dawn warmed the streaked panes of her room and filled it with wan light, she raised herself from the desk, where she had, at some point, laid her head down to sleep, and squinted at the daylight.

She dragged herself up and pulled down the window shades. Not bothering with anything else, she made her way to the bed and fell onto it, yielding to the soft contours of the pillows and allowing her sore muscles to melt into it.

As her eyes drooped shut, her mind raced with the realization that the God of the old Testament; the God of fear and retribution, was not the same God as the God of the new Testament; the God of forgiveness and love, and more so, the God of the Old Testament was arguably not one entity but instead, a legion of diverse characters.

The implications. As her mind swirled with the realization of the changing, mercurial God, she collapsed into exhausted oblivion.

Vatican City

Mary watched the dark cloud of insects envelope the buildings of Vatican City in quiet horror. She was numb.

"You still believe in him," she said, knowing Philo was standing behind her and would answer.

"It's what he believes he must do," answered Philo.

She turned to him. "But you don't believe that."

Philo looked back to the malevolent swarm of Yordon's making which obscured the Vatican buildings behind them. His jaw muscles tightened and his brow furrowed. Finally, the air seemed to escape from him, deflating him. He sighed and returned his eyes to Mary, "No, I do not."

Mary's face softened, feeling a relief and finding a compatriot with which to share her growing doubts, "It all seemed so right at first. I waited a lifetime to meet someone like him."

Philo grunted a short laugh and answered, "And I have spent a lifetime by his side and still I know nothing."

As they talked, Yordon came out of his tent and approached them. He scanned the throng which dominated the area around the Vatican State. It grew larger every day. He seemed satisfied.

"They follow you out of fear," said Mary, coldly.

Yordon frowned. "They understand I speak with God's voice."

"But there's no love here. These people are prepared to kill in your name, but they're not any closer to being enlightened."

Yordon answered, "I need them to be an army right now."

Before Mary could respond, he stepped away and went to join a lieutenant standing by the ruined steps before St. Peter's Square.

"He's a stranger to us now," said Philo softly. "And yet he tells me he still needs us."

"I wonder why?" asked Mary. She was suddenly reminded of her mother. With clarity she saw the possibility that it might have been her foolish, self-involved mother who had pushed her to this place and time -- more than the words of those strange children in Starkenville. Religion had been her salve, but it did not remove her problems. Perhaps she was no different than anyone else in this respect.

She examined her feelings for Yordon and was surprised, but then again, perhaps not so surprising, to find emptiness there. Whatever had happened between them back in D.C was gone. Now she had to find the strength to defy this latest tyrant in her life and walk away free of fear or regret.

Philo raised his hands in an expression of resignation. "My father used to say that one's life can only be understood backwards. But it must be lived forwards, yes?"

Yordon's Encampment, outside Vatican City

The Governatorato's *corpo di vigilanza*, the 120 person police force charged with providing security within Vatican City, made the assassination attempt without waiting for approval from the Special Delegate or the President of the Pontifical Commission. Their captain, Dominio Dilio, had the loyal following of his men and he simply decided that the time for action had come.

They had traversed the chasm between Vatican City and surrounding Rome under cover of darkness, borrowing ropes and harnesses from the construction crews who had been working on one of the residences, and crept about Yordon's encampment until they found his tent. He had been awake and talking with a circle of confidants.

He took the full assault of bullets from Captain Dilio and his men in the chest, legs and face. He did not die. His wounds, it was rumored, healed before the eyes of those who were with him. His anger had been like a heat rising in the room; physically palpable, and as they watched, the men of the *corpo* had literally melted into protoplasm and subsequently vaporized into gas which dissipated in the light breeze of the Roman night.

The next morning, Yordon stepped out of his tent and walked briskly to stand across the gap from the crumbled entrance to the Vatican City State and spoke in a voice heard by everyone within its 108 acres.

"Artieri. Your men failed. And now your guards will die."

As soon as he finished, a cry was heard from the ranks of the Swiss Guard, who had been standing on the other side of the gap at the main entrance.

"*Mio Dio!*" said one of the Guard. He seemed to lose weight as he dropped his weapon and fell to his knees. All the other guards were in similar states of duress. One of them ripped off his blue and yellow uniform, revealing the cause of their suffering. They were dissolving.

As the crowd watched in silent horror, their flesh sloughed off their bones while they stood on their feet. Their eyes shrank in their sockets and their tongues dried up in their mouths. All 101 surviving members of the Guard, and all remaining persons of the *corpo di vigilanza* were dissolved before the eyes of the frightened population.

"He used to save lives, and now he takes them," said Mary, with infinite sadness, as she and Philo watched the spectacle from a distance.

Philo scratched at his head, as if he could remove the discomfort of what he just saw with just a little more rubbing, then abruptly walked away, shaking his head and mumbling to himself.

Papal Task Force Villa, Rome

"I think I'm onto something of potentially enormous importance!" said Karin to her colleagues, as soon as she could convene them in the Salon room.

"And what is this?" asked Goss tartly, looking at the others.

"I did some Bible reading last night, Herr Goss," she turned to Thomas as she spoke, "and I came to see, for the first time, that God, as described in the Bible, is not one entity, but about twenty different characters traveling under the same circus tent!"

Thomas answered, "You're not the first person to posit that."

"Yes, no doubt. But now it's relevant. Really relevant."

"Forgive me for not considering the Holy Bible a 'must-read', as you Americans like to say. Whatever do you speak of Professor Ferguson?" asked Goss.

"Yes and why is this relevant to us?" added Jobson, who was busy with his pipe.

Karin answered, "It's like this. In the Old Testament, God starts out as a dispassionate all-powerful force; creating planets, sunlight, life. As the Bible story unfolds, he turns angry and demanding of his subjects -- kicking them out of paradise, flooding the planet, torching Babel, you know, wrathful. Then as the story unfolds, he turns into a warrior-God, defending the Jews against the Egyptians and anybody else that got in their way. It's only later that he begins to be more of a benevolent father figure. He goes from treating us as his subjects to treating us as his children. Toward the end, he completely recedes into the background, almost disinterested."

Thomas finished it for her, "Until all we had left was faith. That is, until the arrival of his only begotten son, in the New Testament."

"And what about after the Christ figure died?" asked Goss. "What was left? Faith again?"

Thomas nodded, "Yes, but also our redemption from original sin."

Kate interrupted Thomas, "And yet, in the end, still just faith, Thomas, and a human race that is largely unredeemed."

"And perhaps unredeemable?", added Goss with an arch of his eyebrow.

"Until now?" said Thomas.

"Yes, now we have Yordon," said Karin.

"A provocative notion, Professor Ferguson," said Goss through lidded eyes, puffing at a cigarette.

Jobson was rolling the idea over in his mind.

Thomas knew where she was going but bided his time.

Karin continued, "So you see, if the Bible documents multiple personalities for God, that is another way of saying multiple *manifestations* of God, or to take it all the way home, multiple gods! And if the good book is taken at its word, then it could very well be that mankind has been ruled by a pantheon of Gods that we mistake for one."

"The Gnostics wrote about this extensively," said Thomas. "They believed in a pantheon of godly creatures ruling the earth, organized in a hierarchy which they called the *pleroma*. The lesser Gods were called angels or demiurges or sometimes archons. And their children were lesser Gods, in turn."

"That sounds a lot like the Olympic Gods – as in Greeks and Romans," said Dr. Arbolera.

"I'm afraid so, Dolores." said Karin.

"Or perhaps these manifestations are more akin to the Platonic view of Archetypal forms – Unity, Justice, Goodness, Beauty – where these archons make up various aspects of the whole," wondered Jobson out loud.

"Zachary, I think it's possible Yordon is a demiurge or an archon", answered Karin, "And Jesus Christ may have been one too."

Thomas listened in silence. He felt the seduction of his curiosity. To his left, Dr. Arbolera looked distinctly uncomfortable.

Karin could see how difficult this was for the geneticist but she pressed on, "If Yordon is one of these Archons, then it could explain how he is so different from the historical Christ. Just like different sons of the same father can be as different as night and day, it's plausible that different manifestations, or sons, of God could be behavioral opposites."

"But why is he here? Who called him?" asked Arbolera.

"Perhaps it's the power of human expectation that has called Yordon forth. A self-fulfilling prophecy," mused Jobson.

"Could be," responded Karin with a wry smile, "But you don't believe in any of this nonsense, right Zachary?"

"Eh? Right, of course. Merely sharing ideas. Might give us a clue," said Jobson. He puffed at his pipe furiously.

Via Candia, Rome

The *panetteria* that Philo had found for them quickly turned into a favorite stop for them both. It was something Yordon showed no interest in, which both she and Philo liked. It gave them a chance to compare notes and concerns. Philo had initially seen Mary as something of an usurper and possibly even the catalyst of Yordon's increasingly authoritarian manner, but now he had come to regard her as another captive of Yordon's charisma, much like himself. They were trapped, he felt, in a downward spiral as Yordon's actions became more and more belligerent and frightful.

The bakery gave them a place to go and have something of a return to normalcy, simply by being inside the busy shop amongst the workaday hustle and bustle, even though the proprietor would have nothing of their money and treated them with embarrassing reverence.

On this day, Mary had gone alone to the *panetteria*, and while returning to the encampment, hot espressos for her and Philo in hand, that it happened.

286

A group of men, trim but rugged looking, stood in her path on the narrow, winding street, seemingly engaged in banter and horseplay. As she approached, they performed as young Italian men would, whistling at her and making remarks, but just as she was past them, a hand came up and covered her face with a wet handkerchief. As she fell into the murk of unconsciousness, her mind registered the splash of coffee on the ground and then there was silence.

Oval Office, The White House, Washington D.C.

"She's been acquired, sir," said Farrow.

Clement looked up from the papers on his desk. "Excellent. Good work."

"But not by us."

Clement put his pen down. "Say what, Admiral?"

"MOSSAD beat us to the punch." Farrow tried not to blink.

"How?"

"They grabbed her on a side street. Yordon may control an army but he doesn't run it like one. She had left to get coffee."

Clement pushed his chair away from the desk and slumped in it. "It was too easy." He glowered at the Admiral.

Farrow's response was clipped. "Easier than expected. She's in Jerusalem now, we think."

Clement shot upright from his chair and leaned over the desktop. "You *think*? Don't embarrass yourself further, Admiral. You FUBAR'ed the mission before it got off the ground." He worked his jaw as he considered his options. "There's obviously a security leak within our group." He thought a moment longer. "That god-danged Ravessi has to be involved in this. I've never trusted that son of a gun. Get him on the horn right now. And get me Avrahami too."

Papal Task Force Villa, Rome

A few days had passed and the members of the Papal Task Force were once again gathered in the salon room when Max Ravessi, looking uncomfortable for once, announced the news.

"President Clement has asked me to report to you that Mary Maccabe has been captured by MOSSAD and is believed to be in Jerusalem at this time."

"But that wasn't the plan?" responded Jobson in a half-question, looking to Karin.

"Clearly not," she answered.

Without moving from his chair and without looking up, Goss casually asked the room. "How could MOSSAD have found out?"

Ravessi answered levelly. "Perhaps the salon is bugged. Or microwave antennae are aimed at us? There are innumerable ways to achieve this sort of thing."

The corners of Goss' mouth upturned slightly. "I see."

Karin, oblivious to their collusion, asked, "What is Clement planning to do now?"

"Nothing," answered Ravessi.

Thomas grunted, "That doesn't sound like Adam Clement."

"Or Farrow," added Karin.

Ravessi shook his head, "President Clement chooses to do nothing for the moment because he has been persuaded by the Israeli Prime Minister that it is to this task force's advantage to have her far removed from the siege site, and well hidden. Pope Sylvester has been contacted and concurs with the strategy. I am told he expressed pleasure that some action has been taken to counter Antropos."

"But we need to speak with her. To see her," protested Jobson.

"You can easily fly to Jerusalem to meet with her. The major cost is time."

"Which we don't have," snapped Karin. "How much longer do you think those people in the Vatican can last? They must be out of supplies by now."

Ravessi's face was impassive. "The decision is made."

Karin was incredulous, "Take it or leave it, is that it? This is supposed to be our project!"

"We should have involved the Israelis from the start," remarked Goss.

Karin stood up and was about to fire a reply but Thomas cut her off. "Karin, calm down. It's a case of too many cooks."

"Or too many actors not following the script," quipped Jobson.

"Very funny," said Karin. She dropped back in her seat dejectedly.

Ravessi allowed himself to relax. This had been the last of the risks to his position. Goss would want private access to the girl but that was done easily enough. The President had tried to probe him for duplicity but he had been opaque. Clement was smart enough to not make a direct accusation but his thinking was clear. Ravessi was sure to be out of a job as soon as the crisis subsided. He shrugged inwardly. By then it might not matter what Clement did anymore. Ravessi tried to keep his face impassive. Israel had won the day.

Papal Task Force Villa, Rome

The group had broken up their meeting, feeling dejected, shortly after Ravessi's news. Thomas had wandered back to his room within the Villa — normally he would have lodged in the Vatican dormitories but that was, of course, impossible at this time.

When he arrived at his room, he found a cream colored envelope taped onto the door. Thomas recognized the papal seal, grabbed the envelope and hurried inside.

Once in his room he tore open the stiff package and found within it a note, written in Sylvester's own hand.

Thomas, my venerable soldier in God's service, health and apostolic blessing!

I write to you now as the hour grows desperate. We have suffered greatly and though our faith in God is strong, our bodies grow weak. I am compelled to summon you so that you may receive a gift. A gift that will assist you in carrying out your mission. Make haste and come to us as soon as you can. May Almighty God provide sure haven to all who seek the truth and may your journey to us be free of any intercession.

Thomas let the note fall to the ground and stared at the wall. *A gift*. He wondered what such a thing could be.

Chapter Ten: The Disciplina Arcana

Vatican City, October 2020

"Ah, Padre, it will not be easy," shouted the police Capitano.

"I know," said Thomas in the loudest voice he could muster above the noise.

"But for the Papa, we must try, no matter to the risk."

"*Sì*. We must."

It was what he had said to Karin and the others, over their protests, once he made it known what he intended to do.

"You'll be killed!" Karin had shouted at him, a note of plea in her voice.

"Surely there must be another way!" Jobson had protested.

But there was not.

As the police helicopter approached Vatican City, the wind picked up dramatically, making the helicopter buck to and fro. The pilot struggled with the controls. The engine groaned.

The Capitano yelled to Thomas, "It is like this every time. There seems to be no wind and suddenly there is wind. We have been unable to supply the hostages because of this."

"Can we go lower?" yelled Thomas in reply, over the thundering drone of the chopper blades.

"It is dangerous. But, as you say, we must try. For the Papa."

The helicopter heaved suddenly, throwing everyone forward. The pilot shouted profanities as he applied pitch on the stick and worked the engine throttle, trying to get lift.

"You will have to jump. The closer to the ground we are, the worse is this turbulence."

Thomas blinked and tried to feel brave. "Aim for the roof of the Palace."

The Capitano gave him a momentary, measuring look, then nodded crisply and barked orders at the pilot. The helicopter swung reluctantly and made headway toward the Apostolic Palace. As if in acknowledgement of their intent, the wind gusted with ferocious and sustained strength and the helicopter was carried like a leaf toward the perimeter of the island-city, where the wind died down again.

"Amazing," whispered Thomas, gripping the arm of the passenger seat.

"*Da capo,*" said the Capitano to the pilot.

The helicopter swung inwards again and made a determined dash for the drop-off point. The wind responded in kind, but this time the pilot was ready and jammed the throttle. The helicopter pitched forward toward the apartments.

As they were approaching the building, there was a sudden downdraft and the craft dropped like a stone.

"We're going to crash!" shouted the pilot. He pulled on the stick but the helicopter kept dropping. He pulled again and they stalled in their descent for a second.

"Jump, Padre!" was the Capitano's only cry as he pushed Thomas off the plummeting vehicle while they were barely ten meters off the ground. The wind kicked in again, spinning the helicopter wildly.

Thomas hit the ground with a grunt and rolled away as the helicopter crashed into the stones of the square and erupted into roaring flames. A few seconds later the fuel tank caught the fire and the entire wreckage exploded, spewing body parts and shrapnel everywhere. Thomas ducked behind a toppled pillar. After a time of lying there breathless, trying to still his racing heart and wondering how he could be alive, Thomas noticed that the rain of metal had ceased and all was quiet again. He pushed himself upright. With a wince, he realized that he had bruised his entire right side pretty badly. He wasn't exactly a Navy Seal and jumping out of helicopters was not a practiced action. Other than this, he was miraculously undamaged. He cast one more look at the smoking ruin of the helicopter, and stumbled toward the Palace.

The Papal Apartments, Vatican City

"As you suspected, Papa, Yordon may not be what he claims," said Thomas seriously.

They were seated in the Pope's private apartment, which was fitted with cots and supplies and appeared somewhat worse for wear. Sylvester looked tired and disheveled but still bore himself with the dignity of his office.

The Pontiff's eyes went wide. "Then you think he is the Son of Satan?"

"No. It's not that."

"Then what are you saying?"

"Professor Ferguson has a theory regarding the evidence of multiple personalities, all wearing the name of God, acting in the Judeo-Christian histories."

"But we know that God is mysterious," protested the Pontiff.

"There's more."

Sylvester sighed, "Go on."

"She believes that the God of men may be the creation of something greater than he, something unknowable – and, Holiness, that there may be more than one such creature; like a pantheon of Gods which we mistake for one.

"The ancient Gnostics believed something similar; that these Gods were organized into a hierarchy, which they called the *pleroma*. The lesser Gods were called angels or demiurges or sometimes archons. She believes Yordon may be an archon."

Sylvester shook his head disapprovingly. "You speak in heresies, Thomas. I fear you may have squandered your charge. We trusted you to expose Yordon, but instead you destroy us."

"No! But it's not the point. It's shattering, but it's only the beginning. It's necessary to get to the truth about Yordon."

"And what was Jesus then?" questioned Sylvester defensively.

Thomas ignored the Pope's growing anger, carried by his own earnestness. "Perhaps an archon too. That's where it gets interesting. We expect them to be alike but they're not. The story of Jesus is a story of moral redemption. The redemption of mankind by virtue of Jesus' triumph over his own flesh. He was made mortal and yet he was God. His spirit conquered the flesh and he saved us all. With Yordon, the intent may have started out being identical but has turned into the opposite; in his case the flesh is weak and the spirit has become corrupted by anger, ambition and delusion."

"Then he is the Anti-Christ."

"Not *the* Anti-Christ. A kind of Anti-Christ, yes, but not the one of prophecies. If there is a Satan, he's not involved in this."

"How can you know that?"

"Because... because...", he sighed. "I don't. I don't have proof one way or the other. It's that I 'sense' Yordon is not evil. I've met him, like you. There's no deception. He really wants to fulfill his mission of redemption but he's being seduced by his own power."

Sylvester's mood softened. "If it is as you say, how do we stop him?"

"We think the only way is to exploit his human weaknesses and expose his instability to the world. This might break his spell over the masses. Without a following, he may come back to his senses. You'll be on more of an even playing field with him, your Holiness."

Sylvester rubbed at his chin, "Except that I will speak the true, Incarnate Word of God. But how to exploit his weaknesses?"

"Take something away that he values and force him to overplay his hand."

"Ah, the woman." Sylvester went a little pale, "So it is true. He may kill you all for that brash act, Thomas!"

Thomas felt his weariness. "He might, but what choice do we have?"

"My son, forgive me for accusing you of destroying us. Instead you seek to destroy yourself – but with what guarantee of success?"

"If we do nothing, it's Yordon's success that's guaranteed. We have to try."

Before Sylvester could respond, they were interrupted by a rap at the door. "*Entri.*"

Cardinal Matthew Tatian hurried into the room, careful to close the door behind him. Thomas was shocked at the change he saw in the man. He looked gaunt and stooped, and the dark welts beneath his eyes gave witness to his pronounced lack of sleep.

"Padre. Father Prisciotti! So it's true. You are here."

"It's good to see you're surviving this ordeal, Prefect," answered Thomas, trying to find words that would not insult or alarm and also not lie.

Tatian looked at himself. "I am not at my best." He offered a simple smile. "The shock in your eyes acknowledges this, but rest assured I do survive, Father Prisciotti. I am eager to hear your news but I'm afraid I must interrupt your meeting with the Holy Father."

Tatian directed his attention to the Pope. "Holiness, the pretender is making another announcement. Perhaps we should hear it."

Sylvester nodded wearily and took a gentle hold of Thomas' arm. Together they proceeded toward the terrace.

They squinted in the sunlight and observed the multitudes that surrounded the city-state chasm on all sides. Thomas could not believe the high level of control Yordon seemed to have over these people. He didn't think it was unrealistic to say there were a hundreds of thousands of people surrounding the city-state.

Yordon seemed to sense Thomas' and Sylvester's emergence onto the Papal balcony. He swiveled to face them, showing the visage of man possessed, and sternly pronounced, "Your allies have successfully taken Mary from me, Artieri.

Well done, your Holiness. You think this will affect me and give you some advantage. It will not. It will make things much worse for you instead. The time has come to end this siege." Yordon raised his voice to a shout, "I have one final aggression for you and your followers, Artieri. "Your friends will turn against you. They will cry for your blood. You will run like a dog for your life. Behold the plague of madness."

Yordon swept an arm across the expanse of the Square and a howl of unbelievable volume and range that both pierced the upper registers of hearing and at the same time shook one's bowels overtook all the inhabitants. Everyone inside the city-state boundary fell to the ground, covering their ears and bellies with their hands.

On the terrace both Tatian and Thomas collapsed in agony but Pope Sylvester was unaffected. He backed away from their prone forms.

He began to pray. "Precious Lord, protect your people in this time of tribulation. Give us strength and bless us with your glory so we may persevere..."

He was interrupted by the shout of his name from inside the apartment. "Artieerrrriiiii!!!!" wailed two hoarse voices in unison.

Two Pages, once docile young men, now feral and wild-eyed, skulked out of the terrace doors and made a lunge for the helpless Pontiff.

Thomas struggled with the blind welt that sought to separate his intellectual core from his motor functions. He was being possessed. This is what it was. He gritted his teeth and fought for control of his body. In a strobe-like flash of awareness, he saw the Pope backing away from the advancing Pages. He saw Tatian struggling to his knees and shaking his head, a look of animal ferocity on his face.

With a yell of defiance, Thomas jumped toward the encroaching young men. At least the momentum of his weight would put him in their path and give the Pope a few precious seconds. But just as he fell in their path, still essentially helpless and in pain, both from the fall out of the helicopter and the current assault on his sensibilities, another figure came to stand over his body. It was Tatian! Impossibly, he grabbed hold of the two Pages by their collars and tried to hurl them over the terrace ledge. But it was too much for the fatigued Cardinal. The Pages turned on him and threw him over the ledge instead. Thomas blinked and tried to see through the haze of his resistance but he could only hear Tatian's final terrifying cry as he fell several stories to the pavement below. With an attenuated crack, he hit the ground and was silenced.

Outrage fueled his resolve as Thomas strained against the press of evil that sought to crush his mind. Suddenly the blackness clawing at his mind ceased. Thomas snapped upright, breathing hard and puffing his cheeks. He shook his head and thick drops of sweat flew off his face.

The Pages were heading back into the apartment in pursuit of Sylvester. Thomas grabbed one by the shoulder and spun him around. The Page raised an arm to block but Thomas was ready and connected with a right cross. The young man crumpled to the ground and lay still.

He was jumped from behind. A thin hand clawed for his eyeballs. He bent forwards, flipping the other Page over his head, and raised his foot to kick his assailant forward. The kick connected hard, and the surviving Page stumbled forwards head first into the low wall of the terrace. As he was groggily turning around, Thomas punched him in the chin with a roundhouse. The young Page fell backwards against the terrace wall again, hitting his head once more. He didn't move.

Suddenly the terrace shook with the force of a nearby explosion.

Ignoring the anger of his bruises, Thomas ran to the ledge and looked down.

The enraged mob was attacking the surrounding buildings and several walls were breached. Evidently someone had gained possession of explosives. Tatian's body lay sprawled at odd angles on the ground directly below. A few people who had been struggling on the square had leapt on him and were tearing at his clothes like hungry beasts. One of them looked up.

"They're upstairs in the apartment!"

"Get them!"

The attackers bounded toward the entranceway below.

Thomas whirled around scanning for the Pontiff. He was sitting in his throne chair back inside the apartment, sobbing quiet tears. Thomas approached him. He looked up at Thomas.

"It is over, Thomas. How can we survive this?"

"We will, dammit! There must be a way to get by them. Think, Father. Compose yourself. You know this palace."

Sylvester just shook his head.

In a fit of frustration, Thomas grabbed the Pontiff by his robes and pulled him off the throne.

"You're the Prince of the Apostles. The successor of Christ! He may test you as no one's been tested before, but you don't have the option of giving up. Stand up! We've got to escape from here right away. Pull yourself together!"

Sylvester hung limply in Thomas' grasp, eyes closed. Thunderous footsteps could be heard approaching. He looked to the door and slowly resolve reappeared on his face. He took hold of Thomas' fists and pried them off his robes. In a reprimanding voice he said, "You will not threaten the leader of the Holy Roman Catholic Church." Then more softly, "You are right, of course, my son. I have chosen well in appointing you to your special role in these affairs. Come, there's another way out."

Thomas swallowed a smile of relief.

The doors burst open and they were faced with an angry mob.

The ground began to heave as if a huge, invisible hammer were pounding against it. Vases and paintings fell to the ground and shattered. The lights flickered.

"Yordon's doing this. To bury us, like he said," said Thomas as steadily as he could.

"Quickly!" shouted Sylvester.

They ran through the connecting doorway into the anteroom. Thomas cast a glance backwards as he shoved a desk in front of the doorway and could not believe what he saw. The crowd was peopled with familiar faces -- now distorted in expressions of anger and delirium. He recognized priests, cardinals, clerks, men religious, tourists, secretaries and nuns, all driven to this madness by Yordon's will. They were determined to capture him and Sylvester. If that were to happen, he reflected, they would most likely rip them to shreds, as they had done with Cardinal Tatian.

There were several doorways off the anteroom.

"This way!" said the Pontiff as they chose a door connecting to another salon room. The two men ran through the rabbit warren of rooms, frequently changing bearings, until they arrived at a service stairway at the end of an ornately appointed corridor. The rabble could be heard not more than 50 feet away.

Thomas breathed deeply, trying to keep calm. He looked at Sylvester. The Pope looked alarmed but determined.

"Thomas, we must get to the Basilica. This way."

The Pontiff scrambled down the steps. Thomas followed. As they descended, Thomas heard the stairwell doorway above crash open. The noise of the crowd filled the echoing space.

"He's gone this way!"

"Get him!"

"Kill Sylvester!"

Thomas and Sylvester quickened their pace. Thomas resisted his urge to bound in front of the Pontiff and make an escape. Sylvester was the leader of the Catholic church and Thomas had to protect him. There was no one else.

They arrived at the bottom of the stairwell and re-entered the main body of the Palace. Thomas looked about and saw that they were below street level in what seemed to be an access corridor not normally intended for the Princes of the Church to traverse. Most likely it was used by the Palace's maintenance and kitchen staff. The noise of the mob grew louder. They would be in the corridor in minutes.

"Where are we going, Holiness?"

"The Basilica. There's a little known entrance ahead."

"Why the Basilica?"

"Because of what lays beyond. Trust me, my son. We are going to a place few men have seen."

Thomas held his tongue and doggedly followed behind the Pope. He was nimble for someone of his physical stature and advancing years. The pile driver-like impacts against the earth above were muffled, but the light fixtures swayed in reaction to the violence of the blows. Just then the corridor entrance slammed open several yards behind them. Their pursuers poured into the corridor. Thomas and the Pope broke into an outright run.

"There they are!"

"Don't let them get away!"

Sylvester pointed at a nondescript door at the end of the corridor.

Thomas leapt ahead and opened it. It led into a short, darkened passageway of brick and stone that smelled slightly of frankincense. They ducked inside and closed the door behind them. Thomas grabbed a wooden chair and jimmied it against the doorknob as securely as he could. That would give them a few seconds, for what it was worth.

They traversed the short hallway until they arrived at another door, this one of a darker, older wood, set into a wall of brick and stone. Thomas watched in fascination as the wall visibly shuddered from the pounding of the earth outside. Thomas tried the door. It was locked. He turned in half-panic toward

Sylvester. Sylvester was feeling along the wall of roughhewn stones. One of the stones was loose. Sylvester worked it loose to reveal a key. He gave the key to Thomas. It was rusted but with some effort Thomas turned the lock and the door creaked open. The ambience of a large space could be felt ahead. It was the Basilica.

Thomas and the Pope ran into what remained of St. Peter's and ducked below the level of the pews. There was no one present, which was not surprising, given the rapidly deteriorating condition of the antique structure. The walls shuddered in time to the heaving of the ground. One of the huge, hanging chandeliers suddenly broke free of its chains and came crashing down to the floor, spitting crystal and metal shrapnel in all directions. Thomas and the Pope ducked down and waited a few seconds for the dust to settle.

Sylvester looked at Thomas and whispered, "We must make our way to the altar – quickly, follow me to the side aisle."

They skulked along quickly until they arrived at their destination. Hurrying up the aisle like two cat burglars they made their way across the nave and behind the raised area of the High Altar, where St. Peter's chair was situated. This was the sanctuary of the Basilica, delimited by a structure of four ribbed and richly painted columns and a copper roof, the Baldacchino. Sylvester led Thomas to the rear of the sanctuary and down a few short steps into a space filled with mosaics, stone sarcophagi and inscription tablets. Many of them were fallen and broken.

"Welcome to the Sacred Vatican Grotto, Thomas." Sylvester looked at the ruins sadly. "Please follow."

They made their way along the grotto until they found a stone stairway leading to the lower level of the hidden space. It was darker here, and deceivingly quiet, save for the muffled rumbling of the earth. There were sarcophagi stolidly lying in wait, and a statue of St. Peter, depicted as an old man.

Thomas whispered, "The mob must have broken into the Basilica by now."

"They won't know immediately where we have gone," answered Sylvester. "We have eluded them, Thomas, but not for long."

Thomas looked at the sarcophagi in the small space and wondered aloud, "Where to now?"

Sylvester beckoned Thomas over to one of the sarcophagi. "Help me remove this lid."

"But, Holiness! It will be extremely heavy!"

"Please, have faith, Thomas."

Thomas steeled himself for a great exertion but was surprised to find that the stone lid was not nearly as heavy as it should have been. Together, the two men removed the lid and peered into the ancient coffin.

Thomas breathed, "A secret stairway, going lower still – but to where?"

Sylvester gave Thomas a small smile and clamored inside.

"Just come, Thomas. There will be time for questions later."

They pulled the lid back into place and descended down a narrow, earthen stairway. Thomas felt the walls around him and determined they were in a tunnel.

"Do you know where this leads, Holiness?"

"To the Tower of the Winds, my son. But that is all I know. I have never used this passageway. In modern Rome, duplicity no longer requires secret tunnels." His eyes flashed amusement briefly. "The Vatican is replete with such secret passageways. Hurry!"

The tunnel was dank. Their footsteps splashed wetly as they crouched along. They must be near the sewer system, thought Thomas to himself. He fought the feeling of claustrophobia. He swallowed and grimly followed the scrambling Pontiff. As they made their way, the rational mind within him observed the situation and was both amazed and saddened at the indignity the Pope was being forced to suffer. He shook it off and hurried along.

Private Chapel, Vatican City

They arrived at another set of steps and ascended. They quickly encountered a covering, which together they urged off. There was the clatter of spilled objects. It had been the tabletop of a small altar.

They emerged into a space which appeared to be a private chapel. There were a few short pews, and paraphernalia strewn about. It appeared that the chapel was used for storage, rather than for worship. Thomas spotted a skullcap floating just above the upper edge of one of the pews. He tapped the Pope's arm and pointed it out. Sylvester nodded and stepped into the open. Thomas followed.

Monsignor Stanley, prefect of the Vatican Secret Archives, was normally a man of precise articulation and genteel mannerisms, but today he was afraid. His priestly robes, usually worn with a simple elegance, were stained and ripped. He looked at Thomas and Sylvester, wild eyed, as they emerged from the underground passageway into the chapel.

"Monsignor Stanley," said the Pope.

"*Santissimo Padre. Dio Mio!* I am so frightened!"

"You do not have the madness."

"No. I do not know why. Perhaps I was mad already."

"Perhaps we all were," said Sylvester, patting the smallish prelate on the back gently.

Monsignor Stanley smiled adoringly at the Pontiff. "Praise God that you are alive!"

"It hasn't been easy to stay this way," said Sylvester simply.

Thomas grinned at his understatement, despite the gravity of the situation.

"And your associate?" asked Stanley, trying to regain the shards of his dignity.

"Father Prisciotti of the Chicago Diocese. He is accompanying me to the catacombs."

"The catacombs? You are planning to descend during this earthquake?"

The ground shook as if in acknowledgment of Stanley's fear.

Sylvester ignored it. "Lead us to the old entryway."

Stanley hesitated. His eyes grew wide again at the thought of having to travel with all the dangers that lurked throughout the battered Vatican City complex. Then he nodded gravely.

"Of course, *Papa*. This way."

They followed the prefect up the crowded stone stairs and into a darkened corridor that led from the Tower to the main Archive building.

As they walked, Sylvester questioned the Monsignor. "You were hiding. Does this mean the Archives have been sacked?"

"*Si, Papa*. When the madness began. The main Archive is nearly destroyed. The far wall has been collapsed by explosions and the majority of the *fondi* that were stored there have been scattered or burned. It is a tragedy beyond words. I am so sorry. At least I was able to seal off this corridor." The Monsignor's eyes glistened with tears as he narrated this.

Sylvester patted Stanley on the shoulder, trying to offer solace.

"It is not your fault. And the catacombs?"

"As far as I know, they are preserved."

Near the end of the corridor, they came upon a door, locked. The prefect silently produced a key and the door opened with a reluctant groan.

As they entered, he instinctively offered explanation of their whereabouts to Thomas. "Here are kept the most sensitive documents. Recent records, state secrets, proceedings. You are indeed privileged to find yourself here, Father Prisciotti, notwithstanding the regrettable circumstances."

They proceeded in silence along the length of the dusty, shelf-lined room until they came to the opposite wall. There was another door, this one more solid than the last, and judging from the cobwebs that covered it, one that had not been opened in a very long time.

"The key," croaked Sylvester.

"*Papa?*" wondered Stanley innocently.

"You know the one."

"Holiness, it is dangerous to go down there now…"

"The key!" insisted Sylvester with some impatience.

Stanley rolled his eyes, in what would have been a comical gesture in any other circumstance, and bowed to examine his key ring. It was a large ring of black iron, and held many keys of various vintages but he knew the one. In moments he had the key. Muttering to himself, he inserted it and gave it a turn. The lock mechanism released with a muffled squeal of metal.

Stanley turned the knob and the door swung inwards. Thomas and Sylvester entered. Stanley was about to follow but Sylvester stopped him with a raised hand.

"No, Monsignor. Your service to me is done. You have been a blessing to the Petrine office. Find another hiding place! You know this place better than anyone."

Stanley listened with a sorrowful frown but, after a moment of hesitation, he nodded and made to leave.

Sylvester touched his shoulder. "You know I cannot proceed without the other key."

Stanley turned, looking unhappy. "Papa! What do you intend?"

Sylvester was irked. "Monsignor? Do what I command."

"*Santissimo Padre!* You will not live!"

"If such is the will of God, then so be it! Now obey me!"

Stanley reluctantly obeyed. He produced a very old copper key, stained green with age. His hand shook as he handed it over.

"God protect us all from what is to come," he prayed.

"Now go," said Sylvester grimly, ignoring the appeal. "And lock this door behind us."

Thomas scuffled closely behind Sylvester in the resulting darkness. The walls and ceiling rained dust as the ground heaved in response to Yordon's supernatural pounding. He wondered if anything was left standing above ground.

"Holiness, what is this place?"

"A passageway to a very secret location. Soon you will see."

They felt their way in silence. Thomas could sense they were moving downwards on a gradually increasing slope. Suddenly the ground became uneven. Thomas stumbled. He wished there were steps. The two men descended further.

They came to another door. Sylvester worked the door lock with the copper key and pushed against it. It would not give.

"Your assistance, my son."

Thomas heaved against the door. On the second try it swung open in a rain of dirt and detritus. The space, though pitch dark, felt larger. Sylvester ordered Thomas to wait and disappeared into the nothingness. Thomas heard the strike of a match and in a moment, a torch was lit, illuminating the Pope's hand, his raised arm and a half moon silhouette of his face. Sylvester set about lighting several more torches set in wall sconces.

Thomas looked around in amazement at what appeared to be a well preserved, arched gallery. The walls were tiled mosaics. There were statues, paintings, a miscellany of art objects and several heavy chests. More galleries led off from this one in both directions.

"How large is this?" he asked in a reverent whisper.

"The Secret Galleries are a labyrinth. Perhaps no one knows all of them. It is an extremely rare privilege to visit this place. Only Popes and their most trusted confidants have ever been allowed down here."

"And no one speaks of it?"

"The secrets kept down here are powerful and deadly, Thomas. They can destroy as easily as bolster your faith. Take one of the torches and follow me."

They made their way through the galleries. Thomas looked from side to side at the mountains of collected artifacts. Everywhere textiles, jewels, figurines, canvases, ribbon wrapped parchments purple with age, scrolls emblazoned with papal seals and tassels, leather clad volumes and more. This underground collection of rooms must have existed for millennia in secret. As they progressed the rooms became cruder in their appointments and smaller. Sylvester stopped before a huge, iron banded chest, half as tall as a man.

"We are here."

"Where?" puzzled Thomas, looking for a door or a passageway.

"Help me." Sylvester struggled with the lid of the chest. With Thomas' help they opened it. Within the chest, at its base, was a trap door. With an affirming nod from Sylvester, Thomas jumped in. He helped the Pontiff follow suit. Together, they forced the trap door open and found more stairs leading further downwards.

Sylvester urged Thomas forward. "Go ahead, my son. Carefully. You are entering the most ancient of places."

"This is just like in the Grotto."

"It is a favorite trick of ours."

The opening was not large and Thomas had to squeeze his relatively large frame through. He stepped down using cuts made in the rock just below the opening and found himself inside a small hollow. He thought it was an altar, or a shrine. There was a statue of a pagan idol positioned on a raised dais. The statue, a many armed female goddess from the looks of it, seemed to undulate in the guttering torchlight. The shrine smelled musty and faintly fragrant, a flat echo of herbs or scents that had been burned here untold ages ago.

Sylvester grunted softly as he descended. He came and stood by Thomas.

"A Mithraic deity," said Thomas, dumbfounded. His eyes glistened with curiosity. "How old is this place?"

"It dates back to the early Roman empire."

Thomas shook his head in disbelief. "Secrets within secrets."

"It is the way of the Church, my son," answered Sylvester, as he stepped onto the dais and examined the statue. It had numerous holes and small, rectangular slots chiseled into it where offerings had been most likely inserted at one time. He felt for his pectoral cross, and removed it from his neck. Thomas watched in amazement as Sylvester inserted the pectoral cross into one of the slots and turned it. There was a thud followed by a heavy, grating sound and the entire dais moved to the side revealing a smaller room behind it. There was nothing in this room but a rough, wooden table, a long, flat-topped stone bench, and cloth-wrapped object on the table. Wordlessly, Sylvester entered the room and placed his torch into an empty wall sconce. Thomas did the same. The ceiling shuddered and dust trickled down upon them.

Sylvester removed the covering from the object. Thomas could see that it was a book. A very old book.

"What you see here, my son, is something that the church has been protecting since the earliest era of Christianity."

Thomas frowned. "A book?"

"Much more than a book. A conduit. A template for miracles. It's a weapon, Thomas."

Sylvester gestured to the stone bench. "Sit." He handed Thomas the book.

Thomas laid the book back on the table. As he did this, Sylvester spoke.

"This book is a secret which has been kept within the highest levels of the curia since the beginning of the Apostolic succession. It is a secret so vast, and so potentially destructive that the Church has never dared reveal it until now, the time of ultimate crisis. It is the Book of Metatron."

Thomas looked upwards and furrowed his brow as he thought about the name. It was familiar.

"Metatron is Enoch."

Sylvester nodded again. "The grandfather of Noah, who was transformed by God's cleansing and healing fire into Metatron, the greatest of the Angels. The Great Guardian of Heaven. That is correct, my scholarly friend."

"Then is this another Book of Enoch?"

"In a sense, but it is not that book. That one is written by first century Kabbalists. The words in this book are said to be words of the angel himself, transposed directly into this book by the author, who is anonymous."

"Like Mohammed, and his words captured in the Q'uran."

"Yes, but more. This book can do much more, my son."

"What can it do, Holiness?" Thomas held his breath.

Sylvester sat down beside him and reached out with one hand to touch the book. He stared directly into Thomas' eyes.

"This book can summon God, Thomas. This book can bring God to us."

"Do you mean?..."

"I mean his living presence can be conjured, my son."

"Conjured? Like a magical ritual?"

"Unfortunately, yes. Like that." Sylvester looked strangely embarrassed.

"That's amazing. More amazing than the things I've told you. I find it hard to believe such a thing exists."

Sylvester's voice filled the gloomy room, his voice thickening with emotion. "The Church has always been the point of encounter between God and humanity, between the Creator and his creatures. And this is one of the conduits. Nothing more. It is not so large a step from the conceptual to the physical manifestation of such a thing."

The ground above them pounded again, breaking the curious moment of revelation. Sylvester was prodded back into his explanation.

"This book is believed to have been written about 100 B.C., *before* its more well-known 'companion' volume. It is perhaps the oldest original church document of the Archives in our continuous possession."

"It's as old as our faith," answered Thomas.

"And just as real," said Sylvester.

"How could it survive?" Thomas wondered aloud. He was well aware of the disastrous history of the Archives. They had been destroyed and disseminated again and again.

"It is a testimony to the faith and resolve of the men who knew its secrets. Saint Lawrence, the Librarian, was tortured to death for refusing to reveal its location."

"But I was taught that he died defending the location of all the Archives."

"Perhaps that too, my son, but it was this book that he died for. This book can never fall into the wrong hands. This book can never be destroyed for it can never be recreated. It escaped destruction during the sackings of Rome by the Goths in the 5th century, because of the efforts of Innocent and Leo. They say the Huns saw the swords of Peter and Paul playing over the heads of Leo's delegation, and for this reason turned back from Rome. It was the Metatron Codice at work."

"Amazing."

Sylvester continued, whispering in earnest, "It survived the darkest years of the Papacy, when almost all archival records were destroyed or made to vanish in conflict after bloody conflict. Factions, Antipopes, Normans, Saracens, Germans -- even the Roman people themselves – have sacked the Church palaces. The Metatron book was hidden through it all. In the walls of Sant'Angelo it remained through the Crusades, through the Schism, through the

Reformation and the Napoleonic wars. It is one of the few possessions of the Catholic Church which is still maintained under the *Disciplina Arcana.*"

"The discipline of that which is secret. A concealed Christian truth!" whispered Thomas.

Dirt spiraled down from the ceiling and clattered chaotically against the table and the dirt floor.

Sylvester spoke more rapidly. "We fear this book, Thomas. You should fear this book. Because the wrath of God is great. Because the ambitions of mortal men are dangerous. Because no one understands Him. Some of my predecessors have argued that it should never be used, for it will certainly bring forth the Apocalypse."

"But what if it's your only weapon against Apocalypse?" whispered Thomas. He marveled at what he had heard. The Church possessed the power to summon God in response to the entreaties of men. It had been done in the past and it could be done now!

Sylvester' eyes shone in the torchlight. "You have heard of the Third Secret of Fatima."

"Of course. The Marian revelation given to Sister Lucia in Portugal, when she was a child. The substance of that revelation has never been revealed to the public."

"The third prediction of the Virgin Mary has been kept secret all these years because of its implications. The language of it implies the return of God and a great challenge for all men. It refers to an archangel, not Christ, as our ultimate soldier against the forces of evil. It talks about the 'Holder of the Key', who will play a critical role in this drama." Sylvester fingered the pectoral cross hanging around his neck. "We have surmised that reference to mean that a Pope would use this book again. Since the time of John XXIII, the succession of Popes has stood ready to face the challenge. My predecessors and now I have been waiting for events to dictate its use. Until today, my son. Now there is no doubt. The responsibility has fallen upon me."

Sylvester looked pale, despite the darkness, as he uttered these last words.

Thomas turned the facts over in his mind. "So you intend to use it now. Who will answer if we call upon it again?"

Sylvester only shrugged.

The walls around them shuddered. Thomas instinctively crouched down at the next impact. Both their heads were covered with dirt and dust. It was becoming like a rain. The Pope's eyes were a cloudscape of doubt, despair, fear, and incongruously, hope.

Thomas suddenly understood why the Pope was revealing the Vatican's deepest secret to him now. "No, I'm wrong. You don't intend to use it. You said you had a gift for me. This is it. You're giving it to me – to use."

The Pope answered by raising himself from the stone bench.

"Examine the book, Thomas. We have time, though you may not think it. God will protect us."

Sylvester paced the room and began a slow murmuring prayer to himself in Latin.

Thomas turned back to the book and touched its surface. No writing on the cover. A rough but pliant texture, like leather? With a small amount of resistance the leather tongue which wrapped around the book loosened. Thomas unwrapped the tongue carefully, hearing it creak as the dry material gave after centuries of being folded in the closed position. He opened the book.

He gazed with wonderment at the ancient writing. It was written in Aramaic, the common language of the Jews in the time of Christ. Thomas had been trained to read it during his days at Gregorian. He squinted at the angular letters and began the work of deciphering them. He turned the first page, a fine grained lambskin stretched thin into paper-like sheets for the purposes of writing. It crinkled loudly. There were holes in the text where the reddish, iron-based ink once lay.

There were narratives and dissertations dealing with the nature of the heavens, and most interestingly, prayers which read more like incantations. His mind raced. He needed time to properly consider this work.

He looked up. Sylvester was waiting.

"There is much to study here," said Thomas.

"Take it. You have a responsibility to bring the book to safety and to use it."

"But how? Why not you?"

Sylvester shook his head sadly and cast his eyes upward. "No. This is the seat of God's See on earth. *La Citta del Vaticano.* I am his servant. My place is here."

"But Holiness! You'll be crushed to death!"

"Learn the words within the book. The pure of heart and firm of faith can summon angels. You are such a man, my son."

Thomas head swam as Sylvester closed the book carefully and placed it into Thomas' hands. He beckoned Thomas to follow him out of the room.

"Come, now we must go. The collapse of these passages is imminent and you must make your escape."

Together, the two men grabbed their torches, climbed out of the hidden hollow and returned to the level of the secret galleries. There was debris everywhere. Several walls had buckled and their original route was blocked by fallen rocks.

"Is there another way?" asked Thomas.

"I believe so. Follow me," answered the Pope, tentatively.

They moved away from the chest and proceeded deeper into the labyrinth of arched spaces. The walls rained dust and pebbles. Collapse seemed imminent. Oblivious, Sylvester led Thomas deeper into the darkness until they arrived at an ancient stone plug set at the base of a wall.

"What is it?"

"It is another way out. But first, you must move this stone."

Thomas tested the weight of the stone. It was heavy, and firmly seated in place, but movable. "Where does it lead?" he asked.

Sylvester watched him struggle with the plug. "To the deepest levels of tunnels below the city. Deeper than the chasm. Follow it downwards. It will take you to the most ancient of subterranean waterways, formed by the earth itself and discovered by men who lived before the Caesars. It is said that if you follow the course of the waterway, you will arrive at a white cross etched into the brickwork. At that point you will be directly beneath the Lateran Palace, outside of Vatican City proper. There is a way up from there. Go upwards and make your escape."

Thomas pushed on the stone again and it suddenly gave, revealing a profound darkness that nonetheless gave the impression of depth. Thomas smelled the brininess of the air within.

"Come with me, *Papa*," pleaded Thomas.

"That is not how it is to be." answered Sylvester firmly.

Thomas stood erect, and in a sudden impulse, grabbed Sylvester and hugged him as hard as he could.

Sylvester quietly spoke into his ear, his voice subdued but intense with emotion. "Everything depends on your successful escape from this place. Go with God, my son. My prayers are with you."

The Secret Galleries, Vatican City

As Yordon's relentless thrashing of the earth continued, the Sistine Chapel, the Apostolic Palace, St. Peter's Basilica, the Tower of the Winds, the Vatican Library, the Secret Archives, toppled into hills of rubble. Nothing stirred and no one came forth.

Deep below the earth, in the secret galleries, Pope Sylvester III struggled to climb over the wall of fallen rock that separated him from the passageway of their original descent. As he scrabbled for handholds, he imagined Yordon was down here with him.

"Why do you wage war, when you say you are a man of peace?" pleaded the disheveled Pontiff silently to his imagined opponent.

"This not just any war, Artieri. This is a Holy War," said a voice from behind him.

He jerked in surprise, almost falling the entire length of his climb. There, standing at the floor of the gallery and shimmering softly, was Yordon – or an apparition of Yordon. Sylvester wondered about the oxygen levels down this far. He had to be hallucinating. He shook his head tiredly and he returned to his climb, his shaking hands grasping at the stones. Bits of rock crumbled and fell clattering to the tiles below. Sylvester answered the apparition without looking back at it.

"There is no such thing as a Holy War. Only peace is holy. Peace is God's will, not war. You yourself have said to those innocents who follow you that religion should never be a pretext for hate, yet the destruction you have brought in the name of religion exceeds all boundaries."

"In the name of *ending* religion, Artieri. I am sent by God to topple the temples…"

"…only to raise a new one with your name emblazoned on it?"

There was no answer. Sylvester paused in his climb to look back. There was no one there. *Had it been real?* He had no time to wonder further. The entire cavern was collapsing around him. Suddenly the mound of rock he had been attempting to climb shifted and became a rock slide. He scrambled for a hold but it was no use. In moments, he was thrown to the bottom. Rocks crashed down onto his prone form, pinning him face down on the floor of the gallery. He winced in pain. The increasing weight of the rocks pressed down

315

on his body and mercilessly crushed the breath and blood out of him. Sylvester wondered at the horror of his own death as the darkness closed in around him. With his last breath he prayed for Thomas' successful use of the Metatron book, for it would not be as simple as reading a prayer to gain the attention of the Creator.

Ruins of Vatican City

Yordon scanned the smoking ruins of what had once been the center of the Christian world and breathed in his victory.

Yordon looked at Philo from his unblinking eyes. "Now that we have swept away the detritus of the past we can open the minds of men. We are victorious."

Philo reviewed the flattened terrain. Somewhere in there lay the body of Sylvester III, the last successor to the throne of Peter. *The last Apostle.* It was a profound tragedy in Philo's heart. A tragedy that curdled his heart and hardened it into a vantage of objectivity. For the first time, Philo saw his longtime friend and compatriot as something else entirely. He realized that Yordon, for all his noble words and original intentions, had become a monster.

Trying to keep the bitterness out of his voice, Philo asked, "And what do we call you now that you are the absolute ruler of the Christian world?"

Yordon turned to face his companion. "I am who I am."

Chapter Eleven: The Foreskins of Their Hearts

Situation Room, Washington, D.C., November 2020

The Joint Chiefs sat stone-faced around the conference table, several levels below the West Wing, in the White House Situation Room. Clement stood at the head of the table, looking down at the maps and reports on the destruction of Vatican City, while his staff waited. Also present were several Cabinet members and a cadre of Presidential advisers, including Wesley Van Ness and Janine Kelly, the White House Chief of Staff.

"Hell's bells. I just can't bring myself to believe this happened. It's an abomination," breathed Clement huskily. He looked tired.

"It's the ultimate terrorist attack, sir," said Secretary Blaine, his jowls working.

"I think of it more as an act of war," growled Admiral Farrow.

"Wars are between warring parties, Admiral," replied Kent Hanover coolly, "There was only one aggressor here, and that was Mr. Atropos."

Van Ness retorted, "The way Antropos couches it, the Vatican was the aggressor."

"Which makes him, at least in his own mind, a revolutionary," said Janine Kelly.

"Which is a terrorist, if you are on the wrong side of that revolution," answered Blaine.

Clement sighed and sat, placing his hands flat on the table, which directed everyone's attention back to him. "All very interesting, team, and you can parlay that around all day long on your own time, but the question remains, what is the stance of the United States of America with regard to all of this. Vatican City has been destroyed. It's a sovereign state, separate from Italy, and not a member of the NATO alliance."

Hanover added, "And Mr. Antropos is not even sticking around to plant a flag. Italian Military Intelligence reports that he is on the move again and heading East across the Aegean."

"Back to Greece?" asked the President.

"No sir, toward Jerusalem, and that cannot be a good thing."

"Agreed," said Clement. He took a moment to rub at his eyes, then scanned the table. "Janine, let's get the Speaker on the horn. Admiral Farrow, I want the Fifth Fleet positioned off the coast of Israel as soon as possible. And Mr. Hanover, contact the CIC at our Emirates UAV base. We need to move a fresh wing of Predator drones into the region."

3 Kaplan St., Jerusalem

Avrahami sighed inwardly as he watched his ministers bicker over what course of action to take. *Action.* Grabbing the Maccabe girl had been a good tactic but even so, he had begun to lose any sense of connection to what was going on. He couldn't shake the feeling that he was nothing more than an observer. A helpless observer. He coughed, tasting the sour phlegm of the growing bronchial infection in his throat.

"How can this be the same man who stopped the confrontation at Jericho?" exclaimed Secretary General Rosenthal.

"It was a ploy to get our guard down," declared Defense Minister Yaakov. "To let an army of Muslims into the Old City under the pretext of peace. Now we're surrounded, like the Vatican. Only with us, the enemy is already inside the gates!"

The burly Ephrat cleared his throat. "Don't you think Yordon would regard the taking of his woman as an antagonistic act? Why is it a surprise that he should heading to Jerusalem?"

"He's been on a warpath since before that. Look at Rome, like Ben Zion said," answered Avi Grinker.

"And how does he know we have her? How could he know?" added the spindly David Chalutz.

Ephrat shrugged. "Maybe he has spies too. Maybe one of you is a spy."

"Don't do it, Schmuel!" Avrahami barked at his Science Minister. "If we start thinking like that, it's over."

Ephrat was quieted by the warning.

Silver took control of the conversation in the moment of silence. "Yordon is a man. He thinks like a man. Forget about the powers for now. Deal with him like another conventional opponent. If you look at him that way, he's a shrewd politician, nothing more."

"Nothing more?" asked Rosenthal sarcastically.

Silver was unimpressed. "That's right. He changes his position as the situation dictates. He's a master of language. He knows how to rouse a crowd."

Rosenthal stood up, aghast. "They're totally in his thrall! Have you seen the demonstrations by the Wall?"

"Yes, yes. Who can avoid them? But it doesn't change the fact that he's used us -- to establish a foothold in the Middle East and gain the upper hand. The jeep, the IDF guard, all merely convenient until we ourselves became an obstruction to him. It was bound to happen, whether we grabbed the Maccabe girl or not. It's fortunate that we do have her. It gives us some leverage."

The Rabbis Weizman and Chet cast an accusatory look at the Prime Minister. The armed guard had been his idea.

"Now the impetus is on us to regain control of the situation. Yordon's army marches on Jerusalem as we speak."

"Bah! You speak in the same tired language of the soldiers and party bosses that have run Israel into the dirt," retorted Rabbi Weizman. "This is not about politics, Minister Silver."

Silver tried not to show his exasperation. *Here it comes.*

Weizman didn't wait for a response. "This is about the Judgment Day. It's here. It's marching this way."

"There's no use fighting it," agreed Rabbi Chet.

Looking at each other, they both came to silent agreement.

Weizman looked at each face around the table gravely and announced, "Yoram and I have deliberated for many long hours on this and we have come to the decision that even if Yordon is not who he claims to be, he is part of the end-cycle and therefore it is a sin for us to oppose the coming events in any way."

"What? Are you crazy?" protested Rosenthal.

Weizman was unperturbed. "We will instruct our constituencies to make no obstruction to Yordon's army as they enter the city. The will of God must not be hindered."

Papal Task Force Villa, Rome

The bedraggled, dust-covered man who knocked at the door of the villa looked like a Franciscan brother. His name was James. He asked to see Thomas, and was quickly escorted to the Salon.

Thomas felt grief at the sight of the man. He was dirty and bruised and obviously very tired. Thomas ushered him in and offered him water. After a few minutes he gently questioned the man.

"Brother James. You said you have a message for me?"

"What? Oh, yes. The Papal Chamberlain has made contact with the survivors of Vatican City and has advised us that there is nothing more the

Vatican can do for us. He said that at this moment in time, there is no Vatican government."

The man sobbed.

Thomas reached out and held him. He blinked a few times but steeled himself and grabbed James by the shoulders.

"And...?"

James was lost in sadness.

Thomas shook him. "What else did he say? You came here..."

Grimly, James looked up and locked eyes with Thomas. "He said to tell you to use the weapon."

Thomas said nothing. So the Chamberlain knew as well. Perhaps this made sense, since he was one of only two or three senior Curial officials who were sustained across Papal appointments. Thomas suddenly feared the terrible secret he shared would be lost, if he did not use it. And if he did use it what then? It would be known to all the world. Would it work against a living nightmare? What would prevent Yordon from turning it to dust in his hands?

"What is the weapon, Father? Can you tell me? I have no hope left..."

Thomas glared at the man. He felt anger. Then sorrow.

"God is eternal, James. And so hope is eternal. I can't tell you more. Now rest." Thomas looked for the housekeeper, who had been hovering outside the door.

"Take care of him."

Thomas was about to turn away when a voice asked, "What weapon is he talking about, Thomas?"

Thomas blinked again. Karin stepped into the room.

"I don't know what you're talking about, Karin."

"You're lying to me. Don't do that."

"I can't..."

"You have to tell me."

She came forward, stood before him, put her hands on his shoulders, and looked into the darkness of his eyes. He felt his resolve weaken.

"Thomas."

Thomas held his breath. He was entrusted with the greatest secret of the Catholic Church. Sylvester had instructed him to use it. He felt its importance. Yet, he wasn't sure he believed in it. If it was real, the implications were profound. If it was false, it would be crushing. And there was another secret in his heart. And that was that he loved Karin. No, more than that -- he was *in love* with her. Beautiful, tough as nails, irascible, whip smart, caring Karin. The light that had found his heart. He wanted to tell her everything. But that particular secret would have to wait.

He sighed and looked up, into her cobalt blue eyes. "There is a secret of the Catholic Church, Karin. Something of great power."

"What is it?"

"It's a book. The book of Metatron"

"Metatron? You mean the archangel? I've heard rumors about secret books but how is it a weapon?"

"It's like an incantation book. It can summon God."

Karin's nostrils flared and she paled slightly. Her eyes drilled into Thomas, waiting for the punch line, but his expression did not change. *He's serious.*

"We've got to tell the others," she finally croaked.

Papal Task Force Villa, Rome

"If what you say is true, Father, then this book has the power to metamorphose myth into history. We would be like alchemists," said Goss with an air of skepticism.

Thomas had revealed the Metatron book and its purported nature to the team and now it lay on the central conference table in the Salon room. The members of the Papal Task Force stood around it, as if in reverence.

"It's amazing," whispered Dr. Arbolera, reaching out to delicately touch its cover.

"It's poppycock," said Ravessi. "There's no way this is possible. I say we can't possibly rely on this book as some kind of weapon we can use!"

"We've got to try!" protested Karin. "Yordon's going to start a world war if we don't, plain and simple. Yordon's army is marching on Jerusalem as we speak. What do you think the Israeli reaction to an invasion will be?" she asked forebodingly. "We may be the planet's only hope."

"What about pre-emptive military action?" asked Arbolera. Aren't our governments doing anything to stop him before he gets to Jerusalem?"

Ravessi responded immediately. "Admiral Farrow has informed me that the President has approved the deployment of a Carrier Strike Group into the region and that he is prepared to deploy drones and guided missile airstrikes again Yordon's forces in defense of our Israeli allies."

"It will only start a world war sooner," said Karin.

"Has Israel asked for American help?" asked Dr. Arbolera.

Ravessi shook his head. "Not yet. But our Israeli friends are not standing by quietly, waiting for events to overtake them. As you know, MOSSAD has successfully taken the Maccabe girl. She is currently hidden within the city of Jerusalem. They are probably working on her now. Perhaps this will give them some influence when Yordon arrives.

Jobson said unexpectedly, "I'd like to meet with the girl."

"Fly to Jerusalem now? Out of the question," blurted Ravessi.

Jobson answered impatiently, "The Papal Task Force was created specifically to develop counter-strategies against Yordon. Israel's independent actions threaten our success. Aren't we stronger working together rather than attempting to outmaneuver each other? Maybe the girl knows something of Yordon's interest in this book we have. Thomas has said that he knows of it."

Ravessi scowled.

Jobson pressed him, "We're the scholars and scientists, Max, not MOSSAD interrogators. They need us. We need them."

"Will you make contact with them, Max?" asked Karin, more kindly.

Ravessi pondered this, choosing to keep to himself the fact that the Israeli Government already had the entire archive of the Papal Task Force's research, thanks to his efforts on their behalf.

"You're an American, Max," added Karin, seemingly reading his mind.

Ravessi realized his façade of loyalties was wearing thin. He decided to let it all hang out.

"Prime Minister Avrahami is of the opinion that the security risk inherent in divulging her location to any member of this group threatens the secrecy of that location. Our governments would learn of her whereabouts quickly. Shortly thereafter Yordon would know that location too. His followers are everywhere."

Goss was about to protest but found himself silently agreeing.

Jobson was not to be dissuaded so easily. "But Max, only we have the unique insights – and as a team, the ability to continue to make such insights."

"And only we have Metatron," stated Thomas.

"I think Zach is right. We MUST see her!" pleaded Karin.

Ravessi was recalcitrant.

"You can trust us, Max. I'm a scientist! I have no agenda other than to understand the facts. I won't reveal her location. We're on the same side, dammit!" said Jobson.

Ravessi looked into the Jobson's knowing gray eyes and saw the lines of intelligence in the man's face. He knew Jobson was a man of acerbic integrity. He understood the stakes. And the girl just might know something about that infernal book that could help them. He decided he could be trusted.

"Very well. I'll make the contacts -- through the American channels."

"Alright, Maxy!" exclaimed Karin.

Ravessi didn't break eye contact with Jobson. "But only you, Doctor. Only you will be allowed to see her and only under conditions of utmost secrecy."

Mar Saba, Israel

Upon returning to Israel, Yordon rejoined his followers at Mar Saba, a fifth century fortress dug into the canyon walls overlooking the Kidron River. It was an excellent strategic choice, not more than a half hour's drive from Jerusalem.

Yordon grasped the sun-warmed, rough stones of the ledge and scanned the horizon. A commanding view of the Judean Desert and the Dead Sea, hazy in the northern distance, was the backdrop. He found it appropriate that this formidable pile of stones had, amazingly, once served as a refuge for Greek Orthodox monks. Now it served his purpose.

The throng gathered inside the fortress buzzed like hornets. Standing high above them, wearing his familiar white cassock and *skoúfia*, Yordon let his words be carried by the wind to his growing army.

"I am a human being, like all of you."

His followers stirred. Arabs, Israelis, Muslims, Christians and Jews, plus many who had followed him from Italy, waited for his next words.

"And in my mother's womb I was made flesh from seed and ovum, just like you. I was born, I breathed the air, and the first sound I made was a crying. I was swaddled in sleep and nurtured. As I grew, something happened. I prayed, and the spirit of wisdom was given to me. I came to see myself as an instrument of God. He has given me knowledge of the things that are: how the world was made, the turning of the sun, the changing of the seasons, the violence of the winds, the patience of the earth. All such things as are either secret or well known."

He let his words bounce off the stones and dissipate into the air.

"We are all instruments of God's intent. We are his creatures. As such, you must open your hearts to him if you wish to know him in this way too."

A hawk screeched above, the echo filling the emptiness. A flag beat against a sudden breeze. Yordon's voice pierced the air.

"As Abraham was commanded by God to circumcise himself in a gesture of subjugation, now God requires a similar commitment from you. He requires not only your understanding and devotion. He requires your surrender."

Now he shouted and stretched his clenched fists out over the crowd.

"You must undergo a spiritual circumcision. You must remove the foreskins that husk your hearts! Cut away the callus surrounding your souls, and surrender yourselves to him, through me. The moment you make this act of submission you will enter the state of primal innocence and you will be ready to know God. Your soul will be one with God, as the flame is one with the fire."

Philo's eyes widened. *What words. The foreskins of our hearts.* The image was chilling. Cold and surgical, yet bloody and hot with supplication. Yordon was demanding unquestioning loyalty from his army. He was demanding blood from his army. Were these the words of a prophet or a spiritual liberator? Philo stared at the figure gesticulating before the crowd, his air dancing in the wind like a head of serpents, where it was not bound by his *Skoufia*, and could not find his beloved Monk from Athos anywhere there.

Yordon made a fist in the air, and the air crackled around it. He spread his hands out in an arc before the crowd, and a darkness rose up from the earth like a black mist, enveloping the inner courtyard and the hills around the fortress. The crowd grew silent, gaping at the murk that lazily encircled their feet.

"Together we will lick up the face of the earth and deliver it from evil with fire and sword. The hour of reckoning is here."

Yordon's expression was feral as he shouted to the crowd.

"I am the sword of God! We will cleanse the earth of its impurities in preparation for the Last Days. We will march to Jerusalem and stand on the hills which surround her. We will enter through her gates and claim her as the capital of the kingdom of God on earth. She will be called New Jerusalem. From there, we shall tread on the necks of kings and punish the pretenders of the earth. God will reign in Jerusalem and before you, God will manifest his full glory. Then you will clothe yourselves with wisdom like a robe, put knowledge on yourselves like a crown and be seated upon a throne of perception. The kingdom will be yours."

He was breathing hard. Only Philo could hear this. Light radiated from him and the ground rumbled slightly in rhythm to his cadences as he spoke.

"Tomorrow we march into Jerusalem!"

They cheered. They chanted. They danced in the darkening mist.

"To Jerusalem! To Jerusalem!"

And Philo also knew where he must go.

The Citadel, Old City, Jerusalem

They entered the Old City through the Jaffa Gate, one of seven that dotted the ancient battlements, and the main entrance to this deeply historic part of Jerusalem. Jobson looked around in appreciation as they passed the minaret-tipped structure of the Citadel, built by Herod and spared by Titus while he burned the rest of the city. The determined pile of stones looked out to the Judean hills and seemed to say, "Here I will stand until the end of time."

It was dark. The city nestled in her quiet silence. The inside of the Citadel was a dark pool of echoes as their footfalls rang against the stones. Jobson followed the flashlight beams until they passed into a larger area laced with shafts of dim, blue moonlight. They were in one of the galleries of the Museum of the City of Jerusalem, which occupied the body of the Citadel. Jobson craned at the photographs and artifacts inside the glass cases as he was led through the cerulean space by his hosts; a trio of soldiers and the assistant museum curator.

They ascended a flight of narrow stone steps and arrived at one of the tower rooms. It was small, and the visitors severely crowded the space. Mary Maccabe involuntarily cowered against the far wall upon their intrusion.

The slightly unctuous museum curator made the introductions. "Miss Maccabe, I bring you Doctor Zachary Jobson. He is an investigator into the matter of Yordon Antropos."

She stared back at the curator silently.

"He claims to know Yordon."

She turned her attention to Jobson.

Jobson said, "I met him in Tel Aviv."

At that, Mary nodded at the curator and took a step away from the wall.

The escort left, closing the wooden door behind them.

Jobson sat on the nearby cot, not waiting for an invitation. He grunted softly. It had been a tiring trip.

"You're involved in trying to find a way to stop him."

Jobson was taken aback by her directness. "Yes. But also to try and understand him."

Mary laughed skeptically. "Once he's locked away – like me." Her eyes flashed. "Why do you oppose him? He claims to be sent by God. Doesn't that mean anything to you?"

"No," replied Jobson somewhat coldly, then more gently, "What does it mean to you, my dear?"

She blinked and turned away. "It used to mean everything."

"But the game's changed, hasn't it?"

"I don't know. Maybe it's just me." She began to pace the room slowly, biting her fingernail.

Jobson tried to sound casual. "What is it about him that bothers you?"

She stopped and faced him. "The violence. The anger."

"He frightens us too," answered Jobson.

"I'm glad to be away from him." She went to the one chair in the room and sat too, eyes downcast.

Jobson let her be. She was testing the words, the feelings. She had likely not spoken of this to anyone since her abduction.

She looked up again, surprising Jobson with the resignation in her eyes. "But I know he'll come back for me. He's heading here now. He loves me, you know."

"You're important to him. There's little doubt of that." Jobson paused, wondering if he should take the next leap. He decided there was not time for delicacy. "Do you love him, Miss Maccabe?"

She answered absently. "I did once. Now he's a stranger. An alien."

"You mean to you?"

"To everyone. He's…"

"A monster."

She clenched her fists. Then with sudden conviction, "Yes."

She had arrived at a crossroads. It was important for Jobson to bring her all the way to their side now. She needed scope. "Miss Maccabe, it may be that he once believed himself to be what you hoped he would be. But the fact is he's become a belligerent force and he's destroyed many lives. He's coming here to engage the forces of this city in battle. He means to capture it. More will die. It could lead to a global escalation of war if we don't do something."

"But what can you do?"

It was time to ask about Metatron. "Did he ever say anything to you about what it was he wanted from Pope Sylvester?"

"He only said that his actions were necessary before he could move on."

"Did he ever mention a book?"

"No. Not to me. What is this book?"

"A unique and powerful ancient text. A deep secret of the Vatican."

"Do you have it?"

Jobson hesitated a moment before answering, "We're trying to find it. In the ruins."

She shook her head dismissively. "You're lying, or you wouldn't be here."

Jobson sighed and got up from the cot. He went to the tower window and looked down, letting his eyes dance along the labyrinth of winding streets and structures cast in the blue light of the moon. Soon there would be bodies strewn along those way fares and the streets would flow red. It was time for directness.

"We believe the book is a weapon. A supernatural weapon. But it's dangerous. We need to know more, and there's no time."

"I'd like to help you," she said softly, "but I don't know anything about a book."

He nodded, thin-lipped. "Then I will have to seek out Yordon. And I may yet learn something about the book's nature."

Mary looked at him with an expression of alarm. "You'll be killed. He kills easily and casually."

He patted her hand. "It's been a pleasure meeting you, my dear. Members of my group are prepared to assist you in escaping the city before Yordon arrives. They will be here by morning. Please go with them."

* * *

The Israeli army had been prepared for Yordon's assault, but what they had not been prepared for was the large number of defections from within their own ranks.

At the news of the advancing Antropos army, there was a surge of unrest among the troops. Incidents of mutiny and insubordination exploded along the front line like firecrackers.

When the Antropos army arrived on the scene, they knifed through the IDF front lines, taking more than half of the IDF forces with them as spontaneous converts. As they approached the suburban outskirts of the city, the army grew and became better armed so that with little effort, and in fact, little bloodshed, they found themselves at the foot of the walls of the Old City.

The famous Israeli Defense forces, which had triumphed in the Six Day War in 1973, laid siege on the PLO in Lebanon all the way to Beirut in 1982, bombed the Syrian nuclear reactor in 2008, and fought countless, seemingly endless wars throughout the 21st century against its neighbors, had bent like wheat in the wind before Yordon's army.

Near the Dung Gate, Old City, Jerusalem.

It was near the end of day and the sky had clouded over, a rare occurrence in this city of heat and light. The slanted rays of the failing sun angled in beneath the cloud cover to illuminate the low horizon of rooftops that comprised the Old City. It was a landscape of domed and peaked roofs, pale stone and arched windows hinting at cool interiors. The strange combination of clouds above and sunlight below made the city seem miniature, like a child's collection of stones on a seashore.

Yordon's army was camped on the Ophel, a hillside above the Kidron Valley and directly opposite the ignominiously named Dung Gate. Between their position and the walls of the Old City was the large excavation site for the City of David. It was the ancient predecessor to the current city of Jerusalem, more than 3,000 years old, and a site of much religious contention.

Beyond the excavations, the remains of the IDF had heavily fortified the Old City and were waiting tensely for Yordon's next move.

Yordon examined the terrain with searching eyes. He also wondered what had happened to Philo. He was nowhere to be found.

Outside the Golden Gate, Old City, Jerusalem

The next day, in the pink proto-light of dawn, Yordon asked his lieutenants if anyone had seen Philo. No one had. They looked at each other nervously, awaiting Yordon's next command. Yordon seemed puzzled for a moment but then he nodded slowly and stood erect, his face a wall of clenched stone.

Gruffly, he barked, "No matter." Looking enraged for a split second, he snapped orders for his army to process onto the pink granite path leading toward the gates of the Old City and took a position at the head of the column. A former IDF Captain marched up to him.

"The gates to the Old City are heavily fortified. Entrance will be difficult," the Captain paused. "We'll have to fight. Or you could knock the walls down, like in Rome."

Yordon didn't answer the Captain directly but instead looked toward the fortified walls. The loyal core of the IDF waited silently there, weapons at the ready, determined to make their stand.

"No. This place is to be our base, Captain. What about the Golden Gate?" asked Yordon sharply, of the army Captain.

The Captain's face took on an expression of alarm. "But it's well sealed! It has been for centuries."

"How well is that part of the perimeter defended?" insisted Yordon.

The Captain glanced in that direction. "Defenses are relatively light there, but…"

"Captain, I wish to enter the Old City through the Golden Gate," said Yordon more forcefully.

The Captain looked at the sealed entrance with a pained expression and hesitated. He then nodded his acknowledgment and marched off to give the necessary orders.

Old City, Jerusalem, Israel.

After ensuring that arrangements were in place for Mary Maccabe to be safely whisked away, Jobson decided to head in the direction of the Temple Mount on the opposite side of the Old City, where it was widely reported Yordon had amassed his growing cadre of followers and IDF defectors in preparation to enter the city. There might still be a chance to gain an audience with the man.

He pushed past streams of indigents, who were fleeing the area in anticipation of the chaos to come. He stopped now and again to catch his breath, taking cover behind buttresses and in alleyways, to keep himself from being trampled as he pushed against the tide.

As he wended his way toward the Eastern half of the Old City, the crowds thickened and a feeling of panic became palpable in the air. Jobson scanned the crowd, looking for a gap in the flow of people that would allow him to cross the narrow expanse of Chabad St., which bisected the Old City, into the Jewish Quarter. From there he would make his way north, by way of side streets, into the Muslim quarter, where the Temple Mount was located.

He shielded his eyes with his hands, trying to see into the shadows behind the high contrast of the relentless sunlight, when he spotted a familiar face.

Could it be?

Instinctively, he scanned the area nearest to the man he recognized, expecting to see another even more recognizable face, but to no avail. *Strange.*

Finally, impatient with the unyielding throng, and worried his quarry might disappear into the crowds, he shouted out, "Hey, over here!"

Philo looked in the direction of the entreaty. An older, bearded man in khaki pants and short-sleeved, buff colored shirt wearing a broad brimmed hat was gesturing to him to come closer. He knew that time was running out and he needed to make contact with the authorities so that he could surrender himself soon, before the battle began, or before he changed his mind. *Because I am a traitor.* He had to take no chances.

The man waved to him again, and was trying to push past the river of people crowding the cobblestoned street.

Philo was about to turn away, thinking it better to avoid the stranger, when suddenly the man shouted, "Philo! Philo Berith! Is that you?"

Philo stopped hard in his tracks, filling a tingle along his shoulders at being recognized, and slowly turned around. The man had made the crossing and was now standing before him, panting lightly and rubbing sweat off of his brow.

"Who are you?" asked Philo, squinting.

Jobson stared into Philo's face in wonder. "You don't know me but I know you. At least I know who you are. You are Yordon's companion, from Athos, are you not?"

Philo felt a shiver of apprehension rise within him, but he answered, "Yes, I am, or, I was."

Jobson nodded and offered his hand to shake, "My name is Zachary Jobson. I came here to find Mary Maccabe."

Philo's eyebrows shot up, as he tentatively clasped hands with the Papal Task Force scientist. "She is here?"

"Yes, at the Citadel. Or, rather, yes, but not for long. She's being moved to a safe place, away from here."

"By whom? Who are you with?" asked Philo, drawn in by the new information.

"I'm with a special task force created by the Vatican and NATO."

"A task force?" Philo cocked his head at the revelation, not understanding. "To perform what task?"

Jobson looked uncomfortable. Just then there was a burst of automatic weapons fire nearby, causing both of them to crouch lower. "Probably an ill-advised attempt at crowd control," said Jobson. He motioned Philo closer. "Er… to answer your question, our job is figure out the true nature of your friend."

Incongruously, Philo laughed. "That's perhaps unknowable, Mister Jobson, but I do know this much…"

"It's Doctor Jobson, by the way, but you can call me Zachary."

"He is coming and nothing can stop him."

"That may well be, but we have to try." Jobson suddenly stopped himself, "Wait, did you say that you *were* Yordon's companion?"

Philo's face darkened and he slumped a little. Taking a rag from his pocket, he wiped at his face and looked lost for an instant. Jobson could sense a deep sadness coming from the man.

"You've deserted him, haven't you?"

Philo sniffed hard and cleared his throat. He nodded to himself slowly, tasting the words Jobson had spoken.

"Yes, it's true," he answered, "I could not go on supporting him and what he is doing. What he has done."

"So you're here now, in the Old City, by yourself, and he's still outside. Does he know you've gone?"

"By now, he must surely know. It will make him very angry, I think."

"Or disappointed," said Jobson, "in you. You're his oldest friend. So they say."

"His only friend. His last friend. And now he has no one. I fear I may have made things worse." Philo shook his head in anguish.

Jobson grabbed him by the shoulders. "No, no. You did the right thing. You are perhaps the only person on the planet, besides Miss Maccabe, and probably even more so that Miss Maccabe, who can influence him, coax him. Perhaps help us to stop him."

Philo shrugged off Jobson's grip. "You still haven't told me how…"

335

Jobson sighed. "I'm a member of something called The Papal Task Force. It's a group formed in answer to a secret order from the Pope himself to ally with Government leaders to try and put a stop to Yordon's growing world movement. Our job is to figure out his weaknesses and exploit them, be they physical, political, metaphysical, whatever we can muster."

"And have you mustered anything, Doctor Jobson?" asked Philo, skeptically. "Do you have anything that can defeat a God? A mad God? He is crazy now, you know. Bent on destruction. Perhaps he always was, but I do not think that is so. I remember how he was on the mountain, casting his stones into the water, long ago. He was gentle then. Now he is changed. When he revived that woman in America it awakened some madness within him, some part of him that is not human, but demon. And it has been gradually taking over his mind. When Mary was taken, the human part of him was taken too. He stopped talking to people. Even me."

"You loved him," ventured Jobson, feeling the hurt in Philo's words.

Philo suddenly burst in tears, surprising even himself. He sobbed out his next words. "Like a brother. And I know that somewhere inside of him, he loves me still. And I love him still too."

Jobson spoke earnestly, urging Philo forward as he wiped at his eyes, away from the busy thoroughfare and toward the Muslim Quarter. "You must help us, Philo, for the sake of the human that Yordon once was. At least, in honor of the memory of that man. Help us defeat the mad God. Come with me and I will show you something that perhaps may be the means to Yordon's defeat. Something you may even know something about…"

The Golden Gate, Old City, Jerusalem

The 120mm millimeter shell knocked a hole through the stones of the Golden Gate effortlessly. There was an instant commotion inside the walls as IDF forces scrambled to bolster their weak defense, but it was too late. At

Yordon's signal, his army rushed toward the opening and poured into the Old City. Soldiers who had formerly marched side by side now engaged each other in combat. Despite Yordon's bold feat to penetrate the perimeter of the Old City, both sides were hesitant to do further damage to their precious stones. As a result, armored exchanges were kept to a minimum and the fighting was primarily confined to infantry action and hand to hand combat. It was an especially savage scene.

As soon as the area around the wall was secured, Yordon stepped over the rubble and entered through the ragged hole. He was surrounded by his army. They looked through the torn opening in astonishment. They were standing inside a walled compound on Mount Moriah, the Temple Mount, and the location of the Dome of the Rock, in the Muslim Quarter of the City.

A group of Muslims emerged from the gold-domed mosque. Upon seeing Yordon enter the compound through the outer wall, they ran toward them. One of them collapsed at Yordon's feet.

"This is a unique moment, *Imam*. I am elated beyond words! The prophecies have held that the messenger of God would one day return to Jerusalem through this gate. Now you stand here in the *Haram esh-Sharif* in all your glory, having fulfilled that prophecy."

Yordon touched the shoulder of the supplicant man. *"Doqq el-baab qabil ma todkhol, eh?"*

The man heard this and paused, looking puzzled. Then he began to laugh uproariously. He stood, nodding his appreciation, and backed away. "We are your worshippers, *Imam*. Just tell us what to do and we will do it."

Yordon answered, "Brief my captains on all the known IDF positions within the city. Help us make the battle short."

The man nodded and dashed off to speak to his colleagues.

"What was that?" asked a nearby soldier of a comrade, who was smiling at the overheard exchange.

"It's an old Palestinian proverb. 'Knock on the door before entering.'", answered the soldier.

Yordon's forces quickly secured the Temple Mount complex, but the Israelis had good positions. As his men exchanged small weapons fire with the IDF forces hidden in the maze of minarets, cornices and rooftops that faced the silvery Dome of the Rock, Yordon sent a platoon of men to the far corner of the compound, abutting the Jewish Quarter, to the Al-Aqsa mosque. The giant prayer hall straddled a network of underground chambers, known as Solomon's stables. These extended directly beneath an area of trees and ruins that led to the Western Wall. Yordon's men descended and set about excavating and planting explosives at the area closest to the base of the wall.

The IDF was waiting for them and had the Temple Mount enclosure surrounded. What they did not expect was the explosion that produced a massive, smoking hole where the Western Wall once stood. No one had believed such a tactic would be dared. Injured Hassidim lay on the ground all around the area of the explosion beneath the resulting rubble, moaning in pain, shouting in anger, and amazingly in the case of some, praying stoically on.

Taking advantage of the covering smoke and confusion, Yordon's men rushed into the plaza, jumping over stones and bodies, and stormed across the open expanse. They were fired upon from the neighboring Yeshiva but it did not slow them down. From there they clamored up the wide stone steps that led from the plaza into the Tiferet Israel thoroughfare, and set about the block-by-block taking of the city.

Yordon stepped through ruins of the Western Wall into the plaza. Surrounded by his men, he observed the chaos they had wrought. Yordon's men fired into the apartments facing the wall, picking off snipers.

Jobson and Philo arrived on the scene just after the explosions and kept to the shadows, realizing they could easily be killed by random gunshot. They watched in fascination as Yordon strode amongst his troops, still in his monk's robes, seemingly untouchable, impassive of countenance but clearly determined. All around him, men fired weapons at other men and dashed from position to position. The situation was out of control.

From their hiding place, Jobson and Philo listened to the moans of the injured.

"The Kotel!"

"The Kotel is destroyed!"

"We're doomed!"

"Now it is truly a Wailing Wall," said Philo in a brusque whisper.

Jobson nodded silently. He could not believe his eyes. He had to get Philo to safety but he could not tear himself away from the historic events unfolding before him. He also fretted that Mary Maccabe may have not been evacuated yet. The situation was deteriorating very quickly. He realized he might have made a dreadful miscalculation. He had to get back to the Citadel to make sure of her escape, as much as Philo's.

Crouching beside Jobson, Philo's thoughts were as much a chaos as Jobson's, as the scene smoldered around him. Yordon was destroying the icons of old. The entire basis of Western civilization was being cast away and replaced with Yordon's particular stamp. But what was that stamp? He had thought it was a message of enlightenment but here they were dodging bullets. How did the two realities reconcile?

"We have to leave the area, Philo," insisted Jobson suddenly, breaking Philo's momentary reverie.

Philo paused, torn between conflicting impulses, before finally answering, "Yes, you are right, it is perilous to stay. Yordon will discover us."

The Cardo, Old City, Jerusalem

Ariel Engel crouched in the submerged pedestrian walkway several hundred meters back from the Temple Mount and heard the rumble of the collapsing Western Wall. He felt a mixture of fascination and horror. Normally the Cardo was a byway of smart shops and tourists, positioned incongruously next to a trio of Arab Suqs -- old world bazaars from another time, but today it was a trench filled with soldiers and a front line against the invading Antropos army.

"Do we attack, sir?" asked a worried soldier.

Engel shook his head briefly. "No. We wait for them to come to us."

"But then they will be above us, sir. Is that advisable?"

Engel suppressed a sigh. The Israeli Defense Force was known for its independently minded and argumentative troops, but ever since his reprimand for allowing the Jordanian force to enter Jerusalem following the sandstorm at Jericho, and his subsequent demotion to command of a single city defense unit, he found his troops most reluctant to follow his orders. They resented his actions at Jericho. They thought he was a traitor. He was a General, still, but in name only.

He made a decision. "No. You are right. We go to them. Inform the squad leaders. On my signal, plant the mines."

Near the Citadel, Old City, Jerusalem

Mervyn Goss was not one to get directly involved in field actions, but the evacuation of Mary Maccabe was extremely important and the task could simply not be delegated at this juncture. Also, his retrieval of the girl would be a personal coup de grace to end them all. His career as a technocrat would be tempered by the glow of this heroic act.

In truth, he hadn't come to Jerusalem expecting to be involved in a rescue operation, but events had been thrust upon him. He had followed Jobson, concerned about the man's possible actions. Ravessi had given up the location of Mary's secret hiding place easily enough, when threatened with exposure as a double agent. And now the situation was in rapid meltdown. Even though Jobson had arranged for a guard and a car to take Miss Maccabe to the airport, the field operative in him knew they could not wait or rely on those arrangements any longer.

He ran toward the Citadel from his hotel -- a race against time. Yordon's forces were advancing quickly and would soon cordon off the Old City. The gunfire and shouts of men in combat could be heard clearly. He had no idea what had happened to Jobson, but with or without him, he knew he must retrieve the girl and spirit her away, if only to give the Papal Task Force the upper hand again. As he raced, he punched numbers on his cell phone and ordered preparations for his escape.

The Cardo, Old City, Jerusalem

Engel waved his men forward. They were at the intersection of the Cardo and Hashalshelet, the main thoroughfare that bisected the Old City from the Temple Mount to the Jaffa Gate. Ahead were the Suqs, now empty of the usual crowds. His men dashed across the avenue to take cover beneath the awnings and booths of the covered markets.

He also had men positioned in several of the side streets in the Jewish Quarter just before the intersection. They had successfully barricaded the Tiferet Yisrael, preventing further advance of the opposing forces along that route. That left Hashalshelet. Their only chance of containing the incursion was to hold fast at the Cardo trench.

Other IDF troops were moving up the Via Dolorosa toward El Wad in the hopes of executing a flanking maneuver, but the situation was dire. The troops were depleted by defections. The city, a labyrinth of alleyways and rooftops, was difficult to defend once the walls were breached.

Machine gun fire recaptured his attention. The Antropos forces were moving up the main road shielded by several Merkaba tanks in formation. As the tanks rumbled along, the accompanying troops performed reconnaissance and cleanup on the surrounding buildings. There was sporadic gunfire and the occasional explosion. The IDF didn't have any tanks inside the Old City and was ill-prepared to defend against them. Slowly they were being pushed back to the Cardo defense point.

Engel's men had managed to hastily bury several land mines along the thoroughfare. They had also been able to deploy some artillery at the intersection. Engel had full intention of blasting a hole through those tanks as soon as they were near the key side streets he had selected for a three point attack.

"One hundred yards to go!" croaked the field radio.

"Stand ready," ordered Engel. He felt enervated and steady, yet part of him was strangely detached. He wondered if he should have let Yordon live back at the Allenby bridge. He wondered if Yordon could be killed. He also wondered why he was fighting Yordon. Yordon's army was plainly multi-ethnic — Arabs of all nations, Christians and Jews marched side by side. Who had a right to these stones?

"Contact!" barked the radio. Ahead gunfire erupted from several windows. A Merkaba turned its turret toward the defenders.

"Now!" yelled Engel at his artillery-men.

With a "whoosh", the IDF cannons fired their shells directly at the distracted lead tank. The first few bounced off -- the Merkaba was known for its heavy armor — but the barrage was intense and the tank soon buckled under the impacts releasing smoke and cooking the interior. The hatches opened and men poured out. Within seconds the fuel lines were touched by the spreading flames and the tank exploded, showering the surrounding area with hot shrapnel and forcing the Antropos forces to back off. Engel's troops pressed their advantage and surged forward.

Engel ordered more shells directed at the remaining tanks forming the front line of Yordon's advance. Windows shattered and walls trembled under the detonations as the tanks regained themselves and returned fire. In the midst of all this, Engel's troops penetrated the front line and engaged the Antropos forces.

Tank shells exploded above Engel's head and debris rained down on the soldiers inside the Cardo trench. It was time to move more men out. Engel leapt out of the trench.

"For Israel! Attack! Take back every street!" he yelled, more for effect than out of feeling, as he scrambled for cover, knowing the enemy would triangulate on his voice and try to kill him. He waited a few seconds, and then led the charge.

The Citadel, Old City, Jerusalem

Goss had little patience for the guards that tried to block his advance to the Tower room. His credentials were impeccable and yet these uniformed louts hesitated to let him through. Finally he could take it no more. Shells were exploding outside, making the lights sway, and the guard was trying to reach a superior on the phone for confirmation. Goss took out his Beretta – a rarely used ornament -- and shot the man point blank. Grabbing the keys from the man's belt, he let himself into the Tower room.

Mary stared back, trying to look brave. She had expected an Israeli or an Arab soldier but not this patrician-looking man in a tailored suit. He smiled at her – it was clearly not genuine.

"I won't hurt you. I'm here to help you."

"How do I know that? Who are you?

Goss decided to answer the last question. "I'm an ally. Do you wish to escape from here?"

"He'll come for me," she said absently, not sure what to believe.

"Do you want that?" Goss took a cautious step closer.

"I don't know."

"My name is Mervyn Goss. I represent the same group as Doctor Jobson. I believe you've met him?"

"Jobson? Yes. He was here. He went to find Yordon."

"Then he may well be dead," said Goss.

"Dead?" she repeated dumbly looking toward the window. After a moment, she quietly concurred, "Yes, it could be true." She looked up at Goss. "I said I would help him, if I could, but I couldn't help him. He felt he had to go find Yordon."

Goss urged her forward, "Then come, we have no time for reflection. Yordon's army has entered the city and he kills all who stand in his path as we speak."

"Where are we going?" pleaded Mary, resisting Goss' grasp of her upper arm.

"There's no time!" hissed Goss. "If you want to help us you must come now!"

"Okay. "

The Cardo, Old City, Jerusalem

Engel's forces executed their tactics brilliantly and the advance of Yordon's forces was brought to a halt. There was hand-to-hand fighting all around the intersection of the Cardo and Hashalshelet. The street was cratered from the shell detonations. Fires were blazing inside several buildings. Sirens could be heard in the distance. But the tide of the battle had been turned.

Engel and his men advanced along the wide road, firing on the retreating column of interlopers.

"We're doing it, General!" said a lieutenant, honoring Engel with his rank in an unspoken apology.

"So it seems, Lieutenant," uttered Engel grimly. A movement caught his eye as they progressed. A flash of white inside a window of a residence above.

"Continue the advance. Push them right to the wall," ordered Engel as he veered off. He thought he heard a baby crying. In that building ahead. *A mother and child?* They couldn't stay here. Slowly he crept up on the building, sweeping the high windows and dark alleys with his submachine gun. The crying was more definite now. He slammed the door open and rolled inside, panning the room. No one. The crying was upstairs. He climbed carefully. At the top of the landing there was a darkened hallway. The crying was just ahead. Slowly he advanced, listening for anything suspicious.

Abruptly the crying stopped. He instinctively turned to see behind him and was almost shocked out of his uniform by the sight of Yordon standing before him.

"Hello Ariel. I wanted to speak with you."

"How did you do that? And the baby?"

"A trick. Forgive me."

Surprising himself, Ariel lowered his weapon. His body seemed to be out of his control. Yordon came closer and laid a hand on Engel's shoulder. The hand squeezed his shoulder firmly.

"I want you to stop the fighting."

"We're winning."

"No. You're losing the real battle. Do you remember what I said at Jericho?"

"How can I forget? I've been demoted and marginalized because of it. I let those Jordanians enter the city. I cost the state millions in re-armament

345

expense. Everyone thinks I have dove feathers in my head. General Engel, the former falcon of the IDF, now a peace lover."

"You always were. A peace lover. It's your secret. You've always understood the difference between a means and an end. There had to be war to preserve peace."

"Yes," answered Engel slowly.

"This is no different, Ariel."

Engel shook his head, trying to reconcile the colliding thoughts, "You said Jerusalem would be a city for all peoples. A crossroads of peace."

"It will be, if you allow it."

"You said that killing for the sake of religious beliefs is wrong. That religion should never become the oppressor."

"It is the truth."

"Then how do you explain…?"

"This is a battle to *end* religion, Ariel. Do you understand?" Yordon's eyes glowed with intensity.

Suddenly, with the clarity of diamond glass, Engel did understand. He was preventing a cleansing fire that had to burn.

"Stop your troops now. Join me."

The Citadel, Old City, Jerusalem

Goss pulled Mary down the winding stone steps to the ground level of the Citadel. It was mostly deserted now, as the battle came quickly closer. There was a diplomatic car waiting at the Jaffa Gate, not directly in front of the building as he had ordered. At least the embassies were responding to orders, if not perfectly. It was just a few yards but they would have to traverse it in the open. They hurried toward the gate. As they approached the soldiers guarding the entrance aimed their weapons at them.

"Halt."

"I am Mervyn Goss, Deputy Minister of Foreign Affairs for the European Union. I must pass." Goss showed his credentials.

"Who is that with you?"

"A friend."

"A friend?" The soldier peered at them more closely. "Wait, that's the girl from the Tower. You can't!"

Mervyn shot him. Before the other soldier could shoot, he too was felled. Mervyn looked to the source of the second gun's report. The limo driver. Stoically the man nodded and held open the car's door. As more soldiers came running. Goss shoved Mary forward. She kept stumbling, looking back at the dead soldiers.

"Why did you kill him?"

Bullets ricocheted off the car's armored finish.

They were at the car. "Get in!"

Goss hurried her into the back seat and fell in behind her. As soon as the door shut the car began to move.

"To the airport, as quickly as you can."

Yordon approached the Citadel and stopped a few feet before it.

"She's no longer here," he announced to no one in particular.

He turned around to look behind him, where his army waited, restless. They had taken the entire Old City. When General Engel had defected to their side and ordered his men to surrender, a massive hole had been created in the IDF defenses. It had been downhill from there. The battle had ended quickly as the remaining IDF forces were surrounded and routed.

The army captain who had led the Dung Gate attack approached Yordon and reported, "The Old City is yours, sir, but metropolitan Jerusalem is still in the government's control. Soon there will be retaliation."

Yordon looked at the Captain with unblinking eyes and an unexpectedly hard expression. "It is too late for them and they do not realize it. We have our victory, Captain. We have the Old City. Not by divine intervention, but by the will of men. The Old City, and therefore Jerusalem is rightfully ours now. We won her in battle. Now it has an end."

The Captain frowned. "But it's not the end. The Israeli Government, and possibly the Americans *will* retaliate. They won't stop here."

"No, they won't."

The Captain squinted up at Yordon. "Then what do you mean? When does it end?"

Yordon answered, "Soon, Captain, very soon."

Jobson watched Yordon talking to his Captain while standing before the Citadel and felt relief. Yordon had turned away from the structure, indicating to Jobson that Mary was gone from there. *Uncanny how he had known where to look for her.* He looked over at Philo, who was muttering some consoling prayer to himself, eyes closed. *Surely, if Yordon can sense Mary, he can sense Philo?* What if Yordon was deliberately allowing him to observe his actions for some other, ulterior motive? Jobson felt a sudden urgency to leave and he grabbed Philo by his sleeve and led him away in a rapid, crouching run.

3 Kaplan St., Jerusalem

Moshe Avrahami had laid his head on his desk to rest a few moments when the knock on the door came. He was tired and the excitement was making it hard for him to breathe. He preferred to be alone when it got like this, and it had been getting like this all the time recently.

"Come," he croaked hoarsely, coaxing himself upright.

The door opened, revealing Yordon.

"So we meet again. A happy reunion?" quipped Avrahami, unperturbed.

348

Yordon approached him, ignoring his comments. "You're not well, Moshe. You should have taken care of that a long time ago."

Avrahami laughed weakly. "As if there's any time. How did you get in here?"

"Everyone is distracted."

"I'm told you've destroyed the Wailing Wall. You should be punished for that."

"It was a fossil. Such things are not needed anymore."

Avrahami coughed for a long time in response. It was getting much worse. When he was calm again he said, "I feel like an accomplice."

"In a way, you are. You let me do what I had to do."

"And this is how you repay me? Destroy my city?"

"No. The battle is won. I want you to stop the fighting now before it escalates any further."

"You promised retribution for the Jews."

"Not just for Jews."

"Ah well. Details."

"It can't come if we fight."

"You're asking me to surrender the state of Israel."

"I'm asking you to make Israel the capital of the new world I bring."

"And who will be Prime Minister?"

"You can be its Ambassador. Call your generals off. We don't have much time."

Avrahami sat back in his chair. "Sit," he ordered Yordon.

Yordon complied.

A New World. What would a battle accomplish? If he let it continue and his army successfully recaptured the Old City, Israel would be the bitter enemy of millions even more so than she already was. Yordon had won the hearts and minds of half the planet. He had performed miracles — or so they seemed. He had also destroyed the Vatican. Was that the action of a Messiah?

"What are you?" Avrahami asked.

"I am the messenger of…"

"No, no, not that nonsense. What are you, really"

Yordon didn't reply immediately. He seemed to struggle, then quietly he said, "I am… inevitable."

Avrahami considered this, then nodded. "Perhaps you are. But if that is so, what choice do I have?"

"You have one choice left to make – the manner of the outcome."

"And then?"

"You can put aside the affairs of men for good."

"I'm dying," said Avrahami dryly.

"Yes."

Avrahami thought about that. What should be his legacy?

Yordon rose and walked around the desk to stand before Avrahami.

"After this, you can rest."

He touched Avrahami's forehead, and the Prime Minister gasped in relief. He took a deep lungful of air without difficulty and felt his brow unwrinkle as the worries of the past year seemed to rise off his body. His eyes grew moist and he looked at Yordon with new appreciation. He picked up the telephone.

The triumphant throng marched down the Via Dolorosa with Yordon on their shoulders. Jobson watched from the sidelines and wondered if anyone was mindful of the great echo of a similar entrance into the city by a revolutionary of two thousand years ago.

The Prime Minister had called off the armored columns positioned around the Old City. He was found dead at his desk shortly thereafter. Yordon had declared himself the new head of the Israeli government and dissolved all prior appointments. The resulting disarray in the legitimate Israeli Government gave Yordon's forces free reign of the city.

Jobson followed the throng as it made its way through the meandering, ancient streets, in open wonderment over the man's powers. It was really not possible to fight Yordon by earthly means. There was only one possible avenue left. He sighed and walked away from the crowd, making his way back to his hotel. He needed to contact the Task Force.

Chapter Twelve: Metatron

Papal Task Force Villa, Rome, December 2020

With the arrival of Mary Maccabe at the task force's villa in Rome, the remaining members of the group gathered to hear Goss' report.

"Where's Zachary?" asked Karin immediately.

"He is likely dead, Professor," interjected Goss.

"How would you know?" demanded Karin, swiveling to face him.

"I don't know it for a fact, but if he is not back, then it's quite likely he was killed in the fighting."

"You did speak with him?" asked Thomas tentatively of Mary.

"Yes, but I know nothing about the book he spoke of."

"Since you knew nothing, no doubt he went looking for Yordon," said Karin, "and probably got himself killed that way."

"Don't you think you'd better ask me about that first?" said Jobson as he suddenly entered the Salon room, accompanied by Philo Berith.

"Zachary!" yelled Karin, and after gazing at Philo in wonder, almost leapt into Jobson's arms. She hugged him hard, shutting her eyes in relief.

"*Opa!* You are safe!" exclaimed Philo, upon seeing Mary amongst the huddle of strangers. He approached her and they clasped hands, smiling warmly at each other.

"And you've brought with you a most remarkable guest!" said Dolores Arbolera, looking toward Philo and Mary, and then approaching Jobson to put a welcoming hand on his arm. He smiled at her and gently pried himself free of Karin's embrace.

"There, there, Karin, as flattered as you make an old man feel, I think it is of far more import that we have Mr. Berith here with us now."

Thomas moved toward Philo and shook his hand. "Welcome to Rome, Philo! I have to say, I am quite surprised to see you!" Thomas laughed and scratched at his head. Philo smiled back but only hesitantly. Mary held onto his arm, protectively.

"What are you doing here?" asked Ravessi, abruptly.

Philo turned toward him and squinted. The man exuded calculation and Philo's presence here was undoubtedly not one of his calculated outcomes.

"He's defected, Max. He's left Yordon," said Jobson, looking at Ravessi first, then at all the others. "I found him hiding in the Jewish Quarter."

"While trying to get yourself killed by looking for Yordon, no doubt," said Karin accusingly.

Ravessi ignored this and stated, "A most provocative development. Mr. Berith is certainly free to do as he pleases but the girl is undoubtedly here against the wishes of the Israeli government." He stopped to light a cigarette, then stared unblinkingly at Goss.

"It was necessary. Antropos would have reclaimed her," answered Goss levelly.

"I made that choice, Max, not Mervyn" interjected Jobson, "Even if Herr Goss, shall we say, 'expedited' my plans." Jobson cocked an eyebrow at Goss, who nodded briefly in acknowledgement. Jobson continued, "She was not safe in Jerusalem. Surely, even you can see that. For goodness' sake, you don't even work for them! Or do you?"

"Our job is to figure out the Metatron book," interrupted Thomas, losing patience with all the intrigue.

Karin turned to Philo and asked, "Do you know anything about this book, Philo? Has Yordon ever mentioned anything like it?"

"It's just a book, no?" he asked, puzzled.

"No, it's rather more than that," said Jobson.

"It's quite possibly a weapon," offered Dr. Arbolera, "a supernatural weapon."

"A book that is a weapon? That can kill?" Philo shook his head, then suddenly he connected the dots. "That can kill Yordon?"

Thomas answered for the group. "Possibly. At least if Sylvester is to be believed. He staked his life on it."

Philo scratched at his stubble, pensively. "I have always wondered why Yordon was so obsessed with the Vatican. Perhaps it was because of this book. And you have this book?"

They all nodded, in unintentional synchronization.

Karin looked Thomas in the eye and said, "We've got to try and learn how to use the book."

"Unless Miss Maccabe can give us another insight, it's all we've got," added Goss.

Mary shook her head. Philo put an arm around her.

"I suggest you start reading it then, Father," said Ravessi.

"I have been. I think I'm beginning to understand its cosmology, at least. It's controversial."

"Let's sit. All of you, please," said Karin, pulling back a chair for Mary and then for Philo.

"Do go on, Father," said Goss, intrigued.

Thomas continued, "I think we've been on the right track. About God being a multiple entity. This book seems to corroborate some of that. The tracts found within imply a totality made up of many archetypes; each one bearing characteristics making up the whole."

Goss asked, "If this book does what Sylvester claimed, Father Prisciotti, how do we know such an entity would be favorable to us?"

"We don't."

"Can we afford to take a chance like that?" asked Arbolera.

"It's that, or the world according to Yordon," said Karin quietly.

"Yordon has overtaken Israel, but retaliation is sure to come. The Israeli government will call on its allies now," observed Ravessi. "There is sure to be a prolonged period of global conflict, unless we do something to pre-empt it."

Papal Task Force Villa, Rome

Thomas was alone. His colleagues had left him to study Metatron. He sighed and rubbed at his eyes. It was hard to sit here and read when the world was going to pieces. He made himself breathe. It had to be done. It was up to him to understand this book. It was the key.

He doggedly read the crumbling pages of the Codice. The writings had been penned by several men, judging from the changing voices. To read the words was to hear these men, long dead, through fathoms of translation and lost culture. He tried to imagine their simple existence. The universe unknown to them. Everything alive. A desert that thrived with spirits. A people unrooted and living in isolation. A great need for hope. Men who wondered at the stars and the dialogue inside their heads that gave them self-awareness. Men who had sought to explore the nameless country of the mind. From such motivations did these writings emerge.

Thomas resisted the urge to flip pages rapidly. He was getting close to something important but it could not be rushed. Reading these texts was laborious and required careful interpretation and patience. Karin had once said though the writing survived the context was lost.

He turned the page.

And there they were.

The names of the Archons.

The sons of the formless.

… Roeror, Ipouspoboba, Eilo, Gorma, Knyx, Labernioum, Zathoth, Kalila, Jabel, Yordon, …

The list went on for pages. But there he was. Yordon, comfortable amidst the names of his brothers.

An Archon.

Thomas sucked in a trembling breath and continued to read. Slowly, he mouthed the old tongue as he turned the crackling leaves. Apocryphons, Tripartates, tractates, Hypostases, apocalypses, discourses, teachings, steles, testimonies, expositions. All here, one following the other, revealing a hidden structure.

He closed the book and sat back. Then he opened it again almost at once. There would be time to think about all this later. He turned the pages again. Near the end of the collection there was one document, illuminated with gold flake and tempera, and unlike any of the other writings he had seen so far. Illuminated texts were a product of the Middle Ages, long after the formative centuries of Christianity. Closer examination revealed that these particular pages were quite as ancient as the rest of the book but had been illuminated some centuries later. Translating the Coptic text haltingly in his mind, he read on.

In Preparation of Uttering the Cant.

When a man leads a righteous and pious life,
which is pure in intent and without ulterior
motives, his holy breath shall have the power to
evoke the answering angels. Be cautioned --
though they are holy and they spring from the
fountain of God's creation force, they are

summoned by the lips of men and are, because of this, doomed to be imperfect.

These angels are a mystery of God. The quality and dignity of these Archons is dependent on the quality of the man who speaks the words which follow. Use them carefully and with the intention of good acts only. Everything depends on the quality of the human act.

Thomas examined the drawing that accompanied the words. It was a rendering of angels spewing from the mouth of a terrified man. The angels bore weapons and varied in countenance from malevolent to beneficent. They were engaged in battle above the conjurer's head. The image chilled Thomas. The writer had been earnest, even fearful, that his warning would go unheeded.

Everything depends on the quality of the man.

The weight of those words resonated against his fingertips as he softly brushed the Coptic text. Here were the transcribed recitations of the Archangel Metatron, or so claimed the writers. But did this guarantee their veracity? Metatron had been a man before his transformation into the angelic state.

The truth was an onion. The phalanxes of Gods, Demiurges, Archons and Angels in the heavens were complex and multi-layered, forever peeling back to reveal successively more fundamental realities until one arrived at the very precincts of the Absolute.

If he ever arrived at the incandescent core of that onion, Thomas felt that he would burn away, so unfathomable and corrosive would be that knowledge. Perhaps the truth was unknowable by mere mortals. If so, then that left only faith.

But what was faith? He had once read that faith was the assent of the mind to the truths revealed by God. That was his lifelong pursuit. But was that the process or the product? Faith as defined by the Catholic church meant the acceptance of truths that are alleged — the commanding of the will to accept the authority of God, the intellect subjugated by traditions. Some would say that by that route only would the eyes of the mind be fully opened to the grace of God.

The existence of God was an article of faith, a communicated truth by way of Revelation, as per his ideology's dictates. But what if one had not suffered this revelation? Could knowledge of God be gained through reason and intellect? God himself was said to be pure intellect. Was the existence of God then knowable by derivation? The principle of causality. God as the first cause. The evident design and beauty of the universe. The anthropic suitability of the universe to man. The existence of morality. The widespread human testimony to the existence of God in one form or another. Was it all a great accident, an illusion of a watchmaker where there was only randomness and countless eons of time to coax the chaos into a semblance of order? Or were the clues so pervasive, so fundamental to the fabric of reality, as to seem invisible?

But they were no longer invisible, were they? He remembered the apparition of Sabellius. He had said to Thomas that God was knowable, but not with mere intellect. God existed deep within the self, even as he was also a stranger, infinitely alien, beyond our ability to comprehend. Yordon had said, back in D.C., that knowledge of God could only come through an acquired intuition of what lies beyond this physical plane. Thomas understood that what was required was a knowledge beyond words, a knowledge beyond mind. A knowledge requiring one to take *a leap of faith.*

Thomas felt the realization crystallize within him. Yordon existed. He was a creature of the cosmos and, even if he wrongly believed himself the redeemer, he was still living testimony that there must also be a "God". If not the

Creator, then merely the God of men. This was proof to Thomas that the heavens did exist and men played a part in the destiny of the universe. What Thomas did today mattered. Thomas understood with sudden clarity that religion was not meant to be a blind search for God, but rather a response of *faith* to the God who had once and was again revealing himself. But the faith was not in God, it was in man. In himself. In the God-given ability of humans to transcend their weaknesses as Christ had done, and to rise up to meet their God, rather than wait for their God to come and claim them. That was it. That was the meaning of *redemption*.

Moving through the alternating layers of his doubt and his faith, he found the iron core of what he truly believed; what he recognized to be the truth. Having stumbled against its concrete certainty, he embraced it and felt joy. He believed fully and at last.

He turned the page and encountered the prayer. The one that called upon God. Included were the precise instructions for the pre-requisite meditation. He let his mind ride the cadence of the prayer.

After a few minutes he closed the book and stood. It read like many prayers, canonical and apocryphal, that he had encountered in his 48 years of life. But this one was different. He knew. This was going to work. He was shaking slightly. It was time to do this.

Basement Lab, Papal Task Force Villa, Rome

The lab had been outfitted with a glass-lined, cylindrical chamber. Inside the chamber was a podium, on which the Metatron book rested. It was intended that Thomas would perform the ritual inside the chamber. Extensive instrumentation for measuring the phenomena that they hoped would occur was connected by several conduits to the chamber. Thomas would have preferred a less scientific setting, but he couldn't deny his colleagues their desire to understand what was about to happen. They badly needed some empiricism added to the proceedings to lend a sense of reality to the situation.

A partition separated them from the chamber. The partitioned section was crowded with scientific instruments. Dr. Deng's original telemetry was displayed prominently on a view screen and several additional screens displayed real-time readings alongside of it. The Papal Task Force team, with their guests Mary Maccabe and Philo Berith, crowded behind the partition waiting for Thomas to begin.

"I'm ready," announced Thomas.

"This is so strange," said Karin's transistorized voice over the small speaker installed inside the chamber.

"I'm nervous," he admitted.

"Be careful, Father," said Mary Maccabe.

"By the whiskers, I have finally seen it all," added Philo, looking bemused over the entire, elaborate affair.

Thomas watched them through the glass and saw Dr. Arbolera make the sign of the cross to herself. It wasn't a time for atheists, to be sure. Goss and Ravessi watched with tightly controlled façades of cool interest.

Thomas bent his head to the book and found the necessary page. The prerequisite exercise involved visualization. He was also asked to halt the inner stream of language in his head. He was given direction as to how to breathe during the visualizations such that his breath would become a conduit for his awareness to transcend the physical plane and become a channel for the divine influx. His mouth and lips must move as his heart, and his will must soar to where he might encounter the pure unity of the whole. So it said. He breathed.

He read the prayer.

Thomas spoke the words from the book; words familiar, yet strange in their context, unusually juxtaposed against what seemed to be merely sounds emitted from the back of the throat. He breathed, and sang them in a trembling, low voice with the conviction of pure faith. The air grew close. The room seemed very small. Everyone crouched, in animal instinct, waiting for a reaction. Then with sudden force, Thomas raised his arms and exhaled so that his breath became a yell.

Both Thomas and the book erupted into a corona of blinding light. Light flowed from Thomas' mouth and slowly settled onto the book. Thomas slid to the floor, weakened by the effort. Karin ran around the partition to the chamber, slid open the chamber door and dragged Thomas out wordlessly, letting the glass door slide shut behind him. He was pale and breathing shallowly. A cord of light ran from his mouth to the book, ignoring all barriers. His face contorted in what seemed to be pain but he made no sound and gave no sign of awareness of anyone else in the room.

The light in the chamber changed character rapidly, modulating in color and developing a sound like a dull vibration in accompaniment to its undulations. Eventually it formed into an effulgent pillar of light that shot straight up through the roof of the chamber and burned a hole in the ceiling of the lab. Plaster and dust rained down as it raced up the length of the building into the sky. It gave off wisps of smoke like an electric ether. The brightness subsided. The sound resolved into a low hum which was vaguely pleasing. The actinic brightness of the pillar softened into a warm effusion. It widened. The creamy glow was comforting to the eye and completely masked the inside of the glass chamber.

The cord of light between Thomas and book subsided and disappeared. Karin dragged Thomas behind the console. With Goss' help, she propped him up in a chair and returned to looking through the glass partition.

Thomas briefly came out of his trance. "What's happening?"

Karin pointed through the glass.

He muttered. "I guess Sylvester wasn't kidding."

"Karin, Thomas, look at this," said Dr. Arbolera. She pointed at the live telemetry readings coming from the chamber.

Karin looked at the screens and her jaw dropped. "They're identical to Deng's original readings. Some kind of energy without wavelength. Only detectable by its effect on the surrounding environment. See? It displaces the air around it. The pressure readings show it. What is that stuff?"

The glow continued to subside until a vague form could be discerned inside the chamber. The pillar of light slowly dimmed to nothingness. The humming subsided further to more of a sensation of power. The form within could be seen to raise what looked like limbs to its face, as if examining them. It turned its head one way and then another.

"Open the chamber, Herr Goss," Karin heard herself say.

"Eh? Of course." Goss found himself sufficiently to comply. He pressed a button on the console before him.

The curved glass door of the containment chamber slid open silently, releasing a mist into the room. The form within recognized the change and stepped closer to the door. It seemed to test the air. Then it stepped out into the lab. It was humanoid in shape but it had no features. No detail. It appeared to be made of a mercurial, glowing material, like solidified light. And it had awareness – palpable awareness.

It regarded all the people behind the partition in turn, until it settled on Thomas. Wisps of light traveled between Thomas and the entity.

Thomas groaned.

"What's wrong, Tom?" asked Karin, wiping his brow.

"It's… sapping me," whispered Thomas, hoarsely, barely conscious.

The creature stepped toward Thomas, then realized there was a partition between them. The group got a closer look. The creature's face flowed like magma and shone an eerie phosphorescent white, like a sustained flash of lightning. The creature raised its hand and the partition disappeared. It took another step closer to Thomas.

Thomas fought with all his will to look up at it but he felt tired beyond words. His vision was a blur and his head swooned. A trickle of sweat rolled down the curve of his cheek and hung on the edge of his jaw without falling.

The creature spoke in a voice that was like the sound of many waters. "I know why you have summoned me. I know your questions."

"What are you doing to him?" asked Karin frantically, holding Thomas close.

"I must use his essence."

"You're killing him! Stop it!" she snapped.

"You have summoned me. It cannot be reversed. We must proceed with what you want me to do."

"What are you?" asked Mary, fearful and wide-eyed.

It turned to her.

"I am an aeon of the most high, the unknowable. I am Melchizedek of the pleroma. I am Allogenese of the ogdoad. I will release you from the sufferance of Yordon – I will oppose him and destroy him. To you I will be known as Tzedek. That is who I am. Tzedek, the righteous."

"May the righteous know what they are doing," whispered Philo, crossing himself and looking pale.

The rest of them were stunned into silence. The creature knew their entire situation without having exchanged a word with them and its words were expressed with granite confidence. This was their ally and it, HE, had the necessary power and knowledge.

Chapter Thirteen: Apocalypse

The Knesset Building, Jerusalem

Yordon scanned the ranks of his followers from the high vantage point of the forecourt in front of the Knesset building. They draped the hill on all sides and spread into the streets below. He observed with some satisfaction what was now a formidable army. Virtually the entire IDF and the national armies of the surrounding Arab nations were his to command. They stood side by side, Jordanians, Syrians, Egyptians, Israelis, Palestinians and others. They were plainly still wary of each other, but their suspicions were overridden by their certainty that the Messiah had returned and stood on the hill before them.

He spoke.

"There is no longer an Israel."

There was an upsurge of cheering from portions of the crowd.

"There is no longer a Lebanon."

More cheering but primarily from the Israelis.

"There is no longer a Jordan. Or an Egypt, or a Syria. There is only the single land, united under one true God. You are his people and I am his representative."

The crowd's response was huge.

"As I speak, the armies of the world are gathering themselves to oppose us. The exiled government that once occupied this building has made a public appeal for military assistance. This is no surprise; the status quo naturally wishes to preserve itself. But it's fruitless. We can't be stopped. We are God's army!"

The soldiers cheered wildly.

An IDF captain, stepped forward. "How are we to stop the armies of several nations?"

"You won't have to," said Yordon, and with that he raised his arms and conjured a wind which blew in a circle around the Knesset complex.

As the wind blew he spoke again, this time in a voice that could be heard many meters away.

"I will command the elements against them. As God, the Living Silence and unknowable Mind of the Universe, did in the time of Noah, I shall raise the waters and flood the lands and I will blot out from the earth the impure of heart and venal of mind. I shall raise the wind and churn the oceans. I shall blow the desert sands and scour all who dare to move against us. I will prevent them from laying a hand on us. Like this."

Yordon turned in a 360 degree circle with his hand extended. There was a distant roar and suddenly the tangy smell of ocean touched the nostrils of all who were present. From this great distance, they could see the sky above the shoreline on the horizon grow dark as clouds materialized out of nowhere. Lightning bolts flashed in the distance, frequent and violent- looking.

"Our dominion is protected on all sides, while their shores begin to drown under the waters. No one may oppose us. No one can stand against us. No one may approach us."

As he said this, the blue and white flag of Israel was lowered from the flagpole above the main building and a new flag was raised. It was red, with the pinnacle and light-rays icon that had become Yordon's standard emblazoned in white upon it.

The crowd cheered for nearly half an hour before he could speak again.

District Government Center, Haifa, Israel

Avi Grinker didn't look very happy as he gave his report to Natan Silver.

"We've received word from Allied Command in Europe and from the United States, Acting Prime Minister Silver. The news isn't good. Their attempts to divert troops and air support to us are challenged by climactic conditions."

"You mean the polar caps?"

"That's part of it. The coastal cities of the world are experiencing flooding and destruction of property. No one can explain the spontaneous acceleration of the greenhouse melting effect. But there are also reports of tremendous storms over the oceans and violent upheavals in the waters themselves. The only approach left is by land through the Arab countries and they are firmly in Yordon's camp. No one can get to us."

Silver's jaw tensed. "We can guess who's behind it all. He's isolating us. Israel is his."

He wished very hard that Avrahami was still alive. The task of commanding the government in exile was futile. It was simply a losing battle.

Grinker seemed to read his mind. "We still have allies here in the north."

Silver answered with a despondent laugh. "Here in Haifa? Very few. And for how long?" He looked out the window at the pastoral city of churches, quietly nestled in the Galilean foothills. It was tempting to just hide here. But even this bucolic setting would soon feel the effects of Yordon's actions. He dismissed the thought. Hiding was not his way.

"Perhaps Clement will come through…" said Grinker, still holding out hope.

"They won't. The United States is distracted by the self-declared President of the Reborn United States in Texas. They seceded from the USA. Several more states have gone over to him, according to the radio. Very soon they will have a civil war on their hands."

"Then what's left for us to do?"

Silver tried to hide his indecision and present a face of anger to the other Cabinet members.

"We've always fought our own battles. Perhaps we can scramble a squadron of K'firs…"

Grinker shook his head sadly. "We can't. He is somehow causing continuous sandstorms to blow across the Negev, effectively grounding all our planes at Nevatim. And Haifa is totally flooded by the rising waters. We have no other loyal bases left."

Silver threw up his hands in frustration. "We can't just sit here!"

"Sometimes the wisest action is to sit and wait, Acting Prime Minister."

"For what?"

"For a miracle."

Papal Task Force Villa, Rome

"I will take the man and the woman with me," proclaimed Tzedek.

"He means Philo and Mary!" said Karin.

"No! Leave them out of this!" protested Dr. Arbolera.

"They will ease the way into Yordon's stronghold. They must come."

Thomas stared through a haze at the creature. It stood in the center of the lab and spoke to them in that voice that was many voices. There were so many questions he would have liked to ask. As the creature moved, he felt himself becoming indistinct. There was no time.

"Go with him," croaked Thomas weakly, as he looked at Mary and Philo.

"You don't have to go," said Karin, casting a surprised look at Thomas. "Goss and Jobson risked their lives to save you both from Yordon."

"But it was for just such a gambit that we retrieved Mary. She is our leverage," answered Goss, "And now we have the added leverage of Yordon's closest confidant. We have to press this advantage!"

Ravessi voiced his own protest. "We have no way to know what this creature will do. Can we, in good conscience, let these two go with it?"

Mary stepped forward toward Tzedek. "It's okay. Stop fighting. I'll go."

"And I will go too. I must!" spat Philo, gruffly.

Mary continued, "Mr. Goss is right. He or It is our only chance." She looked to the creature. "What do we have to do?"

"Each of you, take my hand," said the creature.

Mary hesitated to touch the miasmic skin of the apparition but she forced herself to take the offered hand. Philo took the other, without pause. In a moment they were gone. The air drafted slightly as it filled the space where they had once stood.

"They're gone!" exclaimed Goss, belaboring the obvious. "Disappeared! And the creature too. To where?"

"To Yordon, wherever he is," said Karin.

Jewish Quarter, Old City, Jerusalem

They materialized in an alley within the Jewish Quarter. Tzedek held Mary steady until she got her bearings. Philo blinked and turned to and fro upon materializing in the alley but get his ground rapidly.

The three of them headed directly to the Temple Mount enclosure.

"That's his base," said Tzedek

"How do you know?" asked Mary.

"I can feel him there."

"Can't he feel you?"

"Not yet. He's not expecting it."

"How will we get in?"

"Like this." Before Mary's eyes Tzedek's flowing outline became solid and took on the color of flesh. As she watched, he metamorphosed into the image of Thomas Prisciotti.

In Thomas' voice, the creature looked at both of his charges and said, "Come friends of Yordon, it's time to visit my brother."

"Mary! Philo!" exclaimed the woman standing guard at the entrance to the Dome of the Rock upon spotting them. She gazed happily at Mary and Philo, then looked suspiciously at Tzedek in the guise of Thomas. "And you have brought a priest with you?"

"Hello Margueritte," said Tzedek, surprising the woman. "I am a friend of Mary's and a familiar face to Yordon. I have brought Mary and Philo back to rejoin with him. May we enter?"

The woman was caught off guard, and seemed about to protest but suddenly relented, upon locking eyes with Tzedek.

They sauntered past her into the mosque's interior. The interior was a large, tiled space encircled by arched columns. There were four main entrances and stained glass windows all around. In the center of the space was another circle of arched columns inside of which was the actual rock for which the mosque was named. According to the Jewish and Christian tradition, this was the place where Abraham set out to accomplish his sacrifice and where, according to the Muslims, the Prophet rose to Heaven. There were a couple of low stages along two of the walls, and a few rooms near the rear. Tzedek, in the guise of Thomas, and his two companions headed directly toward one of the rooms.

Wordlessly, they entered. Yordon was standing at the far end, speaking to several lieutenants and advisors. One lieutenant turned at the sound of their entrance and, upon laying eyes on Mary, shouted, "*Masaalla*! You are found!" Yordon also looked, and upon seeing his two closest companions miraculously returned, instantly strode toward them with open arms.

"Mary! Philo! You have found us!" but then, as he came closer to Tzedek, he stopped and turned pale. "What is this?" he asked, facing the image of Thomas directly, and looking into its eyes. "You are not the priest! Who... What are you?"

Suddenly he moved away from the trio and ordered angrily, "Move away from that creature at once!"

Mary's response was to clutch Tzedek, enraging Yordon even more.

Tzedek gently pushed Mary toward Philo, who advanced a few steps to take hold of her.

Yordon surged forward and came face to face with Tzedek. Tzedek returned his expression of outrage with one of calm. No one dared move.

Yordon spoke first. "What are you?"

Tzedek answered levelly, "Know this, son of Yaldabaoth, I have come to destroy you."

Yordon's nostrils flared, "It is I who will destroy you."

"My power comes directly from God. You are the son of a demiurge and you do not know it. You will be defeated."

"You lie. I am sent by God. You are the demon."

The fruitless exchange stopped abruptly. The two men glared at each other. Philo stared from one to the other. One of them had to be the devil. But which one was it?

"What have we done?" he said to Mary, inching them both away from the confrontation.

Mary answered, "I don't know. But Philo, we've got to get away from here. They're going to kill each other. Maybe all of us too in the process."

Philo nodded his assent and they started toward the nearest door. They walked slowly to avoid distracting Yordon and Tzedek, who were engaged in some silent duel of wills.

Suddenly Mary raised her hands to cover her ears. Philo felt it then too. The air pressure in the room was rising. Their eardrums were pressing inwards. The others in the room began to show discomfort. It quickly became agony. There was a thickness, an opacity, developing around the Yordon and Tzedek as they continued to stare at each other, eyes locked, faces knotted in expressions of concentration.

"We must get out!" yelled someone. Philo was barely able to remove his hand from his left ear as he grabbed Mary's arm and forced her out of the room. He looked back. Inside the room, Yordon and his opponent appeared to be in a curved glass sphere. It began to glow red.

As they approached the exit, Margueritte, the entryway guard, blocked their path.

"Get out of the way!" cried Mary, and promptly tackled the woman. She and Philo scrambled over her kicking body. As they ran away, the toppled woman could be heard to yell.

"Get them! They're the ones that bought that devil here! Kill them!"

Philo and Mary dashed down the steps just as the golden dome atop the mosque erupted in a blast of pure energy. Shards of gilded wood flew everywhere. Philo grabbed Mary and rolled her to the ground. They crouched against a low abutment waiting for the deadly shower to subside.

Philo panted in Mary's face, his face determined and scared all at once. "They'll be up and after us again in a minute. Come, woman!"

He dragged at her. Mary found her feet and they ran down the steps together into the larger, enclosed grounds. People were running en masse toward the gates connecting the compound to the city. Mary paused to look back. Two pillars of light radiated upwards from the mosque. The dome had been blasted open like a paper bag. The light columns collided against each other and emitted angry sparks. At each contact the air around them became flinty with static and the air rumbled.

Philo yelled in her ear. "Come, come, come, come! Look, the gate will be jammed soon. Hurry!"

Philo dragged Mary to the El Hadad gate and together they shoved their way through the growing crowd and spilled onto a crooked street that led directly to El Wad.

There was an explosion above their heads. They looked upwards. Two gigantic, translucent apparitions of vaguely human form were grappling furiously above their heads. Their footsteps as they struggled against each other were like earthquakes. Suddenly one of them reached up at the sky and seemed to grab at the blueness. There was a terrible reverberation, like an empty howl and broken glass together, and the sky rent apart, like fabric. A wind picked up instantly and sucked everything upwards.

"By the whiskers! What's happening?" yelled Philo against the din.

"Philo, it's like a hole in the sky!"

The Thomas apparition, made a slicing motion through the air and more of the sky rent apart. This time creatures came pouring forth, straight out of the worst Dantesque nightmare. Winged and thorned, leathery and slimy, they attached themselves to the Yordon apparition and spilled into the streets of Jerusalem where they grabbed and devoured anything that moved.

"There they are!" yelled someone behind them. It was the guards from the mosque. They had weapons. One of them took aim and fired, shattering a window and barely missing Mary. Mary and Philo ran toward the Christian Quarter, hoping to lose their pursuers in the labyrinth of streets.

Running down the Via Dolorosa, their pursuers close behind, Mary and Philo dodged carts, flying debris, chickens, donkeys, knots of frantic people. Monsters from the sky continued to flap down and pluck people off the cobblestones. Gunshots rang out behind them. Bits of plaster and stone flew into Mary's face. She felt her heart racing in her chest and her lungs burning. The city was losing its atmosphere to the fissure in the sky.

They turned onto a side street dark with overhanging archways, where the chaos was a little less, when ahead they spotted a trio of the gargoyle like creatures advancing on them. Behind them they heard the shouts of their human pursuers.

"We're trapped. We're dead," breathed Mary, panting heavily.

Philo stared grimly down the street. "There must be a way to escape this."

They looked both ways, turning back to back, searching for a way out but there were no alleyways. Philo tried a door but it was locked. They ran to the other side of the street to another door, but it too would not give. They turned to face their attackers. The creatures and guards were approaching from both sides and were just meters away. In a last desperate gambit, Philo threw all his weight against the door, hoping against hope, and miraculously, the heavy, wooden door gave way and they fell inside.

Ignoring the sharp stabs of pain emanating from his shattered shoulder, Philo barricaded the door by pushing a table against it, and not a moment too soon. The door shuddered with the impact of one of the gargoyles as it tried to ram through. There were gunshots and the creature at the door let out a blood wrenching scream. It could be heard to scuttle away. The creature's screams were soon replaced by human screams.

The screams died away too and soon, all that could be heard in the darkened room were Philo's labored breaths and Mary's quiet sobs.

"Oh Philo, it's the end of the world", she rasped quietly, clutching at him, even as he doubled over, nursing in his own pain. His shoulder was dislocated and throbbing pure agony.

He felt himself losing consciousness but he could not leave her alone in her despair. With motes of light dancing before his darkening eyes, he managed, "It is an end, but there is always one more thing. Always, Miss Mary, this I believe."

And with that, Philo passed out.

Papal Task Force Villa, Rome

Karin dragged the inert Thomas beneath a table in the study of the old villa as the ground shook beneath them. Every loose object in the room had been smashed to the ground. Karin held onto Thomas' arm tightly, the rims of her eyes gray and strained with worry. He had passed out shortly after Tzedek had vanished and he seemed to be on the verge of expiring altogether. Her heart beat fast with the very possible calamity of losing him. She had been trying to keep Thomas' body warm while tensely watching the news broadcasts for an indication of Tzedek's actions when the ground started to rumble.

At that moment, the news broadcast had been interrupted to report a strange coincidence of earthquakes occurring around the planet. Before Karin could catch any of the details, the television had rolled off its pedestal and crashed to the ground in a shower of sparks and broken glass.

The table scraped against the floor as the building swayed like a ship at sea. Karin put her arm around Thomas protectively. He came to momentarily, beads of sweat on his brow, despite the clammy feel of his skin. From his half-conscious state he gripped her arm as well as he could and whispered, "We've got to get out of here."

Karin stroked his brow and responded, "But Tom, Thomas, to where? Outside is worse!"

As if to acknowledge her remark, a loud crash was heard outside.

"Downstairs," he breathed raggedly as his eyes fluttered shut once more.

She scanned the swaying room until she located the basement door. Breathing deeply, she shoved her hair behind her ears. *It's up to me to save us.*

Karin took a moment to collect herself, then got up from the floor and determinedly dragged Thomas toward the cellar door, struggling to keep their balance all the way. The door was reluctant, as its frame was out of alignment with the door itself due to the building's movements, but Karin was determined and was finally able to yank it open.

Karin took one look at the rickety stairs and darkness below and said to herself, "This is suicide."

To her surprise, Thomas answered weakly, "Let's argue about it downstairs."

They half tumbled, half scrambled their way down the wooden steps when Thomas suddenly stopped in mid stride.

"What is it, Thomas?"

"The book! In the lab… can't leave it."

Karin felt a spike of pure frustration, "Botheration, Thomas!

Thomas said nothing. He was gone again, a deadweight in her arms.

Karin dragged him the last few steps to the bottom landing of the basement stairs and leaned him against the wall. She stared at him for a moment, as the walls rumbled, her face a changing landscape of emotions, then softly, "Wait here."

Karin struggled back up the stairs and crawled her way to the sitting room, dodging furniture and flying objects. The book was exactly where Thomas had left it, unmoved by the turbulence. She grabbed it and careened her way back to the basement entrance.

Once rejoined with Thomas, Karin scanned the darkness and found what looked to be a supporting beam for the crumbling structure.

She dragged Thomas so that they were crouched beneath the beam, huddled together.

She felt his heart beating, slowly, against her own. Clearly, Tzedek was sapping the life from him more and more, most likely as part of its efforts against Yordon.

Karin held Thomas' head in both her hands, willing him to survive, and suddenly, Thomas came to, but barely. He looked at her with infinitely sad eyes and rasped, "Karin, I may die from this. I want you to know something."

"Thomas, I know," she breathed. Gently she stroked his hair with her trembling hand. "I love you too."

The earth shuddered. Here in the darkness, amidst the sounds of the chaos and destruction waging wildly above them, Karin leaned down toward Thomas' face and bestowed him with a kiss that was full of need and passion and months of unrequited desire. She hugged him tight and lost herself in a swell of emotion for this man. Thomas moved his arms to embrace her, but he was too weak to complete the action. Rivulets of dust trickled down upon them from the upper floor timbers.

They broke apart and listened to the sound of falling buildings, muffled by the stone foundations around them.

Austin, Texas, RUSA (Reborn United States of America)

Francis J. Urban, the President of the Reborn United States, formerly known as Texas, and freshly seceded from the U.S.A., looked down at his audience, who waited cowering under the churning Texas sky, and began to read from his notes.

"The pretenders up north are hiding in fear. They know that the hour of judgment is at hand and it is they who will suffer. We of the Reborn United States recognize Yordon Antropos as the Christ returned to save us and we do not fear the storm. We gather here today in preparation for our coming Rapture. Hear me."

Above Jerusalem

Tzedek willed a bubble of space-time displaced by the barest fraction of a nanosecond around Yordon. This had the effect of creating an impenetrable barrier around his opponent. Tzedek commanded the bubble to shrink, hoping to crush Yordon out of existence.

Yordon removed the physical property of valence in his vicinity, causing a total collapse of all matter and wave particles around him. The bubble dissolved, leaving a hole in the space-time fabric. A hard current of escaping atmosphere rushed past him as he prepared to hurl anti-matter particles at Tzedek in the hopes of annihilating him in the resulting detonation.

Papal Task Force Villa, Rome

Thomas was unconscious again, and huddled against Karin as they lay beneath the supporting beam, in the hopes it would hold and that the shaking of the earth would finally cease. Surely, it had to end. Karin regarded the Metatron book that lay beside her. Incredible that mere words from the crumbling pages of an ancient tome could do this.

But more so, that the creature that was conjured could sap the life from someone. Someone she loved. Karin wondered if Thomas was going to make it. She couldn't imagine not doing everything in her power to help him, and yet here she was just sitting here, with the very thing that was killing him lying on the ground beside her.

She wondered what would happen if she were to destroy the book. Would Tzedek cease to exist? Would Thomas be restored? Even if it did not save him, would it be right to allow this vehicle of the supernatural to continue to exist; a potential weapon that could be used in the cause of evil and much as in the cause of good? Now that there was no Vatican to protect it, who would be charged with its safekeeping? The U.S. Government? A bunch of bald-headed brass buffoons already in the habit of bombing their way out of international tangles. Surely she could not allow that to happen.

Suddenly, Karin realized that Thomas had stopped breathing.

Austin, Texas, RUSA

President Urban found his stride as his voice boomed out of the crackling PA system. Overhead, the sky raced dark clouds across the horizon and thunder rumbled all around them. He had lost his written speech to the vacuum that seemed to want to suck everything upwards, but no matter — he preferred to improvise anyway.

"Behold the days come when He will draw nigh, and visit them that dwell upon the earth, and He will make inquisition of them that have hurt unjustly with their unrighteousness."

Above Jerusalem

Yordon cracked the earth open and summoned mile high walls of lava. Tzedek countered with freezing wind, coagulating the lava into impossibly tall mountains which collapsed under the weight of their impossible geometries and fell from the sky in deadly avalanches onto the helpless populations below.

Tzedek conjured an army of flaming pyres, burning with the intensity of suns, to attack Yordon as he fell backwards in the sky. The atmosphere scorched and flashed as molecules detonated all around them.

Yordon willed the ocean below to rise up and engulf the flames. The water rose in a great mass straight up into the sky, engulfing the pyres. It bubbled angrily, evaporating into steam, creating a continent of clouds and occluding the sun in that hemisphere.

Papal Task Force Villa, Rome

Karin leaned in toward Thomas, until she was just inches from his face, and felt no breath there. She shook him and then slapped him, in an attempt to revive him. He lay there limply, unresponsive. She slapped him again, hard and yelled, "Wake up, Goddammit! I need you to wake up, Thomas!"

A timber fell from the ceiling and the flooring overhead began to buckle. She realized that, for better or worse, if this shaking did not end very soon, they would be buried alive.

Austin, Texas, RUSA

Urban was in his stride now. The audience seemed enraptured by his words. Or was it that they dared not move?

The earth undulated and spit hot magma around the field. Perhaps it was a sign. He felt like he would burst as he spoke of his terrors.

"Then the cleansing of the souls will come, and all the powers of the sea will tremble and dry up, and the skies will be torn asunder and the days will cease and the depths will be laid bare and the stars will grow in size and the sun will vanish."

Urban paused to catch his breath and thought of his sorry counterpart in D.C. He smiled. Soon he would know the wrath of the Lord.

Above Jerusalem

The sky split open in a fury of sound and electrostatic force as Tzedek tried to burn Yordon out of existence with a wall of lightning. The explosions burned away the clouds and ionized the air.

Yordon introduced a lower energy state vacuum in the area around Tzedek, causing a collapse of all higher energy states. The collapsing wave was a bubble that expanded outwards at the speed of light eating everything in its path. Tzedek struggled to contain this horror. He called upon the full life essence of Thomas Prisciotti, for he needed the power to oppose this assault successfully. It would wipe out the planet below as quickly as a match would burn a cloth to ashes.

Papal Task Force Villa, Rome

There was a loud crash as a nearby building collapsed under the unusual stresses of the bucking earth. It was getting worse. Karin wondered if they should take their chances outside. She struggled to stand and took a peek outside through a ventilation slat.

Karin turned toward Thomas' supine form, and even though he could not hear, she said, "It's not safe here anymore. The ground is fracturing outside."

She grabbed Thomas by his armpits and made for the steps as quickly as she could manage. She looked back at the book, which still lay by the support beam, and debated whether to leave it there to be buried and hopefully destroyed in the rubble, but the historian within her welled up in protest and she realized she simply could not abandon it. She went back and retrieved it.

The building shuddered and large pieces of the ceiling came crashing down from the upper floors into the basement.

Karin put the book down and proceeded to drag Thomas up the stairs, one at a time. She was not three steps from the top of the staircase when it collapsed under her weight. Karin grabbed for the threshold of the doorway and managed to grip the ledge but she could not also hang on to Thomas, and within moments, he slipped from her other hand's grasp and tumbled to the basement floor, a broken doll amidst the rubble. Karin began to cry in despair as she dangled helplessly in the air.

Karin yelled for help but no one replied or came to her aid. She looked down at Thomas' crumpled body and as she dripped hot tears from her eyes onto his dusty form, he slowly disappeared, losing mass as his body collapsed inwards, until all that was left was the relatively dust free outline of what had been his body.

"Thomas! Don't leave me! Oh, Thomas!" Karin wept and wailed but still held onto that ledge, against all odds, as the building rumbled in complaint of its failing structural integrity.

The building was coming down around her.

Above Jerusalem

The storms blew full force into each other creating havoc in the sky as the two forces that had been Yordon and Tzedek grappled with each other. They intermingled, trying to will each other's substance into subatomic oblivion. They decomposed each other's nuclear binding forces, they changed the laws of physics around each other in an effort to collapse the other. They blasted pure, destructive energy at each other. The sky burned. The space above them gaped black holes into nothingness. Warrior angels, created by the dueling pure wills, emerged from these openings into the void and did battle with each other. Wheel-like Ofamin, fiery Seraphim, sword wielding Cherubims clashed and fell in battle by the legion and dissolved back into nothingness.

The two divine wills clutched at each other, particle against particle, power against power, will against will, neither willing to succumb to the other's fury. They became one churning, primordial penumbra, broiling above the heads of all who lived on the earth, darkening the sky, fracturing the bedrock, blotting out the sun.

Austin, Texas, RUSA

"Friends shall fight one against another like enemies and the earth shall stand in fear with those that dwell therein," shouted Urban into the microphone, even though the electrical power had long since been interrupted. People lay on the ground and clutched at the grass. Overhead the sky crackled and burned. He snapped himself out of his dumbfounded consideration of the sky and let his words march on, like faithful soldiers of Christ, to their conclusion.

"Whoever remains at the end of all these, shall escape and see his salvation, and the end of the world. For evil shall be put out and deceit shall be quenched..."

Papal Task Force Villa, Rome

Karin screamed as the floor shifted. She looked below. It wasn't far, but the building was about to collapse under its own weight. She would be buried. With a Herculean effort borne of the black hole of grief she felt and the hot anger that resulted from it, she pulled herself up onto the first floor landing and, wiping her face of grime and tears, ran toward the front door of the building.

Above Jerusalem

The combined awareness of the two celestial beings spasmed with self-hate. It was one and it was the other and it was both. They were no longer distinct beings. It tore at itself and screamed indignation at its own actions. With a final shout of victory and horror at its own defeat it exploded in a shower of light particles that dissipated in the sky. All the elements that it had summoned up from the earth and wielded as weapons against itself suddenly lost volition and fell to the ground in blind clumps of dirt and torrents of rain. The winds died, the fires quenched, the wounds in the sky slowly sealed themselves until the air above every city, town, village, hamlet, and wilderness of the earth was quiet once more.

Papal Task Force Villa, Rome

Karin gazed in horror at the landscape of smoking wreckage all around her, once she was outside. The skyline of metropolitan Rome was a ruined caricature of its former glory. Instead, there were broken facades of stone and steel and streets buried in rubble. Amidst the broken stones, bodies and crashed vehicles lay strewn, awash in puddles of blood and petrol. A car exploded not fifty feet away. Karin reflexively ducked but there was nowhere to hide. Behind her the entire Salon building groaned its readiness to collapse. She moved away from it but had nowhere to go. She put her hands to her mouth, feeling the dry bottom of despair.

And then it stopped.

Austin, Texas, RUSA

Urban thundered his next words at the crouching crowd below. "And faith shall flourish and the truth which has been so long without fruit, shall be declared. The days shall be long and the sunshine sweet from that day forward."

Just then the wind stopped, like a switch had been flipped. President Urban looked upwards, as did his audience. The violence in the sky simply dissipated and in moments the sun shone forth.

Urban tried to control the smile on his face. *Was it an omen?* And right on cue, at the end of his delivery. *Oh, baby!*

☐

Chapter Fourteen: Gnosis

Cheyenne Mountain Complex, Colorado, January 1, 2021

President Adam Clement emerged from the Cheyenne Mountain facility and squinted up at the sky.

General Farrow and the remainder of the senior staff had already emerged from the underground complex and were looking around. The view was shocking. The grounds around the entrance looked as if a gargantuan plow had tilled the earth. There were downed trees and damaged structures as far as the eye could see. And yet, though it was unusually thin and cold, the air smelled fresh.

It's really over.

General Farrow came up to Clement and saluted. "Communications channels are heavily compromised, sir, but we do have eyes and ears in most of the major cities and bases. Your speech was well received."

"Thank you, General."

"And, um, Texas Governor Watkins has just called asking to rejoin the Union."

Clement nodded, a small smile on his lips. "More will follow."

"What about Urban, sir? If we mobilize quickly, we can take him out while he's still getting his bearings."

"We'll deal with him later. Right now let's focus on getting our butts back to Washington, General. We've got a lot of important people wandering around here not doing their jobs."

Farrow saluted and marched off, barking orders.

"Happy New Year, sir," said Kent Hanover.

Hanover had come up behind him. Clement glared at him, but secretly harbored a feeling of profound surprise behind the scowl. It was New Year's

Day. *Well, what do you know?* With the troubles of recent, no one had stopped to notice Christmas or the New Year.

Clement put a hand on the younger man's shoulder. It had been a tough year for everyone. "Why don't you find us a chopper, Mr. Hanover? Time to go home, son."

Knesset Building, Jerusalem

Philo and Mary watched Acting Prime Minister Natan Silver's motorcade proceed off the remains of the Ben Gurion highway onto the still navagable approach road to the Knesset. The government had been hastily reinstated once the Antropos government, for lack of a better name, had collapsed. Now that Yordon's spell was broken -- and Philo was increasingly convinced that it had been some kind of spell -- it was glaringly obvious how impractical it had all been. After all the talk of peace and brotherhood, there had to be structure and economics. People had to be fed. Streets had to be cleaned. And yet none of it had seemed to matter at the time. He scratched at his head, feeling puzzled.

Mary was looking at him. He returned her gaze.

"Now that it's over, it seems like a bad dream, doesn't it?" she asked.

"I would not call this destruction a dream. I don't think there are any buildings that are not damaged," he answered, glumly.

"I know, but it seems so unreal, all the same."

A silent column of Jordanian soldiers under IDF escort marched past, on their way out of the city.

"I wonder how things would have turned out if he had lived," asked Mary, as she watched the soldiers pass by.

"You mean, would it have lasted?" Philo shrugged, wincing a little from sling that was wrapped around his shoulder injury.

They stood together in silence, lost in their own thoughts. Philo wondered if everyone on the planet wasn't like this right now. Mary touched his elbow, snapping him out of his reverie, and pointed. Across the road, a ragtag group of demonstrators bearing the red flag with Yordon's icon were heading toward the Old City. It wasn't a large group.

"Some people believe he's going to return. Like Jesus," said Mary.

Philo shook his head disdainfully. "And they will start a new religion around his ashes."

"Maybe. Philo?"

"Yes?"

"Do you think he was the son of God?"

He shrugged again, not taking his eyes off the distant demonstrators. "I don't know. I wonder if he even knew. I think that his actions were eventually beyond his control."

"He became so powerful."

"They say the tongue has no bones and yet it smashes bones," Philo replied, kicking at a stone. He smiled then, remembering his first time speaking to Yordon, long ago in the caves of Athos. "He used to say he was like a stone rippling the waters."

"He could be so poetic."

"But the waters swallowed the stone, and the ripples are gone."

"How sad that sounds, Philo. I feel very sad."

"Yes, I feel this too. Still, I must wonder if Yordon didn't plan it this way. The stone's trace may be more subtle than we know, yes?"

The Israel Museum, Jerusalem

It was a celebration of mixed feelings. So much had happened in the last twelve months. The survivors of the Papal Task Force, joined by members of the Israeli Department of Antiquities, stood before the Metatron Codice. It had been successfully retrieved from the basement ruins of the Papal Villa. It was now encased in bullet-proof glass, hermetically sealed and dimly lit to preserve its delicate parchment. Doctor Benjamin Seibenberg, the curator of the Israel Museum, openly admired the great prize.

"To think this tome saved the world. It's truly amazing. Think of the power."

"But not just anyone can unleash it. And it must never be attempted again. This must be clear or you will have nothing but idiots at your doorstep, Benjamin," said Karin as she glanced at her associates for corroboration.

Mervyn Goss, Max Ravessi, Zachary Jobson and Dolores Arbolera looked back at her doubtfully. She felt momentarily alone as the realization struck her once again that Thomas was not present. *Nevermore.*

Goss stepped forward. "There will be idiots in attendance en masse no matter what Dr. Seibenberg says to them, Professor."

Karin regarded Goss but said nothing. He was unfortunately in danger of being correct.

After the reception was over, Jobson remained behind, talking to the museum curator. Goss and Ravessi promptly got into their chauffeured vehicles and drove off, perhaps never to be seen again. Karin and Dolores Arbolera walked out together, emerging from the boxy structure onto the grounds surrounding the museum. They stopped by a fountain surrounded by toppled statues, which gave the field an ancient cast, like a Roman ruin.

Dolores sat on the edge of the fountain. "That was interminable!"

Karin's eyes exuded sadness but her mouth betrayed small crinkles at the corners. "At the end of a crisis, there's always long speeches. It's inescapable."

Dolores laughed.

"Seibenberg's a good man. He likes to carry on, but with him, Metatron is in responsible hands."

"I hope so. I'm glad." Dolores rubbed the back of her neck and looked around. "This is my first trip to Israel."

Karin sat beside her and followed Dr. Arbolera's gaze across the terrain. "It's a beautiful place. Or it was."

Dolores nodded. "Have you seen the Temple Mount? It looks like a bomb went off inside."

"Ground Zero for Yordon versus Tzedek. That must have been something to see. I wonder what happened to them."

"I supposed they've been 'recalled'," mused Dolores.

Karin became pensive, remembering those final moments with Thomas.

"I wish Father Prisciotti could have been here," said the Geneticist, guessing at her thoughts.

"Oh, I don't know. He would have hated this," said Karin, inclining her head toward the museum.

Dolores watched Karin's expression change and smiled knowingly. "He saved us all." Then after a pause, she tentatively asked, "What do you think he's doing now?"

"You mean, is he in heaven, living in the afterlife? I don't know. He used to muse about souls. Even if souls might be eternal, he would ask me, did that necessarily mean that personalities were also eternal? He wondered if a soul would remember any part of its corporeal life once it was reabsorbed into the celestial whole."

Dr. Arbolera shook her head, "Blasphemous. He was so close to being blasphemous even while he was inspiring. I loved his show, you know."

Karin remembered that first and only kiss, "Blasphemous, indeed."

They sat together in silence and eventually Dolores laid a gentle hand over Karin's. "The new Pope is holding a ceremony in his honor today, at the Lateran Palace," she said.

"Pope Leviticus I, isn't it?" asked Karin, her features softening in response to the comforting gesture.

"I think so."

"It's amazing the church survived. Yordon did his best to dismantle Christianity." She scanned the square, observing various knots of people clearing rubble and collecting refuse, "But already there are cranes and bulldozers unearthing the remains of Vatican City so they can rebuild it. I guess people have got to believe in something."

Dolores asked, "Do you suppose we learned anything from Yordon?"

"I doubt it. Did it change people's minds? Did it change yours?"

Dolores frowned. "It might. But is everything I learned in catechism school wrong? I have to think about that."

"I wish more people would. The fact is, people forget, Dolores," said Karin, "Over time, religious *experience* turns into ritual. Enlightenment turns into superstition. Inspiration turns into intolerance. Salvation becomes the promise of retribution."

Dolores squinted at that. "That's a little too cynical for me, Professor. There's something out there watching over us. We have proof now. There's a Watcher in the Skies. He might not be the Father we imagined. He might not work alone. He might be fundamentally alien to the human psyche, but he, or it, is there. The challenge is to try and understand what it means to the human condition. We touched on something vital and it needs to be explored."

"I wish I could share your optimism. More likely we'll face the future with ignorance and fear and a good measure of sin. That's history. People will gradually turn these discoveries into another ideological cosmic gumbo and in fifty years there will be new temples and new wars of righteousness."

"I'm hoping for evolution, Karin," said the geneticist.

Karin rose. "I'm hoping for some lunch, want to join me?"

University of Chicago, Hyde Park, Chicago

A couple of weeks later, Kate found herself back in her crowded office at the Oriental Institute, typing away at her computer, as snow fell softly outside her office window. She had been away from her normal duties for so long that she almost felt as if she was impersonating herself. And perhaps she was. So much had happened and so much had changed. Not just all the damage done to the infrastructures of the world by the earthquakes that had ravaged all places during the battle between Yordon and Tzedek, but also the damage done to *institutions* and people's systems of belief. The world was like an anthill that had been kicked, and now the ants were trying desperately to re-impose order onto the chaos.

And there were the changes inside herself. The loss of her best and closest confidant. She felt betrayed, but she couldn't figure out by whom. Her feelings for Thomas had been real and heartfelt. She had loved him. Or rather, she loved him still and would forever. But he was gone, except for her memories of him and all their times together, talking about anything and everything, crossing sardonic swords, feeling each other's pull. She missed him so much.

Sighing, Karin slid away from her desk, and rubbed at her eyes. She decided she needed a walk, despite the wintry weather outside. She needed a change of venue. Grabbing her heavy coat and fur hat, she left her office and decided she would try strolling along the Midway. It would be pretty.

Once outside she turned left and walked along South University Avenue toward the long expanse of the Midway Plaisance, a greenway that stretched all the way from Washington Park on the West Side to Jackson Park and the Lakeshore to the East.

She arrived at the Midway and turned left, toward Jackson Park. As she walked along East 59th Street, which ran the length of the Midway, she stopped to admire the gothic grandeur of Rockefeller Chapel and its soaring carillon tower. It was the tallest building on the campus. It was also a chapel in name only, as its dimensions were more like that of a cathedral, occupying the entire square block.

Drawn by its solidity and architectural beauty, for it had survived the earthquakes almost intact, Kate climbed the steps and entered the building. As soon as she was inside she was soothed by the smell of frankincense and myrrh, tinged by the slightest tang of cut lumber that permeated the air. She loved the sound of her echoing footfalls as her low heels clip clopped on the marble walkway. It seemed to give her walking a certain gravity. The air was warm and still, with shafts of colored light stabbing the vast space through the surviving tinted glass windows that lined the walls of the outer aisles. It was a place that made you feel large and small all at once.

The place was nearly empty except for a few stray visitors, lost in their thoughts and meditations. She sat in a pew and examined the interior space of the chapel. It was mostly intact and where there had been damage, scaffolding had been erected and repairs were well underway. The chapel would be restored and perfect again, no doubt.

But what about my beliefs? That would be more difficult. Karin had never been an avid believer, except perhaps as a child, but she had always honored and enjoyed the traditions of her family's religious beliefs and the feelings of unity and fulfillment they provided. She held open the possibility of souls or a life essence that might survive her corporeal existence but, no doubt as a result of her academic dissections of Biblical era writings and artifacts, she viewed all the physical panoply of religion as detritus more than anything else. She supposed she could be called a spiritual skeptic, she thought to herself with a private smirk.

But now, in the aftermath of Yordon, many of her questions about the incorporeal aspects of religion had been addressed, but not necessarily answered, and more had been raised. She contemplated what Thomas would have said, if he could be here with her now. Despite his struggles with doctrinal Christianity, he had always believed in the infinite, the unknowable God. He had always maintained that only man's ability to understand the Creator was flawed. Thomas had privately confided in her that he viewed religion as not so much a divine revelation, but as a series of approximations of the cosmos; an evolving amalgamation of human belief systems that strived to define the place of men in the universe. But, he had said, the agendas of men repeatedly blinded them to the truth.

In the end, Karin mused, Thomas' boundless God, for so long obscured behind a curtain of human design, had been revealed to be something more estimable. Without a doubt, it was not at all what he had expected.

Karin's thoughts twisted around themselves in endless permutations. There was something important to be known here. Maybe Thomas had not been far from the truth. Behind the God of men existed another force. Something that could spawn God-like creatures, almost like afterthoughts. Something without personality. But did that force have purpose? Did existence then have purpose? Or was this dry reality around her -- the dust suspended within the light shafts bisecting the cathedral air, the ache in her hands from having them clenched unwittingly, the people ambling along the chapel aisle, the patient, confident stones of this place -- an afterthought as well?

Shaken by her own musings, she looked around her, almost feeling a small panic and noticed a confessional booth along the outer aisle. She felt drawn to it. She needed to escape into a more private surrounding, to process these expanding thoughts.

Karin slid aside the dark velvet curtain that shielded off one end of the booth and saw that it was empty. She slipped into the space and closed the curtain behind her. Tentatively, she sat on the small, diagonal bench at the back of the cramped space and took in the scented darkness, listening to her own breathing.

After a minute or so she was startled to hear a man's voice from behind the grated screen that lay between the Penitent's portion of the booth and the Priest's.

"How can I help you, my child?"

"Oh, forgive me, Father, I didn't think anyone was taking confessions."

"And why is that, young lady?"

"Well, with all the construction and chaos…"

There was silence from the other side of the partition, which struck Karin as a little strange. Then the priest continued, "Tell me, why did you decide to come and sit inside this confessional?"

Karin hesitated before answering, even though she was hungry to engage with someone to talk this through. But not just anyone. Would a random priest understand her musings? This particular one was certainly not following the typical script for a confession. Perhaps he would do.

She began by asking her anonymous confessor a question, "Father, what do you suppose Yordon really was?"

"Is this what troubles you?"

"Doesn't it trouble you?"

There was a rustling from the other side of the grating. "There are many ways I could answer that, and yet none are sufficient answers," the voice paused, and then, just as Karin was about to speak, he added, "Something more than human."

"And yet all too human," answered Karin, "If he was a God made flesh, then the flesh came to rule him."

Karin heard the priest shift in his seat, as if getting comfortable, "As it rules all of us, my child. Yordon's struggle is the struggle each and every one of us battles in our own search for God. We fight, and sometimes we lose. Our passions overcome us. Our intellect makes us skeptical. We lose our way and, feeling empty, try to find our way back. As you are doing now."

"Am I?"

"Yes. You want to find a way forward for yourself that reconciles what you have experienced with your view of reality but you do not know how to do that."

Karin couldn't believe her shadowy conversant's insight, "That's exactly it, Father. I've never been much of a believer but I have since seen fantastical things that seem to confirm another plane of existence beyond ours. How does it relate to humans?"

"And how does it fit into Christian doctrine?" said the voice.

"Yes, that too. Or any human belief system."

"Fair enough. I see it in this way. Yordon may have damaged our cathedrals and challenged our beliefs, but Christianity, or if you wish, our spirituality, lives on. He could not change the fact that we have souls, my child, and they are eternal. All we have to do is look into our hearts, to find the chrysalis of inner being."

With a start, Karin remembered someone else who had said those very words a long time ago, while sitting in her office, "Wait, only one other person has ever said that to me!"

"No I didn't", said the voice, then, "Okay, maybe I did," followed by a soft chuckle. "Take it to heart, Karin."

Karin gasped, putting her fist to her mouth and felt a surge of emotion threaten to overcome her. She burst out of the confession booth and yanked open the door behind which the priest would be sitting, prepared to leap into Thomas' arms and ask him frantically how he had managed to survive the events in Rome.

But no one was there.

She stood there for a long time as if waiting for him to reappear and say more but after a time, she sighed, collected herself, and walked slowly away, accepting that she and Thomas were done with words.

THE END

Acknowledgments

This novel has been eighteen years in the making. And though I have not actually worked on the story for all of that time – there was a long hiatus in the middle, where I pursued a computer career, raised a family, played drums in a surf band, wrote more stories, tried my hand at teleplays, renovated houses, etcetera – I think it is fair to say that this story, more than any other I have conceived, has always lain in wait in the back of my mind, frustrated by its anonymity, demanding its rightful place as the first debutante of my writing.

I originally conceived the story just before the advent of the Millenium. The original story development and research transpired over a period of two years and by 1999 I had my first, full draft.

My wife, Kimberly Maier, decimated it.

For this, I am profoundly grateful. She was forthright in her criticisms of my excessive pen and florid prose and really helped me to see my effort for the gush of ink it was. She has been supportive and encouraging, and most of all, honest with me throughout this journey. This story owes a lot to her caring and cajoling, and her sharp eye for grammer and style. As with all other things in our shared life, she is my rock and my heart.

My first professional editor and agent, Susan Kelly, was kinder, or perhaps more politic and helped me to cull and hone my storyline from 800+ pages, believe it or not, to more like 400. She was invaluable in her comments and criticisms and I am grateful to her for her lessons in story construction and the use of language, not to mention syntax and punctuation, and for her efforts to market the book to traditional publishers. Alas, we did not succeed, but perhaps that was for the best. This story had more miles to travel.

More recently, my friend of many years and a formidable editor in her own right, Michele Merens, was kind enough to read my tale and present me with a golden, gift wrapped, treasure trove of insightful criticisms and story suggestions, which have influenced the form of this novel that you hold in your hands today, more than any other person involved in the provenance of this story. I am eternally grateful to her and appreciative of her talents. In addition to being a gifted editor, she is also a very talented writer. You can see samples of her work at www.michelemerens.com.

I also owe thanks to Kendall Smith, a colleague at my job of the time, who became an excellent friend, and then my partner in our joint independent publishing venture, Percussion Publishing LLC. He led the way and shone the light on the self publishing process, like a caver with a headlamp in pursuit of his goal. If not for him, this story might have festered in its dusty corner forever. It was he who cajoled me and persuaded me to unlock my muse again and finish what I had started. Through his determination and enthusiasm in pursuit of publishing his own, formidable works of fiction (check out *Vault 2112* – a real page turner about lost Nazi treasure), I found my way to here and now. Thank you, Kendall. You rock.

Thanks also to Jessica Jaffe, who provided the wonderful cover art and was able to translate the spirit of the story into a visual work that I am honored to have grace the cover of my book. It was a joy to work with such a creative and positive individual, who was caring enough to read the entire story and engage me in thought provolng discussion about what message we wanted to convey with the artwork.

There are thousands of books on how to write fiction, and all budding authors have their few on the shelf. In my case, two in particular were catalysts in the refinement of my writing abilities. *Structuring Your Novel*, by Robert C. Meredith and John D. Fitzgerald, and in particular, *Sin and Syntax*, by Constance

Hale. Both are highly recommended for their succinct and practical advice and guidance. They taught me volumes and gave me confidence in wielding my pen.

I also owe thanks to the depth and breadth of the information well that is the Internet, which has made it possible to visualize places far and foreign, not just in terms of cartography and physical locale, but in ambience, history and context, as well. I have never been to many of the places described in this story but with the power of the Internet, which is really the result of millions of human beings typing not just their words, but their experiences and feelings into the ether for others to reference, I think I was able to fake it pretty well!

Without doubt, there are dozens more individuals to which I owe gratitude for their direct or indirect support in my development as a writer and in the creation of this story. To each of you; family, friends, random people who may have said something that inspired a line of dialogue, other writers whose style I admire, teachers of mine of philosophy, history and religion, end times lunatics spouting their froth flecked diatribes on the street, believers and non believers alike, colleagues and cohorts who offered encouragement, to all of you many thanks and a nod in your direction.

I hope you have enjoyed my story.

ABOUT THE AUTHOR

PRESLEY E. ACUNA writes unconventional thrillers, based in reality, but which take unexpected turns into the realms of fantasy, magical realism, science fiction and horror. His aim is to engage the reader in an engrossing mystery or adventure, while simultaneously using the situation to explore the deeper meanings of the ideas behind the story.   When he is not writing, he is working as a systems engineer on the dot com frontier. He is also a musician, and formerly a member of the Supertones. He is a born and raised New Yorker, currently living in Brooklyn, but also enjoys spending time at his cabin, deep in the woods of western Massachusetts, with his wife and the host of critters that always manage to find their way into the house.

www.ingramcontent.com/pod-product-compliance
Lightning Source LLC
Chambersburg PA
CBHW072107250626
47159CB00007B/2341